BERTRICE SMALL

BOND OF PASSION

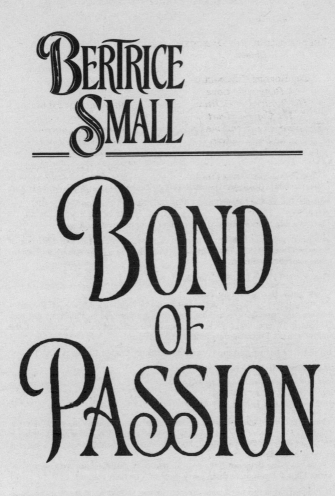

A SIGNET ECLIPSE BOOK

SIGNET ECLIPSE
Published by the Penguin Group
Penguin Group (USA) Inc., 375 Hudson Street,
New York, New York 10014, USA

USA | Canada | UK | Ireland | Australia | New Zealand | India | South Africa | China

Penguin Books Ltd., Registered Offices: 80 Strand, London WC2R 0RL, England

For more information about the Penguin Group visit penguin.com.

Published by Signet Eclipse, an imprint of New American Library, a division of Penguin Group (USA) Inc. Previously published in a New American Library trade paperback edition.

First Signet Eclipse Printing, May 2013

ISBN 978-0-451-23631-9

Printed in the United States of America
10 9 8 7 6 5 4 3 2 1

ALWAYS LEARNING   PEARSON

For my cousin, Millie Warner, with love

Prologue

"He's a sorcerer!" the laird of Rath's wife, Anne, gasped. "You cannot seriously be considering giving our daughter to a sorcerer, Robert. And I am told he holds with the old religion. He's a Catholic. A papist! Only the Gordons and the barbaric Highland families hold to the old faith and refuse to see the error of their ways." The expression on her lovely face was very concerned by her husband's apparent decision.

Robert Baird, laird of Rath, snorted impatiently. "If Angus Ferguson is a sorcerer, wife, then so am I. He's no more a sorcerer than any. As for his faith, 'tis his, not mine. Did the queen not say we might all worship as we pleased?"

"But even here in the eastern borders it is said the Fergusons of Duin practice—"

The laird cut her short. "Said? Said by whom? The Earl of Duin is no sorcerer," he told her firmly.

"Then why does he allow such scandalous rumors to persist, Robert?" his wife wanted to know. "A man's reputation is his most valuable possession."

"He's a man who wants his privacy," came the answer. "By allowing such myths about his family to be perpetuated among the ignorant, he achieves his purpose. This family of Duin is careful in its dealings, Anne. Have you ever heard of their being involved in any kind of disloyalty or treason? Nay! Not the Fergusons of Duin."

"You seem to know much of these people, although I do not," his wife remarked.

"I went to Bothwell," Robert Baird said. "I know him to be friends with Angus Ferguson, for they studied together in France. Has James Hepburn not been attempting to broker the sale of the lands I inherited in the west with Angus Ferguson for the last few years? He has. And you know I would not sell that property to Angus Ferguson, for my kinsman from whom I inherited those lands feuded with the Fergusons. It somehow seemed disloyal to profit from my inheritance under the circumstances. But trust James Hepburn to come up with a perfect solution."

"So marrying our Annabella to Angus Ferguson was the Earl of Bothwell's idea?" Lady Anne's pretty mouth pursed disapprovingly. James Hepburn might be the keeper of the queen's borders, and one of the most powerful men in Scotland, but she like others thought him a great womanizer. He had charm, though, she had to admit.

"Of course it's Bothwell's idea," Robert Baird said. "I wouldn't have dared reach so high, Annie. We're a wee clan with little to recommend us other than an old name."

"Why, Rob," his wife replied, "the Bairds saved the life of King William the Lion, and were given great grants of land. It's a good border name."

He laughed, patting her hand. "A few hundred years

ago, Annie, and how many generations since, with the *extensive* lands being split this way and that? Nay, we're simple folk, and I was fortunate to get you to wife, for you're a Hamilton, a great name today here in the borders and in Scotland. I know Jamie Hepburn is a bit of a rogue, but he's an honorable man, and a good friend."

"How can he be certain the Earl of Duin will take Annabella as a wife? They say he is wealthier than any man living, and the handsomest man in the borders to boot. Our eldest daughter is as plain as mud. Would not Myrna or Sorcha be a better choice?"

"Myrna, Sorcha, and wee Agnes will have no difficulties finding husbands, for they are as beautiful as you are, my dear," her husband said candidly. "'Tis our Annabella who faces an eternal maidenhood. Bothwell himself will speak with Duin. He will not dissemble the facts but be entirely truthful. He has told me that Angus Ferguson's heart is not engaged elsewhere; nor is there any impediment to a marriage between him and Annabella. If he wants these lands that I hold in the west, then he will acquiesce to Bothwell's proposal. I am told Angus Ferguson is in his middle thirties, and like any man with title and property will want an heir or two. At twenty our daughter is almost past her prime, but still young enough to give a husband bairns."

The possibility of her eldest daughter bearing a title, mothering a future earl of Duin, was beginning to seep into the lady Anne's consciousness, along with the advantages such a marriage for Annabella would bring for her family. "If this comes to pass, the Melvilles will no longer be able to look slantwise at Myrna, for her connections will more than make up for her lack of a large dower portion, Rob. She will have Ian Melville and no other, she vows. She is more than ready for marriage, and should wed as soon as possible after Annabella."

"I don't like Ian Melville," the laird of Rath said, "but if she wants him I cannot deny her. The Melvilles are a good family, and stand high in Her Majesty's favor."

"How soon will we know if the Earl of Duin will have Annabella?"

"Within a few weeks," Robert Baird answered his wife. "Bothwell has gone himself to suggest the match."

"Well, as long as he isn't a sorcerer," the lady Anne said, and her husband smiled.

"May she be as happy as we have been all these years," the laird said to his wife.

The lady Anne nodded in agreement. "I pray it," she replied.

Chapter 1

The Earl of Duin was the most powerful and the most feared man in the western borders. His power stemmed from his vast and seemingly unending wealth. The fear was born of the belief that the Fergusons of Duin descended from a race of sorcerers. Angus Ferguson did little to dissuade that conviction. His family was barely known beyond the scope of their lands, which suited the earl quite well. Great wealth had a tendency to attract envy, and envy invited trouble.

At the age of sixteen Angus Ferguson had inherited Duin from his father. His mother had died several years prior. He had two legitimate siblings: a brother, James, and a sister, Mary. Both had sought lives in the Church. James actually had a calling. Angus saw him frequently and was proud to see him slowly working his way up the ladder of the Church hierarchy.

Mary, however, had chosen to enter a cloistered convent. The dark reputation of their family weighed heavily upon her. They had never been able to convince her that the blood of their few ancestors known to have practiced magical arts was practically nonexistent in their veins now. Mary Ferguson felt it necessary for her family's sake to expiate those supposed sins of long ago. He saw her rarely.

At the age of eighteen Angus Ferguson had seen an opportunity to advance his family, and he had taken it. King James V had been defeated by the English forces in the Battle of Solway Moss four years earlier. It but echoed the time some thirty years prior when James's own father had been killed fighting the English, and he had come to the throne a boy ruler. His two sons were now dead, and learning that his wife had delivered a daughter instead of the hoped-for male heir, James V fell into a deep depression, saying, "It cam wi' a lass, and 'twill go wi' a lass." Then, turning his face to the wall, he spoke no more and died shortly afterward.

His French queen, Marie de Guise, was furious at what she deemed her husband's selfishness. A clever and personable woman, she had over the years of her marriage made the right allies from among the contentious Scots nobility, and she had Cardinal David Beaton on her side. She was popular with her subjects, and was able to protect her infant from those who wanted to control the little queen, and betroth her to King Henry VIII's young son, Prince Edward. The English king hoped that with Mary as his son's wife, and the baby in his custody, he would be able to annex Scotland to England.

Marie de Guise did not want an English marriage for her daughter. She wanted a French marriage. To that end and after much negotiation the little queen was to be sent to France and betrothed to the French dauphin Francis. This would make Mary queen of both France and Scotland one day. Mary of Scotland's safety was better guaranteed in France being raised with Francis. The French king, Henri II, agreed.

It was at that point that Angus Ferguson saw his opportunity, and sought an audience with the dowager queen Marie. Riding north to Stirling in early March, he had the guarantee of a private audience with Marie from Patrick Hepburn, the third Earl of Bothwell, who had interceded with the dowager for him. He was to meet his contact, who would take him to the queen at an inn near Stirling called the Swan. When he entered the inn the innkeeper came forward to greet his guest.

"Welcome, my lord. A room? A meal? A mug of fine ale?"

"I'm to meet someone," Angus Ferguson said, his dark green eyes scanning the room. "Someone from the castle," he explained further, hoping the innkeeper would understand and be able to direct him.

"Ah, ye'll be wanting Mistress Melly, my lord," the innkeeper replied.

"Who is she?" the laird asked the innkeeper.

"One of French Mary's personal servants," the innkeeper said. He pointed to a hooded figure seated in a dark corner. "She's there, my lord."

The laird nodded. "Thank you," he said, and made his way across the room to where the woman sat. "I am the laird of Duin," he told her. "I believe you have been sent to bring me to my appointment, mistress."

The woman stood. She was small and sturdy. He couldn't tell whether she was young or old, but two sharp eyes surveyed him. "Well," she said in dour tones, "ye dinna look like a worthless rogue. Come along, then. We've a way to go."

"On foot?" He was surprised.

"Aye. Leave yer beastie here, my lord." She pulled her hood up and her cape tightly about her. Then she hurried across the room and out the door, the laird in her wake.

Mistress Melly led Angus Ferguson down one street, and then another. She turned here, and turned again. He wondered whether he would ever find his way back to the Swan. Above the town the great castle on its massive rock loomed. It was obvious they were not going up to it. Finally they stopped before a house. The woman knocked and they were admitted. "Here he is," Mistress Melly said to the young page who had opened the door.

"If ye'll follow me, my lord," the lad said, leading him down a hallway and to a closed door. Knocking, he opened the door to usher the laird inside.

Marie de Guise was standing, awaiting him. The laird of Duin bowed gracefully, and she was surprised. He was not at all like any border lord she had met previously, even her dearest Patrick Hepburn. They were mostly rough-hewn men in plain practical garments. This man was not only extraordinarily handsome, he was very fashionably garbed, his clothing styled in the latest French fashion. He towered over her, being at least three inches over six feet in height. He was clean shaven, his short hair black as a moonless night, his eyes the changing green of a shadowed forest glade. His carriage attested to his youth, but his face with its high cheekbones, long straight nose, and generous mouth was ageless.

He now took up her hand, kissing it with just the proper amount of respect. "I am honored to greet Scotland's dowager queen Marie, of the great house of Guise." He addressed her in perfect French.

Both Marie de Guise and her companion, a young French priest who served in her household, were surprised. "Your speech, monsieur, is excellent. How is it you speak my mother tongue so well?" she inquired of him.

"My own mother was French, madam, from Brittany, and I had the good fortune to study in France briefly with my friend Jamie Hepburn. I have several languages at my command."

She nodded. Aye, she thought to herself, he was totally unlike any border lord she had ever met, being fashionable, mannerly, and educated. "How may I be of service to you, my lord of Duin?" she asked him, switching to Scots English. She sat down in a high-backed chair now, the priest by her side, the page having silently disappeared.

"Nay, madam, 'tis I who would be of service to ye. It is not often that I admit to it, though it is widely suspected by my neighbors, but I am a wealthy man. Despite my youth I am aware that wealth is useless unless ye can use it to yer own advantage. Ye will, of course, be sending Queen Mary to France shortly."

Marie de Guise grew pale. "That is not common knowledge," she said. "Where have you heard such a tale?"

"It is what I would do were I in your position, madam," Angus Ferguson said, ignoring her question and smiling at her. "The little queen must be protected at all costs, and the English will not stop until they have her. If she is gone from Scotland to France, they must cease their efforts to obtain her, and hopefully their destruction of the borders. Forgive me for being blunt, madam, but I suspect yer purse is not as full as you might want it to be. I realize yer brothers in France will see to the little queen's best interests, but I imagine they will be relieved not to have to bear the expense of their niece's household and personal needs. King Henri as well, and while gifts from these gentlemen would be graciously accepted, wouldn't ye prefer not to have to rely on those gentlemen entirely?

"I am prepared to open my purse to the end that my queen might be maintained in the manner a queen should be maintained. My bankers in Paris, the House of Kira, will see that all of the queen's expenses are paid promptly, quarterly, until the day she weds the dauphin. This would, of course, include her wedding finery and trousseau. I ask only that my part in this endeavor remain secret. The Fergusons of Duin are private people," the laird said. "I do not wish to bring any attention to myself or to my clan."

Marie de Guise was at first speechless at the laird's offer. Then, quickly recovering, she inquired of him shrewdly, "What is it you do wish then, my lord? Your offer is more than generous, but you speak to me like a Breton fisherman bargaining with a goodwife on the quay, Angus Ferguson. What will you have of me in return?"

A brief flash of humor lit his handsome face, but it was quickly gone. "I want Duin created an earldom," he answered her candidly.

"You ask a great deal of Her Highness," the priest sputtered, outraged for his lady.

Marie de Guise, however, laughed, for she completely understood what the young man standing before her was requesting. "Nay, *Père* Michel, the laird requests virtually nothing of me. He does not wants lands, for he has them. Nor does he seek high office, for he prefers his anonymity. Gold he has in abundance, else he should not offer what he has. What he wishes is a title he may pass on to his heirs and the descendants following them. 'Tis nothing more than a piece of paper and a seal."

She looked at Angus Ferguson. "This will cost you dearly, my lord. Maintaining a queen, even a little one, and her entire household does not come cheaply. Remember that my daughter will reign over two great countries. She must be kept in a manner befitting her high station," Marie de Guise said quietly.

"And she will," the laird promised. "She will be sustained royally. Let the French king and the powerful among the Scots lords accept credit for all of this. If you will allow me this great honor, madam, I will gladly accept it. All I ask in return is that Duin be created as an earldom in perpetuity." He paused. "And perhaps yer permission to build a castle, a small castle, of course."

The dowager queen's eyes twinkled. "Why is it that I suspect, my lord, that the castle, the little castle, already exists?"

He shrugged in very Gallic fashion and smiled. "'Tis naught but a rather large house," he explained, "though some might say otherwise, which is why I ask yer permission to have a castle. I cannot therefore be said to be in violation of the law. We Fergusons of Duin do not like drawing attention to ourselves."

"Yet will not your becoming the Earl of Duin raise questions among some?" the dowager queen asked him.

"Not if it is believed that ye wished to balance the power in the west away from certain other families, and raised the Fergusons up with that in mind," he answered her cleverly. "There are some who have taken yer favor and misused it, yet ye are still kind."

They both knew he spoke of Patrick Hepburn, the Earl of Bothwell, who had gained this interview for Angus Ferguson. Though it was known that the *fair* earl, as he was called, loved James V's widowed queen, he was not always loyal to her or to Scotland. Still, he was a very fascinating man, and Marie de Guise had a weakness for him. She had never, however, allowed that weakness to rule her judgment or common sense.

Her mind turned back to the matter at hand. "You are very clever, my lord of Duin," she told Angus Ferguson. "Aye, it will please many if they think I am attempting to dull the Hepburn influence in the west. And your offer to maintain my daughter, the queen, until she is wed is incredibly generous. It is more than worth an earldom. But remember that she is only five years old. It will be at least ten years before my Mary and Francis wed. Scotland's purse is not a heavy one. Your offer is a gift from God, and his blessed Mother for whom my daughter is named, is it not, *Père* Michel?" Marie de Guise's practical French nature was rearing itself now. "Who can verify your wealth for me, my lord? I mean no offense, but this is a serious matter we have discussed."

"The House of Kira, madam. They have people here in Stirling and in Edinburgh, Perth, and Aberdeen," the laird said.

"Send someone to inquire discreetly," Marie de Guise directed the priest. Then she turned again to Angus Ferguson. "I will accept your offer, my lord. If your worth is proven and I am assured by the Kiras of your ability to do what you say you will do, then the parchments declaring your new earldom will be sent to Duin, and word of it cried throughout the borders. When that is done you will direct your bankers in what they must do, according to our agreement. Will that suit you, my lord?"

"The parchments must have the queen's own seal as well as yers upon them," the laird said to her. "And the proclamation posted on the Mercat Cross in Edinburgh."

"Rest assured that they will, and it will be official," she promised him. Then Marie de Guise stood and held out her hand to him again.

Stepping forward, he took the hand and kissed it, understanding that he was now dismissed. "I will pray for the queen's safe journey," he told Marie de Guise. Then he backed from the room, closing the door behind him.

"A very bold man, but then so many of these borderers are," the dowager queen remarked to the little priest. "The woman who weds him will have to be a strong lass."

But Angus Ferguson wasn't thinking of marriage at that point in his life. By late August, when the little queen departed for France, he had his earldom, and had briefly attracted the interest and envy of his neighbors. But when the gossip that his earldom had been created as a balance to the Hepburns was bruited about, everyone laughed. The Fergusons of Duin, magic or no, were not a match for the earls of Bothwell.

And as Angus had hoped, the slight furor had subsided as the business of survival took precedence. The border wars were over. Henry VIII was dead and buried. His son, Edward VI, was crowned, and while his protector, Seymour, was tempted to follow Henry VIII's policies toward Scotland, Mary's removal to France made the efforts futile. The young king died two months short of his sixteenth birthday. He was replaced for nine short days by his cousin Lady Jane Grey, as the Protestants attempted to block Mary Tudor from inheriting her throne. Mary prevailed, but five and a half years later she too died, leaving England's throne to the now twenty-five-year-old red-haired daughter of Henry VIII and Anne Boleyn, Elizabeth Tudor.

Elizabeth spent the first years of her reign consolidating her position as England's queen, and dodging suitors. Her only interest in the poor country to her north was the fact that its young queen, who would be queen of France one day as well, was now calling herself Queen of Scotland *and England*. Mary based her claim on the fact that her grandmother had been Henry VIII's sister, Margaret, wife of James IV. Elizabeth, she said, was merely Henry's bastard by the Boleyn whore. The fact that the English Church had given Henry his first divorce, that Anne had been crowned queen, was incidental to the young girl in France who parroted what her French relations told her.

But then England became less important to Mary, for her father-in-law, Henri II, was killed in a jousting accident. She and her young husband, Francis, suddenly found themselves the rulers of France. France took precedence over both Scotland and England.

In Scotland the Reformation was in full bloom. In no other country in all of Europe had Protestantism taken hold as hard as it did in Scotland. The clans in the north, and certain families, like the Gordons of Huntley and the Leslies of Glenkirk, held fast to the old faith despite the fact that the Reformed faith was declared law, and Catholicism outlawed under the influence of Master John Knox. Marie de Guise, a broad-minded woman who had allowed all faiths to flourish, even sheltering English Protestants from the Inquisition of Mary Tudor, was suddenly reviled for her faith.

Weary with the responsibilities she had shouldered for twelve years, Marie died, leaving Scotland in the hands of her daughter's half brother, James Stewart, the eldest illegitimate son of James V. In France the frail Francis died at the end of the same year. It seemed to Mary Stewart, now Stuart, that her mourning would never end. France's new ten-year-old king was a figurehead behind which his mother, Catherine de' Medicis, stood. She wanted the young dowager queen gone to her French estates, in obscurity. Instead Mary Stuart returned to Scotland to take up her throne there.

Elizabeth would not give her cousin safe passage through England should her ship founder coming from France to Scotland. The lord high admiral of Scotland, James Hepburn, the fourth Earl of Bothwell, had come personally to escort his queen. John Knox preached virulently about women rulers being against God's law, and he preached against Mary Stuart in particular. But Mary came home nonetheless, the swiftness of her passage surprising everyone, so that nothing was in readiness for the queen's arrival. The fact that the port of Leith and all of coastal Scotland was shrouded in a thick fog, a fog that lasted for several days, but gave weight to John Knox's words of doom.

Mary, however, took for her closest advisers her half brother, James Stewart, whom she remembered with great fondness. Marie de Guise had wisely gathered her husband's bastards into her own daughter's nursery. James, the eldest, had been the big brother to whom the tiny queen turned in her troubles. Now he stood by her side as her chief minister, murmuring in her ear along with the man who had served her late mother as secretary of state, William Maitland, the laird of Lethington. Mary had chosen to reappoint him to serve her in the same capacity.

While Mary persisted in maintaining her own Catholic faith, she proclaimed the law of the land to be freedom of worship for everyone in Scotland. It was a clever move, for it robbed John Knox of a major complaint against the queen, although her persistence in worshiping in the old Church infuriated him almost to apoplexy. Mary, unlike her predecessors, traveled Scotland visiting the Highlands, the Lowlands, and the borders, getting to know her people as no king since James IV had. The only place she did not journey to was the lordship of the isles.

Angus Ferguson met her when she spent a single night at Duin one autumn. She was hunting and it was grouse season. He was astounded by her beauty, charmed by her intellect and wit. She rode astride, something she had learned since her return to Scotland. The Scots, it seemed—John Knox in particular—were shocked by her show of leg when she rode sidesaddle. The hunt had been successful, and the roasted birds were served for the evening meal.

"You are indeed the handsomest man in the borders," the young queen told him. "What a pity you have no royal blood in you, my lord, else I should consider you for a husband. Unlike my cousin Elizabeth I am eager to wed again, and have bairns."

"I am, of course, devastated by my unsuitability," Angus Ferguson answered with a smile, "but a simple border lord such as myself could never be worthy of such a queen."

She laughed, but then she grew serious. "Who in Scotland is worthy of me, my lord?" she said softly. "Mayhap I should seek love instead."

"Remember, madam," the Earl of Duin told her, "that it is yer son who will one day rule Scotland, and more than likely England too. Elizabeth loves her freedom, I think, too much to put herself into any man's keeping, so choose wisely when ye marry again." Then he smiled at her once more. "If truth be told, madam, I doubt there is any man anywhere who is truly worthy of ye."

Mary Stuart laughed softly. "You are a dangerous man, my lord," she said. "And when will you take a wife for yourself so Duin may have an heir?"

"I shall wed a wife when you wed another husband, madam," he told her teasingly, and they both laughed.

The queen had departed the next day, and he had not seen her again. Now here it was, several years later, and his friend James Hepburn, the fourth Earl of Bothwell, who stood high in Mary Stuart's favor, had suddenly appeared at Duin. As he was not a man to just visit, Angus was curious, but he waited for Jamie to state the purpose of his visit as they sat in the hall playing chess and drinking the rather excellent French wine Duin always seemed to have.

"The queen is getting married," Bothwell finally said. "She's chosen badly, I fear, but there seems to be no stopping her. No one can reason with her. Not James Stewart, not Maitland. No one."

"Who is it?" Angus Ferguson wanted to know.

"Henry Stewart, Lord Darnley," Bothwell replied. "He's her cousin, and a Catholic, raised in England. Elizabeth Tudor suggested him, and her horsemaster, Dudley. She didn't expect our queen to pick either. Dudley, of course, was an insult, and I'm not certain Darnley isn't either."

"What's wrong wi' him?" Angus asked. "He's obviously got the proper amount of royal blood, which makes him suitable. Wasn't his mam Margaret Douglas, daughter of James IV's widow, Margaret Tudor, by her second husband, Archie Douglas, the Earl of Argyll? And his sire Matthew Stewart, Earl of Lennox?"

"Aye, that traitor," Bothwell snarled irritably.

"What's wrong wi' him then?" Angus repeated.

"He's a weak-kneed pompous fop with a lust for power," Bothwell said. "A tall, gangling lad with golden hair and blue eyes. He's younger than she is too, but she's besotted by him. He has the brain of a flea, and a crude wit."

"Be careful, old friend," Angus warned. "Ye sound like a man in love who has been overcome by a rival."

To his surprise James Hepburn flushed guiltily, but before Angus might say another word, Bothwell spoke. "Enough of the queen's folly," he growled. "That property ye've been trying to purchase from the laird of Rath, I think I have a way for ye to get it, Angus."

"How?" The Earl of Duin was curious. The land in question bordered his, and when its previous owner had died he had attempted to purchase it from his heir, a laird whose lands were in the eastern borders. Robert Baird, the laird of Rath, would not sell the property, despite the Earl of Duin's offer to name his price. For several years now he had been trying to obtain the land, which was particularly good pasturage.

"It's time ye wed," Bothwell said. "Would ye agree to that?"

"Aye," Angus said slowly, "I'll be thirty-five come August."

"Rath is married to a Hamilton. They have a son and four daughters. The eldest lass is twenty. Robert Baird won't let the others wed until she is wed."

"What's wrong wi' her?" Angus asked bluntly.

"It's the damnedest thing," Bothwell said. "Her mother is a beauty. Her three younger sisters are beauties, but Annabella Baird is as plain as porridge."

"She's ugly then," Angus said.

"Nay, not at all. Her face is oval in shape. Her eyes fine. She has a straight nose and a nice mouth, but there is nothing to commend her but her hair, which is the color of midnight, long and thick. It is her finest feature, but ugly, nay. She is not ugly," Bothwell tried to explain.

"But while her sisters are beauties they are ordinary lasses. Annabella Baird has wit and manners. I was introduced to her at a summer games last year. I liked her."

"Ye didn't seduce her, then?" Angus teased his friend.

James Hepburn laughed. "Nay, not a proper laird's daughter. She needs a husband. Ye need a wife, and ye want that land her father possesses. I will wager I can get Robert Baird to give his daughter that property as her dower portion, along with whatever else he was putting aside for her."

"I'll take her for the land," Angus Ferguson said. "I don't like having unprotected acreage on my borders."

It was then that another man in the hall spoke up. "Ye can have any woman ye want," Matthew Ferguson said. He was the earl's bastard half brother. Matthew had been born six months after Angus. His mother had been in service to the earl's late mother, the lady Adrienne. "I have made inquiries, Angus. The girl is respectable, but as Lord Bothwell has said, she is plain of face. Ye could have a great beauty as yer countess."

"A plain woman will suit me very well," the earl said. "She will be grateful to have a husband, and eager to do her duty, which is to give me sons. She will be obedient and bring no shame to the Fergusons, Matthew."

"I suppose ye're pretty enough for all of us," his half brother teased with a grin, ducking the swat Angus aimed at him. But then Matthew grew serious. "Ye'll be kind to her, won't ye? As ye've said, she'll be grateful to have a husband, but even plain women have dreams of happiness."

"I'm nae a monster," the earl said, feeling a trifle offended. "Ye must remember, Matthew, that while some will find love in marriage, the truth is that marriage is an arrangement between families to the mutual benefit of both. Rath wants a good husband for his eldest daughter, and he will get it in me. I want a bit of land that Rath possesses. Taking his lass to wife is no great hardship. We both profit. I'll treat Annabella Baird with the kindness and the respect she will merit as my countess."

"Ye've a soft heart, laddie," James Hepburn said to Matthew. "Be careful it doesn't get ye into trouble," he warned the younger man with a grin, "and listen to yer brother. He's a practical man, wise enough to take a plain virgin in exchange for something he wants. A man's mistresses can be pretty."

Angus Ferguson laughed. "It will be fun to introduce my bride to the joys of the marriage bed. Is it not said that all little cats are alike when you pet them in the dark?"

"It depends on whether they purr or scratch," Bothwell responded with a grin.

"Either way will delight me," Angus answered with a chuckle. "I suppose I should meet Robert Baird face-to-face before I wed his daughter."

"I'll send word to him. He can meet us at Hermitage Castle," Bothwell said.

The Earl of Duin nodded in agreement and turned to his younger sibling. "I'll want you to go to Rath and act as my proxy, Matthew. The few remaining inhabitants of our brother Jamie's monastery are about to depart for France, as they are no longer welcome in Scotland. The abbot has already gone. He left Jamie to conclude the necessary business. I sent to our brother, and he will go with you to make certain the marriage contracts are drawn up properly and to officiate at the ceremony.

Then you will all return to Duin, where this union will be blessed before our clan folk."

"I am honored to act for you in this capacity," Matthew Ferguson responded.

He and Angus had been very close their entire lives. His mother, Jeanne, had been the confidante and tiring woman of the earl's mother, Adrienne du Montverte. It was rumored that Jeanne was her lady's cousin, a poor relation, raised with the du Montverte heiress. Neither woman had ever confirmed nor denied the rumor. Pregnant with her first child, Adrienne had begged Jeanne to service her husband's lustful nature so she would be spared this task while she carried her child. She was a delicate girl, and very much afraid of losing this first child whose birth would cement her place in her husband's life.

But Jeanne was reluctant, despite her love for her mistress. "What if I am rendered enceinte by the master?" she asked Adrienne. "Will you put me out on the road with my helpless *bébé*, madam? Or will you insist that I wed some farmer to cover my shame?"

The good lady, however, had assured her trusted friend that if she had a child by the laird of Duin, that child would be brought up with her own child, following the example of both the Scots and French royal families. Satisfied, Jeanne had agreed, and William Ferguson was not unhappy to have his wife's plump red-haired serving wench to fondle and fuck while Adrienne ripened with his son. The laird of Duin's seed was potent. He impregnated Jeanne, but, less fearful than her mistress, the sturdy serving woman kept the laird's lustful nature well satisfied until her mistress was ready to allow him into her bed again. And, true to her word, the lady Adrienne added Jeanne's newborn son to her six-month-old son's nursery so the children might be brought up together.

The laird of Duin's wife delivered a second son, and then a daughter, secure in the knowledge that Jeanne would keep her husband entertained. Jeanne gave the laird a second daughter. Little Jean grew up with her brothers, Angus, Matthew, and Jamie, along with her sister, Mary. Jean, unlike her sister, was lively and full of fun. It was obvious she had no calling for the Church. Her mother trained her as a privileged servant who would one day look after her oldest brother's bride. Jean Ferguson was eager to meet Annabella Baird.

"About time ye married," Jean had said to Angus Ferguson when he had announced his intentions to her. "At least yer nae as potent as Da."

"I've been more careful than Da," he answered her, laughing. He had always enjoyed the fact that his half sister was so outspoken.

"I'll have quite a lot to deal with on my hands if the poor lass has been filled with the tales of yer escapades here in the borders with the lasses, not to mention those silly stories of our family's magical ways. Matthew says that Bothwell told ye the lass is a plain-faced virgin wi' no knowledge of the world at all." Jean Ferguson was a pretty woman of twenty-two, with her mother's red hair and her father's hazel eyes. She was wed to the castle's captain of the men-at-arms.

"An innocent can be molded to suit my own personal tastes," the earl replied.

"Ye're too arrogant by far," his half sister said, shaking her head. "The lass could be wise beyond her years."

"I seriously doubt it," Angus Ferguson responded. "The daughter of a tower laird? It is unlikely she can even write her name. She will not be educated beyond the skills a woman needs to run her household, which will suit me quite well, Jeannie. What would I do with an intelligent wife?"

"Ye might try talking to her," Jean said sharply.

The earl laughed, showing a flash of straight white teeth. "Do not lead my wife into rebellion, little sister." He chuckled. "An obedient wife is what I seek. If I am kind she will be loyal. Plain women do not get a great deal of attention. Let her be grateful that I am her husband. Then I will not have to concern myself that she will betray me."

Jean Ferguson reached out and put a gentle hand on her brother's handsome face. "Angus, Angus," she said, "it still chafes ye, doesn't it? Elizabeth Kennedy wasn't worthy of ye. Pity poor Adam Douglas, for he canna be sure that even the first bairn she bore him is his own. Certainly none of the others are. The woman canna keep her legs closed to any man with an upstanding cock. Ye would have killed her long since. I don't know why Adam hasn't, except he is still so besotted by her."

Angus Ferguson nodded in agreement with his sister's assessment. The daughter of a neighboring laird, Elizabeth Kennedy possessed a great beauty that was matched by an equally great lustful nature. Although warned by his siblings against her, the young earl had been taken in by her exquisite fair face and delightful playful manner. He had begun to court her, thrilled that she would bestow her kisses upon him. His siblings were wrong. Jealous. They had to be, for when he had declared his affections for her she had responded with delight. At twenty-three he became the happiest man in all of Scotland.

And then one afternoon he had come upon her lying in the autumn heather, her beautiful breasts bared to the sky, and three young lads were taking turns servicing her lusty nature as she laughed, teased, and encouraged them in their endeavors. He had watched, fascinated, unable to fully comprehend what he was seeing. His Elizabeth. The lass he loved and wanted to wed was nothing better than a common whore. He struggled to disbelieve the evidence of his own eyes, but how could he? The labored grunts of the men using her, the cries of pleasure she made, finally slammed into his consciousness, forcing him to accept what he was seeing.

With a roar of fury he made his presence known. The three men gaped in shock, but then, recognizing him, jumped up and fled. Her mouth bruised with the kisses of others, sloe-eyed Elizabeth Kennedy had beckoned to him, smiling a slow, seductive smile. At that moment he had wanted to fall on her and fuck her until she was dead. He had believed her a virgin. He had been so gentle in his wooing of her. To see other men enjoying what he had denied himself was galling. But instead he had dragged her up, taking her home to throw her at her father's feet, disclosing her perfidy.

The little bitch had attempted to lie, claiming that the earl had misunderstood what he had seen. She had been set upon and raped, Elizabeth Kennedy told her father. Lord Kennedy's face had grown pale as he listened to his daughter, but it was quickly obvious that he believed the Earl of Duin. What Angus had wondered at that point was, did Kennedy really know about his daughter's character? The older man's face now grew deep red in his uncontrolled fury as, reaching for his cane, he grasped his daughter by her long unbound hair and beat her until her screams shook his hall. He ceased his punishment only when his weeping wife begged him to stop.

Lady Kennedy had escorted her wayward daughter

off, while Angus Ferguson tendered his regrets to the Kennedy laird that he had had to bring him such unpleasant news. "I canna possibly consider Elizabeth for my wife now, knowing and seeing what I have this day," he told him. Kennedy had nodded his understanding. Two months later Elizabeth Kennedy was wed to one Adam Douglas, delivering a bairn seven months afterward. A weak man, Adam Douglas basked in the knowledge that he was wed to the loveliest woman in the borders, and ignored the gossip about his wife's many lovers.

Angus Ferguson never forgot that at the age of twenty-three he had been betrayed by a beautiful woman and made to look the fool. Everyone, he later learned, had known of the Kennedy lass's proclivities but him. He had been taken in by a fair face just like any damned green lad, and he should have known better. After that, he had avoided the topic of marriage, amusing himself with a variety of lovely mistresses, for mistresses were supposed to be beautiful, and only briefly faithful. The volatile nature of a mistress was no threat to his pride.

He met with the laird of Rath at Bothwell's castle of Hermitage. Robert Baird had been totally honest with him. Aye, his oldest daughter was a virgin, an obedient and good lass, but she had not beauty to recommend her. But it was his duty to find her a husband, and not just any husband. Annabella, the laird told the earl, was quite dear to his heart. Her husband must be able to forgive her lack of beauty, and be kind to her. If the Earl of Duin wanted those lands bordering his that Robert Baird possessed, he would have to take Annabella as his wife, and guarantee the laird his assurances that he would be good to the lass.

"I dinna want a beautiful wife," Angus Ferguson had told his prospective father-in-law. "I want an obedient wife who will do her duty by me." Nay, he didn't want a wife who would be the envy of other men's lust. A woman who would use her beauty to betray him and break his heart. He wanted a woman he could respect, who would be faithful to him and to his wishes. "Yer daughter's reputation is pleasing to me, my lord. I believe she will suit me quite well."

"I must ask," Robert Baird said, "the rumors of sorcery . . . are they true, my lord?"

"Nay, they are not. I am no sorcerer; nor do I practice the dark arts," Angus Ferguson said.

"Then I am satisfied ye'll be a good husband to my daughter. If ye'll have her, the land ye desire is yers. It will serve as her dower portion," the laird of Rath said.

"Agreed!" the Earl of Duin responded, and the two men shook hands. "I'll send my half brother, Matthew, to Rath as my proxy. He will travel in the company of our other brother, James, a priest. Jamie will see to the marriage contracts and perform the ceremony. I know ye're of the Reformed faith, but I remain a son of Holy Mother Church."

Robert Baird nodded. "I understand and have no objections," he said. "We were of the old faith until the law was changed, but the queen says we may all worship as we see fit. Annabella will conform to yer wishes, my lord."

Indeed she would, the laird thought. He had found her a good husband when he had not ever thought he would. And she would not just be a wife. She would be the Countess of Duin.

Chapter 2

$\mathcal{T}$he laird of Rath had gathered his family in the hall of their tower house. He signaled to his servants to bring wine. It was poured into the two silver cups that belonged to the lord and his wife, and five small round earthenware cups for their five children. Robert Baird raised his cup. "Let us toast your sister, Annabella, who is soon to be wed," he said, enjoying the look of surprise on his daughters' faces.

"To Annabella!" they all said, drinking deep from their cups.

Annabella Baird had never liked surprises. Especially when they involved her. She would have preferred it if her father and her mother had told her of this marriage privily before announcing it in the hall for all the world to hear. She could but imagine how relieved her parents were to have finally found her a husband. Annabella Baird had no illusions about herself. She knew better than most just how plain of face she was. Finally regaining her composure she asked, "Who am I to wed, Da?" Who indeed?

"You are to marry the Earl of Duin, Angus Ferguson. He is your senior by fifteen years, but has never taken a wife," Robert Baird told his daughter.

Annabella's next-younger sister, Myrna, snickered, and then whispered something to their next sister, Sorcha, who immediately giggled. Sorcha was by nature a giggler. Annabella found it quite annoying.

"What is so amusing?" she demanded of Myrna.

"The laird of Duin has had no time for a wife, it is said, because he spends all his time chasing pretty lasses," Myrna replied. "Blessed Mary, Annabella, he is said to be the handsomest man in the borders, as well as a sorcerer!" She brayed her laughter. "The plainest face in the borders to wed a handsome sorcerer. Maybe his magic can make you fair." Myrna cackled again at her own wit.

"If sorcery could sweeten your nature, sister, I should be forever grateful," Annabella returned sharply. "Won't Ian Melville be surprised to learn what a shrew ye are, Myrna." She turned back to her father. "Where is Duin, Da?"

"In the western borders on the sea," Robert Baird answered his daughter.

"I am nae a shrew!" Myrna said angrily.

Sorcha and their youngest sister, Agnes, giggled as Annabella shrugged but did not take back her harsh words.

"Now, now, my lasses, ye're sisters. Make yer peace wi' one another," their mother said. "Very soon Annabella will be gone from us, and who knows when we will see her again." She smiled warmly at her eldest daughter.

"Probably never," Myrna said almost smugly. "We shall be much too busy with our own lives to go traveling across Scotland to see Annabella and her sorcerer. I am so glad that Sorcha, Agnes, and I will wed closer to home, so we may be near our mother."

"Though you three will be near," the lady Anne said, "'tis Annabella who is making a great marriage and bringing honor to the Bairds of Rath. The distance between us is several days, but we will see one another again," she reassured her eldest daughter. Then she smiled at them. "Now, because time is short we must begin to prepare your sister for the journey to her new home. In just a few weeks the Fergusons will come to claim her and take her back to Duin."

"Ohhh," Myrna said. "Will we get to see the sorcerer?"

"Daughter," Robert Baird said to Myrna, "Angus Ferguson is no sorcerer. Ye must cease referring to him that way. I now find myself grateful he will not be coming to Rath, but sending his proxy."

The next few weeks were busy ones, with the ladies of the household packing Annabella's few possessions into an iron-bound oak trunk. Her dower consisted of linens for both bed and table; two fine goose-down pillows; a down coverlet; a silver spoon and cup; and a fine wooden box filled with ointments, balms, salves, potions, and healing herbs, along with her clothing and small bits of jewelry. A special gown was to be made for the bride to wear on her wedding day. Afterward it would serve as her best garment.

She tried to picture this unknown man she was to wed so soon. He would be tall, of course. Short men were not usually highly praised as handsome. Was he fair or dark? What color were his eyes? Myrna, who always seemed to know everything, could say only that the gossip about the Fergusons of Duin said they were magical folk, and kept much to themselves. It was the earl's handsome face that caused the telltales to chatter.

"He is said to enchant any woman he wants with a

mere look," Myrna related in hushed tones as she crossed herself.

"It is something to talk about besides the English raids and the destruction they have wrought here in the borders," Annabella responded. She was a practical young woman. "Babbling about a handsome man is much nicer than wondering how we will feed ourselves in the coming winter." But for all her brave words, she worried. Still, it was a far better match than she could have ever anticipated.

"They say hc has many mistresses, for once he has loved them, they do not—will not—leave him," Myrna chattered on. "I'm sorry we will not get to see him, but perhaps 'tis better this way. After all, we are so beautiful, and ye're so plain, Annabella. The earl might regret his decision if he saw us together."

"What a mean thing to say," young Agnes spoke up in defense of her eldest sister.

But Annabella, used to Myrna's thoughtless tongue, just laughed. "Ye're jealous," she taunted back. "I am to be the Countess of Duin, and ye naught but Mistress Melville. As for the earl's many mistresses, they may come in handy if he is not to my taste. I am required to produce an heir for my lord, to keep his house in good order, to stand by his side and chatter pleasantries when he entertains. I can do all of that, Myrna—and a handsome husband is much to be appreciated."

Myrna shrugged. "Ye're a strange lass," she said. "I should be furious if my husband strayed. Indeed, I should scratch his eyes out so he didn't ever cast them on another woman again. But then I suppose ye're just grateful to have found a husband at all. I wonder ye did not go to the old church to spend yer days in prayer."

"I have no wish at all to spend my days in prayer,"

Annabella said. "I'm grateful that Da found me a husband, but I can't help but wonder how he did it. We live in a stone tower that has stood for several hundred years, and housed many generations of Bairds. We cannot be said to be poor, but neither are we rich. How hard our father must scrabble to find dower portions for four daughters. How has he done it? Where is it coming from? And how on earth did he find an earl for me? Why would such a man have the daughter of a simple tower laird of no importance for a wife?"

She looked at Myrna. "Ye're good at ferreting out information." Then Annabella added the spur she knew would encourage her sister to go snooping. "I can only hope that Da has not taken from your dowers in order to gain this earl for me."

Myrna paled as her breath caught in her throat briefly. Recovering, she said, "Ian remarked to me recently that his father was not pleased with the size of my dower. He said his son's bride should do better. But he also said I am healthy, and he believes I will be a good mother."

"Ye're not breeding stock," Annabella said, irritated.

"Aye, I am, and so are ye," Myrna replied. "Our dowers and our ability to give our husbands sons are our great value as women."

"Jesu, Jesu, ye're listening to those traveling churchmen again. Reformed Church or old Church, they all have the same opinion of women." Annabella swore.

Myrna's Cupid's bow of a mouth pursed itself in disapproval. "I intend to be a good wife to Ian Melville," she said. "I shall birth a son for his family as quickly as I can. Ye had best do the same for yer earl, sister."

Annabella sighed. Why couldn't a woman just *be*? she silently asked herself. Why was her only value in her ability to reproduce, and in the coin she would bring her husband? But she was curious to learn what Myrna could find out about Duin and its earl, because the day was drawing nearer and nearer when the Fergusons would come to take her away to the west, and the stranger who would be her husband.

Myrna, however, could learn no more information about the lord of Duin. Nor did she learn how their father had managed to gain the dower to betroth Annabella to an earl. With the Fergusons just a few days from Rath, Annabella went to their mother and asked, "How did Da find a dower large enough to satisfy an earl, Mama? I pray he took nothing from my sisters to do it."

"Ye should really not ask such questions, Annabella," her mother said. "It should not matter to ye how the deed was accomplished, and naught was taken from yer sisters."

"But I have asked, and I want to know," Annabella persisted.

The lady Anne sighed. Then she said, "I suppose there is no harm in yer knowing. It was nothing more than a wee bit of good fortune that put ye in the earl's path. I will not pretend that it has been easy to find a good husband for ye, Annabella. Yer da was actually despairing over it, for a lass wi' a plain face and a small dower has a difficult time of it. But then Lord Bothwell came to yer da and suggested that he offer the Earl of Duin that bit of property in the west yer da inherited, as a dower portion for ye. The earl has been attempting to purchase that land from yer da for several years, but Robert would nae sell, for the kinsman who left it to him feuded with the Fergusons of Duin. The land borders his own and is particularly good grazing land. The earl raises cattle.

"Angus Ferguson is ready to take a wife. He doesn't need a rich wife, for riches he has aplenty. He doesn't object to having a wife whose features are modest in appearance. But most important, he wants that acreage that yer father holds, and so ye have gained him for yer husband in exchange for that land. Land has always been an acceptable dower, Annabella. Yer da has rented that land to Duin since he inherited it. The coin he earned for the rental has been put aside for yer dowers.

"Last month when yer da and the earl met, Robert was assured that Angus Ferguson wanted only the land in exchange for making ye his wife. He declined any purse, saying the land was more than enough value for a wife. Yer da and I will take the coin we saved for ye and now divide it among yer sisters."

"Nay," said Annabella. "If the earl declines my purse, then it should be mine, Mama. What if he dies, and I have need of another husband? Ye cannot take back the land ye have given the Fergusons, which leaves me in poverty wi'out my gold. I will not be left helpless to the Fergusons, and married off to some retainer for their benefit. If the earl does not want my gold, I do."

Her mother was surprised by her daughter's clever reasoning. She saw the wisdom in Annabella's words. "Say nothing to anyone, my daughter," she told the girl. "I will speak wi' yer da. Ye will have what is yers; I promise ye. Ye will be far from the Bairds of Rath at Duin. You do need to be able to protect yerself."

"My sisters have inherited yer beauty, Mama, but I seem to have inherited yer wisdom," Annabella remarked to her mother.

The lady Anne smiled. "Thank ye, daughter," she said. "Now learn this from me as well. Men, husbands in particular, dinna like discovering that their wives are intelligent. Keep this knowledge from yer bridegroom, and always keep yer own counsel. Ye will have a happier marriage if ye do, Annabella."

"How will ye get Da to let me keep my gold?" the girl asked, curious.

"By letting him believe 'twas all his own idea," her mother said mischievously.

Annabella laughed. "Oh, Mama, ye're really quite wicked," she teased her parent.

"Being a wee bit wicked," the lady told her daughter, "can also intrigue a husband, as long as he does not feel threatened by yer behavior. Now, there are other things we must discuss if ye're to be properly prepared for yer marriage bed."

"I know a man's form is different," Annabella said. "I recall that ye bathed Rob and me together when we were little ones. Yet girls dinna have breasts as children. They grow them as they grow older. Do men grow anything extra?"

"Nay," her mother said, "but their man parts do grow in keeping wi' the rest of them. Some sprout hair on their chests, while others do not. We are all furred in many of the same places."

"Myrna says the earl has many mistresses," Annabella told her mother.

"Aye, a man will have his extras," the lady Anne said calmly.

"Does Da have a mistress?" Annabella asked her mother. "How do you bear it?"

"Your father has not the means to keep a mistress." Her mother laughed. "But I know he tumbles the village lasses now and again. It means nothing. He is my husband, and my lord. He gives me his love and his respect. I want nothing more."

"The earl is rich enough to keep a mistress," Annabella said thoughtfully.

"Aye, 'tis said he is rich," her mother responded. "But if he keeps a mistress you will never acknowledge her, my daughter, should you learn of her existence. Give yer husband the bairns he wants and must have. Give him yer loyalty. He will respond in kind, no matter his wandering eye. You may even fall in love wi' him."

"Will he love me?" Annabella wondered aloud.

"If ye're fortunate, perhaps he will," her mother said, "but his respect is more important. A woman respected by her man is secure in her place."

"Do ye love Da?" the girl boldly inquired.

"Aye, I suppose that I do, and I've always enjoyed our bed sport," the lady Anne said. Then she smiled. "But we have strayed from the knowledge ye must have for yer wedding night."

"I think I know what I must," Annabella said, suddenly a bit shy. "I've seen the creatures making the beast with two backs, Mama."

The good lady laughed softly. "'Tis a bit different when a man mounts his woman," she said. "Ye'll be on yer back, not yer belly. There is an opening between yer legs where his manhood will be fitted. Some think of it as another form of riding. The first time he enters yer body will hurt, but only briefly. That is because his cock will pierce yer maidenhead. When he has pleasured himself, and hopefully ye as well, he will water yer womb with his seed. The seed will not always be implanted, but once it is, a bairn will grow within yer belly, and after several months, usually eight to ten, the bairn will be born. Being my eldest daughter and second child, ye've seen the process of birth, so I need not tell ye of it. Do ye have any questions, Annabella?"

"Nay, Mama, thank ye," the girl said politely. Actually she had several questions, but she was too embarrassed to ask her mother.

"'Tis better ye not be too knowledgeable," the lady Anne said. "Yer husband will want to lead the way, and ye should let him."

And finally her possessions were packed and ready. Her wedding gown was sewn. And on a fine morning toward the end of September, Matthew and James Ferguson, in the company of their sister, Jean, arrived at the tower house of the laird of Rath. They came with a large troop of men-at-arms wearing the blue-and-green plaid of the Fergusons of Duin, with its thin red and white stripes. Two pipers accompanied them, and Jean Ferguson, riding astride like the men she rode with, led a pristine white mare. From the moment they had entered onto Baird lands, they had been accompanied by the bride's clansmen. There would be no delay. The marriage would be celebrated this very day, and on the morrow the bride would depart with her husband's kin for Duin.

"Ohh," Myrna squealed, gazing from a window on the arriving visitors. "What a fine mare! Who is the woman leading it, do ye think?"

"The Fergusons are well garbed and well mounted," Sorcha noted.

Agnes began to weep. "We'll never see our Annabella after today," she sobbed.

"Ye're not promised, nor will Da permit ye to wed until ye are at least sixteen," Annabella said quietly to her youngest sister. "Ye shall come and visit me next summer, Aggie." She put a comforting arm about the girl. "I'm sure the earl will permit it, and send a fine escort for ye too," she promised.

Agnes sniffled, but then, looking up through her wet lashes at Myrna and Sorcha, both of whom were always lording marriage over her, she said, "Ye two will probably be wed by next summer, so ye'll not get to visit our sister in her fine new home, but I will!" There was an air of triumph in her voice. Then she added, "Maybe Annabella will even find a rich husband for me."

Myrna and Sorcha looked distinctly put out by Agnes's words, but then Myrna said meanly, "If I were our plain-faced sister, I would certainly not invite my beautiful little sister to visit. What if the earl fell in love wi' ye, and magicked our sister away so he could have ye?"

"Oh, Annabella, I wouldn't steal yer man!" Agnes burst out. "I swear it!"

"I'm sure ye wouldn't, Aggie," her elder sister said, "and if my husband turned out to be that fickle, I wouldn't want him. As for ye two, eventually ye'll come to Duin to see me. Ye'll always be welcome, sisters."

Their brother, Rob, entered the chamber. "Da wants you downstairs in the hall immediately, Annabella," he said. "Ye should be there to greet yer bridegroom's kinfolk." He was a handsome young man of twenty-two, with their mother's blue eyes and their father's dark hair. "Ye three are to remain here until ye're invited into the hall," he told his younger sisters. No need for the Fergusons to be blinded by their beauty until they had grown used to Annabella, Rob considered.

"Do I look all right, Rob?" Annabella asked anxiously. She was wearing the gown in which she would shortly be wed. It was lovely, but not quite the right color for the pale girl. The bodice was a light gray velvet embroidered with silver threads and black jet beads. The heavy silk skirt was a blue-gray. On a lass with golden hair it would have been stunning, even if it was a bit old-fashioned. But it did not really suit Annabella's coloring at all. Her dark hair was left loose to proclaim her innocence.

"Ye look fine," he said dismissively.

Brother and sister descended down the narrow staircase that led into the hall.

Once there, the laird waved to them to come quickly forward, indicating they should stand with him. The lady Anne reached out to take her eldest daughter's hand in hers, giving it a little squeeze of encouragement as the Fergusons entered the hall.

"Welcome to Rath," Robert Baird said, smiling.

"Thank ye, my lord. We have not met, but I am Matthew Ferguson, the laird's half brother, and steward of Duin. This is James Ferguson, the laird's brother, a priest come to inspect the contracts and perform the ceremony." Matthew bowed politely.

The laird greeted both men cordially, noting that the priest did not wear the robes denoting his office. A wise move, he thought, considering the recent law of the land outlawing the old Church. Then Robert Baird introduced his wife, his son, and, finally, Annabella.

Matthew and James acknowledged each introduction pleasantly. Then Matthew turned, nodding to his sister to step forward. "This is the earl's half sister and my sister, Jean, my lord. She has been raised to serve my brother's wife. Angus thought that since the journey back to Duin is one of several days, his bride would feel more comfortable in the company of another woman."

"How kind!" Annabella exclaimed before anyone else might speak. She would indeed enjoy having another woman with her. Her family could not send a female servant with her, for she and her sisters had always been taken care of by their old nurse, who was too ancient now to leave Rath. "I must thank the earl as soon as we arrive," the bride said. "To send me a companion was a most thoughtful gesture."

"I commend your good manners, Annabella Baird," James Ferguson responded. "My brother is a man who values the courtesies." He already liked this young woman. There appeared to be no deceit about her. As a priest, he had learned to quickly assess those about him. Despite Matthew's concern over her lack of beauty, his eldest brother's bride seemed a sensible lass, which would serve Angus far better than some flighty beauty. He turned to the laird. "I have brought the marriage contracts with me, my lord. May we sit and go over them? Then, with Matthew standing proxy for the earl, I will perform the ceremony making your daughter Angus Ferguson's wife."

The four men moved off to sit at the high board, where the marriage contract was now spread out upon the long rectangular table. The lady Anne and her daughter moved away to seat themselves by the hearth.

"Who are the mothers of these men?" Annabella asked her mother. "Did the earl's father have a second wife?"

"Nay," the mother told her daughter. "The earl's mother was a Frenchwoman. The story told is that when she was enceinte with her first child, she begged her young serving woman, a lass who had been raised with her and come with her from France, to fulfill her husband's manly needs, for he was a lusty man. She swore to raise any bairn born of such a union with her own bairns. She gave her husband three, and her serving woman gave him two. That is the tale your da told me, for the earl told him when they met at Hermitage several weeks ago. The five were raised together."

Annabella was shocked. "How could the old laird's wife bear to keep such a servant? Did ye not tell me that if my husband takes a mistress I am not to acknowledge such a woman?"

"'Twas the earl's mother who suggested the arrangement, for she trusted her servant. She did not want her husband in the clutches of another woman. The laird was always respectful of his wife, and she loyal to him. There was no conflict between mistress and servant over this matter. I am told the old laird had several other bastards whom he acknowledged over the years of his life. Those bairns, however, remained wi' their mams. Men will be men, Annabella, but unless your husband's behavior threatens you or your bairns, ye would be wise to look the other way. The wives of the Stewart kings certainly have, and those bairns who are born on the other side of the blanket are useful and loyal to their sire's family. It is the custom among the high nobility to raise their bastards as trusted servants and confidants. Queen Mary is advised by her half brother, Lord James Stewart, whose mam was once King James's mistress. And the Earl of Duin's half brother serves him well, as you see. His half sister will serve ye, and will prove a valuable ally for ye, my daughter."

"I am not certain I am comfortable with my husband's half sister serving me," Annabella admitted to her mother.

"Do not worry yourself," the lady Anne advised. "Jean Ferguson has been raised to fulfill this position. She will take pride in it." She turned to look about the hall and see where Jean was now, and, finding her standing quietly across the hall, the lady Anne beckoned to her to come and join them.

Jean came immediately. "How may I serve ye, my lady?" she asked politely.

"By reassuring my daughter that although you are the earl's half sister, you are glad to serve her," the older woman said.

Jean Ferguson smiled a sweet smile. "Do not be uncomfortable, my lady Annabella," she said, looking the girl directly in the eye. "My own mam was the lady Adrienne's serving woman. I was raised to one day serve my brother's bride. I am honored to do so," she told her new mistress, curtsying.

"Having a personal servant is new for me, and I am used to a simple life," Annabella replied.

"Life is not overly complicated at Duin," Jean reassured her new mistress.

The lady Anne arose from her seat, indicating that Jean should take it. "Why do not you two become better acquainted," she said, "while I go and fetch your sisters? As soon as your father has approved the contracts, you will be formally wed." She hurried off.

"Do you think the earl will like me?" Annabella asked shyly.

"Of course he will. Angus is a good man, my lady," Jean said.

"I realize 'tis that bit of land he really wants," Annabella remarked.

"Aye, he does," Jean replied, "but it is also past time he took a wife. He has no legitimate heirs. He did not obtain the earldom to have it expire on his death. My brother wants to found a dynasty, and he needs a wife to do it."

"He's being forced to the altar," Annabella said softly. "I hope he will not hate me for it."

Jean laughed. "All men are *forced* to the altar, my

lady. Few go willingly. Marriage is about gold, land, and power. These are the things that make a family strong."

"He will certainly be disappointed in me, for I have no beauty," Annabella said bleakly. "I have never before wished for my sisters' beauty, but I do now."

"Aye," Jean said candidly. "Ye're plain. There's nae denying it. But ye're nae ugly. Yer features are neat. Yer skin is clear, and"—she reached out to catch a length of Annabella's sable hair between her fingers—"yer hair is glorious. My brother has been told of yer deficiencies, and did nae object."

Annabella didn't know whether to laugh or cry at this bit of information, but then her father called her to come to the high board. She rose and hurried to his side.

"Look here in the marriage contract," the laird of Rath said, pointing. "Here is where it is acknowledged that ye possess ten unclipped gold coins, and that they are yers in perpetuity to do with as ye will."

Annabella's gray eyes scanned the parchment. "Aye, Da, I see the clause. Thank ye for that."

"Ye read, my lady?" James Ferguson asked her.

"Aye, sir. I read, I write, and I have been taught to work simple numbers," Annabella admitted to the priest, hoping the earl would not disapprove of her knowledge. *I need no more deficiencies*, she thought.

Well, well, well, Matthew Ferguson considered. *Perhaps there is hope for the lass after all. She does not appear unintelligent, and with these small skills may be of use to us in more than just her ability to breed. 'Tis all to the good. Angus should be pleased.*

"Are the contracts to yer satisfaction, my lord?" James Ferguson asked politely.

"They are," Robert Baird said. "Everything is as it should be."

"Since all has met wi' yer approval," James responded, "let us sign the contracts now, and when that is done I will perform the ceremony." He looked to Annabella. "Ye will want to sign for yerself, my lady. There are three copies: one for yer father, one for the earl, and the third will be kept by the church."

"They must be wed in the Reformed kirk as well," the laird of Rath said. "I want no one doubting my daughter's status, nor that of her bairns. While the old Church may recognize only its own rites, it is no longer legal in Scotland."

James Ferguson sighed. While the queen might proclaim religious tolerance, John Knox and his ilk had made the new kirk the law of the land. "My brother understands this, my lord. Lady Annabella will be wed at Duin in the Reformed kirk. My brother wishes no disputes over his marriage either, which is why he sent a proxy to Rath rather than come himself. This way his own people can proclaim the marriage legitimate under the laws of Scotland, having seen it performed at Duin kirk with their own eyes."

Robert Baird nodded, satisfied. While he found John Knox's lack of tolerance for the Catholic Church objectionable, the Reformed Church appealed more to him and his kin.

The lady Anne now reentered the hall in the company of her three younger daughters. The lasses curtsied prettily as they were introduced to the three Fergusons.

Myrna flirted with the two men, unaware at first that James was a priest. Sorcha giggled nervously, as was her habit when faced with young men.

But it was fourteen-year-old Agnes who caught Matthew Ferguson's eye. He thought her utterly adorable and lively. She was almost ready for marriage, but not quite. Yet in another year or two, he might very well come courting the lass. She had to notice his interest, but if she did she gave no indication of it at all. Matthew didn't know whether he should be amused or offended. The lass obviously had spirit.

The women waited patiently as the contracts were signed. A fresh quill with its sharpened point was inked and handed to Annabella. She signed each copy in a neat, legible hand. Her father also signed, as did Matthew Ferguson, both as witnesses. Then James Ferguson carefully sanded each signature so that it would not smudge, but dry easily. Annabella noted that the Earl of Duin had already signed the contracts before sending them off to her father. His signature was a strong if impatient one. He was obviously doing what he had to do, she thought. Taking a wife was a duty for him.

Annabella felt another flutter of worry, but she was not allowed any time for her fears to build up. With her family and her servants about her, and Matthew Ferguson standing by her side as proxy for his older brother, Annabella Baird was married to Angus Ferguson by the local pastor of the Reformed kirk without any further delay. James, however, pronounced the blessing himself. Her mother had been correct, the bride realized sadly. Marriage was not about romantic love. Did romantic love even exist?

Marriage was all about alliances and trade. Daughters had no other use than that. Whether a union was between a man and a woman, or a woman and the old Church, daughters were born for this sole purpose. The Fergusons had accepted her as the earl's bride in exchange for a piece of land. She would be expected to produce bairns for her new family. Sons, preferably. There was nothing more to it. And she could hardly consider herself abused for having just been wed to a wealthy nobleman. She found she was suddenly eager to meet this mysterious man and learn the truth of him herself.

As Annabella, Countess of Duin, she now presided over the high board with a smile, seated in the place of honor at her wedding feast. While her father's table was usually simple, with one or two dishes and bread and cheese, today was different. There was broiled trout and poached salmon set upon beds of green cress. A large roast of beef had been packed in rock salt, roasted, and set upon the board, along with sliced venison, goose stuffed with apples, and a large pie filled with game birds and topped with a flaky crust. There was a potage of vegetables, a rabbit stew, fresh bread, butter, and a small wheel of hard yellow cheese. Cider, ale, and wine were for drinking. And finally, a large dish of poached pears in marsala wine completed the meal.

The Baird's piper, along with the two Ferguson pipers, entertained them after the meal had been cleared away and the trestles below the board set to one side of the hall. Jean and Matthew Ferguson sang several songs, delighting the Bairds, for their voices were particularly sweet. In exchange, the four sisters danced together most gracefully for the small gathering.

Outside the tower house, the last sunset of September blazed across the border skies, and night came. The Ferguson men-at-arms had encamped outside of the house. It was not cold yet, but two fires burned to take the chill away. Matthew and James joined them, understanding that such a small dwelling as Rath could not hold much company. Jean Ferguson was settled comfortably into one of the two bed spaces in the hall near the great hearth. The laird and his wife went to their bed. And in their small bedchamber, the four sisters huddled together in their large bed, chattering softly.

"Well," Myrna said, "I suppose Mama has told ye everything you need know."

"Enough to get me started," Annabella admitted. "She said it isn't wise for a virgin to be too knowledgeable. We spoke of other things."

"There's nothing to it," Myrna informed her, sounding more knowing than she should, Annabella thought. "All you have to do is lie on yer back, open yer legs, and he'll do all the rest."

"Not at all like the bull and cow," Annabella teased.

Sorcha giggled. Agnes was silent but alert with her curiosity.

"Nay," Myrna replied with a chortle. "All ye have to do is lie upon yer back, and he'll put his cock into ye," she repeated. "We have a wee opening in our bodies for it."

"And how is it that ye're so well-informed?" Agnes demanded to know.

Myrna flushed with guilt, saying, "Ian Melville told me. After all, we will be wed before the snow flies, now that Annabella is married."

"Be careful, sister," the new bride said softly to her sister.

"Ye let Ian Melville speak of such things to ye?" Agnes was shocked. "I don't think Mam would approve, nor our da." Then she said, "Ye let him touch ye too, didn't ye?"

Sorcha giggled again, for she knew the truth of her sister's involvement with her laddie. They had best be wed soon, she thought, for their games out on the moor could prove dangerous sooner rather than later.

Myrna said nothing in reply to her youngest sister.

"Ye'll all have more room in the bed once I've gone,

and then Myrna," Annabella said in an effort to turn the conversation from the present subject. Aggie was curious, for the lads were beginning to flock about her. She was enjoying their attention, but Annabella didn't want her bartering her chastity, as she suspected Myrna had already done. She would speak to her before she departed on the morrow. "I think it's time for us to sleep now, sister," she said. "The Fergusons have informed me that we will depart as soon as it is light. We have several long days' journeying ahead of us."

"Aye," Myrna agreed, realizing that she had perhaps revealed a little too much knowledge of her relationship with Ian Melville. Aggie was not above telling tales. "I'll miss ye, Annabella," she said.

"I also," Sorcha added.

Agnes began to cry.

Laughing softly, Annabella drew her little sister into her warm embrace, smoothing her cheek with a loving hand. "Remember that ye're coming to visit me next summer, Aggie," she reminded her. "Now go to sleep, my bairn." Then she began to hum an old lullaby that she had hummed to Agnes when the lass became too large for her cradle and had been put into the big bed with her three older sisters. Agnes relaxed in her sister's arms, and shortly after, all four Baird sisters were sleeping soundly.

Chapter 3

The first day of October dawned chill and gray. Annabella was up before the first light began to dapple the sky. She had not slept as well as she might have, being anxious and nervous about what lay ahead. Her three sisters were snoring softly, burrowed beneath the down quilt. Using the night jar she pulled from beneath the bed, she set it aside. Then, pouring some water into the pewter basin, she quickly washed. The water was icy cold and drove any thoughts of sleep from her.

She had laid her clothing out the night before on a chest at the foot of the bed. Capable of riding astride, she had taken Jean Ferguson's suggestion from the evening before, and dressed warmly. She tucked her chemise into a pair of woolen breeks, pulling on thick wool socks to wear beneath her worn leather boots. She put on a light wool undervest lined in sheepskin, then a linen shirt over it, followed by her doeskin jerkin with sleeves lined in lamb's wool. Unless it rained, she wouldn't need a cloak.

When Annabella had dressed, she stopped to look slowly about her. This was her bedchamber. The only one she had ever had. High in Rath Tower, she had slept here her entire life. It was a simple room, modest in size, just large enough to hold the big bed and four little wooden trunks holding each sister's personal possessions. Her trunk was now packed into a cart to depart for her new home.

She couldn't help the little sigh that escaped her, along with the thought that she wished her new home were closer to her old home. At least her sisters would have that advantage, even if she didn't. She considered waking her siblings but decided against it. It was far earlier than their usual rising hour. Myrna would complain. Sorcha would giggle sleepily, for she was always the hardest to wake. It was unlikely she would even recall saying farewell. And little Aggie would weep, for she was such a tender creature, and as the baby of the family had long ago learned that crying gained her the most attention. Annabella looked down at them, smiling. They were so damned beautiful.

"Farewell, my dearies," she whispered softly to them. Then she left the bedchamber, descending into the hall through her brother's chamber, and then their parents' chamber.

Pale light was beginning to show through the hall's two windows. The servants were already bringing in bread trenchers of oat stirabout to the high board, where the three Fergusons sat with her brother, Rob, and their parents. The trestles were filled with men-at-arms eating fresh-baked bread, cheese, and the cold meats left over from yesterday's bridal banquet. She greeted the others at the high board as she took her place. There was virtually no conversation in the hall.

Annabella spooned up her oat stirabout, noting that the cook had added bits of dry apple to the mixture. She must remember that, she thought, as she poured a large dollop of cream onto the hot cereal. Then, knowing her day would be a long one, she took advantage of the unusually large meal, for breakfast at Rath was never quite as lavish as it was today. There were eggs poached in heavy cream and dill, along with rashers of bacon. Annabella helped herself and ate heartily, adding bread, butter, and cheese along with a cup of cider. She ate quickly, watching the Fergusons as she did. She would not be the cause of any delay, but the Fergusons were also eating vigorously.

When the meal was over, Annabella and Jean Ferguson retired to see to their personal needs before the departure. Now, in the little courtyard, the bride looked about her, experiencing a brief moment of panic. Suddenly she didn't want to leave Rath. She would rather die unmarried, a virgin, than leave her home for a stranger's house. Nay. Castle. What did she know of living in a castle?

But then, seeing her mother struggling to hold back her own tears, Annabella gained a mastery of her own emotions. She had made a brilliant marriage for the daughter of an unimportant tower laird. Especially considering her lack of beauty. How ungrateful would it be to fling this good fortune away? She stepped into her mother's embrace, accepting her kisses and kissing her back.

"Now, Mama," she gently scolded her parent. "Dinna be like our poor Aggie, who weeps at any- and everything. I am going to my husband. All is as it should be."

"I know, I know," the lady Anne murmured. "Ye're the Countess of Duin now. I am both proud and happy. I could but wish ye were nearer, my daughter."

Now her father was taking her by her shoulders. He kissed her on both cheeks and nodded silently. Annabella was surprised, for she had never known Robert Baird to be at a loss for words. Rob hugged her, whispering in her ear that if she ever needed him, she was to send a messenger to him with the little ring he now fitted on the littlest finger of her right hand. Annabella blinked back the tears that sprang to her eyes and nodded at him. Her farewells were now finished.

Jean Ferguson quickly led her brother's bride to the waiting white mare before the family could grow any more maudlin. "This is the earl's first gift to you," Jean said.

"What is she called?" Annabella asked as she easily mounted the beast.

"The earl said ye were to name her," Jean replied.

"Then I shall call her Snow," Annabella said. "She is quite pristine, and shows no color at all." She turned in her saddle as the others mounted up. Raising her gloved hand, she bade her family a final farewell. It was instinct that made her lift her eyes to the top of Rath Tower, where her three beautiful sisters now stood upon the rooftop, waving to her and clinging to one another. She could clearly make out Aggie's little woebegone face. Annabella smiled up at them and waved back.

"Are ye ready, my lady?" Matthew Ferguson asked her.

"Aye, I'm ready," Annabella responded, looking forward over the mare's head now as she urged the animal onward.

Given the signal to move out, the large mounted party led by the two Ferguson pipers departed Rath. Behind them, the small baggage train carrying the bride's possessions followed. The sun was now climbing over the eastern hills, a faintly shining ball through the pearlescent skies of the cloudy day, and so it remained for the next few days of their travels. They were fortunate, however, not to be burdened by rain.

They rode from dawn until dusk each day, stopping briefly at midday to rest the horses. Each evening, when they halted their travels, a small pavilion was raised for the two women to shelter within. They ate cold food, because a fire would have attracted any nighttime raiders, and the Fergusons preferred to avoid confrontations. The countryside about them still showed the ravages of the recent border wars with England, although the farther west they went, the less damage had been done. Much of the land was desolate and lonely. The weather was chilly but not unbearable.

Finally, on what Matthew Ferguson promised would be the last day of their journey, the sun shone in a cloudless blue sky. There was a tang to the air that grew stronger as they traveled. It was a fresh and clean smell, such as Annabella had never known. The horses seemed lively. When she asked about this new scent in the air, Matthew told her that it was the smell of the sea.

"I've never seen the sea," Annabella admitted. "Is it like a loch? Is it big?"

"Endless," was his answer.

"Beautiful and dangerous," Jean added.

"How far are we from Duin?" the bride asked her escorts.

Matthew looked about him, then to his sister. "About two hours," he said.

"Aye," Jean agreed. "We must stop soon so that Annabella can change into her gown. A different saddle must be placed upon Snow. The countess must greet her new husband as the lady she is, Matthew."

"There's a grove of trees on the hill before we reach the castle road. That should allow me time to send a man to Duin so that Angus knows we're arriving, and give the lady a chance to change her garments," he said.

"I know the place ye mean," Jean said. It was about half an hour's ride from Duin.

They finally reached the designated spot. A rider broke away from the group, galloping away down the road, while the men-at-arms took the time to dismount, relieve themselves, and rest their horses. Matthew took Snow off to replace her saddle with a sidesaddle, which was more appropriate to a woman in skirts. Jean led Annabella deep into the grove so she might have her privacy while she changed from her traveling clothes into her wedding gown. Annabella fretted that her best gown would stink of horse.

"Ye'll not be wearing it that long," Jean assured her. "I'll air it afterward."

"I'll need a bath after all this time on the road," Annabella said. "I stink of both horse and my own sweat too. I wish I didn't have to meet the earl until after I was bathed and my hair washed so 'twould be fresh and clean." She sighed as Jean pulled off her boots. "What a grand impression I shall make upon yer poor brother. Plain as mud and smelling of horse to boot." She shook her head in despair as she stood up in her stockinged feet and drew off her breeks.

Jean had to laugh at the picture her companion had painted. "I know," she said. "It's a difficult position ye've been put into, my lady, but my brother Angus is not a man faint of heart. Nor is he stupid. He will understand, and he will make you feel quite assured of yerself; I promise ye."

"Jean, I am not some wretched lass impressed by her own importance. For all the circumstances of yer birth, we are kinswomen now. I want ye to call me Annabella.

I am not used to being 'my lady.' It is too formal between us."

"Thank ye," Jean Ferguson said. "In private we shall call each other by name, but in public you will receive the respect due my brother's wife as Countess of Duin, Annabella, and be 'my lady.'" Jean had quickly come to like this young woman. There was no artifice about her. If her brother was as wise as she had always thought him to be, Annabella's lack of physical beauty would not disturb him once he came to know her.

Now dressed but for her embroidered bodice, Annabella sat upon a small folding stool that had traveled with them, while Jean brushed out her long dark hair, then fixed it into an elegant chignon that quite suited Annabella's oval face. Then, helping her mistress into her bodice and lacing it up, Jean set a small light gray velvet cap with a narrow pointed eagle's feather upon the girl's head. The feather was held by the Baird clan badge, which had an eagle's head in the center.

"Where did that come from?" Annabella asked.

"Yer mam gave it to me just before we left Rath. She said ye were to wear it when you rode into Duin, and to never forget from whence ye sprang. It's quite charming." She stepped back. "Are ye ready, Annabella?"

"Aye, I suppose I am," her companion agreed, pulling her riding gloves back on her hands. Together, the two young women emerged from the grove, where Snow was now waiting with an elegant saddle and bridle upon her. Matthew helped Annabella to mount, steadying the mare as the young woman settled her leg over the pommel and her skirts about her. She took the reins from him.

"For pity's sake, get her to smile," Matthew whispered to his sister. "She is such a solemn little puss."

"She's nervous," Jean whispered back. "She'll shortly meet her husband for the first time, and he's a total stranger to her." Men! They could be so unfeeling, she thought. But not Angus. Angus's charm and ability to understand women were his strong points, as Annabella would soon learn. She would not be nervous for much longer.

Led by the Ferguson pipers, the bridal party topped the last hill, stopping briefly so that Annabella might glimpse Duin in all its glory for the very first time. The castle, for it was indeed a castle, stood below them on a rocky promontory overlooking the sea. Annabella's mouth fell open with surprise, but she quickly closed it not to look the fool. It was a dark gray stone structure, rectangular, with four tall round towers, each with a slate witch's-cap roof. The walls connecting each section of the castle were made for defense, although Annabella could not imagine anyone attacking Duin. It was set in such a way that it could be accessed only on one side across a drawbridge. Beyond and around it, the bright sun danced on the dark blue waters, catching the foamy curl of the waves. It was beautiful and seemed to have a magical air about it.

"Duin," Matthew said in an understated manner.

"It looks impressive at first glance, I know," Jean said, seeing the look on Annabella's face, "but I promise it is very comfortable within. You will be happy here."

They descended the hill on the castle road, the pipers playing a cheerful march ahead of them. Then from out of the castle and across the drawbridge came a party of riders. Two outriders rode with gaily colored flags flying. Matthew grinned and Jean laughed, delighted. A cheer went up from the men-at-arms escorting the bride.

Leading the welcoming party was a tall man on an

enormous dappled gray stallion. Annabella knew in an instant that this had to be Angus Ferguson. Her party had stopped, and as the other group of riders drew near, she saw his face for the first time. They had not lied. She almost wept then and there. He was without a doubt the handsomest man she had ever set eyes upon. She felt her plainness now more than she had ever before felt it. This beautiful man shouldn't be wed to her. His wife should be some glorious female whose beauty matched his.

He had a sculpted face with high cheekbones and a long straight nose. His chin was squared, not with hard lines, but soft ones. There was the faint impression of a dimple in the exact center of that chin. His mouth was long and just full enough without being big. She could not see the color of his eyes yet, but his hair and brows were every bit as dark as hers were. *God's mercy, how envious Myrna would be,* Annabella thought.

Angus Ferguson's stallion came to a halt. He dismounted, going quickly to where Annabella sat upon Snow. She couldn't look at him for fear of weeping. Seeing him, she wanted him, but he would certainly send her back having seen her. A little gasp escaped her when, reaching up, he lifted her from the back of the mare. A single finger slipped beneath her chin, raising her head up. Deep green eyes met her startled gray gaze.

"Welcome to Duin, madam," a deep voice said.

How she found her voice, Annabella wasn't certain, but she heard herself replying, "Thank ye, my lord. I am glad to be here."

He smiled a quick smile at her, then, turning to both mounted parties, said, "Go home. The countess and I shall walk the mile together." Then his big hand gripped her small one. "Come, madam," he commanded her. "We will walk and talk so we may come to know each other better."

The horses and riders galloped off immediately, leaving the newly wedded pair alone. They began walking down the road to the castle.

"Ye're twenty, I am told," he said.

"I am," she answered him.

"I am thirty-five, and said to be set in my ways," he answered.

"Most men are set in their ways by the age of two," Annabella replied.

He laughed aloud. "Ye have a quick tongue, madam." Aye, she was plain, he thought, but not ugly; and he was already finding her interesting, which was to the good.

"I am said to be forthright in my speech," she admitted. She was finding him easy to talk to, and that was a small comfort, Annabella considered.

"Are ye in love with any other?" he demanded to know.

"Nay!" Her tone was genuinely indignant. "My father should not have made this match between us if I were."

"Yer father had something I wanted," the earl said candidly. "And he needed a husband for his eldest daughter. Gaining an earl for a tower laird's wench was quite an achievement for yer family, madam."

"Had my heart been engaged elsewhere, my lord, I can assure you, even if ye were a king, my father would not have acceded to this match. Neither of my parents would have forced me to the altar had I not wanted to go."

He was silent for a brief time as they walked. Then he said, "Were ye ever in love, madam?"

"Nay," Annabella told him. "There has never been

any to take my fancy. Nor, were I a member of the old Church, would a convent have been for me. I thought I might be one of those women who never weds but remains home to care for her aging parents. With the border wars these many years, it was difficult to socialize among the border families in the east, thanks to the English. And fewer young men to meet, as so many were killed," she explained.

"There was less trouble here in this region of the west," the earl said. "We have little that the English want."

"Yet it is said ye are a wealthy man," Annabella replied. "How does one gather wealth from nothing?"

He chuckled. "The Fergusons are said to be magical folk," the earl told her.

"My sister said if ye were magical ye would make me as beautiful as ye are, my lord," Annabella challenged. "Should we not be a matching pair?"

He stopped but he did not release her hand, rather turning her to face him as he looked down at her. "Ye are not ugly," he said quietly. "And I did not want a beautiful wife. I wanted a wife who would respect and be loyal to me, madam. I have been in love. I learned that beautiful women are vain, selfish, treacherous. I did not want a wife like that. Ye will be the perfect wife for me," he assured her.

"Ye are called the handsomest man in the borders, my lord. Yer reputation, however, is not that of a vain and selfish man. My sisters are beautiful, and while they can be silly, even foolish sometimes, they will be good wives to their husbands, because they have been raised by a good mother. As for respect and loyalty, they are not gifts easily given. They are earned and must come from the heart."

"Will ye be a good wife to me, madam?" he asked her.

"By yer reasoning, my lord, I will, for I am not beautiful," she answered sharply.

"God's bones!" he swore, surprised. "I believe I have disappointed ye," the earl said to her.

"Nay, my lord, ye but surprised me. I am no fool. It is obvious ye have been disappointed by beautiful lasses. I am not beautiful, but if I were I should still endeavor to be a good wife to ye," Annabella told him.

He raised to his lips the small hand he held, and kissed it. "Madam, I apologize, for I have offended ye. It is not a good way for us to begin. Will you forgive me?" He smiled a little smile at her.

Unable to help herself, Annabella smiled back, showing him a row of perfect little white teeth. How many women, she wondered, had given in to that smile? "Ye're forgiven, my lord. This walking and talking was a wise decision. Now tell me what ye have planned for today. I am anxious to conclude the formalities so I may bathe. I stink of the road and of my horse. I want a hot bath more than anything."

"I had planned to have the ceremony immediately, but ye cannot be wed to me in that gown. Whoever chose such a color for you did you no kindness," the earl told her. "Yer pale skin needs clear, bright colors, not this dull gray. Duin has its own church, and my people will be crowded into it to get their first glimpse of their new lady. I would have them see ye at yer best, madam."

"I fear my other two gowns are as drab," Annabella informed him. "One is brown, and the other is black."

"Ye will find a complete new wardrobe in yer apartments, madam," he told her. "Yer mam was kind enough to send me the measurements I required. There may be some small adjustments needed, but ye shall have a fine gown to wear at our wedding ceremony. Ye will have yer bath first, and then Jean will garb ye in yer new finery."

"But how did ye know which colors would suit me?" Annabella asked him.

"I was told ye were as pale as the moon, with hair like ebony," he said. "It was enough. Tell Jean to choose something particularly festive." He smiled down at her again, and she felt her knees weaken. "Now we are almost home, madam, so let us hurry."

They continued on down the castle road, finally crossing over the broad oak drawbridge. There was no moat, Annabella saw, but rather beneath the drawbridge was a chasm that fell to the sea itself. Duin Castle, she now realized, stood upon a great cliff separated from the land. "Where is yer village?" she asked him, curious.

"Look to yer left," he said. "Ye can see the church tower from here. The village was built around St. Andrew's. Ye can inspect it in a few days. Our people farm and fish." He led her beneath the great iron portcullis and into a large courtyard. "Welcome home, madam!" he said to her. "Welcome to Duin!"

Looking about her, Annabella could see the lines of the original house that had become a small castle. Her curiosity aroused, she looked forward to exploring it and learning all about it. "Thank ye, my lord," she said, accepting his welcome.

Jean came forth from the house, smiling.

"The countess will bathe and change into something more suitable," the earl told his half sister. "Help her choose something festive, Jeannie. When she is ready we will celebrate the formalities at St. Andrew's."

"Aye, my lord," Jean answered him. Then she said,

"My mother is here to meet yer bride. She'll want to help."

"Ye'll like old Jeanne," the earl said. "She is a second mother to me." He raised her hand to his lips once more, kissed it, and then released it.

Annabella felt suddenly and strangely bereft at the loss of the strong fingers that had wrapped themselves about hers just a moment before. "I will try not to keep ye waiting too long, my lord," she said as she curtsied to him.

He smiled a brilliant smile at her that seemed to light his whole face. "A woman preparing for her wedding cannot be faulted if she takes her time," he said.

"Bothwell is in the hall, and he's in a rare temper," Jean told her brother before she turned away to escort Annabella to her apartments.

The earl nodded and hurried off.

"The Earl of Bothwell?" Annabella asked as they hurried into the castle and up the stairs to her apartments. "James Hepburn?"

"Aye," Jean said. "He and Angus have been friends since they were lads. His da, the fair earl, fell in love with Marie de Guise and divorced his wife so he might woo her. Of course, it was useless, for Marie's sole reason for living was her daughter. Eventually Patrick Hepburn betrayed Scotland. I think that is why his son is so loyal to it. It's as if James Hepburn is attempting to make up for his father's treason. His sister, Janet, is married to John Stewart, another bastard son of King James V. He controls and has the income from the priory of Coldingham."

They walked down a hallway lined in windows on one side. They had reached their destination. Jean flung open one side of a double door and ushered her mistress into her new apartment. Annabella was enchanted. The dayroom was paneled in warm wood. There was a stone fireplace flanked by stone greyhounds that was blazing with a bright fire. The leaded windows over-looked the sea and were hung with burgundy-colored velvet draperies. The furniture was warm golden oak, the settle and straight-backed chairs cushioned. There was a red-and-blue carpet upon the wood floor. Her mother did not have a dayroom, although they had heard of such chambers, and she had always believed a dayroom was for the rich. Then she recalled that her husband was a wealthy man. And as his wife, she now had a dayroom. She could not help but think that Myrna would be very jealous.

An older woman resembling Jean came forward. She curtsied politely to Annabella. "I am Jeanne, my lady. I served the earl's mama until her death several years ago. If I may be of service to ye at any time, ye have but to ask. I live in a cottage in the village, tending to my two grandchildren."

"Thank ye, Jeanne," Annabella said. "I didn't realize Matthew was wed and had two bairns of his own."

Jeanne chortled. "I doubt I shall ever live to see my son wed. The bairns I care for are Jeannie's. Both she and her man are in service to the earl."

"But I should not take ye from yer bairns," Anna-bella said to Jean.

"Aye," Jean replied, "ye should! Mama is much better with them than I am."

"All here is as it should be, my lady," Jeanne told An-nabella. "I have served my time with my mistress, Ma-dame Adrienne. We were girls together in Brittany. I chose to come to Scotland when she married the laird. Now it is my daughter's time to serve ye. My grandsons are my joy. Now, having met ye, I will leave ye, for it is past time for ye to prepare for yer wedding to the earl." She curtsied and departed.

"Ye have a special chamber for bathing," Jean said to her. "I can pump cold water into it, but we must send for hot water." She reached for the bellpull near the fireplace and yanked on it. A maidservant immediately appeared, and Jean gave her instructions. The girl hurried off. "Let's choose yer gown," Jean suggested. She led Annabella to a small windowless room off the dayroom. There were two large wooden wardrobes against a wall inside the chamber. Jean flung open the doors to the tall chests. "Here are the gowns the earl had made for ye. There is a burgundy velvet I particularly like, but ye must pick yerself."

Annabella caught her breath as she looked at the beautiful gowns hanging from pieces of carved wood within the cabinets. What luxury! At home, their gowns had been packed in their trunks until needed and set out the day before wearing to air and lose their wrinkles. The colors were wonderful. Bright and clear. Scarlet. Rich deep green without a hint of yellow or blue. Sea blue. A sunny gold, tawny orange, deep bright pink, lavender, violet, apple green. But it was a cheerful yellow velvet skirt that caught her eye. She looked about for a bodice to go with it and found a cream velvet one embroidered with copper silk butterflies and fat bumblebees.

She took it out. "This one with the yellow skirt," she said. "I've never seen anything so lovely in all my life."

"Aye," Jean agreed. "It's a perfect choice for ye." She set out the two garments. "Let's go and see how yer bath is coming along now."

She led the way to another room, where Annabella

was surprised to see a large square stone tub half-sunk into the floor of the chamber. There was a fireplace with a hot fire burning in it on the wall opposite the tub. There were two doors: the one they had entered through, and another. Annabella was surprised to see a maidservant taking bucket after steaming bucket from an opening in the wall and dumping it into the tub.

"'Tis Angus's invention," Jean explained. "These were once his mother's rooms. She loved to bathe. When he became the Earl of Duin he designed this little device to bring hot water to her from the kitchens so the servants did not have to run and up and down, spilling half the water by the time they reached their destination. He made her a separate bathing chamber with a fixed tub. The pump at one end of the tub gives only cold water, but the tub has a drain that can be opened to empty the tub directly into the sea." She walked over to the tub, looked in, and said to the little maidservant, "A dozen more buckets should do it. When it is ready call me, and I will mix the cold water into it for my lady."

The servant nodded, and, opening the second door, Jean led Annabella into her bedchamber. It was a lovely chamber with a large bed hung with rose-colored velvet. She saw her trunk was already there, but the space was also furnished with tables, chairs, and a chest. The fireplace was flanked by stone fairies with sweet faces and dainty wings. The windows overlooking the sea were also hung with rose-colored velvet and had a window seat with a tufted cushion. She had never seen such a beautiful room.

With Jean's help, Annabella divested herself of her garments, her boots, and her stockings, which after several days' travel seemed to be welded to her feet. The tiring woman now hurried back into the bathing chamber, and Annabella heard the sound of water gushing.

"It's ready now," Jean called. "Ye can come in now."

Naked, Annabella walked into the bathing chamber and got into the stone tub. It was long enough for her to actually sit down and stretch her legs out. The water flowed up to her chin, and was fragrant. "God's mercy," she breathed with a sigh. "Surely something this marvelous has to be a sin."

Jean laughed. "Despite what the priests and the pastors of the new kirk say, I think being clean is no vanity."

There was an alabaster jar of sweet-smelling soft soap on the narrow rim of the tub. Annabella loosened her hair, dunked her head beneath the hot water, and, taking a handful of the soap, she washed her long black tresses. When she had finished she wrung her hair free of excess moisture and, taking a pin from Jean, affixed her hair atop her head. Then she washed her body thoroughly. The fragrance from the soap was astonishing in its seductive elegance.

"Who made this soap, and what is the fragrance?" she asked Jean as she finally finished her bath.

"My mother makes it with ingredients she imports from Provence," Jean said. "The scent she chose for ye was that of moonflowers, because she said if ye were indeed a plain lass, ye would need an extravagant perfume to make ye memorable. Moonflowers bloom only at night in the light of the moon. The earl's mama preferred the fragrance of violets, for it reminded her of her home in Brittany." As Annabella stood up, Jean held out a large, warm drying cloth for her mistress to wrap herself in. "Come and sit by the fire so we may dry your lovely hair." She led her to the bedchamber, handing Annabella another drying cloth so she might get the moisture from her long hair. Then she gave her a silver hairbrush fitted with boar's bristles.

Annabella sat quietly, drawing the brush slowly through her damp hair. The heat from the fire felt wonderful as it seeped into her bones. The long journey in the crisp autumn air, and sleeping beneath the little pavilion that even the charcoal brazier hadn't been able to heat, had left her wondering whether she would ever be warm again. She had never, it seemed to her, known a hearth so delightfully toasty. Her long locks dried quickly.

Poor lass, Jean thought, watching the girl. *She's exhausted.* She saw the motion of the brush Annabella was wielding grow slower and slower. Catching it before it dropped from the younger woman's hand, she gently shook her mistress, who was falling asleep. "When ye're ready, Annabella, I'll get yer stockings, chemise, and petticoats."

Annabella started, opening her eyes, then laughing softly. "I was falling asleep, wasn't I?" she said. "I didn't realize how tired I was until now."

"I don't know why Angus couldn't have waited until tomorrow to go through all this folderol," Jean said. "He can be so impatient." Kneeling, she rolled the pretty white silk stockings onto the girl's legs, securing them with plain silk garters. A chemise and two petticoats, one heavily stiffened with starch, were donned. Next came a cream satin underskirt, the embroidered panel of which would show through the divided yellow velvet overskirt. The embroidery of bumblebees and butterflies done in bright copper threads matched the design on the bodice.

"I can't wait to give ye a more elegant coiffure," Jean said, "but ye know that today ye must wear yer hair unbound to give testament to yer virginity." She brushed the long tresses free of any remaining tangles. Then she placed a bejeweled gold circlet about Annabella's head. "There! Now let's get yer overskirt and bodice on."

The remaining garments were quickly donned. The pale yellow velvet skirts settled over the underskirt and petticoats in a bell shape. The bodice with its copper embroidery and puffed sleeves was just right. When Jean had finished lacing the garment, she turned Annabella about and nodded approvingly.

"Ye look quite lovely," she said. "Much better than the gray."

The bride laughed. "I thank ye for the compliment, Jean. I have never before heard the word *lovely* directed toward me."

"Come and see! Come and see!" Jean insisted, taking her by the hand and leading her to a tall, narrow mirror set in a gilt wood frame.

Annabella looked nervously into the mirror. Her only looking glass at Rath had been a piece of highly polished metal that had a tendency to distort whatever it reflected. Staring into the smooth glass, she was surprised by the difference fine clothing made in her appearance. Oh, she was still plain of face, but somehow it seemed to matter less with her beautiful garments. And while she shyly admired herself, Jean placed pear-shaped pearl earrings in her ears and slipped a rope of creamy pearls around her neck, from which fell a jeweled silver and-gold crucifix. "God's mercy," Annabella gasped softly.

"The earl wanted you to wear these today," Jean told her. "They are now yers." Then she said, "Just yer shoes, and ye'll be ready. We haven't been too long. Angus canna complain at us," Jean said with a chuckle.

Annabella slipped her feet into a pretty pair of yellow kid slippers decorated with pearls that Jean had set out for her. She stretched a leg out to admire the slipper. "I can't believe such lovely bounty is now mine. The earl does indeed possess magic to make me feel almost pretty."

Jean smiled at the girl's words. "Perhaps he does," she agreed, but then added, "or perhaps he is just a thoughtful man with the means to indulge his bride."

Annabella paused, but then, unable to help herself, she asked, "Is he really a sorcerer, Jean?"

"If he is," Jean replied, "I have never in all my life seen any evidence of it."

"Then why is it said that this clan are magical folk?" Annabella inquired.

Jean sighed. "Some ancestor several hundred years ago either actually had magic or convinced everyone that he did. The Fergusons of Duin have chosen not to let the legend die. People are fearful of us, and it has allowed us to avoid entanglements with our neighbors. There is too much feuding in the borders. It leads only to death and destruction. We have the English for that. The fear of our alleged magic keeps people afraid, and thus we can avoid difficulties."

"I am surprised the Church has not interfered wi' ye," Annabella said.

Jean laughed. "We have always been generous to the Church. Even the pastor of the Reformed kirk in our village trusts us, and ye surely know how virulent they can be. Besides, no act of magic can be attributed to us. The reputation we have gained is simply assumed to be our way. Indeed, here in the west we are considered the mediators for others. It is thought our judgments are impartial and equitable."

"I can see the Fergusons of Duin are extremely clever," Annabella remarked.

"We are." Jean laughed. Then she said, "We must go down now. We are riding into the village, where Jamie will marry ye to Angus in the kirk surrounded by our clan folk. Afterward, there will be a feast in the hall, and gifts for all."

"But we were married at Duin when Matthew stood proxy," Annabella said.

"Aye," Jean replied, "but Angus will not feel properly wed to ye unless the rite performed is that of the old Church. Fortunately, Jamie is here, as we no longer have a priest at Duin. But soon Jamie will leave Scotland. He has been invited to Rome. Our sister Mary's convent has already relocated to France. For all the queen's generous words, the old faith of our ancestors is no longer welcome in Scotland."

Of course he wanted to be wed in the faith he practiced, Annabella considered. She had been baptized in the old faith, but when John Knox managed to make the Catholic faith illegal, her parents had quietly turned to the new kirk. Annabella had never been quite comfortable with the hard man preaching such a hard faith. She followed Jean back through the windowed corridor and downstairs to the hall. She could see through the windows as they passed by that the afternoon was advancing quickly.

The earl and Lord Bothwell had already gone on to the church, but Matthew was awaiting her. Leading her outside into the courtyard, he settled her upon her horse, then put Jean upon another beast before mounting his own horse. They departed the courtyard, crossing over the drawbridge and onto a narrow path that led to the village.

"Your yellow skirts are very pleasing," Matthew noted of the velvet now spread over Snow's plump flanks.

"Thank ye," Annabella said. The afternoon sun was warm on her face.

No one spoke again as they rode toward the village. They saw no one, and, entering Duin, Annabella found the streets deserted. Arriving at the church, Matthew dismounted, then lifted the bride from her saddle. Jean slid from the back of her horse easily. She hurried into the church, followed by her brother and Annabella. It was filled with the Ferguson clansmen and -women, and she was suddenly grateful for her new finery. She had seen the difference it had made in her appearance when she had looked into the mirror. Plain she might be, but she now looked every inch how she thought a countess of Duin should look. A little lass stepped forward to hand her a small bouquet of white heather.

Annabella bent, whispering to the child as she gently touched her pretty face, "Thank ye, my dearie." She kissed the rosy cheek of the child. Then, standing again, she allowed Matthew Ferguson to lead her down the aisle of the church to where the earl stood waiting for her. Angus Ferguson, she noted, had also changed his garments. He was now garbed in rich brown velvet with a fine velvet doublet that was embroidered in gold and copper threads, its slashed puffed sleeves showing cream-colored satin.

He took her hand, and together they knelt before the priest, James Ferguson, while the ceremony was performed and lengthy prayers were intoned for their long life together along with a fruitful union. A copy of the marriage contract was displayed, and then read to those in attendance. The clan folk were asked if they approved their lord's acceptance of both the terms and the virgin

Annabella Baird. The clansmen and -women answered in the affirmative, not that they would have said otherwise. The question to them had been a courtesy practiced by the Ferguson lords for centuries. Then Annabella and Angus were pronounced man and wife. The blessing upon their union was pronounced. Rising, they turned to face their audience.

"Kinsmen and -women, I present to ye yer countess," Angus Ferguson said.

Annabella smiled a shy smile as those in the church cheered enthusiastically.

Then, hand in hand, the bridal pair walked from the church to their waiting horses and began the return to the castle, led by the two Ferguson pipers, who were now playing a lively tune as they marched ahead of the newly wedded couple. Behind them, the entire village followed, laughing and chatting. Their earl had finally taken a wife. Oh, she was plain, they all noted, but her kindness to the wee lass who presented her with her bridal bouquet had been noted with communal approval. Plain the bride might be, but instinct told the clan folk that her heart was good and true. And God's mercy! Was not Angus Ferguson beautiful enough for them all?

Chapter 4

As they rode back to the castle, he complimented her. "Ye did well, madam. Thanking little Una and kissing her cheek will be remembered kindly. Ye have made a good beginning with our clan folk."

Annabella felt a flush of warmth at his words. "I am glad if I have pleased ye, my lord," she told him.

"I like the gown ye chose. It suits ye far better than that drab gray with its black beading. Why did ye pick such an unflattering color?" he asked her.

"It was the only material remaining in my father's storeroom," Annabella said. "Da has not yer means, my lord, and two of my sisters will soon wed. I could not take the fabrics I knew they wanted, but because I was to wed wi' ye, the embroidery and beading were lavished upon me. Their gowns will be much simpler, for all the threads and beads are now gone. Aye, the color was dull, but there was much love in that gray gown."

He was not used to being scolded, and in so gentle a manner too. His plain-faced bride had spirit, and was obviously used to speaking her mind. "Ye shall send yer sisters a generous supply of such fripperies at once then," he told her. "The chatelaine's keys will be given to ye this very day, and Jean will take ye to my store-rooms. Ye will know best what will suit the materials yer sisters have chosen for themselves."

"Ye are too good!" Annabella exclaimed, delighted. "I know such small things do not overly concern a man, but they are so important to a woman. Thank ye!" They had reached the drawbridge of the castle once again. "Oh, stop!" Annabella cried. She stared past the low stone walls to where the sun was beginning to set over the dark sea.

"Ahh," he said, understanding, a smile touching his sensuous lips. "Aye, 'tis beautiful, isn't it? I never grow tired of the sunsets at Duin."

The autumn sky was aflame with vibrant color: rich deep orange, fiery scarlet, and rich dark purple streaked with lavender and yellow. A wash of peach running into the pale blue sky was topped by pink clouds edged in gold. A tinge of pale green just above the horizon was touched by the great red globe of the sun preparing to set.

"I have never seen such a sunset," Annabella said softly.

"'Tis the sea that makes it diffcrent," the earl told her.

After a moment or two more, remembering the entire village was bchind them eager for the wedding feast, Annabella urged Snow forward again. In the courtyard her husband lifted her from the mare. The sensation of his strong hands about her waist sent a blush to her pale cheeks. He noted it but said nothing.

In the great hall, the four stone fireplaces with their great metal andirons, with bronze heads fashioned like dragons, held enormous logs now fully ablaze, warming the space. The trestles were laid with fine white cloths, with pewter cups and spoons for each guest to use and, afterward, take home as their very own. The guests thronged in, men, women, and scampering children.

The earl escorted his bride to the high board, which was set with an embroidered white linen cloth edged in fine lace. Upon the table, tall carved golden candlesticks holding pure beeswax candles had been set, along with a silver gilt saltcellar in the shape of a thistle. By each place setting was a fine linen napkin, a gold spoon, and another implement she did not recognize that had a gilt handle from which sprang three slender gold prongs. Angus Ferguson seated his wife on his right. Jean was seated next to her, with Lord Bothwell next to the earl's sister and Matthew and James to the earl's left. Pastor Blaine found himself next to Matthew. A modest man, he was a bit taken aback to find himself at the high board. He was no kin to the Fergusons, and had not expected to be invited. Still the earl was a fair-minded man. So when asked, the pastor stood and offered the blessing in a voice easily heard at the back of the hall.

"These Protestants are surely heard as far as heaven itself when they open their mouths in prayer of any kind," Jean murmured softly to Annabella, who giggled.

The servants were now streaming into the hall with bowls, dishes, and platters of food. Annabella had never seen such a variety. There were oysters, which the men enjoyed, cracking open the shells and swallowing down the slimy mollusks. Annabella didn't think they looked very appetizing. The prawns had been steamed in white wine. There were platters of fresh salmon and river trout. There was a bowl of creamed cod.

She saw a side of beef crusted in rock salt carried in on its spit, which was set between two iron holders and later carved. A roasted boar, an apple between its jaws, was brought into the hall on a great silver server that sat on the shoulders of four brawny serving men, who paraded it among the trestles before presenting it to the high board. There were a good half dozen legs of lamb, several bowls each of venison stew, and rabbit stew with bits of carrot, celery, and herbs flavoring the wine gravy.

There were capons in plum sauce, geese and ducks roasted until their skins were crisp, the meat beneath succulent and juicy. There were lettuces braised in white wine, tiny onions in a cream sauce flavored with dill, and bowls of late peas. Each table had its own bread, butter, and small wheel of cheese. October ale, cider, and sweet wine flowed generously.

"I have never seen so much food in one place at one time," Annabella exclaimed.

"I thought our union worthy of a great feast," the earl answered her.

"Oh, tell the lass the truth, Angus. We eat like this every night," Matthew teased.

Everyone laughed, even the solemn Pastor Blaine, who knew the earl to be a careful and prudent man, even if he stubbornly persisted in holding to the old faith. The lord of Duin was a good master, and a charitable one. The pastor could find no real fault with him, although he would wager that John Knox would. Still, John Knox was far away.

The hall was noisy but reasonably free of smoke, for the four large fireplaces burned cleanly. Somewhere a harp was being played most sweetly, but Annabella was fascinated by the conversation going on at the table. Lord Bothwell was in high dudgeon.

He had brought them word of the queen's marriage in late July, and his opinion of Mary Stuart's bridegroom was not a kind one.

"Damned fool woman fancies herself in love wi' the pretty creature she wed. Pah! He makes me sick," James Hepburn growled.

"Whom has she wed, my lord?" Annabella asked. She wondered why Bothwell was so irate.

"Her cousin Henry Stewart, Lord Darnley," came the answer. "She even got a dispensation from the pope because of the degree of kinship between them. Her grandmother, Margaret Tudor, James the Fourth's widow, remarried. Her daughter from her second marriage, Margaret Douglas, wed Matthew Stuart, Earl of Lennox. This barefaced boy, Lord Darnley, is their offspring."

"What's wrong wi' him, Jamie?" Angus Ferguson asked.

"He's a conniver, a liar, a fop. He fancies himself king now that he has wedded her, but she's nae said it. The little turd makes me want to puke," Bothwell snarled. "The kirk is not happy, I can tell ye. Knox is fit to be tied, but he's a fool if he thought she would take a Protestant for a husband. And Elizabeth Tudor is horrified that her mischief making has resulted in this turn of affairs. She hardly expected Mary Stuart to take her advice in the matter of marriage."

"What the hell has the queen of England got to do with this?" the earl wanted to know. "I would think she had enough trouble seeking a husband of her own."

"Our queen thought it prudent to ask her queenly cousin for advice in the matter of a prospective husband. I do not believe the English queen is interested in marrying herself. Certainly not with the example her father set. Two queens executed. Two shed by legal means. One dead of a childbed fever. But neither does she wish to see Mary remarried, for Mary stands closest to Elizabeth's own throne. Indeed, there are those who still question the legitimacy of England's queen, and believe that Mary Stuart is the rightful heir to Mary Tudor," Lord Bothwell said.

"But if the English queen has no heirs and our queen has no heirs, then who stands to inherit either throne?" Annabella asked.

"I don't believe Elizabeth Tudor cares, as long as she may rule unfettered," he answered her. *How interesting,* James Hepburn thought. *Angus's wife seems to understand the complexities of the political situation.*

"How did Darnley come to the queen's attention then?" the earl asked his friend.

"Mary asked her cousin to suggest suitable gentlemen for her hand. Elizabeth, egged on by that clever devil William Cecil, I've nae a doubt, suggested two men. The first was Robert Dudley, the Earl of Leicester, her horsemaster, and rumored to be her lover, though I think that is but gossip. The Tudor lass is far too canny to be compromised by anyone. The second man was Darnley, for he is Elizabeth's cousin too, and stands near her throne as closely as does our queen. Neither man was a suitable suggestion, and Dudley would not even come to Scotland to be inspected. Henry Stuart, however, did.

"One look at the laddie and she fancied herself in love. Ye've nae met her, Angus, but she is a tall woman, standing six feet in height. It but adds to her queenly stature, but few men stand tall enough to meet her eye." He chuckled. "How Knox hated meeting with her, for she made it a point to always stand when he was in her presence, and he was forced to look up at her. Lord Darnley, however, stands a wee bit taller than the queen.

"He is very tall and slender. He has golden curls, and

eyes the blue of the sky. He is all rose and white, more like a lass in features. He simpers. He minces. But his French is absolutely flawless, and 'tis the language she learned to speak from infancy, although she speaks perfectly good Scots English. He writes poetry for her, and recites it before the court in praise of her. The queen is a romantic lass at heart, and Darnley has enchanted her. She has not seen him drunk and in his cups, as I have. He tends to sulk when he cannot get his own way. Against her councilors' advice, she has wed him. Now the young fool struts about demanding he be treated like a king. I could not remain at court and watch.

"The queen is no fool, and when she comes to her senses she will see that she has wed a buffoon and a fool, but it will be too late. Unlike her great-uncle Henry, she will not dispose of this unsuitable husband that she has shackled herself to, but will rather bear him, and his boorish behavior, until something, God only knows what, happens to rid her of this mistake in her queenly judgment."

Lord Bothwell's gossip and his opinion were fascinating, but Annabella was starting to feel the effects of the last week. She felt herself beginning to wilt as exhaustion set in, and she struggled to keep her eyes open as she nibbled upon a sweet sugar wafer. She had eaten little, for the quantity of food had overwhelmed her. She was simply too tired to cope with making choices. She was also overwhelmed with homesickness, and wished her whole family had been here to share this day with her.

Suddenly the earl was whispering in her ear. "Ye must gather yer strength but one more time today, madam. We must dance before ye may be excused."

She didn't dare turn to look at him, for his face was

so close to her ear. She nodded. Annabella knew that their guests were expecting to see her dance with Angus. They would be disappointed if she did not. "Can it be soon?" she asked him softly.

"It can be now," he answered, standing and drawing her up with him.

A cheer went up, and then the hall grew silent as Angus Ferguson led his bride to the open space between the high board and the trestles. The music—a harp, a drum, a flute—began to play. Annabella looked up at her new husband, giving him a tremulous smile. He smiled his gorgeous smile back at her. Then together they began to dance. They moved slowly at first, weaving a pattern across the stone floor, her left hand and his right one raised palms out but not touching as they swayed back and forth. Then the tenor of the music grew livelier as a bagpipe joined in. They pranced and capered across the floor while the guests began to clap around them. He lifted her up off the floor, swinging her as her yellow skirts blossomed about her. Then, as suddenly, he set her down, leaning forward to kiss her mouth. The music stopped. The guests cheered.

Covered in blushes, Annabella looked up into his handsome face. She felt an odd burst of emotion, although she could not have said what it meant, or from where it had come. Green eyes met gray eyes as she suddenly realized that this was a truly good match she had made. She lowered her eyes, her dark lashes brushing her pale cheek.

At that moment Angus Ferguson suddenly realized that it mattered not at all that his bride was plain of face. To his surprise he became aware of the feeling that by some odd stroke of fate they seemed to match. She was as thoughtful and careful as he himself was.

She appeared kind. She seemed to understand the concept of duty, and was ready to accept her position as his countess, with all of its responsibilities. He doubted any other bride and groom had ever begun as well as they had.

As for the concept of love, he wasn't even certain such a thing existed. A man could not be bothered with such foolishness. Respect. Duty. These were the things that made a good marriage. And then he recalled an odd occurrence as his mother lay dying. As he sat by her side, she had called out the name Giles several times in her delirium. He had asked Jeanne about it, but her eyes had gone blank, and she shrugged. She knew of no such person. But Angus had heard the passion, the longing, in his mother's voice. Had she come into her arranged marriage with his father loving another? If she had she had nonetheless been faithful and loyal to his father.

Realizing they were still standing before all in the great hall, the earl said, "Well-done, madam. Ye may be dismissed now if you so choose."

Annabella stepped back up to the high board, briefly bidding each of her guests good night, thanking Pastor Blaine for his service and the blessing he had offered earlier.

Then she joined Jean, and the two women departed the great hall, hurrying upstairs to Annabella's new apartments. Once there, Annabella could not suppress her yawns as Jean divested her mistress of her beautiful garments. The bride quickly washed her face and hands, rinsed her mouth with mint-flavored water, and was dressed in a silk-and-lace night garment.

She almost fell asleep as Jean brushed out her long hair, undoing any tangles it might have encountered during the course of the afternoon and evening. "Shall I braid it?" she asked, and her mistress nodded sleepily. Jean's quick fingers wove the long, thick hair into a single plait. Then she tucked Annabella into the big bed with its lavender-scented sheets and down pillows. "Don't be afraid, Annabella," she told the younger woman. "Angus is reputed to be a skilled and thoughtful lover. He will treat ye gently, for he knows ye're a virgin. Would ye like the taperstick left burning, or is the firelight enough for ye?"

"Snuff the stick," Annabella said. She struggled to remain awake. She had one more duty to perform this day, and she would not shirk that duty.

"Good night then," Jean said, and she hurried from the bedchamber, closing the door softly behind her as she went.

It was such a big bed, Annabella thought. Her sisters would fit quite comfortably into it. Her sleepy eyes scanned the chamber. It was a gracious space at least four or five times the size of the little room she had inhabited at Rath. Jean had not drawn the bed curtains. The hearth opposite her bed burned brightly, warming the room. There was a large upholstered chair set at an angle by it. The floor, like the one in the dayroom, was covered in a wool carpet, this one dusky blue and cream in the firelight. She would be interested to see whether the colors held in the daylight. It was a lovely room.

Hearing the click of a lock, she turned her head toward the sound. The earl stepped into her bedchamber through a small door that had been hidden in the paneled wall. He was wrapped in a brocaded robe, but his feet were bare. Annabella realized that beneath the dark silk he was undoubtedly naked. He must have worn the garment for her sake, believing that the sight of a male body might frighten her. She felt her fingers clutching at the down-filled silk coverlet as he seated himself on the edge of the bed.

"We have one final duty to perform this day, madam," he said.

"I know," Annabella replied.

"And ye are prepared to fulfill it, madam, are ye not?"

"Aye, my lord, I am," she answered him.

"Yer mam has told ye what is required of ye?" He waited for her reply.

"I am to lie upon my back with my legs open to ye," Annabella responded.

"God's blood!" he swore softly, and then he laughed. "I think, madam, we shall leave this duty for another time," the earl told her. "Ye're exhausted by yer long journey, and coupling wi' a man ye have known but a few hours will not be pleasant for ye. I have no desire to have to deal wi' a tired little virgin tonight. We both understand that the purpose of our union is to create heirs for Duin. There is time enough for that, lass," he finished as he reached out and stroked her face with a gentle hand.

But instead of being reassured by his words, Annabella was horrified and found herself near tears. "Is it that ye find me so displeasing, my lord, that ye canna bring yerself to do what needs be done?" she asked him in a tremulous voice.

"Nay, nay, madam," he sought to reassure her. "I am a man of great carnal appetites, lass, but never have I forced a woman to my will. That is what I would be doing tonight if I insisted on deflowering ye. I want us to get to know each other better, and when we do what will come next will come naturally to both of us. I dinna find ye displeasing at all. Ye have surprised me and ye quite delight me, for ye have charm, manners, wit, and intellect. What is beauty in comparison to those?"

"Do ye speak of love?" she queried him. She didn't quite understand what he was getting at. She had wed him. It was their wedding night. Why was he was turning away from her? And yet . . . She paused in her thoughts, realizing that she was actually finding herself relieved that she should not have to take the next step with him tonight.

"I know naught of love, madam," he said honestly. "I know of lust, and ye will discover that delightful emotion quite soon, for though I will give ye time to grow used to my presence, we shall kiss and caress at will, which will give rise to your lust. It is ye who will lead the way for us as ye seek more and more knowledge of a passionate nature. Soon enough, the time will come when we will do what is expected of us, madam. Do ye understand better now, and agree wi' me? Or will you insist that I mount ye now? I will do whatever ye choose, madam."

"Aye, I understand ye," Annabella said, and she did. He was a strange man, she thought, wondering whether any other bridegroom would have been as thoughtful.

"Give me yer hand," he said. Without hesitation, she obeyed him. He took the hand in his own, kissing first the back of it, then placing lingering warm lips upon her palm and her wrist.

She shivered with delight but said nothing.

The dark green eyes twinkled at her. "I can see ye're going to be an obedient wife, madam," he told her.

"I will do my best to please ye, my lord, but there may be times when I displease," Annabella said candidly. His lips on her flesh had been deliciously disturb-

ing. A frisson of emotion had shot through her that she
did not recognize when his flesh had met hers.

Angus Ferguson saw the brief confusion upon her
face. He was surprised. A virgin, aye. But one so artless?
It had become more and more obvious to him that she
had not dissembled in any way when she told him she
had never been courted. Had there ever been a time
when he had known such pure and perfect innocence?
Releasing the small hand in his, he reached out with his
other hand to cup her face in his big palm. "Will ye trust
me, madam?" he asked her softly.

Again Annabella felt that unfamiliar stirring within
her. His dark green eyes were like a pool in the depths
of a deep sunlit forest. She wanted to immerse herself
within that pool until she became one with it. His touch
both warmed and aroused her. "Aye, my lord," she told
him low. "I will trust ye."

They called her plain of face, and yet he thought the
solemn little face now looking up at him with wary eyes
had a sweetness about it that touched him. Leaning
forward, he brushed her lips with his own, but then the
very sweetness of those lips aroused a ferocity within
him that was difficult to control. A hand cupped her
head. His mouth pressed down hard on her soft mouth
and his kiss became demanding. To his absolute surprise
she met the wild kiss with a fierceness of her own until
he broke the embrace, saying, "I shall bid ye good night
then, madam." Angus Ferguson arose and returned
back through the little door in the paneled wall, ducking
his head as he went to avoid hitting the low arch.

Her lips still burning, Annabella lay back against her
plump pillows. She didn't know whether to rejoice or to
weep. She knew so little about bed sport, and yet should
she have known more? Her mother had said a virgin

should not be knowledgeable. She had been vague in her explanations. Was Myrna's blunt explanation closer to the truth?

When she had repeated it to her husband, he had laughed ruefully. Why?

But she had to admit that she was more comfortable knowing she might sleep in peace this night. Although she had not shown the emotion to anyone, fearing to be thought a weakling, she had been very frightened of leaving Rath to travel across Scotland and into the keeping of a virtual stranger known as a sorcerer, as well as the handsomest man in the borders. It was a relief to find that Angus Ferguson was a kind man.

It had been such an amazing day, and a day filled with so much activity. Duin Castle was so beautiful. It made the tower house where she had been raised look so poor and sparse. Yet she had never felt a lack of anything, and her girlhood home had been filled with love and happiness. She hoped that in the weeks, the months, the years ahead, she would be able to bring that same sense of warmth to Duin, to her husband and their children. Then, clearing her mind of random thoughts, Annabella softly whispered her prayers and fell into a deep, dreamless sleep.

On the other side of the little door in the paneled wall, the Earl of Duin was not so fortunate. Angus Ferguson had returned to his own bedchamber, part of a spacious apartment that matched his wife's. He had seen the relief on her face when he had suggested they come to know each other better. The truth was, he was equally relieved not to have to deflower Annabella this night. She was a stranger. An intriguing one, but nonetheless unfamiliar to him. He had always taken the time to know a woman before they became lovers. His French mother had always insisted that the hunt, and the seduction that ensued, brought about a greater satisfaction when one worked at it. Quick couplings were to be avoided at all costs, and forcing a woman was unforgivable.

His new wife was a true innocent. Who the hell had told her that lying on her back and opening her legs to him was all that was required of her? Her mother? A serving woman? Annabella might not be a beauty, but he would treat her with the greatest care nonetheless. Her position as his wife made her particularly worthy of his regard.

She had not been aware that the coverlet she had clutched so tightly had slipped down while they talked. He had been treated to a shadowed glimpse of her breasts beneath the sheer silk and lace of her bed gown. They were dainty, perfectly round little breasts with small nipples. He had quickly looked away so she had not been aware of his interest, but his hands had actually itched to reach out and cup those breasts. Even now, the memory of them caused him to imagine their weight in his palms.

His body servant had been dismissed for the night, so no one would know he had not done what was expected of them. Jean would see. Like everyone at Duin, she was anxious for him to produce a legitimate heir. She might question him, but should she find out, he knew she would understand. He realized all at Duin would be pleased if midsummer of the new year brought them the birth of the next generation of Fergusons. However, he would not force the issue. Annabella needed to be slowly seduced so that when the right moment came for her to give up her virginity, she would do it gladly and without tears. He wanted her filled with the passion his lips had drawn from her this evening. He wanted to be filled with that same passion her lips had surprised him with earlier. He slept fitfully.

Up early and down in the hall the next morning, he found Jean. "Tell yer lady that we will ride together this morning," he said to her.

Jean looked at him, surprised. "Will she not be too fragile?"

"Nay," he replied, and the look he gave his sister warned her to ask no questions.

Jean did as she was bidden, waking Annabella and helping her dress. She saw the lack of blood upon the sheets, and looked to the younger woman, who blushed. It was then that Jean realized her mistress was yet untouched. As to Angus, she said nothing.

She realized that her brother was giving his bride an opportunity to know him. She remembered the sage advice regarding lovers that the lady Adrienne had given to them all when they were growing up. Only Mary had fled away when such things were discussed.

And so Angus and Annabella rode out together most mornings. They rode the hills about the castle. They rode the beach along the sea below it. They rode without an escort, for it would have been a foolish man who attempted accosting the Earl of Duin on his own lands. Angus Ferguson wanted to be with his new wife. He wanted to know more about her. Realizing his intent, Annabella spoke freely with him. In doing so, she learned as much about her husband as he learned of her. They were making a good beginning, and becoming friends.

Matthew was directed to help Annabella become quickly familiar with the household, which was hers to manage. He complied, quite content to have the new lady of Duin take up her womanly duties. Suddenly Annabella found herself conferring with the cook on meals, and directing the maidservants in their duties. One morning, down in the kitchens, she saw a little lass and, recognizing Una, the child who had given her the white heather bouquet on her wedding day, she greeted her.

Una's small face lit up at hearing the countess address her by name. She curtsied.

"What brings you to the kitchens, little one?" Annabella asked.

"I've come to deliver the clean polishing clothes," Una replied. "My mam is the castle's laundress, my lady."

It was then that Annabella realized she had seen many children toiling in Duin village at one simple task or another. The winter was coming, however, and soon those children would spend most of their days penned up in their family cottages in idleness. It was then that she decided to teach the children at least to write their names. She went to Matthew Ferguson, asking, "Is there anywhere in the village where I might have a place to teach the bairns this winter?"

"Teach them what?" he inquired of her.

"To write their names, mayhap to read," Annabella told him.

"Why would ye teach cotters' brats to read and write?" he said. "They have no need of such things. Have you spoken to my brother of your plans, my lady?"

"I had not thought it necessary to ask him," Annabella said, irritated by Matthew's presumption. He might be the steward of Duin, but she was its lady. "However, now that ye have brought it up, let us go and ask Angus what he thinks."

He was surprised that she had forced his hand, and

had not yielded to his authority as the castle's steward. "Angus is out seeing that the cattle and sheep are brought safely into the home pastures," he told her.

"We shall ask him when he returns then," Annabella said sweetly.

Matthew was further astonished when his brother agreed to Annabella's wish. "There is no work to be done in the winter that cannot give the bairns time to learn. There is no harm in it. Besides, there might be among those bairns one who is clever, and for whom a slight bit of knowledge will prove useful to me eventually. Come the spring, they will return to their regular duties in the fields, helping their elders where they are needed."

Matthew offered the lady a tiny uninhabited cottage, its former tenant now deceased. "I'll have the roof repaired and the place swept out. What else will ye need?"

"Wood for the fire, stools for the children, and a table and chair for me," Annabella told him. "And make certain the chimney is open."

The clan folk were wary of Annabella's plans, for while they liked their new mistress, they didn't understand why she would want to teach their children to read or to write. What good were these skills to simple folk?

The first day, Annabella came down from the castle to discover the little cottage was overflowing with lads and lasses. She quickly discovered they had come more from curiosity than a desire to learn. Over the next few days, her pupils faded away, until by week's end she was left with only two: little Una and the blacksmith's youngest son, a lad called Callum.

Curious, she asked them, "Why have ye remained when all yer friends have gone off?"

Callum immediately spoke up. "My two older brothers already work with our da in the smithy, my lady. They will inherit the forge one day. I have no taste for it, however; nor do I wish to be a soldier. If I can learn to read and write, Pastor Blaine says there are more opportunities open to me. I can go out in the world and earn my bread."

Annabella nodded. "'Tis true," she agreed. "And when ye have learned both reading and writing, I will teach ye yer numbers, Callum Ferguson. Then ye will have three skills to offer a master." The lad was respectful, and had an intelligent look about him. He could prove useful to Duin if he were capable of learning. She looked to Una.

The little lass spoke up now that it appeared to be her turn. "I dinna want to follow my mam into the laundry, my lady," she admitted. "I want to go to Edinburgh and work in a fine shop. If I can read, write, and do my numbers, I can do this."

As there were no shops in Duin village, and it was quite unlikely that the lass had ever been farther from her home than a few miles, or even gone past the borders of the earl's lands, Annabella was curious as to how little Una even knew of shops. "Who has told ye of Edinburgh?" she asked.

"There is an old peddler who comes to Duin now and again. My mam always gives him a place to sleep. He has told me stories of the town, and of the beautiful shops where folk can purchase wonderful goods from foreign lands. I should rather earn my bread doing that than doing the castle laundry," Una said, blushing. "I mean no offense, my lady, but I hate the laundry."

Annabella suddenly had an idea. Why should she come to the village when she could teach these two bairns more comfortably in the castle? "Would ye both be willing to live in the castle while I teach ye this winter?" she asked them. "I will find places for ye both so ye may earn yer keep, but the snows of winter will not keep ye from yer learning if ye're at the castle."

"Aye!" the two would-be scholars chorused, grinning at her.

"I shall have Matthew Ferguson speak wi' yer parents," Annabella told them.

Again, Matthew Ferguson was not pleased when the lady of Duin made her simple request. "I must speak wi' the earl," he said in almost surly tones.

"Why is it ye are so against my teaching these two bairns?" Annabella demanded of him. "I've freed this wee cot now for some deserving soul. Is that not better?"

"Are ye wi' bairn?" Matthew asked her bluntly. "Are these the fancies of a breeding woman?"

Annabella was astounded by his query. She blushed furiously, a flash of scarlet flooding her pale cheeks. She spoke before she could think. "Nay!"

"Well, ye should be by now," Matthew replied. "My brother's prowess is proven by the two little lasses he has fathered. The mistress he put away before the wedding was wi' bairn. She will deliver any day, I am told."

Annabella was almost speechless with anger now. "I will speak to my husband," she said in frosty tones.

"He married ye to gain legitimate heirs," Matthew persisted heedlessly. "Ye need to do yer duty instead of trying to teach two cotters' bairns to read and write."

"Ye're dismissed, *steward*," Annabella told him. She was near to weeping, and she would be damned if she would allow Matthew Ferguson to see her weep. Then she felt Jean, who had been by her side this whole time, squeeze her hand hard. She drew a long, deep breath. "Go!"

Surprised by her harsh tone, Matthew turned, only to be stopped by his sister's voice. "Apologize to yer lady, brother, for yer presumption," Jean told him. "She is gracious, and yer breach of good manners will remain between ye, but I will not hesitate to speak with the earl, our brother, if ye do not tender yer apologies to our mistress immediately. If I tell our mother, ye'll never hear the end of it, and ye know it."

Flushing, for he knew he had overstepped his bounds, Matthew turned and bowed to Annabella. "Ye have my regrets, my lady, for speaking out of turn," he told her. Then he left the two women.

Chapter 5

They watched him hurry from the hall.

"His apology is almost as gracious as he is," Jean murmured.

Annabella laughed weakly. Matthew's words had unnerved her. "The trouble is that he is right," she said.

"A bairn is more easily conceived when two people come together," Jean replied softly. "Surely ye are more comfortable wi' him now. It has been two months."

"*Ye know?*" Annabella was embarrassed to learn her secret was revealed.

Jean patted her mistress's hand. "Aye, I know. There was no blood the morning after yer wedding night. Now, that might have been because ye were nae a virgin after all, but I dinna believe that is the case. But no one else, including my nosy brother, is aware of the private relationship between ye and the earl."

Annabella sighed. "Since that night he has not come to my bed. He is kind, yet I fear my lack of beauty is what keeps him from me."

"Has he said it?" Jean inquired, although she refused to believe Angus was that cruel or stupid.

"Nay, he says he would give me time to know him.

Still, I suspect my lack does nothing to encourage him," Annabella mourned. "Have ye not noticed that he has never once called me by my name? He addresses me as *madam*."

"Even in yer bedchamber?" Jean was shocked. What the hell was the matter with Angus? Then she asked, "Have ye ever called him by his name?"

"Nay! He has not given me permission to do so," Annabella responded.

Sweet holy Mother, Jean silently thought. She would have to speak to Angus, or Duin was apt to never have an heir. "My brother is wont to be gentle wi' ye because he respects yer innocence," she told Annabella. "Perhaps ye should swallow yer fears and encourage him to do what needs be done."

"I don't think I know how," Annabella admitted, feeling like a perfect fool. "Do ye like it, Jean, when yer husband . . ." She paused. Did she know of what she spoke?

"Aye, I do like our bed sport. And really, all ye need to do is kiss the man and caress him to encourage him. He'll do all the rest." She chuckled. "Ye do know that the first time will hurt? But after that there is little but pleasure for ye both."

"My sister Myrna told me I should lie on my back and open my legs," Annabella ventured. "When I told the earl that, he laughed."

"Well," Jean allowed, "she is right, in a manner of speaking. There is an opening for yer husband to put his cock into ye. And it is between yer legs, but yer bodies will find the right way to allow him this access. Let Angus lead ye. He will not harm ye. The longer ye put this off, the more terrifying it becomes, and 'tis not. Once ye have made love ye will discover ye want to do it again and again. And if I know my brother, ye will." She smiled at the younger woman. "The morning after, ye will see how silly all of yer fears have been."

"Is it truth?" Annabella asked. She actually felt encouraged by Jean's speech.

"'Tis truth," Jean reassured her. "Tonight invite yer husband into yer chamber, and welcome him into yer bed. Put yer arms about him, kiss him, and let what should happen, happen. And dinna let him leave ye until dawn on the morrow. Duin needs an heir."

But to make certain there was no difficulty, Jean sought out her eldest brother before the meal. She found him in his small library. He smiled in welcome as she came into the chamber, closing the door behind her.

"Sit," he said gesturing to a chair opposite his by the hearth. "Ye have yer serious face on today, Jeannie," he teased.

"It is past time, Angus," Jean began. "She thinks it is her plain face that keeps ye from her bed, and from consummating yer marriage. I know ye have been patient, but it is past time now. The longer ye both wait to do what needs doing, the more difficult it will become for her. Tonight ye must go naked into her bedchamber. Ye must get into the bed wi' her and kiss her protests away as ye do what must be done. Duin needs an heir."

"I know, I know, but I don't want her to hate me," he said. "Can ye imagine having to live wi' a woman who hates ye?"

"Ye're a fool, Angus," Jean told him. "She admires ye. I watch her as her eyes follow ye in the hall. I suspect for all yer lack of intimacy that Annabella is falling in love wi' ye. Why do ye think it troubles her so that ye have not made love to her? Annabella knows what is expected of her, but she does feel neglected by ye, brother.

And dinna say I told ye, but this morning Matthew accused her of not doing her duty, saying your prowess was proven, given the evidence of yer two bastards, and the one soon due. She was very hurt by his accusation, but ye would have been so proud of her. Every inch yer countess, she gave him no quarter but immediately dismissed him wi'out comment as regally as any queen might have done."

"Must I kill Matthew?" Angus growled.

Jean laughed. "Sweet Mary! Do ye care for her then?"

"She's my wife, and I will allow no one, even my brother, to disrespect her," he answered.

"Oh, my." Jean chortled. "The handsomest man in the borders is falling in love with his plain-faced bride. I can see, however, that ye're not ready to admit it, Angus, so I'll tease ye no more. Don't bother wi' our brother. He did apologize. Just make love to Annabella tonight, and get an heir on her."

Afterward, as they sat at the high board, Jean noted that both the Earl of Duin and his countess were more silent than talkative, thoughtful and introspective. Would her interference prove fruitful? If it did not, she would have to ask her mother for advice. As was their custom after the evening meal, Annabella and Angus sat at the same game table playing chess. He had discovered, to his pleasure, that she was a skillful player.

Now, as she moved to capture his bishop, he put a large hand over her small one.

Annabella looked up, surprised, and met his gaze. "Tonight," was the only word he spoke. She colored, but said nothing in return. She could hardly refuse him. Shaking his hand off of hers, she took the dark green agate piece.

With a positively wicked smile, he checked her queen. "That was careless of ye," he teased her. "Ye're not paying attention, lass."

"Or else ye are playing better tonight, my lord," she teased back. "But ye're correct. I do have other things on my mind. I would bring the blacksmith's youngest lad, Callum, and little Una to live at the castle this winter. Of all my pupils, they are the only ones remaining. Both of them are intelligent. Pastor Blaine told the lad that the ability to read and write would take him far in the world. I've begun to teach them their numbers as well."

"To what purpose?" the earl wanted to know.

"The smithy will go to Callum's two older brothers. He has no interest in it, nor in being a soldier. He's intelligent, Angus, and if educated could be of use to ye. Ye have ships trading in the New World, and even the East Indies now. Surely a place could be found among yer enterprises for such a lad."

"What about the blacksmith?" the earl inquired of her. So she was aware of his shipping endeavors. How much did she know? It wasn't something he had considered discussing with her. Her place as his wife was to supply Duin with heirs.

"With two sons already working by his side, Callum will be no loss to the blacksmith," Annabella told her husband. "Matthew can find a place for him here in the castle so he will earn his keep."

"And the little lass, Una? She will have her mam's place one day, won't she?"

"She says she doesn't want it, my lord. The old peddler who visits Duin has told her tales of Edinburgh and of shops," Annabella explained. "She wants to go to the town one day and work in a shop. She can have a place with me, and be responsible for keeping my clothing fresh and neat. Jean is willing to teach her. And she can take my laundry to her mother and bring it back. I'm sure there's another lass in the village who would be willing to help the laundress. With both these bairns here in the castle the winter long, I can concentrate on teaching them. I doubt Una will ever get to Edinburgh, although perhaps she will. Or we might help her to open a shop here in the village. It would be a great convenience for our clan folk."

Her arguments were well thought out, and he felt a surge of pride to be married to such a clever woman. Then he said, "Ye've a thoughtful heart. Aye, ye have my permission to bring these two bairns to the castle. I will speak with my brother, the steward, myself. And I will speak with the smith and the laundress of the opportunity we are giving their bairns."

"Thank ye, Angus," Annabella said. Then she arose from the game table and withdrew from the hall.

The earl watched her go, his half sister a step behind his countess. Jean was right: It was time for their marriage to be consummated. It was time for them to get on with the important business of getting an heir. For two months now he had courted her, riding out in the mornings with her, walking the beach below the castle with her many afternoons, playing chess with her in the evenings. They had talked and talked. He was surprised by her intellect but decided that it was pleasant to have a wife with whom he might speak on matters other than domestic. And she made him laugh.

Standing up, he sought out his brother at the other end of the hall with several men-at-arms. Drawing him away, he said, "Annabella has spoken to me of her plans to bring two of the village bairns to the castle. I have approved it, and will speak with the smith and the laundress myself so they understand the honor bestowed on their bairns."

"Better yer wife be raising her own bairns than another's," Matthew muttered.

"Why are ye being so hard about this?" Angus demanded of his younger sibling.

"It is not usual for ye to take so long to impregnate a wench," Matthew replied. "She should be wi' bairn by now, yet she ripens not. Perhaps she is infertile as well as plain. Ye might have had a beauty, an heiress."

Angus Ferguson swallowed back his anger. Matthew was just anxious for Duin's future. Having been recognized both personally and legally by their father, he was extremely loyal to his family. From his youth he had worshiped his elder brother. "Annabella will be enceinte soon," Angus promised Matthew. "Her mother was fertile, and she will be as well. She traveled across Scotland to be my wife. It's been only two months. She needs time to acclimate herself to Duin, to me. I am happy wi' her."

"Silis delivered ye a lad this morning," Matthew said.

"And ye're just now bringing me word of it?" the earl said, irritated.

"The messenger arrived during the evening meal. I didn't think yer wife would want to know that yer former mistress delivered ye a firstborn son this day," Matthew said. "What gift will ye bring the laddie tomorrow when ye go to see her?"

"Silis has been well taken care of, Matthew, and ye know it. I gave her a large cottage on the moor, for she didn't want one near her family's in the village. I furnished the cottage, gave her a servant to help her and a generous yearly stipend. I will visit my son when I have the time. If I go tomorrow, she will take it as an indication that I wish to resume our former relationship. Send the messenger back with a small silver cup. 'Twas what I gave the mothers of my daughters. Silis is aware of that, and can read nothing more into that.

"She'll take a lover soon enough, for she's a lass who cannot live wi'out a manly cock to entertain her. I'm actually not sure that this bairn is mine at all. I caught the blacksmith's middle son sneaking out of her da's cottage one day when I went to see her unexpectedly. I told her that same day that I was bored wi' her, and would no longer be coming to visit her. And she told me she was expecting a bairn, swearing 'twas mine, but I have never been entirely satisfied that was the truth. Silis is a whore at heart. I learned that the blacksmith's lad visited her at least twice a week last winter."

Matthew flushed. "I knew," he admitted, "but once ye told us that she was to have a bairn, I dared say naught to ye."

Angus laughed ruefully. "The bairn could be mine," he replied.

"When ye see him, look for the mark," Matthew said. He referred to a tiny round birthmark that all their father's male children bore on their testicles.

Angus laughed. "When I go to see the bairn, I will look," he replied. "Say nothing to Jean or Annabella."

Matthew nodded. "I'll say nothing," he promised his brother. "But they are bound to hear of the bairn sooner than later."

"Jean, mayhap," Angus agreed, "but 'tis unlikely Annabella will go into the village now that she is to have Callum and Una here wi' her. Silis and her bairn should be of no concern to my wife. 'Tis past."

"As long as Silis understands yer wishes," Matthew said. "Perhaps I should deliver the silver cup to her."

"Nay, yer presence would have her believing that I still care. Send the cup with the messenger," the earl told his brother. He would, of course, have to go and see the bairn sooner or later. It would be expected of him. His former mistress was the daughter of a fisherman, who had lived in the village with her aunt, for she could not abide the smell of fish. She had flirted with him boldly, and finally he had indulged his curiosity. She had given herself to him freely, and for a time she had amused him with her beauty and her greed for any bauble he gave her. Finally bored with her and concerned by the faint rumors of her faithlessness, he had ended the relationship. Her news, however, led him to act honorably. He had not seen or heard of her again until this evening.

He considered whether he should tell Annabella of Silis and her bairn, but decided against it. It was hardly the kind of conversation a man wanted to have with his bride before deflowering her and spending the night in her bed. Tonight of all nights, their thoughts and emotions should be only for each other. "Good night, Matthew," he said, and, leaving the hall, hurried up the stairs to his own apartment.

Within he found that his body servant, Tormod, had prepared a hot bath for him in the bathing chamber. He bathed quickly, saying little, yet he could not help but wonder how Tormod had known he wanted to bathe this night, for he had sent no order to him. The servant wrapped a towel warmed by the fire about his master when he emerged from the stone tub. He knelt to pare the earl's toenails, and then with a smaller towel dried his short-cropped dark hair. Back in his bedchamber, Angus dismissed the servant. "I will not need you again until the morning," he said.

Tormod bowed. "Aye, my lord," he said. Then he was gone from the chamber.

Had there been the hint of a smile upon the man's lips, or had he imagined it? Angus wondered to himself. He was ready to join Annabella, but now he became assailed with doubts. What if her lack of beauty caused his lust to lie dormant? What a disaster that would prove to be. Still, her bedchamber would be lit only by firelight. She was not ugly, nor deformed, and she was a sweet lass who might be shy but was more than willing to do her duty. Of course he would perform properly. It could not be otherwise.

He decided against wearing a nightshirt or house robe. It was always awkward removing such a garment in the heat of passion, and there would be passion. How could it be otherwise when a man held a tender, warm body in his arms? Angus Ferguson walked across his bedchamber and, opening the door in the paneled wall, ducked his head to avoid the top of the doorjamb as he stepped into Annabella's bedchamber.

She turned as he came into the room, gasping with surprise at his nudity. The dimness of the chamber showed little more than his shadow, the firelight touching his skin here and there. "My lord," she murmured.

He could smell the intoxicating fragrance that surrounded her. She was wearing a silk-and-lace garment that, rather than concealing her figure, revealed her entire body to his sight. And to his great surprise, it was an absolutely beautiful body. He felt a tightening in his groin. Her limbs were long and shapely. Her charming little breasts almost made his mouth water with anticipation at the thought of the thorough licking and sucking he would visit upon them very shortly. Her belly had just the faint hint of rounding, and below it was her smooth plump mons. He walked slowly about her to discover that her buttocks were delightfully curvaceous. His hands itched to grasp those charming mounds.

If God had denied Annabella Baird the face of a goddess, he had certainly given her the body of one. The dancing flames of the firelight offered him a most perfect view of it. His cock tingled at the thought of possessing that body. She was his! His alone! No one but him would ever know the secret that her clothing hid. He almost laughed aloud at this wonderful discovery. Then he greeted her. "Good evening, madam," he said.

She did not demur. "Will we couple tonight?" she asked him.

"Aye," he told her.

"Then, as we are about to become intimate," Annabella said softly, "perhaps ye will call me by my given name, my lord. Since ye're about to shortly take my virginity from me—yours by right, my lord—I should like to hear ye speak my name, and not address me quite so formally as *madam*."

"Take off yer garment, *Annabella*," he replied to her.

"As ye will, my lord," she answered him, drawing the long, loose garment over her head and dropping it to the floor.

"Undo yer hair for me, Annabella," he next commanded, watching as she slowly unplaited the thick braid, fluffing her hair out once it was undone. Plunging his two hands into the thick, silky mass of her sable tresses, he drew her toward him so he might kiss her a deep, slow kiss. A surge of lust raced through him as her soft lips met his, and she kissed him back. Releasing her lips, he looked down into her gray eyes and smiled. Then, reaching out, he cupped one of her small breasts in his palm, rubbing the nipple with the ball of his thumb until the rosy flesh stiffened into a peak.

Annabella drew in a sharp breath. "Angus," was all she could manage. She was absolutely fascinated by all that was happening. He was so gentle with her.

He put an arm about her, drawing her close. Their naked bodies were now fully touching, and he felt her quiver. "God's mercy, sweeting, ye're lovely," he told her softly, squeezing the little breast nestled in his hand.

Her eyes filled with tears. "Don't mock me, Angus. I could not bear it," she whispered to him in a tremulous voice.

"Annabella," he said, "while there is no denying that ye're plain of face, ye have the most outrageously beautiful body. I'm already afire to possess ye!"

"I do?" She sounded honestly surprised. Then she asked him, "How can ye know that, Angus?"

He chuckled. "Because, lass, I have known many female bodies in my life," he told her. He turned her so that they were facing the beautiful full-length mirror that had once belonged to his mother. "Look for yerself, Annabella," he said.

Her eyes fastened on the images in the glass. It was the most erotic sight she had ever seen. He stood behind her, his big naked body pressing against her naked body. His two big hands cupped her two small breasts. Their bodies were both golden and shadowed in the light of the hearth's dancing flames. The odd stirring she had experienced once before was suddenly filling her. Her head fell back against his shoulder, and she watched, mesmerized, as his thumbs began to rub her nipples. She shocked herself by pressing her buttocks back against him, gasping again as she felt his manhood awakening.

His dark head bent and he placed a kiss upon her rounded shoulder. His lips followed the curve of her neck. "Ye're wickedly tempting, Annabella, Countess of

Duin. I am filled wi' my desire for ye. Are ye ready to yield yerself to me, sweeting?"

Her head was spinning from the new sensations suddenly assailing her.

"Wha . . . what do ye want me to do?" she finally managed to grate out. Her voice kept getting caught in her throat, and her mind was confused. How was it possible for a man to wreak such havoc with a touch, a kiss, a sensuous word?

"Tonight ye will do naught but accept the homage of my passion for ye, Annabella. Eventually I will teach ye the things a woman can do to pleasure a man, but not tonight. Tonight I would introduce ye to passion. I would explore every inch of yer luscious body. Finally, when ye are ready, I will join my body wi' yers so that we may attain the ultimate pleasure." He turned her about so she was now facing him again, his arms wrapping tightly about her. Then, before she might say another word, he began to kiss her.

He began with soft, gently playful kisses that he scattered across her mouth, her cheeks, her closed eyelids. Then he concentrated fully on her lips, pressing his against hers as one kiss blended into another and another and another as her resistance gave way, finally permitting his tongue to plunge into her mouth. Her tongue shyly retreated, but he hunted it down with his, cornering it, stroking it over and over until she could not help but respond to the flames of desire now licking at her body.

Angus could feel that the girl in his torrid embrace was near to swooning with her newly aroused excitement. Breaking off his passionate kisses, he caught her up in his arms, walked to her bed, and set her gently upon it. He stared down, briefly enchanted by the voluptuous picture she made as she lay upon her back, her body slightly curled, one arm shielding her eyes from the sight of his powerful masculine body, his manhood now engaged and fully aroused.

Then, before she might grow frightened, he joined her in the bed. He lifted her arm away from her face, saying, "Look at me, Annabella."

She wanted to refuse, for the elegant man she had married two months ago suddenly seemed so fierce and dominating. Oh, she was very aware that he was holding himself back for her sake. That he was being kind, and patient, but still . . .

"Annabella!" The voice was now commanding.

Her eyes flew open to find his handsome face staring down at her. "Angus?"

He smiled that wonderful smile of his at her. "Kissing, sweeting, is an art. I find ye're an excellent scholar," he said. "Now I will show ye other places where kisses may be enjoyed by both husband and wife." His dark head moved to one of her breasts. He covered it with little kisses, then moved to the other breast, which he kissed as ardently.

Annabella found herself sighing with genuine pleasure, but then his lips closed over one of her nipples. The tug of his mouth on that most sensitive portion of her flesh caused her to cry out softly. "Oh! Oh!" *Sweet Mary!* She could feel a corresponding tug in that secret place between her legs. "Angus?" she murmured questioningly.

He raised his head, his green eyes staring into hers. "Hmmm?"

"I . . . I . . ." She didn't know what to say, too shy to ask whether the feelings overwhelming her were those that should be felt.

Again that smile lit his face. "Sweet wife," he said, his hand caressing her face. "Ye're surely not afraid of me, are ye?"

"Nay," she said, shaking her head, "but everything is so strange to me."

He kissed her mouth, a deep kiss. Then he said, "I sense that you have a talent for passion, sweeting. Let me awaken it, Annabella. Do not question; just follow as yer heart, yer body, and mind dictate," he suggested to her as he began to kiss her naked body, his mouth moving slowly, lingering first here and then there, obviously enjoying himself. His kisses covered her torso, her belly, her legs, and her feet. He nibbled at her toes, causing her to giggle. Smiling, he turned her over and, beginning with the soles of her feet, his lips worked their way up her shapely calves and thighs and across her rounded buttocks to the small of her back.

Annabella gasped as she felt his warm tongue licking its way up her spine, across her shoulders, and finally reaching the nape of her neck, which he bit gently. "Oh! Oh!" It was all too delicious. He claimed that she had a talent for kissing? Certainly he far surpassed any budding skill she might have, Annabella thought, relaxing beneath the warm mouth that seemed to enjoy her body. When he turned her over again onto her back she hummed a small protest at the loss of his kisses.

Her eyes were closed, and he admired her lovely long, thick eyelashes.

"Surely I haven't put ye to sleep, Annabella," he teased her, and delighted in the color staining her cheeks. She was adorable. Delectable. He was amazed at his own patience in waiting to possess her, for his cock was hard and ready.

"Nay," she answered him, opening her eyes again. "I

find I am enjoying yer kisses and caresses perhaps more than I should."

He laughed softly. "With passion, enough is never enough, my sweet." He began to stroke her as he might a small cat. His hand moved down her torso until he was brushing her plump mons. She watched him, shyly fascinated, but then his palm pressed down upon that mound of flesh. A bolt of sensation shot through her, and she stiffened.

"Ahhh," he said, seeing the look of both panic and curiosity in her eyes, "now, sweet wife, ye're beginning to understand passion." Leaning forward, he began to kiss her again, delighted when her lips met his eagerly.

She felt just the tiniest touch of fear as he ran a finger along the slit dividing her nether lips. She tried to distract herself from what he was doing, because she knew he would not harm her, yet that finger was unnerving. The finger pushed between the slit, seeking, seeking. Seeking what? *Mother of mercy!* "Ohhh!" What was he touching, and why did it feel so exciting, so wonderful? "Ohhhhh!"

He had found her love bud and caressed it gently, and then with a stronger stroke.

Her little cries excited him. Unable to help himself, he bent low, kissing that sentient nub of flesh. Her gasp was audible, but then he was burrowing his finger deeper, and finding the opening of her love passage, and gently inserted his finger to the first joint.

She gasped again, and bucked beneath him.

"Dinna be fearful, Annabella," he reassured her as he pressed his finger into her to his knuckle. His voice was thick with his desire.

"I'm not," she lied, pressing her lips together to keep from screaming.

He moved the finger back and forth gently. His own cock was so hard now that he feared a simple touch would shatter it into a thousand pieces. He had to take her soon. "Yer love juices have begun to flow, sweeting," he told her. "Ye're ready to be mounted."

"So soon?" she whispered, realizing that the moment had come.

Without another word he withdrew his finger from her. Swinging himself over her body, he looked down into her plain little face. Her lack of beauty meant nothing to him. He wanted her as he could never recall wanting another woman. He had to have her. *Now!* Her eyes were squeezed tightly shut. Her beautiful body was tensed and braced for his assault. He almost wept at this last sight of her innocence. He leaned forward and began to kiss her—deep, soft kisses to distract her from what was to come.

His lips! *Holy Mother!* His lips were wonderful. She had never imagined kissing could be so incredible. She lost herself in those kisses, his tongue dancing with her tongue. It was heaven! Wait! What was happening? He was pushing himself into her love sheath. He was too big! Too big! Annabella's eyes flew open. "Nay! Stop!" *Oh!* He was pushing himself deeper into her body, tearing her asunder, invading her very soul. "No! No! Angus! No!" she cried, struggling beneath him, her small fists beating at his chest and shoulders.

God forgive him, but he could not cease now. Her untried sheath was very tight, but it was yielding to him. Her pleading almost broke his heart. There was nothing for it. He had reached the barrier of her virginity. He could feel how tightly lodged it was. Drawing back, he quickly thrust himself through it and deep into her body. Her shriek almost brought him to tears, for he was not a man to visit pain upon a woman. Having torn her maidenhead asunder, however, he rested a moment, kissing the tears on her cheeks. "It's done now, sweeting," he murmured in her ear. "The worst is over, and 'twill be better now; I promise ye."

She didn't believe him when he said it, but as he began to piston her, his long, thick cock flashing back and forth within her, the burning, stinging pain quickly dissolved, to be replaced by a new sensation that could almost be called pleasurable. Annabella made a small sound of enjoyment. When she did, his big body stiffened atop her. He groaned as she felt his seed being expelled into her. It was at that moment that Annabella realized she was no longer a bride. She was a wife.

After a few moments he withdrew from her body. "I'm sorry for the pain," he told her. "It won't happen again now that yer maidenhead is gone. Wi' yer permission I should like to remain wi' you tonight."

Annabella nodded. "Aye, I would like it if ye did," she admitted. "After the pain I felt the beginnings of pleasure, Angus. Will ye come to my bed every night now?"

"If it pleases ye," he told her. "There is more, ye know."

"What more?" she queried him.

"Ye should feel great pleasure when we come together. Tonight ye were frightened with the newness of it all, but ye say ye felt the beginnings of pleasure, which is encouraging. My own desire for ye was so great tonight that I could not take all the time ye needed to reach yer own delight. I will not let that happen again, sweeting."

"I felt that if it went on just a bit longer," Annabella confided, "I might fly."

He smiled, pleased. "Next time I will see that ye do,"

he promised her. Reaching for the coverlet, he pulled it up over them, and they slept in each other's arms.

When he awoke he could see the false dawn beyond the windows of the bedchamber. He realized he was hungry for her body once again. The fire was burning low. He arose, and fed it generously. Then he attempted to sleep once more, but he could not. Her sweet bottom pressed into his groin, its cleft almost cradling his stiffening cock. He needed to satisfy his passion at least one more time this night.

Turning her about, he kissed her awake. "I need ye again," he growled in her ear, nipping the tender lobe.

Annabella could actually feel her breasts grow firm, her nipples puckering at the sound of desire in his deep voice. "I have not the right to deny ye, my lord," she said, meekly pressing herself against his hard body.

"I want ye as filled with lust for me as I am for ye," he said fiercely.

"Then," she boldly taunted him, "make me feel that lust!" What on earth had come over her? Annabella thought. But then she pushed all thoughts of propriety aside. This big, handsome man was her husband. He wanted to possess her body, and to her own surprise she realized that she was as eager to be possessed as he was to possess her. She sensed there was a great deal she had to learn from him. She knew she was going to prove to be an apt pupil. "Make love to me, my lord of Duin!" she commanded him.

Her words sent a jolt of surprise through him. To find her so suddenly eager made him more than happy to comply with her whispered wishes. Especially when she wrapped herself about him, her hands boldly stroking his back and buttocks as he had stroked hers earlier. Delighted, he rolled her onto her back, kissing her until she was gasping for breath. His knee pressed between her legs, and she opened herself to him. He groaned when she surprised him further by reaching down to cup him. Her hand began to pull away from him.

"Nay! Nay!" he almost begged her. "Dinna remove yer hand from me, sweeting. I need yer touch." He caught the little hand, drawing it back down to his cock and balls.

"Ye're not angry?" she said softly. "I so wanted to touch ye." Her fingers caressed him ever so gently. "It grows bigger wi' yer lust, doesn't it."

A wave of heat washed over him. "Aye," he managed to answer. Jesu, he was getting so hard! Had he ever been this hard this quickly? What magic was it that aroused his passions so quickly, so greatly? He now regretted every moment of the last two months when he might have been making love to her—but nay. He had been wise to wait, to give her the opportunity to know him better. The loss of her virginity had opened Annabella to the passion within her.

Her fingers stroking the length of his cock were wreaking an incredible and delicious havoc on him. He didn't know how much longer he could bear this sweet torture she was inflicting upon him. Finally he took control again, drawing her arms up above her head as he mounted her and plunged into her wet, hot sheath. He groaned as its walls closed tightly about him. Annabella sighed with the intimacy of their contact. She was sweeter and warmer than any woman he had ever known.

Her legs wrapped about him as she reveled in his need. So this was passion. No wonder women were unable to speak clearly about it. It was indeed indescribable. He had released his hold on her hands, and she was now able to hold him closer to her. Her fingers kneaded his broad shoulders.

He wanted to be gentle, for she was still newly opened, but he simply couldn't restrain himself when her legs closed around him. He began to thrust into her. Deeper. Harder. Deeper. Harder, until she was making little sounds of pleasure that only encouraged him to greater efforts. Her nails raked down his back as her body almost rose to meet his every thrust.

He had said it would not hurt again, and it didn't this time. His fierce, passionate need sent her senses reeling with delight. She could have never imagined that coupling would be as delicious as it was. Her head was spinning. Her body felt as if it were going to explode with pleasure. How could that be? But then it did. Her body seemed to erupt from the inside out, leaving her overwhelmed by a riot of emotions she couldn't sort out. She soared. She flew. It was simply too much for anyone to bear.

Angus roared with his own release as his throbbing cock exploded its juices deep into her, flooding her secret garden with his lustful tribute. He shuddered, then groaned a deep sound of utter satisfaction.

Annabella burst into tears.

"Jesu! Have I hurt ye?" His cock was still tingling, and he was not yet able to withdraw himself from her.

"Nay! Nay!" she reassured him through her sobs. "It's just that I have never known such pure pleasure as I have now experienced. Tell me you have known this happiness too, and I have not greedily taken it all for myself. That would be so unfair."

He laughed weakly. "Oh, sweeting," he told her, "I cannot ever recall having been so pleased by a woman. I look forward to sharing many more such moments as we have just had. Your innocence last night was a great gift, Annabella. I thank ye for it. But to awaken before dawn to find you eager for passion was a gift I had not expected. I thank ye again." He was now able to roll off of her, but when he did he drew her into his embrace, kissing the top of her head as he did so. The delicious fragrance surrounding her assailed his nostrils again. Plain of face his wife might be, Angus Ferguson thought. *But what a wife I have been given. I want bairns of her body, and we shall have them.*

They fell asleep again in each other's arms. When Annabella finally awoke she found herself alone. The light outside of her bedchamber window told her it was well past dawn. She realized that she did indeed feel a bit sore between her legs, and her limbs were a trifle stiff. Blushing, she remembered her boldness with him, but he had been content with her behavior. Still, was it permissible for a wife to be so bold with her husband? After the initial shock, Annabella had decided that she enjoyed coupling. She wanted more of him. *Mother of mercy!* Was such desire on her part a natural thing? She had so much to learn, and Jean would certainly be able to elucidate it all for her.

The door to her bedchamber opened. "Ye're awake," Jean said smiling, "and none the worse for wear, I can see," she teased. "The earl would like to know if ye're of a mind to ride out wi' him, though it be close to mid-morning."

"Aye," Annabella said, and she jumped from her bed, heedless of her nudity.

Jean's eyes widened briefly, for although she had served her young mistress for two months now and seen her in various states of undress, she had never seen her fully as nature had fashioned her. *Oh, my!* she thought. And then Jean chuckled to herself. No wonder Angus had come into the hall whistling that morning. Were men not simple in their needs? Angus had discovered his plain-faced wife had a beautiful body, and it was obviously more than enough to content him. "Ye'll want a bath," she said.

"Tonight, but for now I will use my basin. I dinna wish to keep my husband waiting," Annabella said, already pouring water into the basin.

"Be sure to cleanse the blood from yer thighs," Jean advised, then turned quickly away to gather up the bloodied sheets from the bed. *Gracious*, she thought at the sight of the brown stains. Angus had indeed done his duty to Duin quite thoroughly, and Annabella did not look unhappy for it. Rather she looked very happy this morning. There was a small smile upon her lips, and she was humming to herself as she bathed using the basin.

Jean laid out a fresh chemise, stockings, breeks, a linen shirt, and a fur-lined, sleeved jerkin. She set her mistress's boots by the bed, where Annabella was now quickly dressing. "Shall I go tell Angus that ye'll be down shortly?" she asked.

"Aye, but then come back to help me wi' my boots and my hair," Annabella said.

Jean hurried out, carrying the sheets. She brought them to the castle laundress, who, seeing the bloodstains, looked questioningly at the countess's tiring woman. "Not a word," Jean warned her. "The deed is now done, and 'tis all that matters."

The laundress nodded silently. She wasn't about to gossip, lest she harm her daughter Una's chances with the lady of Duin.

Jean went back up to the hall and, seeing her brother,

said, "The lady will be down as soon as I get her boots on and plait her hair, my lord."

"I'll await her in the courtyard," Angus Ferguson replied.

Jean ran back up the staircase to her mistress's apartment. She helped Annabella with her boots. Then she brushed out her sable tresses, braiding them into a single plait. "Dinna ride too far," she warned Annabella, handing her a pair of doeskin riding gloves that had been dyed a bright red. "Ye'll get sore. He's in the courtyard."

Annabella hurried down the stairs and out into the courtyard, where the earl was already mounted. A stableman helped her into her saddle. Snow danced skittishly, eager for her morning run. "I'm ready, my lord," she said, her eyes meeting his.

They rode out, and Annabella saw that the flocks of sheep and the herds of cattle were now back from the sheiling, as the summer meadows were called, and safely settled in the home pastures. The animals were fat with their months of grazing. When the snows came the earl would have them moved into the barns to protect them from the wolves that would boldly roam the winter hills.

"Ye're well this morning?" he asked her politely as they rode.

"As well, I hope, as ye are, my lord," she answered him.

He chuckled. "Then ye were content wi' our bed sport, madam?"

"As well, I hope, as ye were, my lord," she replied.

He glanced sharply at her serene face. Her twinkling gray eyes met his and he laughed aloud. "Ye're a bold wench, madam," he told her. Then his eyes went to her little round breasts, and he felt his cock stirring. How sweet her flesh had tasted in his mouth last night. Had the morning not been cold with a sharp wind coming from the north, he would have been tempted to take her on this hillside amid the heather. Briefly he pictured her spreading herself for him, moaning with pleasure as he filled her. He was once again surprised by his desire for her. He could hardly believe his need. He could not wait until nightfall to have her again. But did he have to wait until then?

"We've gone far enough for today," he said, turning his stallion about.

"I'll race ye!" Snow leaped forward.

Surprised, he urged the stallion into a canter. Mischievously, she had taken advantage of him. They raced, and she was across the drawbridge and into the courtyard, just barely ahead of him, as he thundered after her. There were no stable lads in view. Laughing, Annabella slid from her mare, leading Snow into the semidarkened stables to her stall. He followed with his own beast.

Without a word between them, they unsaddled their horses, rubbed them down, and filled their food bins with oats and hay. As she exited Snow's stall, drawing the gate shut as she did, the earl came up behind her, wrapping his arms about her lightly. She protested faintly as he pulled her farther into the darkened stable, pushing her facedown over a bale of hay.

"There is more than one way to couple, madam," he growled in her ear, as, reaching about her, he fumbled with the buttons on her jerkin, unlaced her shirt, and yanked her breeks down to reveal her tempting bottom.

"Angus!" she squealed. "What are ye about?" She heard him undoing his own breeks, heard them drop to the stable floor.

"My thoughts of ye last night haunt me," his voice whispered harshly into her ear. "I must have ye, Annabella! *I must!*" He fisted her thighs apart, grasping her hips.

Her heart was hammering wildly in her chest; she was more excited than afraid. Then she felt his engorged cock sliding into her love sheath.

"Jesu! Ye're already wet for me," he groaned, pushing himself deep, her rounded buttocks pressing against him. Reaching around her, he took her two breasts in his hands as he slowly began to piston her. Her sheath tightened about him, setting his lust aboil.

Instinctively she arched her back for him. This was delicious madness—being ravished from behind in a dark stable like some milkmaid or servant lass. But oh, oh, oh, it was wonderful! His thrusts grew quicker and deeper. Her head was already spinning with her own lustful appreciation of his efforts. His hot breath scalded her ear. "Oh, Angus," she half sobbed. "It is good! So good! Dinna stop!"

What a jest God had played upon him, Angus Ferguson thought as he enthusiastically fucked his wife. He had given Angus a maiden who appeared as meek as a lamb, but was in reality the most passionate woman he had ever known. She was like fire, and she scorched his very soul.

"Oh, aye! Aye!" Annabella cried out as her excitement began to peak.

"Jesu! Jesu!" he groaned as he felt himself ready to burst with his pleasure.

The passion between them exploded. They sprawled upon the bale of hay, their breath coming in painful little gasps as they both attempted to regain their sanity. His fingers squeezed her breasts as the last drops of his juices spurted weakly, and she attempted to prolong the delight.

Finally, Annabella sighed a gusty sigh. "Someone may come," she said softly.

"Aye," he agreed, pulling himself slowly to his feet. Pulling his breeks up, he fastened them. Then he drew her up, helping her to regain some order in her garb. He couldn't help kissing her before he released her. Then they walked from the stables as if nothing had just happened between them.

"So one may fuck anywhere," Annabella said in a perfectly calm and conversational tone of voice as they entered the castle again.

"Aye," he replied. "At any time or place."

"I always thought such activity was confined to the bedchamber in the dark hours only," Annabella responded.

"Would ye prefer it so, madam?" he asked her.

"Mother of mercy, nay, my lord, I should not!" she told him. "I shall look forward to more of yer delightful surprises. Ye have promised to teach me what will please ye, and I promise ye that I will be a most attentive scholar, husband."

"Cease, for pity's sake, madam," he begged her. "Ye but arouse my lust again, and I have work to do this day."

"Then do not keep me waiting tonight, my lord," she cautioned him. "I am so eager to learn." She curtsied to him and, turning, hurried away.

Angus's head spun with the lustful thoughts her words aroused in him. Again he wondered what was the magic she was using that made him feel as randy as a young bull in high summer? Then he realized that he didn't really care. Wasn't his lust for her, and hers for him, a good thing? Certainly they would produce bairns at a rapid rate if they continued on as they had this day. Women were cautioned by both the old and the Reformed churches that the coupling of a husband and wife had only one purpose: bairns.

Yet he knew for a fact that his dour father and his gay French mother had fallen in love and enjoyed their bed sport. Could he ever come to love Annabella? Or would his emotions for her be confined to simply lust?

December came. Annabella made it an extremely happy month at Duin, for there were many feast days to be celebrated. Pastor Blaine wanted to disapprove of all the gaiety, but the young Countess of Duin would not let him. "There can be no wrong in celebrating the coming of our Lord and his birth," she said.

"So much feasting and dancing is wicked, my lady," he said, distressed.

"Is it wrong to thank God for sending us his beloved son, Pastor? Is it wrong to feed the poor, and give gifts to those who have served us well? Nay! I cannot sanction such thoughts, and certainly ye do not believe such a thing," Annabella told him.

Her words were so reasonable, and how could God be offended under the circumstances? Pastor Blaine acquiesced. He had heard there was to be venison for dinner, and the earl would be broaching a keg of his own whiskey. "But we must always remember to keep God in mind as we feast," he said.

"Do ye not give the blessing each time ye're at the high board?" she reminded him.

"Aye, but when I am not there, who does it?" he demanded to know.

"Why, my husband, of course," Annabella told him.

Satisfied, the pastor even helped decorate the hall

with pine and holly. He oversaw the bringing of the Yule log into the hall, and agreed with the countess when she appointed the steward, Matthew Ferguson, as the lord of misrule. Each day was a feast, but for the few ember days still observed by the old Church, as the Fergusons were still Catholic. Pastor Blaine found himself approving of those days of prayer and fasting, much to his surprise.

Angus Ferguson could hardly keep his hands off of his wife. Not a day passed, except for those few when her link with the moon was broken, when he didn't find his cock foraging between her legs at least two or three times daily. He had her in his library on the floor before the fire. One afternoon he pulled her into a deep and dark linen cupboard to fuck. The stables had become a favorite trysting place. Scarcely had the meal been cleared away in the early evening before the lord and lady were gone from the hall.

"Ye're like a lad wi' his first wench," Matthew said disgustedly one afternoon. He had earlier heard Annabella giggling and his brother growling in a dark corner of the hall.

They hadn't heard him, but it was damned obvious what they had been about when the earl, almost strutting like a rooster, appeared from the dimness. "Can ye nae confine yer lusts to the bedchamber in the evening?" Matthew demanded to know.

"'Twas ye who encouraged me to greater efforts," Angus said with a grin. "Are ye telling me that ye confine yer lusts to a bedchamber in the evening?" Then he laughed uproariously at the look on his younger sibling's face.

"I suppose I'm amazed that such a woman can rouse you to such passions," Matthew said bluntly.

Angus chortled knowingly. "Annabella's face may be plain, little brother, but the body that God gave her is magnificent. I have but to think of her, and I am ready to fuck. And my sweet wife is a most enthusiastic and willing partner. It is impossible to resist her, and as I see nae reason to, I shall not. I am beginning to believe ye would not be half as sour if ye had a wife to keep ye company these long, cold winter nights."

"Bah!" Matthew said. "Get the wench wi' bairn, Angus, and stop enjoying yerselves so damned much."

The earl laughed. "In God's good time, little brother. In God's good time."

Chapter 6

Twelfth Night was scarcely gone when James Hepburn, the Earl of Bothwell, came to Duin. "I've come to take ye both to court," he told Angus and Annabella. "The queen is wi' bairn. Darnley is a pig and behaving badly because she will nae gie him the crown matrimonial, and the earls appear restless, which is always a bad sign."

"And ye would drag us into that situation?" Angus said. "Nay."

"She needs a distraction and new faces about her. She asks about ye often, Angus, and would meet the man who made her childhood in France such a comfortable one," Bothwell said.

"How do ye know that?" Angus demanded. "Even yer father didn't know the cost of Duin's earldom."

"Nay, he didn't. She told me," Bothwell replied.

"Ye're that close to the queen, Jamie?" Angus was curious. "Ye play a dangerous game then, and I think ye should not."

"I am loyal to the queen. No other man in Scotland who knows her can claim that distinction, even her own dear brother, James Stewart, the Earl of Moray, who has a curious habit of disappearing whenever something wicked is about to happen. My father allowed his love for Marie de Guise, and his disappointment at her refusal to wed him, to turn him traitor and brand the Hepburn name. I have spent my whole life attempting to erase that stain upon our family. Whatever Mary's fate, I will remain at her side, loyal until death."

"What of the wife ye are to take shortly?" Angus asked candidly.

"Ye'll come to the wedding, of course," James Hepburn said, avoiding the query. "The queen will be there, and 'twill be the perfect time to join the court. Remain wi' her for a few weeks, gain her favor, and then return to Duin. 'Tis simply a courtesy, Angus. Nothing more. Besides, my sister, Janet, will be there. She will enjoy having another ear into which to pour her complaint about this marriage. Until I have a legitimate son, 'tis her wee lad, my nephew, Francis, who is my heir. She's determined to have my earldom of Bothwell for him," James Hepburn said, laughing. "She need not worry. This marriage between myself and Jean Gordon is nae a love match. The queen and George Gordon want it. Gordon feels he gains more influence wi' the queen through me. The queen feels that she gains the loyalty of one of the north's most powerful earls. The Gordons are now being forgiven for their last uprising."

"And Jean Gordon?" Annabella asked quietly.

Surprised that she had insinuated herself into the conversation, James Hepburn turned to look at Angus's wife. Aye. There was something different about her that he could not put his finger upon. "My betrothed is in love with another," he said. "An Ogilvie, but once the queen decided to unite me with Lady Jean Gordon, the young man was quickly married to another."

"Poor lass," Annabella murmured.

"Where's the wedding to be held?" Angus asked, hoping to cover his wife's bold words.

"Edinburgh. In the kirk at the Canongate. The queen wanted a Catholic ceremony in the Chapel Royal, for the Gordons, like ye, still cling to the old faith. But I am a Protestant now. The Gordons dinna object, and Knox is quiet for a change."

"We'll be there," Angus said, with a quick look in his wife's direction, stifling any protest she might make. James Hepburn was his friend. He was obviously in favor with the queen, and he was marrying the sister of the Earl of Huntley, a most powerful northern lord.

"Ye're nae pleased," Bothwell said to Annabella.

"I dinna like travel," she admitted. "But I canna deny it will nae harm Duin for us to go and pay our respects to the queen. We shall have to leave shortly, for yer marriage is less than a month away, and Edinburgh far. I shall barely have time to pack my finery."

James Hepburn chuckled. "Ye're a good lass," he said. "Dutiful and loyal."

"So ye approve of my lass, do ye, Jamie?" Angus said.

"Aye, I do. I think, madam, that ye will do well with Lady Gordon, for like ye she is educated, although apt to be a wee bit pedantic for my taste," Bothwell said.

He remained with them for another day, and then left. Jean and Annabella began to pack for their journey, for Jean would go with her mistress. Angus sent Matthew to Edinburgh to find them a house, for he was not of a mind to live in a public accommodation, and they were unlikely to be given a place at Holyrood Palace, where the pregnant queen was living.

Annabella had not felt well in recent days, but there was no help for it; they must go to James Hepburn's wedding, and then join the court to please the queen. Matthew returned, having managed to lease a house for three months on a street off of the Royal Mile. It had a view of Edinburgh Castle, and a large garden. The owner was in France, but the servants remained. Matthew had also arranged for the places they would stay during the nights of their journey. And to Annabella's delight they would spend two nights at Rath.

They left Duin on a cold but sunny morning. The gulls flew overhead, skreeing noisily as they departed over the drawbridge. They had prayed for good weather, for it would take them a good week or more to reach Edinburgh. They traveled with two dozen men-at-arms. The baggage carts had gone on several days earlier, escorted by another dozen armed men. Hopefully they would all arrive in the town at the same time, for the carts could not travel as quickly as the mounted riders could.

After several days they reached Rath just as a snow began to fall. Annabella had warned her husband that her family's tower house was small in comparison to Duin Castle. "We will probably sleep in the hall in the bed spaces by the fireplace," she told him. But to her surprise they did not. While the earl and his brother would have the bed spaces, Annabella would share her girlhood chamber with her sister Agnes and Jean Ferguson.

Her parents greeted her warmly, but Annabella immediately noticed that everyone at Rath seemed subdued. "Where are my other sisters?" she asked.

Agnes began to cry.

"We hoped to spare ye the shame," the lady Anne said. "Myrna allowed herself to be despoiled by Ian Melville. Then he would nae wed her, marrying one of my Hamilton cousins instead. Both lasses were wi' bairn by the dirty lecher, but the Hamiltons were able to offer a higher dower to old Melville. Myrna miscarried a son. She was held up to ridicule in the kirk. Only yer da's standing as laird kept her from the stocks."

"Oh, Mam, I am so sorry," Annabella said. She remembered her sister's bold and knowing words the night before Annabella departed Rath for Duin. She had wondered about Myrna then, but there was naught she might have done to save her sister. "What of Sorcha? Is she all right?"

"She was wed to Gilbert Elliot in December. Thank God the Elliots looked the other way, but they knew Sorcha is a good lass," Robert Baird said.

Agnes sniffled.

"What has happened to Myrna?" Annabella persisted.

"Gone. Married to a Highlander my sister sent down from the north," the laird told his eldest daughter. "I had written to my sister about Myrna, and one day in early January, a man named Duncan MacKay appeared. He's kin to my sister's husband and came with a letter written in my sister's hand."

They were all seated about the fire as he told the tale. They had hardly expected any visitor at this time of year, the laird began, let alone a giant of a red-haired clansman.

"I've come to wed yer daughter," the deep voice boomed at the startled laird and his wife. He had a bushy red beard that matched his hair.

"I hae four daughters, and two already wed, sir," the laird of Rath replied.

"Ye've one who's been despoiled, I'm told," came the surprising answer. "'Tis that lass I've come for, my lord.

I am Duncan MacKay, the MacKay of the Cairn, kin to yer sister's husband. I've land, a fine stone house, a wee village, thirty-two men whose loyalty is to me first, and a fine herd of cattle. But I cannot seem to keep a wife, and I must have one."

Fascinated in spite of himself, Robert Baird had asked, "Why can ye not keep a wife? How many have ye had?"

"Three," Duncan MacKay said mournfully. "And each dead and buried. One in childbed of a stillborn bairn. One who drowned when she fell into the loch, and the third from a winter ague. Now no one will gie me a lass to wed, for they say I bring misfortune to the lasses who wed me."

"Indeed," the laird of Rath had said, not quite certain what else to say at this point.

His wife discreetly signaled a servant to bring refreshment. "Please sit, sir," the lady Anne invited their visitor.

He sat and, leaning forward, asked the laird, "How and why was yer lass despoiled, my lord?"

And then Robert Baird had found himself explaining to Duncan MacKay.

"He nodded, and his eyes were genuinely sympathetic," the lady Anne said.

"I told the MacKay that Myrna was not wanton. She was simply foolish," the laird explained. "Melville rejected her for a larger purse, she was held up to public shame, and none would have her. Still, this clansman would have her. He said he would find no fault in her for what had happened, for it was Ian Melville who was to blame. He said he thought the other lass was fortunate that her family could pay a large dower to keep their daughter from facing the shame that Myrna had to face. Then he asked to see her. Before I agreed I reread my sister's letter to gain a better understanding of just who this man asking to wed Myrna was, but if truth be told, I considered him the answer to our prayers."

"What happened next?" Annabella asked her father. "Do ye remember what your sister wrote?"

"I committed it to memory, for it was Myrna's salvation. The missive read:

Brother, ye hae asked for my help. I commend to ye my husband's kinsman Duncan MacKay, to be a husband for my niece Myrna. He is considered a good man, a worthy opponent, a dangerous warrior on the battlefield. His weakness has been in choosing silly lasses to wed. If Myrna remains strong of character, as ye hae written to me, then she will make Duncan a good wife. If ye gie him my niece, be assured that I will be nearby to guide her. Yer loving sister, Jane.

"I sent for your sister to come to the hall while warning Duncan MacKay that she was beautiful, but had a tongue that could cut wood, it was so sharp. He laughed and told me he liked a lass wi' a bit of spice in her."

His listeners now laughed too.

"MacKay's jaw dropped as he gained his first look at Myrna," the laird continued. "I had reacted the same way when I first saw yer mam. I told Myrna that this man now with me was to be her husband. Myrna declared she should never wed, but MacKay just laughed and told her that aye, she would marry him. She then scorned him for a Highlander, and said that she would wed no northerner. At that point I lost my temper wi' her. I told her that if she had nae been so vain and foolish she might have had the Melville lad, for all he was a cowardly cur. I told her that Duncan MacKay was kinsman to her aunt's husband and was willing to have her despite her faults. I told her I would not have her behavior cause our family's good name to be besmirched further. I told her that the pastor would see to the contracts immediately, and that she would be wed before nightfall. Then I left the two of them together in the hall, but as I departed I heard Myrna shout that he was to come no closer, he was not to kiss her, and then silence."

"A formidable fellow," the Earl of Duin remarked with a chuckle. "And so yer second daughter was wed to this Highlander?"

"Aye! I went directly to the kirk, where the pastor fell on his knees and praised the Lord for Myrna's good fortune. He drew up the marriage contracts, then came back to the hall wi' me, where we found Myrna now resigned to becoming the wife of the big Highlander. The pastor agreed wi' us that he seemed a reasonable man, and that Myrna was fortunate despite her shortcomings to get such a fine husband."

"It was hardly the future she envisioned for herself, Da," Annabella said. "She saw herself at court, because Ian's kinsman is the queen's adviser."

"'Tis unlikely," the lady Anne spoke up. "For all their pretensions, that branch of the Melville family has no real distinction. And despite his rough Highland manner I found I liked Duncan MacKay in spite of our short acquaintance. There was a kindness and an honesty about him that gave me comfort. I know Myrna will be happy with him."

"He accepted her dower?" Annabella said.

"Ten gold pieces, a chest of linens for bed and table, a down coverlet, two silver goblets, six silver spoons, a small gilt saltcellar, a little bag of salt, and two small rolls of velvet," the laird recounted to them. "Duncan MacKay was most impressed, and told us he had never had so well-dowered a wife. I had no need to apologize, as I had had wi' the Melvilles. I heard the Hamiltons gave a purse of twenty-five gold pieces to stave off their lass's shame."

"I hope she births a daughter," young Agnes said venomously. "They made poor Myrna so unhappy that she miscarried her son. She cried for days after."

"Agnes!" her mother remonstrated. "Where is the charity in yer heart?"

"I have nae charity for fools," Agnes said fiercely.

What an interesting little wench, Matthew Ferguson thought.

"They were married that day, Da?" Annabella asked her father.

"Aye, as soon as the contracts were signed. Myrna was surprised that MacKay could write his name. He was equally surprised that she could write hers. But once the agreement was signed the pastor wed them."

Agnes spoke up again. "She was wed in her skirt and a white blouse."

"I'm relieved that all ended well," Annabella said, smiling.

The meal was served. It was a simple one: venison stew in a red wine gravy with leeks and carrots, a roasted capon, and bread, butter, and cheese. Afterward, there were baked apples. When the meal was over, Annabella sat by the hearth with her mother and Jean Ferguson. Agnes, however, was engaged in a game of chess with Matthew Ferguson. She crowed with delight at each move she made, considering herself very clever.

"Ye smile more now," the lady Anne said to her daughter. "Ye're happy."

"I am," Annabella admitted.

"Everyone at Duin loves her," Jean spoke up. "She is a good lady to her folk."

"I am pleased to hear it," the lady Anne replied. "At least the eldest of my daughters behaves as she was brought up to behave. I canna believe that Myrna behaved so improperly. Still, it saddens me to have lost her."

"Aunt Jane had only lads, Mam," Annabella reminded her mother. "Myrna will be like the daughter she never had, and I will wager that my sister proves a good wife to her Highlander, Mama."

In the morning they departed Rath at first light for Edinburgh, arriving two days later. The house Matthew had rented for them was surprisingly comfortable, and Annabella saw immediately that the servants were well trained and friendly. They rendered Jean Ferguson their aid as she unpacked and prepared her mistress's gowns. Bathing, however, proved a different matter. Duin's bathing chamber was a unique accommodation. Angus was not at all pleased by the little round wooden bathing tub that was brought forth. He sent immediately for a cooper, carefully elucidated his requirements, and two days later a tall round wooden tub was delivered to the house. It would require buckets of water to fill, but the earl enjoyed his bath, and Annabella had come to enjoy a large tub as well.

"We shall save the servants the toil of filling the tub twice each day," he told her. "We shall bathe together, sweeting." He gave her a quick kiss.

"How thoughtful of ye, my lord," she murmured sweetly.

The tub was filled that evening after the meal had been served. Jean helped Annabella disrobe. The tub was made of hard oak. There were two steps that could be used to mount and descend into the tub. Jean helped Annabella into the water, and then said, "I've nae ever seen my brother wi'out his breeks, and I'll not do so now. Will ye need me again tonight, Annabella?"

Annabella giggled. "Nay," she said. "My husband will help me to bed."

"Not until after he's helped ye in the tub," Jean said pithily. Then she was gone.

Annabella enjoyed the hot water finally easing the soreness in her muscles from their long journey from the western borders. There was a door between the two bedchambers inhabited by the lord and the lady. It opened, and Angus came through as naked as the day he was born. Without a word, he climbed into the tub with her.

"Good evening, madam," he said with a grin.

"My lord." She inclined her head at him.

"A messenger came just before I came upstairs. I am to be one of Bothwell's groomsmen tomorrow. Matthew will escort ye to the church."

"He does ye honor," Annabella said.

"I dinna like being known amid these foxes and wolves," Angus remarked.

"We will remain until spring, and then go home to Duin," she said. "The queen is being generous and courteous to invite us, but we are nae so important that it will be necessary for us to remain more than a month or two."

Reaching out, he pulled her into his arms and kissed her mouth.

Annabella enjoyed the kiss, but then pulled away from him. "Ye need to bathe before ye play, sir," she scolded him. "If ye are to be in the limelight tomorrow, then ye must nae have a dirty neck or ears."

He pulled her back into his embrace, cupping a breast in his hand as he did.

Annabella whacked him gently with a bath brush.

"Ow! Madam, ye hae injured me sorely," he complained, rubbing the side of his head with a big hand. But he had released his hold on her breast.

"Nonsense," she told him. Then, picking up a cloth, she soaped it, washed his face, ears, and neck, and rinsed them free of the lather. Then, picking up the brush, she pushed him about, scrubbing first his shoulders and back, spinning him around again, then washing his broad, smooth chest. When she laid the brush aside, he pinioned her arms to her sides, pushed her back against the tub, and kissed her hard.

Releasing one of her arms, he growled in her ear, "Fondle me, wench. I have a need to fuck ye." Then he kissed her again, groaning into her mouth as her hand played with him, stroking his cock, teasing his balls with skilled fingers. Her small round breasts against his chest aroused his lust. He felt her thighs against his as his hands reached about to cup her bottom and lift her up to impale her on his manhood.

"Ohhh, Angus." Annabella sighed as she felt him filling her. It was too delicious. She wrapped her arms about him, enjoying every stroke of his manhood until finally they both achieved pleasure.

"Damn, wife, ye can render me a helpless bairn wi' your sweetness," the earl said to her. He kissed her mouth hard. "Shall we continue this in our bed?"

Annabella was breathless as she recovered from their passion. She laughed weakly. "Once, but nae more, Angus. We must be on time to the wedding."

"Twice," he growled into her ear. "Am I some old man, then, that I cannot appreciate my wife's loveliness more?" He climbed from the tub, taking a warmed drying cloth from the rack near the hearth and toweling himself before heading for their bed.

Annabella followed, exiting the tub, drying herself off, and climbing into bed to snuggle next to him. Mother of all mercies, she surely had to be the most fortunate woman in all the world, she thought as his arms wrapped around her. They made love a second time, for Angus Ferguson was of no mind to be denied. They slept and indulged themselves a third time before falling asleep for the night beneath the down comforter. When she awoke she found Jean laying out her clothing for the day, but Angus nowhere in sight. "Where is he?" she asked sleepily of her tiring woman.

"Gone to Bothwell's house," Jean said.

"Is it that late?" Annabella sat up.

"Nay, nay, ye've plenty of time. I've brought ye a tray, and ye're to eat every bit of it," Jean said. "Heaven only knows when ye'll eat again. I hear the wedding feast is to be at Holyrood."

"Nay, Bothwell would not have it so. 'Twill be at a place called Kinloch House. 'Tis the home of a wealthy merchant who owed Jamie Hepburn a great favor. It is said that the bride and groom will honeymoon at Seton."

"They say the Earl of Bothwell is crude in his many amours," Jean said. "Pity the poor bride."

Annabella smiled. "Aye, I suspect Bothwell is hurried wi' a serving wench, but I am sure he will be more delicate wi' his wife. Still, he is a handsome fellow. Now tell me, what was Angus wearing when he left? I made some suggestions, but ye know him. He will nae always do what he should."

Jean laughed aloud. "Aye, he's a stubborn man, but

he was in his finest. His doublet was of plum-colored silk brocade. The puffed sleeves were slashed to show a lavender silk. His short velvet cape was plum velvet. He wore that heavy gold chain with the Ferguson bee on a thistle."

"Then I shall wear my lavender velvet gown," Annabella said. Then she began to eat the food from the tray Jean had brought her. An egg poached in cream and marsala wine. A rasher of bacon. A slice of warmed bread with butter and cheese. The cider was not as sweet as Ferguson cider, but it was probably not stored as well. When she had finished her meal, Annabella quickly washed herself in a basin, and then with Jean's aid she dressed. The gown's bodice was cut very low, with just a ruffle of lace from her chemise showing over the top, although it did little to conceal her swelling breasts. She had noted that her breasts seemed to be increasing in size of late.

Seeing her mistress staring into the looking glass, Jean asked, "When are ye going to tell him?"

Annabella turned, a puzzled look on her face. "Tell who? And what?" She admired the bodice's puffed and slashed sleeves showing a cream silk underneath.

"Ye're expecting a bairn, lass," Jean said. "Are ye nae aware of it? That's why yer breasts are getting larger."

"I wasn't certain," Annabella said slowly. "If I had said anything Angus would hae used it as an excuse nae to come. I canna allow him to offend the queen or Bothwell. My lord may avoid politics and hide us away in our western borders, but he canna allow Duin to offend any if we are to remain safe." She slipped her feet into short fur-lined boots with a fur trim. It was winter, and her footwear was fashionable if not formal.

Jean nodded her agreement. "Ye're far wiser than my

brother, although we shall nae allow him to know it, Annabella." She put Annabella's beautiful hair into a chignon.

Annabella laughed. "I think it best too, Jeannie." Then she finished dressing. She was particularly pleased with the underskirt of cream-colored silk brocade, with its narrow silver stripes that showed amid the heavy lavender velvet.

Jean clasped a necklace of purple amethysts and pearls about her neck. She affixed large pearl ear bobs in her mistress's ears. Finally she set a heavy, dark violet velvet cloak lined in rich marten on Annabella's shoulders, and handed her a pair of soft silk-lined leather gloves dyed the same color. "Matthew is waiting in the hall."

She found Duin's steward in sober black and white waiting for her. The horses were waiting for them outside of the house. They mounted and rode the distance to the kirk at the Canongate.

"I canna go inside wi' ye," Matthew said. "'Tis a sin, and I hae enough sins on my conscience."

"Then ye hae another," Annabella told him. "If yer brother can serve as one of Bothwell's groomsmen, then ye can enter this Reformed kirk. Ye canna expect me to go inside unescorted, Matthew. I am the Countess of Duin."

He looked as though he wanted to argue.

"The queen is coming, and is she nae the first Catholic in the land?" Annabella said. "And her husband will be wi' her too. If the queen can sin, and yer brother can sin, then so can ye sin, Matthew Ferguson."

He made a grimace but, handing the reins of their horses to a liveried lad, escorted Annabella into the dark stone church. "I'll hae good company in hell," he muttered, looking about the church and seeing more than one Catholic nobleman. The queen and her husband were already in the royal box. An official stepped forward, blocking the way. He glared at the couple.

"Give way for the Countess of Duin," Matthew said.

"I dinna know the earldom of Duin," the official replied.

"Well, Lord Bothwell does. The Earl of Duin is among his groomsmen. I am the earl's brother, and this is his wife. Now step aside, ye officious Edinburgh man, so we may find a place before the bride arrives."

Before the official might argue further, a little page hurried up and murmured something to him. The official nodded, saying, "The lad will bring ye to yer places, madam, sir." Then he turned away from them to question another pair of arrivals.

They followed the young boy and were given places. The church was abuzz with chatter, for this new kirk frowned on music. There was a small foreign-looking gentleman sharing their space. The bishop of Galloway, who was to marry the couple, appeared before the altar. Then James Hepburn came forth garbed in his wedding finery, his groomsmen surrounding him. The chatter ceased suddenly as Lady Jean Gordon came down the aisle in a gown of white silk and cloth of silver.

"From the queen's own stores," the man next to them said softly.

The bride was pretty, with brown-blond hair and light eyes, but she was no beauty. Annabella didn't think she looked wildly happy, but then she remembered that this marriage had been arranged by the queen herself, with the purpose of uniting an important border family and an important Highland family. Mary Stuart knew that she could trust James Hepburn. She hoped this marriage and the honors she had lavished upon both him and his bride's family would bring the Gordons back into the royal fold.

The church was filled to overflowing. The bridal couple's vows could scarcely be heard by most. But then the bishop in a loud voice pronounced that they were man and wife. The church quickly emptied as the guests poured outside to find their horses and make the short ride to Kinloch House, where the wedding feast would be held. It was there that Matthew left her as Angus came to claim his wife's company. Together they went to congratulate the newlywed couple.

"Ye have caused quite a stir among the court," the new Lady Bothwell said to Angus.

"I would hardly think the court would concern themselves with an unimportant man from the west," Angus answered.

"The handsomest man in the borders and his plain wife, my lord, aye. Everyone is fascinated as to how such a union came about, for as beautiful as the lady of Duin's clothing and jewels are, she is still very plain, while ye are very handsome."

"Love, I am told, madam, is often blind," Angus Ferguson said, squeezing his wife's hand, for Annabella had gone pale at Lady Bothwell's thoughtless words.

But while she was shocked, Annabella was perfectly able to defend herself. She smiled sweetly at the bride and said, "Yer husband said he thought I should like ye, madam. Alas, he was wrong." Then with a curtsy she moved on, with both Angus and Bothwell containing their laughter, for the look on Jean Gordon's face was quite amazing.

"I shall be careful not to quarrel wi' ye, wife," the Earl of Duin said.

"She is arrogant!" Annabella fumed.

"She is a Gordon of Huntley," he replied. "They are all apt to be arrogant."

"She has no manners. I pity Jamie Hepburn having to wed her."

"The queen wished it, and James is loyal wi'out question. Besides, the bride has brought him a very large dower portion, and the queen has gifted him for his unquestioning obedience with more lands," Angus said.

"He can't possibly love her," Annabella replied, still fuming.

Just then, the gentleman who had sat next to them in the kirk came up to them. He bowed politely. "I am David Riccio, the queen's secretary," he introduced himself. "I have come to take ye to the queen. She tells me that long ago ye rendered her mother a great service." His voice was tinged with a slight accent when he spoke. He was a small, elegant man with just a touch of hauteur about him, but his quick smile was friendly.

"My service to the late Marie de Guise has never been made public," Angus said, "nor would I want it to be known, Master Riccio. Some of us prefer to perform our good deeds in private rather than seek acclaim."

Riccio chuckled. "Ye are a wise man, my lord, to avoid the scrutiny of those who believe themselves more powerful, and use violence to maintain their positions."

They had now reached the high board where Queen Mary, her husband, and the bridal couple were seated. The queen was dressed in scarlet velvet and cloth of gold far overshadowing the bride in her silver and white. Annabella had the oddest feeling that Mary had planned it that way.

"Madam, I bring you the Earl and Countess of

Duin," Riccio said. Then he quickly withdrew back into the crowd of guests.

Angus bowed his best court bow, while Annabella sank into a deep, graceful curtsy, her lavender skirts blossoming out about her.

"Rise, my lord, my lady," the queen said. Then she stood up. Both Lord Darnley and Bothwell also jumped to their feet, but she waved them away, holding out a hand to Angus Ferguson to help her from the dais. "Remain, my lords," she said to her husband and James Hepburn. "I prefer to speak with Duin and his wife alone." She stepped down and, walking slowly, led Angus and Annabella from the hall at Kinloch House and into a private chamber.

"Who are *they*?" Darnley demanded of James Hepburn. "Why is she seeing them alone? What is it that I have not been told?"

"Calm yerself," Bothwell said. "Angus Ferguson long ago and privily rendered the queen's mother a great service. She invited them to court so she might thank him personally. Duin is in the western borders on the sea. 'Tis nae an important place."

"I saw him among yer groomsmen," Darnley said suspiciously.

"Aye, ye did. Angus Ferguson and I were friends growing up. We studied in France together years ago," Bothwell responded.

"His wife is no beauty," Darnley noted with a slight sneer.

"Nay, she isn't, but she hae a good heart, my lord," was the reply.

"And undoubtedly a fat dower, else why would he have her?" Darnley snickered.

"She hae a sharp tongue," the bride said. "She spoke rudely to me."

"Ye spoke rudely first," Bothwell murmured. "Ye insulted her."

"I meant nae harm," Jean Gordon said. "I speak my mind."

"Ye pride yerself on yer intellect, madam," Bothwell replied. "Does that quality nae allow ye to form yer words for courtesy's sake? Annabella well knows her deficiencies, and does nae need reminding of them. She is a good lass."

"What did he do for her mother?" Darnley demanded to know.

"I was nae ever informed, for it was a private matter," James Hepburn lied. "I'm sure the queen will tell ye if ye ask, my lord. Dinna fret. She should not be long."

But of course they were longer than suited the queen's husband. When they had reached the small private chamber, Mary invited both the earl and his wife to seat themselves near the blazing hearth with her. "Does yer wife know of your generosity to me, my lord?" Mary asked him.

"It was a private matter between yer late mother of blessed memory and myself," the earl said, crossing himself.

The queen turned to Annabella. "Without yer husband I should not have had the wonderful childhood in France that I did," she began. "I was not yet six when I departed Scotland for France. It was Angus Ferguson who saw that my household was furnished, my household servants and staff paid, my wardrobe and that of my four Marys supplied. Never once was I allowed to wear clothing that was too short or too small. Everything that I was garbed in was lavish and of the finest quality. I had jewelry and pocket money. I had the finest horses to ride and to hunt with, as well as a fine kennel of dogs. There was nothing I wanted that I was denied. My mother's mind could be at peace where I was concerned, although the burden of Scotland fell upon her shoulders."

"She carried that charge very well, madam," the earl said to her. "Ye should be proud, but remember that I gained something in exchange."

"A piece of parchment creating Duin an earldom," the queen replied. "Parchment and ink in exchange for the devoted care ye saw I had, relieving my dearest mother of that worry. Ye had the lands, and ye had the gold. Ye paid dearly for that title."

"It was my privilege, madam," Angus responded quietly.

"My lord, I am curious," the queen said. "There are rumors that yer family practices sorcery. Where does yer gold come from, and so much gold that it could support a queen for over ten years?"

"Madam, I will tell ye what even my wife has not known until now, but I would beg ye keep my secret," Angus Ferguson said to the queen.

The queen reached into a deep pocket in her skirt and drew out her rosary. Holding it up she said, "I swear that I will keep the secret of your wealth, my lord, unto the grave itself." She kissed the rosary's small silver crucifix before slipping it back into her pocket. Then she looked to the Earl of Duin.

"My mother," the earl began, "was a Frenchwoman, even as yer own mother. She had an older sister who was married into Spain to the Duke of Casarosa. Sadly, the children born of their union died either at birth or before they reached the age of five. They took a great interest in my brother James and my sister Mary. James now serves in Rome, as his monastery was confiscated recently. Mary, a sister of the order of St. Andrew's, is now in a convent in Spain, as the nuns were driven from Scotland by Knox."

"That damned man who claims to speak for God," the queen said sarcastically.

Angus Ferguson chuckled, then continued with his tale. "My aunt and uncle died within a very short time of each other. Plague, I believe. It was then that I learned I had inherited the duke's wealth. He had great interests in the New World, which are now mine. Two ships a year arrive at Duin to unload barrels of gold coins that have been minted in the Spanish colonies. Some of the gold I retain in my own storehouses. The rest I invest in the East Indies in spices and gemstones. I also export fine woolen cloth and whiskey. That is where my wealth springs from, Majesty. There is no sorcery involved in it at all."

Queen Mary nodded her understanding. "There are always those anxious to defame others," she said, "but why do the rumors of sorcery persist where Duin is concerned? There is always a soupçon of truth in rumors."

He chuckled. "Several hundred years ago a laird of Duin was said to dabble in sorcery. He had a wife reputed to be a witch. Together they are said to have held back a terrible storm that raged across the sea in Ireland and was coming in our direction. It is said that the storm, in sight of Duin's coastline, suddenly dissipated and was gone, sparing Scotland. That laird's wife was also a great healer. So the legend began, and we have allowed it because we Fergusons of Duin are very private people. Because it is believed we are magical folk, we are given a very wide berth."

"How clever!" The queen laughed, clapping her hands. "I wish I might do something like that and make most of the earls and their contentious lords disappear."

"I think, madam, I should first make Master Knox disappear if I could," Angus Ferguson said with a smile.

The queen laughed again and then turned her gaze on Annabella. "What is it like being married to such an amiable and clever man, madam?" she asked her.

"He is the best man in the world, to my mind, Majesty," Annabella said. "I consider myself a fortunate woman. But Yer Majesty has greater good fortune in that she carries Scotland's next king. May he be born safe and strong. I will pray for it."

"Thank ye, my lady of Duin," the queen said. "Perhaps ye will join me and my ladies during the next few days. Do ye play games?"

"I do, Majesty," Annabella said, "and I am honored ye would accept me into yer circle of great ladies."

The queen nodded graciously, then looked to Angus. "Duin, I have spoken much, but not yet said those simple words that can hardly serve for the great kindness ye did for me. Thank ye, my lord. Thank ye."

"Madam, I would beg a simple boon of ye," the earl said to her. "Tell no one of my part in yer childhood, for I would keep my wealth a secret. Wealth draws envy. My wife and I will shortly return home, where we live quietly. It is best that Duin be forgotten, and no one be drawn to it, for all our sakes."

"I will keep the secret, but I must tell my husband something, else he grow suspicious," the queen said.

"Tell him, then, that I arranged a loan for yer mother

through my own French relations so ye might have the necessities when ye went to France," the earl suggested.

"Aye, ye're clever," the queen replied. "I am glad Bothwell has ye, my lord of Duin. He has few real friends, but ye, I believe, will always be loyal to him."

"I will, Majesty," Angus said, "if for no other reason than the evenings we spent together roistering about Paris in our youth."

"Ohh, I should have liked to have been with ye!" the queen exclaimed as there came a knock upon the door of the chamber. "Come!" she said.

A little page appeared. "The fireworks are scheduled to begin, madam, and the king would like ye by his side."

"Of course," Mary said, and she hurried out with the page.

"I thought Darnley was not king," Annabella said, confused.

"She allows him to be called such, but he has not the crown matrimonial," Angus explained. "Without that, he is not really king of anything. She does it, I suspect, to soothe his ego, but is clever enough to withhold it until he proves worthy, which he has not."

"He is a pretty fellow," Annabella said, "but he drinks too much. I watched him in the church, all proper and dutiful, but once he reached the high board he was swilling from his cup, which was being refilled quite often. He doesn't look particularly intelligent, Angus. In fact, I think there is a sly look about him."

"He's ambitious without the intelligence to back it up," the earl said. Then he asked her, "Were ye surprised to learn the source of my wealth, Annabella?"

"I will admit to wondering where yer gold came from, but I have seen no one taking coins from the air or spinning straw into gold at Duin. I might hae asked ye eventually, my lord, but I know the only sorcery about ye is that which ye weave about me, Angus," Annabella told him.

He chuckled. "Ye flatter me, madam. 'Tis ye who have enchanted me."

"I hae never seen fireworks," she said blushing. "I dinna believe we are meant to remain in this wee chamber." She took his hand, and together they went from the room, hurried to the hall, and took their places by the tall windows to watch the sparkling reds, blues, silvers, and golds of the exploding fireworks celebrating the marriage of James Hepburn, the Earl of Bothwell, to Lady Jean Gordon, sister of the Earl of Huntley.

Chapter 7

rue to her word, the queen welcomed Annabella
into her small circle of ladies. The winter was bitter and long. The women spent their days sewing and gossiping, for the queen's pregnancy kept them from other pursuits, such as riding, hunting, and hawking. Three of the queen's Marys were still with her. The Italian secretary, Riccio, kept them amused, but the truth was that Annabella found the days boring.

It was obvious that the queen and her husband were not on particularly good terms. The more Annabella saw of Darnley, the less she understood why Mary had married him. True, he was handsome, and she heard that in days past he had been considered quite charming. She saw none of that charm, however. What she saw was an ignorant young man with a thirst for power, who, had he been actually made king, would not have been capable of ruling anything, as he was incapable of ruling even his own emotions. And he was jealous of his wife's friendship with David Riccio.

Annabella didn't think a great deal of the Italian either. He had charm, she was forced to admit, but no common sense. He delighted in being the queen's favorite, and used his small position to flaunt himself before the rough and mostly dour powerful Scots lords. His manner of dress was fashionable to the nth degree but did little to alleviate the fact that he resembled a small and very self-important toad. But Mary was deeply fond of him, and foolishly overlooked his faults, for he amused her. And little else did these days.

Annabella's days among the mighty were numbered now as March came. She and Angus would leave court by the middle of the month to return to Duin. Hopefully the weather would turn toward the spring by then. Two nights before they were to leave, she finally shared her happy secret with her husband. They lay abed after a particularly satisfying bout of passion. Cradled in his arms, she spoke softly.

"We will have an heir by Michaelmas, my lord. Does that please ye?"

At first he was not certain he had understood her, and then he said, "Ye're with child?"

"Aye." She snuggled closer to him.

"How long have ye known?" was his next question.

"It was Jean who told me, for I have never had a bairn." Annabella attempted to conceal her sin.

"And when did Jean suggest to ye that ye were with bairn?" His voice had grown serious, and he moved to look into her face.

"J-just before we came to Edinburgh," Annabella responded, and then continued in a rush, "but I didn't want to tell ye, because then ye wouldn't have come, and the invitation was from the queen herself, and I knew Bothwell wanted ye here too, Angus."

"I see." His voice was cold.

"I am not some fragile flower to be encased in cotton wool just because I am expecting a bairn," Annabella defended herself. "Coming to court would nae harm the bairn at this stage, but it was important to ye and to Duin that we come."

"'Twas a decision to be made by me," he told her. "Ye're carrying my heir."

"Ye would have said nay, and then Bothwell would have been offended and, more important, the queen. And now we're going home, so where is the harm in it?"

"Ye should have told me," the earl insisted.

Annabella wanted to argue with him. She had never seen him so stubborn, but he had made his point. They would be leaving for Duin in just a few more days. Still, she could not help saying, "I did what I thought was best for ye, and for Duin, Angus."

Angus Ferguson could not help laughing aloud. "Ye're hardly a biddable woman, Annabella," he told her. "Still, no harm is done, and I'll find a comfortable vehicle for ye to travel home in. We'll travel more slowly this time, but we'll get there nonetheless."

"I can ride," she said. "And I want to get home quickly. Did I not promise my sister Agnes that she could come and stay wi' us this summer? She will be good company for me. I am looking forward to seeing her. I want Matthew to go and fetch her from Rath."

"Ye'll travel home in a padded cart, madam," her husband told her. "And ye'll nae ride again until after the bairn is birthed."

Annabella was silent now. There was no use arguing with this man. She was doomed to a boring trip. They would not stop at Rath this time, but go straight west from Edinburgh across Scotland and then south. "Aye, my lord," she muttered dutifully.

Angus chuckled. He knew how much that murmur of obedience cost her, for Annabella was a proud woman, and every bit as stubborn as he was himself. Stroking her sable head, he bent and kissed it. "There's my good lass," the earl said.

The next day, their last in Edinburgh, the Countess of Duin was invited to Holyrood in late afternoon to say her farewells to the queen. Annabella was surprised as she dismounted in the courtyard of the palace to see old Patrick Ruthven, Lord Ruthven. When their eyes met briefly he quickly ducked from her view. *What a pity*, Annabella thought. *I had heard he was on his deathbed. His death would have been a great relief to the queen, for he is not an easy man, and has made difficulties for her.* Then with a shrug she made her way to the queen's private apartments.

There she found that Mary was entertaining a small group of her friends. The three remaining Marys were there, as were Riccio and several others. They had eaten an early supper in the apartment's tiny dining room and now returned to the queen's dayroom, where a fire burned in the hearth, although the icy north wind blowing through the cracks in the windows made it difficult to heat the chamber. They welcomed Annabella warmly, having come to like the plain-faced but charming Countess of Duin.

"I have come only to say farewell," Annabella told them. "We leave for Duin on the morrow. Angus is anxious to return home."

"Back to the dull borders," Riccio said.

"Living in a beautiful small castle on the sea might prove dull for ye, but it isn't for me," Annabella answered.

"Sing a final song for us, madam," the queen said. "I have come to enjoy yer voice and the simple songs ye have introduced to us. David, accompany the countess."

They had discovered in the weeks she had been with them that Annabella had a lovely voice, and prevailed upon her often to sing for them. She sang simple songs of the borders and of Scotland. Going over to Master Riccio, Annabella told him the song she would sing, and the Italian tuned the strings on his instrument in preparation.

Lord Darnley entered the queen's rooms, surprising them all, for he rarely came to see her any longer. Smiling warmly in an effort to ease his obviously nasty mood, the queen beckoned her young husband to her side as Annabella began to sing.

Early one morning just as the sun was rising, I heard a maiden singing in the valley below. Oh, do not leave me. Oh, do not grieve me. . . .

The lute suddenly screeched with discord and crashed to the floor.

Annabella looked up and saw Lord Ruthven pushing into the queen's chambers, and behind him a group of armed men. They had obviously overcome the queen's guards to reach this sanctum. Ruthven pointed a bony finger at Riccio, who jumped from her side with all the agility of the amphibian he resembled to get behind the queen. The look of fury on Lord Darnley's face as the little man struggled to hide himself was terrifying.

"Give us the Italian!" Lord Ruthven said in a dark voice.

"How dare ye enter my chambers uninvited, my lord," the queen said.

"Give us the Italian!" Lord Ruthven demanded a second time.

"To what purpose?" Mary wanted to know. "It is obvious to me that ye come here with no good outcome in mind. Leave me at once!"

God's bones, Annabella thought. *She is so brave, and I am terrified.*

"Not wi'out the little rat whose service does ye nae credit. He needs to be put down, madam, and we shall do it this night," Lord Ruthven said. "We dinna want this papal spy in yer service turning ye from what is right and just for Scotland."

"Ye are mistaken, my lord," the queen said. "David is no spy. If ye believe he has done some wrong, then present your proof, but of course ye cannot, for there is none."

Lord Ruthven's face grew almost purple in his rage. He took a threatening step toward the queen, and as he did Annabella flung herself, arms outstretched, in front of Mary Stuart. "Remove that bitch!" Ruthven roared.

Several men jumped at his command, attempting to pull the Countess of Duin away from her defensive position in front of the queen. Annabella fought them furiously but was finally pulled away and flung to the floor of the chamber. She struggled to regain her feet, but Lord Darnley stepped forward and delivered several brutal kicks to Annabella's form, forcing her to remain where she was. Then he restrained his wife as the screaming and shrieking Riccio was dragged from the chamber. Ruthven and his party plunged their daggers into the little man over and over again.

Annabella could not hold on to consciousness after that and slid into darkness. When she managed to regain her senses she was still on the floor, Mary Beaton, one of the queen's maidens, leaning over her, waving a burning feather beneath her nose. The young woman's eyes were filled with a mixture of sympathy and admiration. She put her arm about the Countess of Duin's shoulders and helped her to a seated position.

"Ye were very brave," Mary Beaton said low.

"What has happened?" Annabella asked. She felt a sticky wetness between her legs and a cramping in her belly. *Dear God! Not the bairn! Not the bairn!*

"Ruthven and his ilk have gone," Mary Beaton said. "The townsfolk gathered before the palace, but that snake Darnley told them all was well, and that a papal spy in the pay of the Spanish king had been discovered and slain. The people dispersed, but Bothwell's men are battling with the Earl of Morton's men to reach the queen as we speak."

Annabella's glance went to the queen, who was weeping over the murder of her secretary and friend, her head in her hands. "Mistress Beaton," Annabella said. "Help me from this chamber quickly." Then she groaned low.

"Ye've been hurt by Darnley's blows," Mary Beaton said, genuinely distressed.

"I am losing the bairn I've been carrying," Annabella said. "I cannot do it before the queen, lest my misfortune cause her to miscarry too. Please, I beg ye, get me from this place now, and find my tiring woman who came wi' me."

"Can ye stand?" Mary Beaton asked.

"I must," Annabella said, struggling slowly to her feet. The cramping was worse now, and she felt blood drizzling down her legs as Mistress Beaton slowly helped her from the queen's chamber.

Once outside, Mary Beaton spoke to the young guard, who was now disarmed and rubbing his head from the blows he had received when Ruthven and his band had broken into the queen's apartments. "The Countess of Duin has been injured in the melee. Find and fetch her tiring woman, Jean Ferguson, to her. She will be in my chamber."

The guard nodded, and went off.

"'Tis not far," Mary Beaton said as she aided Annabella down a narrow corridor.

Annabella said nothing. How could this have happened? She had come to bid the queen farewell, and got caught up in a maelstrom. They reached Mary Beaton's chamber, and with the help of Mistress Beaton's tiring woman, Annabella was able to reach the bed, where she lay down just as she began to weep.

"What has happened, my lady?" Mary Beaton's serving woman asked fearfully.

Quickly, the young woman explained the situation. She then bent over Annabella, whose eyes were closed, although tears were slipping down her face. "My Susan will stay with you. Your Jeannie will be here soon." Then she hurried toward the door just as Jean Ferguson dashed into the chamber.

Mary Beaton quickly explained what had happened, and then she left.

Hurrying to Annabella's side, Jean lifted her mistress's skirts, gasping at the profusion of blood. "Holy Mother!" She crossed herself, but then, recovering, she began to direct Mary Beaton's servant. "Can you fetch me cloths to take up the remaining blood? And a basin of cool water, please." She bent down. "My lady, dinna weep. What's done is done. Weeping will change nothing."

"Darnley," Annabella said, opening her eyes. "Darnley did this, Jeannie! Angus must know if I die."

"What do ye mean, my lady?" Jean glanced quickly

about to see whether Mistress Beaton's servant had heard, but the woman was on the far side of the chamber.

"I stood before the queen to protect her from the ruffians who had broken into her chamber and were threatening her as they attempted to catch the Italian, Riccio. When they were finally able to pull me away, I was flung to the floor. I attempted to get up, but Lord Darnley kicked me several times, preventing it. He is responsible for my loss." Her eyes blazed with anger. "I shall have my vengeance upon him, Jeannie. I shall!" Then she fell back as a wave of dizziness overcame her.

"Dinna upset yerself," Jean cautioned. "If it's revenge ye would have, then ye must live to take it, my lady." Taking the small knife that hung at her waist, Jean cut away Annabella's bloodied skirts and removed her bodice.

Mary Beaton's serving woman returned to Jean's side with the basin and a stack of cloths. "I'll make some yarrow tea to help strengthen her," she said. "And I've also brought ye a small stone jar of comfrey balm."

"Thank ye," Jean said. Then she quickly went to work wiping away the layer of blood to see better what had happened. The large clots told the tale. Annabella had indeed lost her bairn. Tears came to her eyes, but she blinked them away. Both her brother and his wife were healthy. There would be other bairns. Carefully, she rubbed the comfrey balm into her mistress's genital area.

"Here's one of my mistress's chemises for yer lady," the kindly serving woman said. "Ye tuck her right into that bed now. My lady is unlikely to return here tonight."

She held out a small earthenware mug. "The yarrow tea," she said.

Jean thanked her, and when she had reclothed Annabella in the chemise and settled her beneath the coverlet, she put the cup to her mistress's lips. "'Twill be bitter," she said, "but it's strengthening, my lady."

Annabella sipped, making a face, for the tea was bitter. She began to cry again. "I've lost my bairn," she sobbed. "I've lost my wee laddie."

"There will be others," Jean said low. "There is a bond of passion between ye and my brother that makes it impossible to believe otherwise."

"Where is Angus?" Annabella asked.

"Probably wi' Bothwell and his men fighting Chancellor Morton and his men," Jean said. "I saw Morton's men in the courtyard."

"Poor queen," Annabella sad sadly. "She can trust no one."

"She can trust Bothwell," Jean replied. "Now go to sleep, my lady. Ye're safe, and I will sit by yer side."

"I want to go home," Annabella said low.

"Soon," Jean promised. "Soon."

But it was not as soon as they wished. Mary Beaton did not come back, and after telling Jean to remain as long as she liked, the serving woman, Susan, disappeared. Holyrood Palace was suddenly very quiet but for the occasional tramping of booted feet in the corridors outside.

When morning dawned gray and drizzly, Jean Ferguson, assured that her mistress would not awaken for some time, made her way to the kitchens to fetch them some food. The queen's French cook and his assistants were surprised to see her, but glad to share what news they had, along with some food.

"Bothwell and Huntley are gone," the cook told her in his mixture of French and Scots English. "Ze queen's attendants have all been dismissed."

Jean, whose own mother was French, understood him, and was able to communicate with the cook. "Who is left in the palace?" she asked.

"*La reine*, and the craven coward she wed who calls himself *le roi*," the cook responded. "The old dowager of Huntley, who is caring for our mistress. Ruthven's and Morton's men. They say the Earl of Moray has returned from exile, and will reason with his sister. How is it ye remain? Almost everyone was sent away."

"My mistress was gravely injured in defense of the queen," Jean said. "She has miscarried her bairn. She insisted on being taken out of the queen's sight lest she cause the queen distress. Mistress Beaton offered her chambers."

"Your mistress lived through the night?"

"She is young and will survive, but I must bring her nourishment to help strengthen her so we can leave this place," Jean explained.

"Sit down," the cook said. "I will prepare something myself for *la pauvre*."

Jean sat, and immediately a mug of cider and a bowl of hot oats were given her. She ate quickly as the cook prepared a meal for Annabella. The tray she carried back upstairs to Mistress Beaton's quarters contained an egg custard, a soft fresh roll, butter, jam, and a cup of wine with herbs. The few guards she passed glanced briefly at her, then nodded for her to go on. Reaching her destination she slipped back into the chamber, setting the tray aside, and seated herself back down next to the bed, waiting for her mistress to awaken.

In midmorning, Annabella opened her eyes. At first she was confused as to where she was, and why. Then the memory of the previous evening flooded back, and she sat straight up. "Jeannie!"

"I'm here," her tiring woman said. "I've brought ye some food."

Annabella shook her head. "I canna eat! I want to leave this place."

"Eat what I've brought ye," Jean said quietly. "Then I will find a way for us to return back to the house." Bringing the tray, she set it on her mistress's lap. "The queen's own cook made ye this nice egg custard. 'Twill strengthen ye. And the wine has healing herbs for ye." She sat back down and, spooning a bit of the custard, held it to Annabella's lips. "Come, now, my lady; eat," she coaxed.

Taking the spoon from Jean, Annabella ate. She wasn't a silly bairn. She had suffered a needless loss, but she was alive. Alive to plot her revenge, and she would.

"I will find a litter for ye, and we will return to our house as quickly as possible. I have nae doubt Angus will be worried," Jean said. "I know ye're weak, but if we can reach the house I can nurse ye better."

"Find someone to carry us there," Annabella said. "I dinna want to remain here. What word of the queen?"

"Her French cook says she is confined to her apartments wi' old Lady Huntley to watch over her. Her servants have been dismissed by Morton, but they've nae gone far. The rebels conspire wi' one another, and the Earl of Moray will come soon. They believe that, even though she sent him away, he is the one who can best reason wi' her."

"He has arrived rather quickly from his exile in England," Annabella said dryly.

Jean snickered. "Aye. He hae been waiting in the background during all of this, and was certainly involved in the plot to murder the little toad man. I saw his body at the foot of a flight of stairs. They had stripped him naked and he was covered in stab wounds. I hope someone has the kindness to bury him."

"He was a fool," Annabella said in a hard voice as she spooned the egg custard into her mouth. "He made no effort whatsoever to placate those in positions of power who resented his influence wi' the queen. Indeed, he flaunted himself about. But God knows I should not have wished such a fate upon him as he suffered last night."

Jean nodded in agreement. Then she said, "Will ye be all right if I leave ye alone in order to find us some transport?"

"Aye," Annabella replied.

Suddenly, however, the door to Mistress Beaton's chamber was flung open. A soldier stepped into the room. "What are ye two doing here?" he demanded to know. "My lord Ruthven gave orders for the palace to be evacuated yesterday, save those needed to sustain the queen."

"This is the Countess of Duin," Jean said. "She was sorely injured in the *incident* that took place last night. Mistress Beaton offered her chamber until my lady was strong enough to travel."

"Ye must get up from that bed, dress, and go now," the soldier said.

"My lady has miscarried her bairn," Jean replied, "but we are willing to leave. However, we must have transport, for my lady can scarcely walk. Can ye help us?"

The soldier hesitated briefly; then he said, "I will fetch a litter for ye. It will await ye at the postern gate. Ye'll have to get her that far, lassie."

"Thank ye," Jean said to him. "We'll hurry as quickly as we can."

The soldier grunted his acknowledgment and then, leaving them, closed the door.

"I hae no clothing," Annabella said. "Ye cut it off me last night."

"Mistress Beaton will have something ye can wear, for she did not return to collect any of her belongings," Jean replied. She opened the trunk at the foot of the bed and rummaged through it impatiently.

"She's taller than I am," Annabella said. "See if she has a long cloak I can put over this chemise, and something for my feet. The house is not that far from the palace."

"Here's a nice fur-lined cape," Jean said, pulling it out of the trunk. "It must come to her knees, but 'twill fall longer on ye, which is to the good. And a pair of house slippers. Her feet are just about yer size, which is small for a lass who is tall."

"Is there another chemise?" Annabella asked.

"Aye, 'tis a good idea, my lady." She pulled one out, and then set about helping her mistress to dress. The second chemise would add warmth to the first, which was now lightly stained with dried blood. Jean had no cotton wool to make a pad to contain the ooze from Annabella's miscarriage. She would be able to better take care of her lady when they regained their town house. She put the slippers on the younger woman's feet and helped her stand.

Annabella swayed slightly, but then steadied herself with the help of Jean's strong arm. The cape was set onto her shoulders. It was of heavy wool, dark in color, and lined in fur. She was relieved to find that it had a fur-trimmed hood, which she pulled up.

"I'm ready," she told Jean, who was now garbed in her own hooded cloak.

Together the two women left the shelter and safety of Mary Beaton's chamber. Slowly they made their way through the dim, silent, and empty corridors that were usually bustling with life. After a few minutes, Annabella felt a weakness beginning to fill her, but she gritted her teeth and moved ahead into a narrow passage that led to an inside courtyard and the postern gate. Opening the door into the courtyard, they found the same soldier who had spoken to them earlier.

"Ah, here ye are at last," the man said. He scooped up Annabella, running across the cobbled space with Jean right behind him. The postern gate was already open, and outside was a litter large enough for both women, manned by two bearers. The soldier set Annabella carefully inside the vehicle, and Jean climbed in after her.

"Thank ye!" Jean said.

"Aye," Annabella echoed. "Thank ye, sir."

"Take these ladies to . . ." The soldier looked to Jean.

"Burnside House," she said.

"Burnside House," the soldier repeated.

The litter was lifted, and the bearers set off at a trot. They never broke stride, and Holyrood faded behind them as they got deeper into town. Finally, after a few twists and turns from the Royal Mile to a side street and the private lane upon which Burnside House stood, they arrived. The servants were immediately out the door to help them. One very tall footman lifted Annabella up and carried her into the building and upstairs to her chamber. Jean came behind after paying the litter bearers.

"Where is the earl?" she asked him.

"Hasn't come home," the man answered. "What is happening? We've heard all sorts of rumors, good and bad. Ye were there."

"Let me get my lady settled, and then if ye'll all

gather in the hall, I'll tell ye what I know," Jean promised.

"Angus?" Annabella asked weakly from her bed.

"Still wi' Bothwell, I suspect," Jean answered. "One of the bearers told me that he and Huntley withdrew their forces from the town because it was not possible to reach the queen wi'out endangering her and the unborn child. He'll nae linger wi' Bothwell. He'll want to know that ye're safe, and he'll want to go home. Fergusons dinna involve themselves in such disturbances as are now occurring. Dinna fret." She struggled to divest Annabella of the two chemises, sliding a clean one onto the younger woman's frame.

"I know," Annabella said. "He can take care of himself."

"Aye, he can. Now, let's get you tended to properly," Jean told her. Then, with the help of two of the housemaids, she inspected her mistress's genital area, and, satisfied that there was no sign of infection, she dressed the area again with a mixture of healing herbs and rendered goose fat, placing a pad of cotton wool between Annabella's thighs to contain any leakage. Drawing the down coverlet up over her mistress, she said, "I'll send a messenger to Bothwell to seek Angus. Ye are to rest."

Annabella nodded. "I think I can now. I feel safer here than at Holyrood Palace."

Jean drew the bed curtains, and in the company of the two little maids left her mistress to sleep. As she had promised she dispatched a messenger to the carl immediately. It was another two days before Angus Ferguson returned to Burnside House. He had already departed Bothwell's encampment before the messenger arrived, and gone to Holyrood in search of his wife. It was there the messenger caught up with him to tell him his wife was at Burnside House. He hurried to reach her.

"Where is she?" he demanded of Jean when he entered the dwelling.

"Upstairs, resting, my lord," Jean told him, reaching out to catch at his sleeve before he might dash upstairs. "Angus!" Her voice was low. Sisterly.

Angus Ferguson turned to look at her questioningly.

She led him into the little hall, signaling to a servant to bring him a dram of his whiskey. "Sit down, brother," she instructed him. "Before ye see yer wife, there is something ye must know." She waved the serving man away when he had brought the earl's dram. "Annabella was with the queen when Lord Ruthven broke in with his minions and murdered Riccio. When Ruthven threatened the queen, it was yer wife who flung herself before the monarch to shield her with her own body. They dragged her away and to the floor. It was that cur Darnley who kicked her several times. Annabella has lost her bairn, brother. She is in a fragile state right now."

"She will live?" he asked softly. His eyes were suddenly hard, however. Darnley! That drunken, lecherous fop who fancied himself king, and expected everyone else to do so as well. He had brutalized Annabella without a single regret. Well, he would pay for that error. *I don't know how, or when,* the Earl of Duin considered, *but one day he will pay for our loss.*

"Aye, she will live, and ye will get another bairn on her, brother."

"If we had not come to court, this would nae have happened," the earl said grimly.

"Dinna say that, for in doing so ye blame yer wife for yer bairn's loss," Jean said. "She has already done that, and plots revenge against Lord Darnley. Ye could nae refuse the queen's invitation to come to court, Angus."

His shoulders slumped as if in defeat. "Nay," he agreed, "I could not refuse."

"Drink yer whiskey," Jean said, "and then go to Annabella. Her wee heart is broken, and she needs ye."

"How is it that ye're the youngest of us, and yet the wisest?" Angus asked his sister.

Jean laughed. Then she stood up. "I'll go tell her ye're home, and coming to her." She bent to kiss the top of his dark head and then hurried off.

Angus swallowed down his dram, letting the whiskey hit his stomach like a ball of fire. He wanted to go home and never leave Duin again. That, however, was going to be impossible. When he had arrived at Holyrood Palace today, he had learned the queen had escaped the night before with Darnley, aided by Bothwell. The rumor was that they were already ensconced at Dunbar Castle, a full twenty-five miles from the city. The traitor lords had immediately fled Edinburgh and were headed south into England or back to their homes. Many others would flock to declare their loyalty to the queen as she rode to take back the town. He would have to be among those lords. With the rebels fled there would be no resistance, for Edinburgh was loyal to Mary Stuart.

He was not going back to Duin until late spring. Annabella, however, was a different matter. As soon as she was able to travel, he was going to see that she was sent home. Matthew would accompany her, and then his younger brother would fetch little Mistress Agnes Baird to keep her sister company. He would escape the political machinations of the more powerful lords as quickly as he could. Setting the empty dram cup aside, he hurried to his wife.

Annabella's eyes lit up as he came through the bed-chamber door. "My lord!" She held out her arms to him.

The earl went immediately to the bed to embrace her. As soon as his arms closed about her, Annabella began to weep. "Ahh, sweetheart," he said soothingly. "We shall have more bairns, and great joy in creating them."

"If we had not come . . ." she began, sobbing.

"We had no choice, Annabella," he told her.

"Darnley did this to us, Angus." She snuggled against his shoulder.

"And we will have our due on him; I vow it," the earl replied.

"I want to go home, Angus," Annabella said softly.

"And so ye shall, as soon as Jeannie says ye're fit to travel," he promised. "But now ye must get well and strong to do so." He did not tell her he was leaving again at first light to join the queen's army now marching toward Edinburgh. Instead he crawled into bed with his wife, and together they slept in each other's arms for several hours.

When Annabella awoke the following morning, the imprint of his head was still visible in the pillow next to her, and she imagined she could still feel his strong arms enclosing her. She sighed happily, stretching herself like a young cat. She felt better already. Certainly she would be ready to travel home to Duin in a few more days.

"Good morning!" Jean entered with a tray.

"Where is Angus?" Annabella asked.

"He had to return to join the other lords pledging their loyalty to our queen. He rode out at dawn."

"Will there be fighting?" Annabella asked nervously.

"Nay, the people love Queen Mary, but there will be retribution," Jean said grimly, "against all who turned traitor against our queen."

"Darnley must be punished!" Annabella said in a fierce voice.

"I'm certain he will be," Jean replied.

But Lord Darnley was not censured for his part in David Riccio's murder, much to Annabella's fury. Four thousand men had rallied to the queen's side, including the earls of Crawford, Atholl, Glenkirk, Sutherland, Duin, and, of course, Bothwell. Lords Seton, Livingstone, and Fleming, brothers of three of the queen's Marys, joined forces with Mary Stuart. Together with their clansmen they descended upon Edinburgh, where the town's population came forth to cheer their queen's return.

The very next day the queen's council met. They outlawed all who had taken part in the murder of the unfortunate Riccio. Chancellor Morton, lords Ruthven and Lindsay, and all of Clan Douglas were outlawed. Those not at the murder itself, but believed or known to have been involved in the plot, including Maitland, were warned to keep from court and the queen's sight until asked to return. But the queen's husband, Henry, Lord Darnley, swore before the council that he had no part whatsoever in the murder of David Riccio. He was vindicated of any wrongdoing, and documents to that effect were publicly posted all over Edinburgh clearing his name.

Annabella was outraged. "He most certainly was involved! He was there! He imprisoned the queen so she could not defend Master Riccio. He followed every order that that old devil Ruthven gave him. How can he in good conscience swear he knew nothing of the plot and was not involved? He hated Riccio. Was jealous of him. He even suggested once that the bairn the queen carries might be Riccio's."

"And it was partly because of that accusation that he was spared. The bairn to be born is Darnley's. But until it is born, and Darnley formally accepts it as his own blood, its legitimacy could be questioned. Darnley is a childish coward, and it is unlikely he would make such a claim. But we cannot endanger the rights of Scotland's future king. Darnley must be placated and declared innocent. Once the queen's bairn is born it will be a different matter," Angus answered her.

"The queen hates him now," Annabella said. "She will not miss him."

Nay, she would not. Angus Ferguson had seen the way Mary Stuart looked at James Hepburn. He had seen his friend's hidden desire for the queen warring with his honor. But if Henry, Lord Darnley, the man who styled himself Scotland's *king*, were no longer alive, he believed that Bothwell's scruples could be overcome, despite the fact that he was newly married, and he would pursue the queen. The marriage between James Hepburn and Jean Gordon had been a political match. There was no love between the two, and Angus Ferguson knew that Bothwell was already considering a divorce that Jean's brother, George Gordon, would not object to as long as his sister came out of the marriage a rich woman.

But he kept this knowledge to himself. Annabella was recovered from the loss of their bairn. April was coming to an end, and it was past time for them to return to Duin.

He sent a messenger to Matthew, who had returned to Duin weeks ago, that they would be coming. Another messenger was sent ahead to see to the accommodations for their trip.

They left Burnside House on a clear and sunny

morning, traveling slowly, for Angus did not want his wife's recovery to relapse.

Ten days later they stopped upon a hill to view the towers of Duin Castle. Beyond it the deep blue sea sparkled in the May sunshine. The hills were dotted with flowers and their flocks of sheep. In the meadows their cattle grazed placidly. Angus Ferguson felt his heart expanding with his pleasure. Reaching out, he took Annabella's hand in his.

"At last!" she breathed.

The joy on her plain face delighted him. She loved Duin as much as he did. And he loved her as much as he did Duin.

Chapter 8

𝒜 week after they had settled back into their home, the earl sent Matthew Ferguson across Scotland into the eastern borders to Rath to fetch Mistress Agnes Baird. Matthew carried with him a letter from Annabella explaining the loss of her bairn. The laird and his wife were saddened by the news, and outraged that Darnley had played a part in robbing them of a grandchild.

Agnes was now fifteen, and the prettiest of her sisters. She had dancing eyes, the blue of a summer's sky, and fluffy brown hair filled with golden highlights. Matthew could not help but notice how trim her figure was, with its dainty waist and generous bosom that had not seemed quite as voluptuous six months ago. *Odd*, he thought to himself. *She was interesting the last time I saw her, but now she is delectable.*

It took several days for Agnes's belongings to be packed for her visit, as she had not been certain when her escort would come. Matthew and his men were content to wait. And then a week after his arrival at Rath they were ready to make the long return journey. Agnes was filled with excitement as she mounted her horse.

Lady Anne and her husband bade their youngest daughter farewell. "Be helpful, and dinna impose too greatly upon yer sister, my child. I know yer visit will delight her."

"I promise to be good, Mama," Agnes said dutifully as her father gave her a wink. She was anxious to be off on this adventure she had waited so many months to attain. And she was anxious to be free of Rath. It had been very dull since her three older sisters had wed and gone off with their new husbands. Myrna now lived in the far north. It was very unlikely Agnes would ever see Myrna again. Sorcha lived nearby in much the same style as the Bairds. There was no excitement there. But Annabella lived across Scotland in a castle on the sea. Agnes had never seen the sea, and she was most anxious to do so.

And to be escorted to Duin by a handsome man might prove delightful, she decided.

Matthew Ferguson gave the signal to depart, and the journey to Duin began.

To Matthew's surprise Agnes Baird turned out to be an excellent and uncomplaining traveler. Whether it was her nature to be so or simply the novelty of the journey, he didn't know, but he was grateful. Anxious to see her eldest sister, Agnes had even pushed Matthew to travel faster. Liking her spirit of adventure, he had gladly obliged her. They reached Duin a day before he had anticipated that they would.

Annabella and Angus were awaiting them in the courtyard. Agnes jumped down from her horse and ran to her sister. The two siblings hugged.

"Let me look at ye, Aggie," Annabella said, setting the girl in front of her at arm's length. "Oh, my! Ye've grown taller, and ye finally have breasts! Come into the hall. Ye'll tell me everything that has happened at Rath in these last months since I saw ye."

The earl stepped forward and kissed his sister-in-law's rosy cheeks. "Welcome to Duin, little sister Agnes," he greeted her.

Agnes curtsied politely. "Oh, thank ye, my lord! And thank ye for sending yer brother to escort me. Matthew proved a delightful traveling companion, even if he is a bit slow a-horse." Then, linking arms with her sister, she entered the castle.

Matthew Ferguson's mouth fell open at being called poky a-horse.

"All is well at Rath, I assume," Angus Ferguson said, chuckling at both Agnes's remark and his brother's reaction to it. He could see that his young sister-in-law was going to prove a lively addition to his household.

"Aye," Matthew said. "The laird and his wife are well, saddened by yer loss, but hopeful that another bairn will soon be on the way."

"So Mistress Agnes considers ye a delightful traveling companion," the earl teased his younger brother.

Matthew flushed. "She's an interesting little minx," he said.

The two men joined the two women in the hall, where Agnes was taking a cup of wine from a servant.

"I think ye are no longer quite so plain, Annabella," the men heard Agnes say. "Ye're actually beginning to look pretty."

"I am happy," Annabella said quietly.

Angus Ferguson sat down next to his wife on the settle by the great hearth. Taking her hand, he gave it a little squeeze, which she reciprocated.

He loves her! Agnes thought to herself. *That's what I*

want. A man who will love me. How fortunate my sister is, but she deserves her happiness.

"Mama writes that ye have many suitors," Annabella noted.

"They only want me because I am beautiful," Agnes said scornfully, "and they want my gold dower. They do not want *me*. I have never been like Myrna, who was content in her beauty and thought it was enough. Nor am I like Sorcha, who is pleased to have married into a family more important than the Bairds. And I am not like you, Annabella. You were happy to have been given a husband at all, for no one thought such a plain lass would ever wed. It was believed ye would remain at Rath looking after our parents as they aged, and thus free any wife Robbie took from that burden."

Although the earl bridled at his sister-in-law's thoughtless tongue, Annabella merely laughed. "And yet I was given the greatest prize of a husband," she said. "One never knows what will happen, Aggie. Dinna despair. Ye and yer true love will find each other one fine day. Ye are, after all, only fifteen."

"Sorcha was sixteen when she wed," Agnes reminded her sibling.

"Then surely within the next year something wonderful will happen for ye," Annabella teased. She reached out to touch her sister's cheek. "I am so glad ye're wi' me, Aggie. I have missed ye, and I have a great deal to show ye here at Duin."

Agnes Baird had arrived at Duin at the end of the month of May. Her sister's home was a wonder to her. Like Annabella, she had never before lived in so large a dwelling; nor had she seen the sea. The water, the waves, the soaring gulls all delighted her. She loved the vivid sunsets. One clear day Annabella had insisted that Matthew take Agnes to the rooftop of the castle to see the magnificent view.

With much grumbling Matthew Ferguson climbed the narrowing staircase to the very top of one of the square towers. Agnes was right behind him. Opening a small door, he carefully stepped out, then reached back to take her hand and pull her up onto the rooftop. Together they walked to the stone parapet that bordered the edge of the tower.

"Look out across the sea and tell me what ye see," he instructed her.

Agnes stared, seeing in the distance something she had never noticed before when she looked out over the water. "Is that land out there?" She looked up at him for the answer. "Is it an island?"

"Nay, 'tis the northern end of Ireland," he told her. "On a very clear day like today ye can see it. The Irish used to raid Scotland. They haven't come to Duin in my memory, although I understand they still raid this land. Perhaps we are too strong."

"Could we take a boat and sail there in a day?" she asked.

"Aye, wi' a good stiff breeze we might just make it," he said, admiring her spirit of adventure. "But why would we go?"

"To see what's there," Agnes answered him. "Why don't we?"

"Because I am the steward of Duin. I have my duties to perform daily, Aggie. 'Tis the way of the world. A man toils. The woman keeps the house and bears the bairns," Matthew told her.

"Then I might just have to go myself," Agnes said

pertly. She looked up at him and smiled. "Would ye miss me if I went, Matthew?"

He gulped. There was no way she could know that he had been thinking a great deal about her ever since she had arrived at Duin over a month ago. "Nay," he boldly lied. "I should not miss ye." He waited for her to either weep with disappointment or castigate him for his words.

But she did neither. Instead Agnes Baird smiled a knowing little smile at him.

Matthew Ferguson was suddenly uncomfortable. "If ye've seen enough, then," he said in a tight voice, "I hae more important duties to attend to, mistress. We will return to the hall." He went down the steep ladder that led from the roof to the stone floor of the tower's landing first, then reached up with both hands to help her down.

June slipped into July and August. Agnes Baird was quite comfortable in her sister's house. It was Angus who suggested she might want to remain for several more months. Annabella agreed with her husband that it would please her greatly, and Agnes was delighted. A messenger was sent off to Rath, and returned with permission. The sisters rode out daily. They hunted with the men, and shot at the archery butts set out in the courtyard. They spent lazy September afternoons lying in a meadow talking.

The days were becoming cooler and shorter. The warm hall was very welcoming in the evenings, when they would play chess with Angus or Matthew. The earl had been careful of his wife since the loss of their child, but now with the long nights he felt his need for her rising, and sensed that she felt the same. Catching her briefly alone in the hall late one afternoon, he took her hand up, kissed it, and said, "I miss ye. I need ye in my arms again, Annabella."

Her gray eyes filled with warm laughter. "I thought ye would never ask," she surprised him by saying. "I hae missed ye too. Jeannie said I was well healed several weeks back, but ye seemed more interested in the possibility of English raiders and the cattle than ye did in me, my lord."

"I was making up things to divert me from how much I wanted to be back in my wife's bed," he said, grinning.

"Then come to it," she said softly.

"What of the evening meal?" he asked her, looking to the servants, who were now setting the high board and dragging the trestles for the men from the side alcove, where they were kept after meals.

"It will be served whether we are at the high board or nae," Annabella said, smiling. "But if ye would prefer to wait until after ye hae supped, my lord, I shall abide by yer decision." She curtsied and, turning about, left the hall. Once inside her bedchamber Annabella undid the fastenings holding her bodice to her skirt. The skirt dropped away to the floor. Undoing her petticoats, she stepped from the pile of material, kicking her shoes off as she did. Unable to reach the laces of her bodice, she waited for him. He would, Annabella knew, enjoy doing it. She undid her long dark hair and began to brush it free of tangles, restraining her laughter when he burst through the door of her bedchamber. "Undo my bodice for me," she greeted him before turning her back to him.

He acquiesced, unlacing the bodice, pulling it off of her, tossing it aside. Fascinated, she watched his hands coming about her to undo the ribbons holding her chemise closed. It fell away from her. He pushed the delicate garment from her shoulders, his hands slipping beneath her beautiful breasts. He groaned low in her ear as he felt the weight of them settle in his palms. His fingers tightened about the firm flesh, rubbing the nipples with the rough balls of his thumbs.

Pressing her against the bed, the earl knelt so he might undo her garters. Slowly he rolled the gossamer stockings down her shapely legs, his expert tongue following his fingers down the warm, soft flesh of her thighs as he divested each leg of its silken covering. As he drew each stocking from her feet he kissed each one, nibbling at her toes, which caused her to giggle.

Every inch of her seemed to be throbbing. With a great effort she stood up so she might undress him; he had entered her bedchamber in only his breeks and a shirt. She undid the ties of the shirt, pushing it off his shoulders. Then Annabella pressed her own naked breasts against the smooth, warm flesh of his chest, rubbing her nipples against him quite wickedly.

"Woman," he growled low in his throat. "Do ye mean to try my patience?"

"Aye," she whispered in his ear before she licked it. Her hands moved to unfasten his breeks. He wore no drawers beneath, and as they fell away she reached about him to cup his firm buttocks in her hands, squeezing them lightly. "Have ye truly missed me, my lord? If ye would hae me believe it, ye must show me how much." She took a hand and stroked the length of his manhood, reaching beneath it to cup him.

The earl groaned as fiery pleasure engulfed him. A brief year ago she had been a shy but curious virgin. He had taken that curiosity and taught her to satisfy him, to satisfy them both. She had proven to be an incredible pupil. *Jesu!* He groaned again as she fell to her knees to take him into her mouth. She had learned her lessons well, he considered as a bolt of wicked sensation shot through him. His long fingers tangled themselves in her thick hair, kneading her scalp as she brought his cock to raging life with her mouth, her tongue, and the skillful fingers that teased his balls. He closed his eyes briefly, savoring her delicious attentions.

In the early months of their marriage he had actually come to like her for the qualities that had nothing to do with her gorgeous, tempting body. He saw kindness, thoughtfulness, and intelligence. It was her clever mind that he found truly pleased him, and her instant loyalty to Duin. Then, when they had finally joined their bodies, he had been astounded by the perfection of her body. It had aroused in him a passion such as he had never known. Some might have thought it lust, and perhaps in the beginning it had been. But not now. He was in love with his wife, and could not imagine his life without her. To his relief she had responded in kind to his passion. "Enough, sweetheart," he begged her.

Annabella arose gracefully, slipping her arms about his neck, her lithe body pressing against him. "Dinna play the lover, my lord. I need ye inside of me. Deep inside! Afterward we will sport ourselves with kisses and caresses, but now I very much need to be fucked, Angus, my lord and husband."

He pressed her back against the edge of the bed, pushing her down, drawing her legs up and over his shoulders. "I am happy to oblige ye, madam," he said thickly, guiding his engorged cock into her with an audible sigh of pleasure.

Wet and hot, her sheath enclosed him eagerly, squeezing the long, thick peg that plunged itself into her right to the very hilt.

"Is that what ye desire, madam?" he demanded of her. He stood very still now.

"Aye!" *Holy Mother!* His cock throbbed with life as he stood over her. Her eyes were shut to better experience the sensations, and she repeated, "Oh, aye, Angus! But 'twill be even more perfect, my darling, if ye will . . . Ahhh! Oh! Aye! Just like that! Dinna stop! Dinna ye dare stop!" Her hands fisted themselves into the coverlet beneath.

At first he moved with slow and majestic strokes, pushing as deep as he could, slowly withdrawing almost all the way until he could see his tormenting was beginning to drive her wild with passion. After a time he increased his tempo, his cock flashing furiously back and forth with great rapidity. Her pleasurable moans of delight increased his own desire. He felt invincible. As if he could go on like this forever and ever.

They were both panting as each stroke of his cock brought them closer and closer to pure perfection. Annabella burned and froze with her need for him. She tightened herself about him again, wresting a cry of delight from him. Knowing that he wanted her, needed her, every bit as much as she did him excited Annabella. The rapture began to build, swiftly rising up to overwhelm her. She opened her mouth to scream her satisfaction as she was rocked by spasm after spasm after spasm.

Angus roared in reply as his love juices burst forth in a torrent of excess. For a few moments he remained buried within her, unable to withdraw, for she was so delicious. Finally he withdrew his temporarily appeased manhood from her momentarily gratified body. "Are ye content for the moment, ye lustful vixen?" he asked, smiling down at her.

"Aye, for the moment," she teased back. Then she said, "Do ye think we've made another bairn, Angus?"

"There is time for us," he answered.

"Nay, I have nae done my duty by ye or by Duin until I have given ye an heir. I wonder if the child I lost was a lad or a lass," Annabella said. "I have often wondered."

"Get under the coverlet," he said, and he joined her. "Dinna think of it, sweetheart. God will provide us with an heir when the time is right." His arms went about her, and he stroked her head comfortingly.

Ohh, she loved him! She had never thought it of herself that she could fall in love with a man who didn't admit to loving her. But why on earth was she complaining? Annabella considered, as she drifted into sleep. Angus Ferguson was a good husband.

He kept no mistress and treated her with kindness and respect. But she loved him. She wanted him to love her. Could he love at all? Could he love her? Ever?

It was October when word finally reached Duin that the queen had been delivered on the nineteenth of June of a fair son who was to be called James, and would be the sixth of his name. But the queen remained estranged from her son's father. Though he had been cleared of any culpability in the murder of David Riccio, Mary had come to despise the degenerate drunk Henry, Lord Darnley, had become.

"Poor lady," Annabella said.

"She wed him willingly," Agnes replied.

"What a hard-hearted little minx ye are," Matthew Ferguson remarked.

"Well, she did," Agnes retorted. "No one wanted her to wed him, but she insisted. Now she has discovered the truth of what he is, which her advisers saw beforehand. Didn't Lord Bothwell say it the last time he visited?"

"She was in love," Annabella told her sister. "A woman in love sometimes makes foolish choices."

"Which is as good a reason as I can think of for this nebulous thing they call love having naught to do with marriage," Agnes said. "Marriage has always been a practical matter between families, and so it should remain. The queen will have Darnley for a husband until death parts them."

"He'll drink himself to death sooner rather than later," the earl said. "And Bothwell says he is riddled wi' the pox."

"He is one to talk, considering his amours," Agnes said boldly.

"Aggie!" Annabella was shocked. "James Hepburn is a fine gentleman, and a close friend of this family. It does not become ye to repeat the tittle-tattle ye have heard from the servants, who no doubt tittle-tattle about ye. Perhaps ye should return home to Rath, for it would seem the freedoms we have allowed ye here at Duin have gone to yer head," the countess said sternly.

"Ohh, dinna send me back to Rath!" Agnes Baird pleaded with her sister. "I couldn't bear it, Annabella. It is so dull there, and our parents will be seeking to find a suitable husband for me. Robbie will nae chose a wife for himself until we are all wed, and Da grows anxious for another heir for Rath."

"Well . . ." Annabella pretended to consider.

"Send the troublesome chatterbox back," Matthew said mischievously.

Agnes turned on him furiously. "Oh! Ye!" she sputtered. "Ye're only saying that to irritate me."

"Please tell me that I have succeeded," he teased her.

"Why do ye persist in being mean to me when I can see that ye'd rather kiss me?" Agnes taunted him. "Why don't ye?"

Matthew Ferguson blushed bright red. Her instincts were correct, although he was not of a mind to admit to it yet. What if he did and she mocked him, as she was teasingly doing now? "Ye're not old enough to be kissed," he said loftily.

"Hah!" Agnes countered. "I'll be sixteen in December!"

"Enough," Annabella said quietly. "Behave yerself, Aggie, and ye may remain at Duin. Matthew, stop baiting her. My sister is nae too young to be kissed, but ye are too old to tease her in such a manner."

Watching her gently chastise their siblings, Angus Ferguson grinned. What a woman she was, his Annabella!

October was gone with its grouse hunting. November came, and the pigs were slaughtered for the winter, save a few. Then it was December, and they celebrated Agnes Baird's sixteenth birthday on the feast of Saint Nicholas, which fell on the sixth day of the month. Matthew Ferguson pulled her into a dark corner later, and gave Agnes her first kiss. She surprised him by kissing him back. January came, and then the short month of February.

It was at the end of that month that Bothwell appeared briefly at Duin. Closeted with Angus Ferguson in the earl's privy chamber, he said without preamble, "Ye must nae be the last to know. Darnley is dead. Murdered. And there are those who would lay the blame at my door, but I swear to ye that I dinna do it."

"Do ye know who did?" Angus asked his friend, pouring them two dram cups of his own smoky whiskey. He handed one to Bothwell. "And how?"

"I suspect Moray and Maitland had a hand in it. The queen's half brother did his usual disappearing act before it happened, a sure sign that he was involved," James Hepburn said dryly. "The queen had gone to the wedding of one of her servants. I was there too. We had visited Darnley earlier, for she will nae have him in the same house wi' her any longer, and he has nae been well. He was lodged at Kirk o' Field house. Someone filled the cellar wi' gunpowder and blew it to smithereens. They found Darnley and his servant in the orchard garden. The servant had his throat cut, but it appeared as if someone had strangled Darnley as he fled."

"Jesu!" Angus Ferguson swore softly. "And the queen?"

"Shocked and saddened, and totally unaware of how Darnley's murder can be used against her," James Hepburn replied. "Now that there is a male heir, *they* have decided to make her unessential. But they can't dispense wi' her as long as I am there to protect her, and I will be until my death."

"The prince?"

"She put him wi' John Erskine, the Earl of Mar. They are housed at Stirling. They won't harm the bairn. 'Tis Mary they would be rid of, Angus," Bothwell said.

"Ye must first defend yerself, James," the Earl of Duin advised. "Ye canna help her if they tangle ye up in legalities. Maitland, for all his qualities as a good servant, would be the queen's *only* trusted adviser, as Cecil is to Elizabeth. He is clever enough to manage Moray, but ye are a different animal. Ye're in love wi' her, and our queen hae not Elizabeth Tudor's knack for survival. She is ruled by her heart, and she trusts too freely."

James Hepburn, Earl of Bothwell, flushed at Angus Ferguson's suggestion that he loved the queen. He did love her. He had ever since he had met her at the French court years earlier. But a Hepburn would never be considered worthy of Mary Stuart. He might be a man in love, but he was not a fool. "I have to protect her," he said. "My honor will nae allow me to do otherwise, Angus."

"Then first make certain they affix the blame for this murder on someone else, James. Whatever happens, I am yer friend and yer ally," the Earl of Duin said quietly. "As ye will nae desert the queen, I will nae desert either of ye. I will keep the faith."

Bothwell swallowed down the remainder of the whiskey in his dram cup in order to have time to regain control of his emotions. Finally he said, "I am grateful, Angus, for I know how much ye Fergusons of Duin prize your anonymity."

"Send a messenger to me with updates of what is happening, so I may be prepared for whatever comes," Angus told his friend.

Bothwell nodded, and then with the Earl of Duin by his side, took the offer of a fresh horse, departing to return to Edinburgh.

"What did he want?" Matthew Ferguson asked his brother afterward.

Angus shook his head. "Nothing," he said. "He just came to bring me word that Darnley has been murdered."

"Did he do it?" Matthew asked.

"Nay."

"Ye believe him?"

"I have known James Hepburn since we were wee lads. Is he capable of killing? Aye, he is. They want to blame him, for he is the queen's best defense."

"We should nae be involved in these matters," Matthew said.

"I agree," Angus replied. "But James Hepburn is my friend. Remember that, little brother. I dinna gie my friendship lightly, but I will also protect Duin."

Annabella agreed with both her husband and with Matthew. A close friendship must not be betrayed, but neither must Duin be put in any danger. She was glad to be an unimportant woman married to an unimportant border lord. She had seen what power and the desire for ultimate power could do the night she had witnessed the murder of David Riccio. She felt great sympathy for her queen. Few women had her strength of character, or were capable of ruling over a land constantly fought over by a group of contentious lords and their families.

The queen's cousin, Elizabeth Tudor, had learned the lessons of survival well in her difficult childhood. Mary, however, had been cosseted and pampered at every turn. She had been wise enough upon her return to Scotland to seek good counsel from her half brother, James Stewart, whom she had created Earl of Moray; and from William Maitland, whom she had made her secretary of state; but when her desires conflicted with that counsel, trouble was certain to ensue. Annabella wondered whether that trouble would now overwhelm Mary Stuart, and lead to her eventual downfall. Only time would reveal the answer to her question.

Chapter 9

True to his word, James Hepburn kept his friend Angus Ferguson fully informed of what was happening in Edinburgh with regard to the matter of Lord Darnley's murder. Although Mary had never formally given him the crown matrimonial, she had allowed him to style himself king. He was buried with royal pomp and Roman Catholic rites and interred at Holyrood in a grave next to King James V. Mary had gone into official mourning, but after a few days had departed Edinburgh to mourn more privately by the sea.

No sooner had the queen departed than men holding up scandalously painted posters had begun to travel the streets of the city, crying that Bothwell had killed the queen's husband—that the queen was in league with him in the murder. Darnley's father, the Earl of Lennox, demanded that a trial be held to determine the murderer of his son. The queen was informed of all of this at her seaside residence. Finally there was no other solution than to try Bothwell to determine his guilt or his innocence in the matter, and silence the rumors.

On April twelfth the trial was held at the Tolbooth in

Edinburgh before a panel of Bothwell's peers. It was noted that James Stewart, the Earl of Moray, was absent from the proceedings. The trial began at ten in the morning, and lasted until seven o'clock of the evening. As no formal charges had ever been filed in the matter, and there was no evidence produced connecting Bothwell with the murder, the Earl of Argyll, who was the presiding judge, acquitted James Hepburn of any complicity in the murder of Henry, Lord Darnley. The court then adjourned to a nearby tavern, where the innocent man treated everyone to a good supper.

"God's blood!" Matthew Ferguson swore. "Is there a bolder man in the borders?"

Angus laughed. "Nay, I do not believe there is," he agreed. "Nor on this earth."

"The matter is settled then, and perhaps Duin can now concentrate on its own business, and not Bothwell's," Matthew said.

"Why is yer brother so hostile to James Hepburn?" Annabella asked her husband afterward, when they walked in the castle's gardens. The gardens overlooked the sea.

"He doesn't know James as well as I do," Angus said. "James's father, Patrick Hepburn, defected to England, casting shame upon the family name. Some say Patrick did it because Marie de Guise, whom he loved, refused his suit. Of course, Marie forgave him and pardoned him so he could return, but James never forgot the betrayal. He has spent much of his life proving the loyalty of the Hepburns to the royal Stewarts."

"I think his care of the queen is because he loves her," Annabella said quietly.

"Aye, he has told me so," her husband admitted.

"Matthew fears your friendship and loyalty to Bothwell could endanger Duin, doesn't he?" Annabella said. "He may be correct, Angus."

"It's over now," the Earl of Duin told his wife. "James is acquitted of Darnley's murder, and my need to go to Bothwell's aid no longer exists." He put an arm about Annabella as they looked out over the blazing sun sinking slowly into the sea.

But it was not over. Another messenger came from James Hepburn to Angus Ferguson, asking the earl to join him with a small force of his clansmen at Dunbar Castle.

The Earl of Duin did not hesitate, for his loyalty to his old friend was yet great. He rode out the next morning with fifty men. Matthew Ferguson was beside himself with worry.

"What mischief is Bothwell up to now that he needs to drag Angus into it?" he said.

Annabella was as worried as Matthew was, but she soothed him, saying, "Dinna fret, brother. Bothwell will nae put Angus in danger." Please God he wouldn't, for she was certain she was with child again.

It was a beautiful spring. The trees bloomed and leafed. The hillsides were covered with flowers. She, Jean, and Agnes walked out together most afternoons. It was during one of these walks that she told her sister and Jean that she was now certain she was enceinte. "The bairn should come before year's end," she said.

"Then I shall remain at Duin," Agnes said. "Ye'll need my company now more than ever."

Jean smiled to herself. Agnes Baird had been at Duin for a year now. She would never leave Duin, especially if Matthew had anything to say about it. Matthew was in love with Agnes, but Agnes was proving a difficult girl to court. Unless Matthew soon took the initiative, they would spend the rest of their lives sparring with words instead of kisses, Jean thought. "We should tell Matthew about the bairn," she said. "He'll be relieved to know there will soon be an heir of Duin."

Annabella laughed. "At least he's stopped fussing at me about it," she said. "Aye, let's tell him. Perhaps it will lighten his spirits, for he worries that we have nae heard from Angus. I worry too."

Her news did please her husband's brother, and it was followed by a messenger from Angus Ferguson. They gathered in the hall that evening so Annabella might read aloud to them the letter she had received from her husband. Seated at the high board, the Countess of Duin unfolded the parchment written in his own hand and began to speak.

" 'My good wife, may God have mercy on us all, and upon Scotland. We reached Dunbar, traveling with all due haste, to learn that Bothwell had kidnapped the queen.' "

Those listening gasped with shock.

" 'They spent several long days and nights locked together in a tower,' " Annabella continued, " 'and we have now traveled on into Edinburgh, where Bothwell will be granted a divorce from Jean Gordon so he may then wed the queen. They are openly and desperately in love. There is no reasoning with them. I will attempt to make James understand that while my friendship for him remains, I can no longer endanger the Fergusons of Duin by being a public party to this event. The earls are now dividing themselves into two parties that are called the Queen's Men and the Prince's Men. Moray is not, as ye may well imagine, among his sister's adherents. There is certain to be civil war. Look for me to return to Duin as quickly as I can. Your loving husband, Angus Ferguson, Earl of Duin.' "

The hall was silent as Annabella laid the parchment

upon the table and, reaching for her cup, quaffed the remaining wine in it. "That is all," she said to those who had been listening. "I hope ye will all pray for Scotland this night," she told them.

"Madness!" Matthew Ferguson muttered. "And he has involved Angus."

"He has involved others as well," Annabella said in an attempt to calm Matthew.

"The others, I wager, are more important, more powerful names, who cannot be punished. We are nae important," Matthew responded.

"Neither Angus nor the Fergusons of Duin were among the kidnappers. Angus was called to Dunbar after the fact. He is leaving before the marriage is celebrated. His friendship can be taken only so far, even by James Hepburn. His loyalty to Duin is greater than anything else," Annabella told him. "He will come in just a few more days."

And he did. The messenger had preceded his master by only two days. Angus Ferguson, however, was grim faced at his arrival. He climbed wearily from his stallion, flinging the reins to a stable lad, and, putting an arm about Annabella, kissed her hard. Reaching up, she caressed his grimy cheek silently. Their eyes met in understanding.

"My lord must bathe and eat," the Countess of Duin dictated. "Then he will tell us everything." Without another word she led him into the castle and upstairs to his apartments, where menservants were already seeing that the bathing room tub was filled with steaming water, and feeding the small raised hearth so that the chamber remained warm. Annabella undressed her husband, and as the servants exited she helped him into the stone tub.

Angus closed his eyes briefly and emitted a deep sigh as the hot water sank into his tired body. He opened them as Annabella stroked a wet cloth over his face.

"Ye look exhausted," she said, meeting his gaze.

"I am. Once I had spoken with James I did not delay in departing Edinburgh," he said. "God's blood, sweetheart, this time he has overreached himself. They won't be satisfied until they have slain him or driven him from Scotland for good and all."

"He understood why ye had to leave him?" Angus was probably correct in his assessment of the situation, but Bothwell had always been clever at wriggling out of tough situations. It was entirely possible he could outride this storm, and if he did she did not want the Fergusons of Duin on his bad side.

"Aye, he understood. I asked him why he had called me to Dunbar when he did not really need me. Do ye know what he answered? He said that because he knew the great risk he had taken with the queen he wanted one true friend by his side, if only briefly." The earl's eyes teared with the memory, but then he continued. "When I said it seemed to me that all of his friends surrounded him at the moment, he laughed. He said they were none of them true friends. They would remain with him as long as it appeared he had a chance of winning, but once it was decided he could not win this particular fight, they would disappear like so many rats scuttling back to their holes."

"Oh, Angus, how sad!" Annabella said, and she kissed the tears from his cheek.

"He's wagered it all this time, sweetheart."

"Does he really love her, or is it just the power he seeks?" she asked.

"Nay, he loves her. Madly. Passionately. And she returns his love. She has already said she will not make him king, or give him the crown matrimonial," Angus told his wife as she washed him. "He feels their marriage is the only way he can protect her from Moray and the others. Because he is one of them, and because he has always been strong, he thinks he can manage to keep them in check as her husband. I do not. They know she will be influenced by him to a certain degree. Ye know the earls. Each a cock on his own dunghill, crowing. They are afraid of him because individually he has the power to keep them at bay so Mary Stuart may rule. None of them has that charisma. They all need one another to defy her. And now they will with a vengeance."

"Did they wed?"

"Aye, but it was nae easy. He gave Jean Gordon everything she wanted to be free of her. The queen's confessor had been forbidden by the pope from performing the marriage, and has withdrawn from her side until she gives Bothwell up, but in this even the Church cannot prevail. The queen is wildly in love for the first time in her life. Darnley was but a foolish infatuation. James Hepburn is another matter altogether. But even Edinburgh's most distinguished pastors of the Reformed kirk would nae perform the ceremony. They finally found one who accepted a large bribe to formalize the marriage. I left Edinburgh at dawn the morning of the wedding, which was performed at Holyrood's chapel."

"But surely now the deed is done Moray and his cohorts will accept the queen's decision." She quickly washed his dark hair and rinsed it free of soap.

He arose and stepped from the large stone basin. "I dinna remain to find out, but I doubt it. Moray is but for an accident of birth the man who should be king. He is nae about to give up his position at the top of the hierarchy. He'll fight, and many will fight wi' him. The question is, can Bothwell gather as many forces, and overcome him."

Annabella toweled her big husband dry with several towels warmed on a rack by the fire. "I'll leave Tormod to get ye dressed again," she said, referring to Angus's servant. "They'll be waiting in the hall to hear all of what ye have told me. Ye'll nae be going away again soon, will ye?"

"Nay, I'm home to stay, sweetheart." He pulled her against his naked body, and kissed her a long, sweet kiss. "I've missed ye," he said.

She lingered a moment in his embrace, but then drew quickly away, her hand brushing down his long cock, which was showing strong signs of interest in her. "There is nae time, my lord, for they are waiting in the hall. Afterward, however, I shall be pleased to entertain yon eager laddie. I have some news that should please ye well. By year's end we'll hae an heir." Then, with a quick smile, she turned and left him.

Angus Ferguson wanted to shout with his joy. He was home! Duin was safe! And Annabella was going to give him a son. "Tormod!" he shouted as he opened the door back into his own apartments. "I need clothes!"

She heard him as she hurried down into the hall, and Annabella smiled. While she felt a strong sympathy for Mary Stuart and James Hepburn, she didn't want the Fergusons of Duin involved in what was certain to be a very volatile matter, and would surely become worse. They would be safe in their haven here in the southwest borders. The summer was almost upon them, and she would have her bairn in safety.

But while peace surrounded Duin, the queen and her bridegroom found themselves facing a great wall of opposition to their marriage. On June fifteenth, a month to the day after their marriage, the forces of the queen were defeated at Carberry. Bothwell fled north into the isles, while Mary was taken first to Edinburgh, and then imprisoned at Lochleven, where she miscarried of twins on the twenty-third of July. This served as proof to all that Mary and Bothwell had been adulterous lovers. The next day the queen was forced to sign a document abdicating her position in favor of her year-old son, James. The little king was crowned five days later at Stirling, and his uncle, James Stewart, now ruled Scotland as the king's protector. But at Duin none of this was known until several months later.

The summer faded away into autumn. Annabella grew large with her bairn. The earl was openly solicitous of his plain wife. Their amusement came from the constant battle between Matthew Ferguson and Agnes Baird. Agnes would be seventeen at year's end, and there was no hiding the fact that Matthew wanted her as his wife. The laird of Rath and his wife would be coming before winter to be with their eldest daughter when she gave birth. Matthew intended to ask the laird's permission to marry Agnes then. He had, however, said nothing to Agnes; nor would he until he had spoken with Robert Baird.

Finally, in mid-October, a messenger arrived to say the laird and his wife were but a day behind him. Annabella was overjoyed, for she had not seen her parents since their fateful journey to Edinburgh almost two years prior. Agnes was not as pleased.

"I hope they do not want me to return to Rath," she said.

"Ye're welcome to remain wi' us at Duin," Annabella replied, "but as ye're soon to be seventeen I suspect our parents are concerned that ye hae no husband. There is no court for ye to visit, and so a husband must be found for ye among the border families near Rath. Ye must be wed, Aggie. The old Church is nae longer an option, so it is wed ye must be. I'm sure Da will have a suggestion as to a husband for ye."

"I dinna want to leave Duin," Agnes insisted. "I love it here. I love being wi' ye."

"Then if a husband canna be found for ye at Rath, one must be found at Duin," Annabella said mischievously, looking directly at Matthew Ferguson, who looked away.

Agnes saw her look and sniffed scornfully, but said nothing, to her sister's surprise.

The Bairds of Rath arrived, to be greeted by both of their daughters. Anne Baird looked upon her eldest daughter's big belly, exclaiming, "Are ye certain this child is to come in December?"

Annabella laughed. "Sometimes I wish it would come now, for I am as fat as a well-fed shoat, and I can no longer see my feet."

"I think it is a good thing we have come now," the lady Anne replied.

Robert Baird, however, after greeting his two daughters, was eager to know whether he and Angus would be hunting grouse anytime soon. He was delighted to learn they would be going out on the morrow. "Not today?" he said, not keeping the disappointment from his voice.

"'Tis past the noon hour," Angus told his father-in-law, "and the sun will be setting soon, Robert. The grouse will be awaiting us tomorrow."

The laird's glance turned to Agnes. He looked her up and down. "Ye've grown some since we last saw ye," he said. "Ye'll be needing a husband, Agnes." Then, turning, he followed the rest of his family into the castle's hall.

The entrance to Duin Castle across the worn oak draw-bridge had given the laird of Rath pause. He had known that his son-in-law was a wealthy man, but the solid stone walls and the iron portcullis had come as a bit of a surprise. Inside, however, the house proved to be gracious and warm. More important, Annabella was obviously very happy.

There was a fine hot meal to greet the guests: rabbit stew, venison, a roasted capon, fresh bread, two kinds of cheese, and butter. There was a choice of wine or ale.

And apples baked with cinnamon were served when the rest of the meal had been cleared away. "Ye keep a good table, daughter," the laird of Rath praised his daughter.

Afterward they gathered about one of the two large fireplaces in the hall to exchange news. Sorcha had delivered a son, and her husband's family was well pleased. Nothing had been heard from Myrna in the north, although the laird's sister had written once to say they had arrived, and Myrna seemed to be settling into her new home. The lady Anne expressed her disappointment at not having heard from her second daughter.

"Be glad, Mama," Annabella said. "If she were unhappy the whole of Scotland would know it by now. She is obviously content wi' her lot and wi' her man."

"Else she would hae filled our ears wi' her complaints by now," Agnes said mischievously. "Her Highlander is probably wondering what he got himself into."

They all laughed, but Annabella was more sympathetic. "Aggie, dinna say it. Pray our sister and her husband will live a long and happy life wi' many bairns."

"Myrna was foolish," Agnes said without the slightest hint of remorse. "She gave away her most precious possession to that cad Melville. A man who was already deceiving her wi' another. I will never do such a thing! I will preserve my virtue until my wedding night."

"But will ye preserve it after yer wedding?" Matthew Ferguson said wickedly.

The laird of Rath shot a quick look at his wife, confused to see her suddenly smile a very knowing smile. What was this all about? he wondered silently.

Agnes Baird gasped with shock at his question. "How dare ye make such inquiry of me?" she demanded of him. "Do ye imply I would behave dishonorably after I am wed?" Her cheeks were pink with her outrage.

"I simply wish to learn whether ye will be a willing and faithful bedmate once we are wed," Matthew responded calmly.

"*Wed?*" Agnes practically screeched. "How dare ye even presume to think I should wed ye, Matthew Ferguson?"

"If I can gain yer da's permission, Aggie, of course ye'll wed me," he said, and he looked to the laird. "May I have the honor of yer daughter Agnes's hand, my lord?" he asked Robert Baird. "I have become quite fond of the lass these two years past that she has been wi' us at Duin. I am my brother's steward. He will tell ye that I serve him to his satisfaction. I hae the means to care well for Aggie. We will live here in the castle, where she will hae her sister for good company. Our bairns will hae their cousins for playmates. If this dinna suit yer daughter I will build her a stone house on lands that I own nearby. I have more than enough coin for it."

"Do ye hae yer brother's permission to ask for my daughter's hand?" the laird asked, knowing the answer but preserving the formalities.

"Aye, my lord, I hae Angus's permission," Matthew replied.

"I'll nae wed him!" Agnes shouted, jumping up and stamping her foot.

"Be silent, lassie!" her father roared back. Then he looked to his wife.

"We will speak in private," she told him.

"'Tis a most generous offer, sir," the laird of Rath said to Matthew Ferguson. "My wife and I will consider it. We will gie ye our answer in due time."

"I am satisfied to await yer answer," Matthew responded politely.

"Well, I am nae satisfied!" Agnes said.

"Be quiet, daughter!" the laird of Rath snapped.

"Aggie, do gie over, and cease yer turmoil," Annabella chided her sibling. "Ye're tired, overexcited by this long day and our parents' arrival. Ye hae our permission to seek yer bed, dearest."

"Aye, Agnes," the earl spoke up, backing his wife's decision. "Go and rest, lass."

Agnes Baird looked briefly as if she were going to cry, but then she turned, running from the hall. When Matthew made to follow, his brother bade him remain. The laird of Rath was pleased by the firm hand with which the earl ruled his household and his lands. He spent many a pleasant hour in the weeks that followed in Angus Ferguson's company, coming to like his son-in-law better and better with each passing day. And the lady Anne's previous concerns of sorcery were erased entirely. Both parents were touched by the devotion between their daughter and her husband.

When November was half-gone, the matter of Agnes Baird's betrothal came to the forefront once again. The laird of Rath was willing to accept Matthew Ferguson's proposal for his daughter's hand, but both Annabella and her mother felt that Agnes had to be allowed to make the choice to wed him or not.

"I'll nae return to Rath," Agnes said stubbornly.

"The scandal over yer sister has long died," the laird told her.

"And there are several fine young men seeking wives," the lady Anne added. "There are Bobby Lindsay, Ian Scott, Alexander Bruce, Jamie Elliot, and several of our Hamilton cousins who look most favorably upon ye, Agnes."

"But I like it here at Duin. As for the swains ye offer me, Mam, Bobby Lindsay has a nose like a turnip! I'm taller than Jamie Elliot, and he stammers every time he looks at me. I thought Alex Bruce was to wed Mary Douglas. If that light-skirt cried off I certainly wouldn't want him. As for Ian Scott, he has a face full of pock-marks, and lips that are much too big. He always looks like a salmon gasping for air."

"What of our Hamilton cousins?" Annabella said sweetly.

"Never! They may be our kin, but one of their ilk stole my sister's laddie. I'll hae nothing to do wi' any of them," Agnes said angrily.

"Ye're getting a bit long in the tooth for us to marry ye off well," the laird noted.

"Annabella was twenty when she wed Angus!" Agnes snapped. "I'll just be seventeen next month, Da. I certainly hae time."

"Yer brother will nae take a wife until all of his sisters are wed and gone," the laird told her.

Agnes laughed. "'Tis but an excuse for Rob to play the tomcat, Da."

"'Tis yer brother who will inherit Rath one day. It is important we find him the best match, which we canna if I must worry about ye. Besides, I want to see another heir before I die. I'm nae a lad, daughter."

"Bah!" Agnes laughed again. "Ye're nae old, Da."

The laird sighed. No one knew how to irritate him more than his youngest daughter. "I canna hae ye causing a calumny like yer sister," he told her. "There is a certain willfulness in ye, Agnes. What respectable family will gie us a well-dowered daughter for yer brother if ours is considered a scandalous household? Ye'll settle on a husband here or I'll take ye home and pick a man for ye," Robert Baird threatened her. "Yer mam was fifteen when she wed me. Seventeen is nae too young to marry."

Agnes burst into tears, sobbing piteously, but her father was not moved.

Annabella put a comforting arm about her little sister. "Why will ye nae accept Matthew when I believe that ye love him, Aggie?"

"He doesna love me! He has nae said it! He never asks. He only tells me what I am going to do! I'm nae his servant!" Agnes said.

Blessed Mother! Why was it that beautiful girls thought they could have their way in everything? But Agnes was correct in one thing: Matthew was too bossy and set in his ways. But it would be up to Aggie to change that. No one else could do it for her. Annabella sighed. "Ye hae to tell him," she advised Agnes. "If ye care enough for him ye canna refuse him. I dinna want ye unhappy, Aggie, but I do believe ye care."

"He is the only man who can make me angry," Agnes said slowly, "but he also makes me happy," she admitted. "And he is so very handsome. Not as handsome as the earl, but handsome enough to make me the envy of many a woman in the borders when I become his wife.

But I've been so mean, Annabella. Will his offer to Da still stand?"

"We'll only know that if Da gives him an answer," Annabella said.

Agnes looked up at her father. "I'll wed him, Da."

"Good!" Robert Baird said. "I'll be glad to hae this drama over and done wi'."

The earl echoed his father-in-law's sentiments. "Now my brother can stop hiding his love for the wench. I'm tired of his moaning about over her." He sent for his sibling.

"Let us sit together by the fire," Annabella suggested to her sister, taking her hand and drawing her over to a cushioned settle, where they sat down. Their parents remained at the high board with the earl, awaiting Matthew's arrival. "Now you will learn the fine art of patience," Annabella told her sister.

"What is happening?" Agnes wanted to know.

"All is well," Annabella responded reassuringly.

Matthew came into the hall and went directly to his brother. They watched as the four heads at the high board came together. They could not even hear an echo of what was said, but Annabella could well imagine.

Then Matthew came over to where the two young women sat. He bowed politely to them. "Will ye consent to walk wi' me, Agnes?" he asked her, holding out his hand.

"I will," the girl said, taking his hand, standing up.

Then together they walked to the far end of the hall, where they appeared to be engaged in animated conversation.

Annabella got up from her place by the fire and joined the others at the high board. As she reached it she heard her father saying to her husband, "Aggie's dower isn't large, my lord. Each of my daughters has had the same dower, excepting Annabella, who brought ye the land ye wanted instead."

"If such a dower portion was good enough for me, and yer two other sons-in-law, then it is certainly good enough for my brother," the earl reassured the laird. "Especially since Matthew's birth on the wrong side of the blanket dinna bother ye."

"I've come to learn that he is a fine young man, and he hae yer favor," the laird said. "I am content in the match."

"I'm glad," the earl replied. "Agnes's presence is good for Annabella, especially now. I would suggest we hold the wedding sooner than later."

"Agreed," the laird said.

Matthew and Agnes returned from the end of the hall. They were both smiling.

They were in favor of having their wedding celebrated quickly. The marriage contracts were drawn up and signed. On the eighteenth of November the marriage was celebrated in the Duin village kirk. The bride wore a pale blue velvet gown with a cream-and-gold-colored silk damask underskirt. Her beautiful straight brown-blond hair was left loose, but topped with a wreath of dried white heather. A small feast for the family was held afterward. Both Matthew and Agnes seemed calmer now for their union.

A week after the wedding Annabella went into labor. The day had been oddly warm for late November. They watched as a storm blew up seemingly from nowhere, lightning forking down into the green water out over the sea. The storm, Jean said, would blow itself into Ireland, and not disturb them. Under the circumstances Annabella had felt the urge to take a leisurely ride to the village in the dog cart. She had been very restless these past days, which worried the lady Anne.

"'Tis good of ye to visit old Margaret," Jean said, referring to a cottager in the village. "She and her Sim were wed for over forty years. His death was quite a surprise for us all. He seemed indomitable."

"What happened?" the lady Anne asked.

"He just dropped down dead hauling wood the other day, but he was old," Jean said. "Well past seventy, I believe."

They entered the village, greeted by each person they passed. Annabella spoke to all by name, and with a smile. Her mother was impressed by her daughter's gracious behavior, for there were a goodly number of clan folk. The dog cart came to a halt before a small neat cottage, where a smiling elderly woman stood waiting to greet them. Jean and the lady Anne helped Annabella from her transport.

As the Countess of Duin's slippered foot made contact with the earth, there was an odd little sound. Annabella gasped, a look of shock upon her face. She looked down to discover herself standing in a puddle. "Holy Mother!" she cried. "I think my bairn is coming! 'Tis too soon! Holy Mother! Holy Mother! I can feel it."

The two older women took Annabella by her arms and hustled her past the startled old lady into the cottage. Instructing her to lie upon the bed, Jean pushed her mistress's skirts up to see what was happening.

"Holy Mother!" she echoed Annabella. "I can see the head. The bairn is indeed coming."

"We must get her back to the castle," the lady Anne cried, thinking of the well-scrubbed birthing table, the feather bolster and down pillows for her daughter's shoulders and head, the waiting cradle.

"There is nae time for that," Jean said. "If we attempt it Annabella will hae the bairn out on the moor."

"Ohhhhh!" Annabella groaned as a hard pain assaulted her.

Jean shook her head in the negative. "Nae time, madam." She turned to the cottage's tenant. "Margaret, we'll need hot water, and some clean rags if ye hae them."

Margaret nodded, and hobbled about collecting the required items. She also added a bit of ribbon from her sewing box. "To tie the laddie's cord off," she said.

Between them Jean and thc lady Anne quickly stripped Annabella down to her chemise, which Jean then pushed up, revealing her mistress's enormous distended belly.

"Push yer legs up so I can see what's happening." She peered down. "Holy Mary! The wee thing is about to be born! Can ye push, Annabella?"

"Mother of God, if I dinna, I fear I shall burst," Annabella exclaimed. Then she bore down with all of her might and pushed.

"Again!" Jean said. "And again! Ahh, here's the bairn! We hae a lassie!" She held up the bloody infant, who began to squall loudly.

"Let me see her! Let me see her!" Annabella said. But then suddenly she cried out again. "Sweet Jesu! The pain! The pain!"

Jean handed the crying infant to her grandmother. Old Margaret pulled her aside to where she had laid out a basin of warm water, some lamb fat, and a rag to bathe and soothe the infant before she was swaddled.

Annabella screamed aloud. The urge to push down again was building up once more. What was happening? She had already birthed her child. "Jeannie," she cried out. "Help me!" She groaned.

Bending, Jean saw a second head just crowning. "We hae a second bairn!" she said excitedly to the others.

"Twins!" the lady Anne exclaimed, cradling her now swaddled granddaughter. "Ye were a twin, Annabella."

Jean nodded. Obviously Annabella's mother had lost her other bairn, but no nccd to point that out as her young mistress labored to deliver that second bairn.

"Ohhhhhh!" Annabella groaned once more, but her second child was as quick to be born as its sibling had been. It slipped from her body after but two pushes.

A smile lit Jean's face. "'Tis a laddie," she said. "They're both wee, but they're both strong." She turned back to attend to the afterbirth.

And as if to prove her point, the newly born infant began to howl as loudly as his sister had, extremely annoyed at having been pushed from his mother's comfortable, warm, and dark womb. His little face squinched itself into a red wrinkle, and his balled little fists waved in protest. He was quickly bathed and wrapped tightly in swaddling clothes before being placed in his mother's arms.

Annabella was astounded as she looked from one tiny face to the other. Neither of them seemed to have inherited her plain features. These were her bairns. She was a mother now. Her eyes grew wet, and tears slipped down her cheeks as her mother came to kiss her and praise her accomplishment.

Someone had had the presence of mind to send up to the castle. The Earl of Duin had come immediately, and now burst through the door of Margaret's cottage, his handsome face filled with concern for his wife.

"We hae twins, Angus!" she crowed triumphantly. "A lad and a lassie!"

Angus Ferguson glanced at the infants and saw they

were healthy. But it was his wife's face his eyes sought. Kneeling by her bedside, he took her hand in his, kissing it fervently. "Thank ye, sweetheart!" he said to her. "Thank ye!"

"Are they nae beautiful?" she cooed at the babies. "Are they nae perfect?"

"Ye're beautiful in my eyes," he said to her. "Ye're perfect."

"I love ye, Angus," Annabella said boldly to him. She had not until now felt brave enough to admit it to him.

"I love ye more," he surprised her by replying, for neither had he ever until now admitted the emotions that had been filling him for the last months.

"What will ye name them, my lady?" old Margaret said. She was very proud that the earl's heir and daughter and been born in her humble cottage.

"The lad shall be James Robert," the earl decided. "James for the king and Robert for my lady's good sire."

Annabella smiled up at him. She knew the James was for James Hepburn and not the toddler king. "With my lord's permission I should like to name our daughter Anne Margaret," the Countess of Duin said. "Anne for my mother, and Margaret for ye, good dame, in whose house my bairns were born and first saw the light of day."

"Ohh, my lady, such an honor." And the old woman wept.

"We must get my daughter and her bairns back to the castle," the lady Anne said. "When I think of all the preparations made for this birth, now useless . . ." She sighed.

"We'll need a second cradle," Jean said in practical tones. "How did ye know to come?" she asked her brother as she washed up from her labors.

"Little Una ran all the way up to the castle and came to fetch me," he replied.

"Bless the lass," Jean said, nodding. She had thought Annabella a bit sentimental when she had taken the girl in to educate, but the eight-year-old lass was showing a great deal of promise, having been the only one in the village to go for the earl.

A litter was brought down from the castle. It contained a woolen blanket and some furs. Annabella was well wrapped and carried from the cottage, to be put in the litter. The twin infants were snuggled down in the furs with their mother, and the litter was quickly carried back up to the castle. Jean remained to help old Margaret put her dwelling back in order. She sent one of the clansmen up to the castle to fetch fresh bedding for their hostess, for what was there was now wet with blood and birth fluids.

The two afterbirths, which had been saved in a basin, would be buried beneath an oak tree near the castle. They had dug the hole for it just a few weeks prior, lest the ground be frozen too hard when the time came.

Agnes was waiting with her father to greet her sister's return. The laird of Rath voiced his approval at his daughter's success in providing Duin with not just an heir but an heiress. Agnes cooed over the twins, marveling at their miniature perfection.

"Perhaps I'll gie them a playmate one day," she said coyly.

"If I hae not already gotten ye wi' bairn after this week of trying, I am not the man I used to be," her husband boasted, grinning.

"*Matthew!*" Agnes scolded, blushing.

Weakened as she was, Annabella giggled, for, despite being given quarters in an isolated part of the castle,

Matthew was a noisy lover, and his efforts were heard by many.

"Annabella needs to rest," her mother said. "Put the twins in their cradles by the hearth in their mam's bedchamber," she instructed the two little maidservants who stood anxiously nearby. Then she considered. "Has a second cradle been found?"

It had been, and the newborns were now settled within, each lying upon a thick piece of sheepskin that had been set beneath the tiny feather beds for warmth. Miniature down coverlets were placed over the sleeping infants. Annabella was now settled in her own bed, half-asleep, while her mother directed everyone.

The cradle rocker insisted she needed no help. "I hae two legs and feet, my lady," she said. "Two are as easy to rock as one."

"As ye will, then," the proud grandmother said. How well Annabella had done. Despite the tragic loss of her first bairn she had still managed to give her husband two children within two years of marriage. Duin's legacy was safe.

Chapter 10

*W*ith Annabella safely delivered of her bairns, and the weather still favorable, the laird of Rath and his wife departed for their own home. Annabella was sad to see them go, but their visit had been a happy and successful one. With Agnes now wed it was time to seek a wife for their only son and heir. The laird would not be happy until Rob had produced an heir for Rath.

Agnes turned seventeen. The winter set in. Christmas came, then departed. On the feast of Candlemas in February, Agnes announced she was enceinte. The winter dragged on with no visitors and consequently no word of what was going on outside of their little world. The snows piled up in the courtyard. Lambs were born. The days were becoming noticeably longer, but the wolves still howled out on the hillsides in the dark of night, reminding them that winter was not ready yet to relinquish its grip.

One afternoon a large vessel anchored in the cove beneath the castle. A small boat was rowed ashore, to be pulled up on the rocky beach. Its single occupant got out and slowly climbed the barely discernible narrow path up to a small door in the stone walls. He pounded upon the door for a time before someone finally came, opening the small grilled hatch to demand what it was he wanted.

"I've a message for the Earl of Duin from one James Hepburn," the sailor said.

There was the sound of a key turning in a lock, and the hinges creaked resentfully as the small door slowly swung open. The seaman stepped inside and followed the man-at-arms who had opened the door down a long dark corridor lit only by the flickering torch the man ahead of him carried. The walls of the passage were covered in hoarfrost.

The visitor wondered whether it ever melted. They climbed three flights of stairs, finally exiting into a well-lit corridor that led to the hall. At the high board were seated what appeared to be a family.

"My lord," the man-at-arms said, "here is a messenger come for ye."

Angus Ferguson waved his guest forward. "Are ye off the ship now anchored in my cove?" he asked the man.

"Aye, my lord," the sailor answered, pulling off his cap and bowing. "I have a message for ye from a James Hepburn." The man spoke English but his accent indicated it was not his native tongue.

"Where are ye from then?" the earl asked him.

"Orkney, the isles," was his reply.

"Where is Bothwell now?"

"Imprisoned in Denmark, may God hae mercy on him," the seaman responded. Reaching into his shirt, he pulled out a carefully folded parchment tied with a bit of string and sealed with a small blob of wax. He handed it to Angus Ferguson.

Gazing down at the parchment, the Earl of Duin saw Bothwell's rabbit crest imprinted in the wax. Looking up, he said to the messenger, "Find a place for yerself at the trestles and eat." Then, turning back to the parchment in his hand, he broke the seal and slowly unfolded it. There was Bothwell's impatient writing upon it.

Angus, all is lost. I have failed my dearest wife, Mary. I have failed Scotland, and I have failed myself. With no gold or influence left there is no one who will come to my aid, for far too many fear me, and wisely so. I have named my nephew, Francis Stewart, my heir, provided he take the Hepburn name, which I know he will when grown, at his mother's behest. Help my Mary if you can without endangering Duin. I regret little but that I shall never ride my beloved borders again. Remember me, old friend. Bothwell.

Angus felt tears welling up as he read the brief letter. James Hepburn, his friend. The most loyal of the queen's men, gone from Scotland, never to return. Imprisoned. Never to be free. He remembered with a brief smile their days as young men in Paris. He remembered a brave, bold, and dashing man with little tolerance for fools, and yet it was the fools who had triumphed over them all. What a tragedy!

"What is it?" Annabella asked, seeing the play of emotions across his face.

He handed her the parchment. "Read it," he said.

She did, and her own tears slipped down her cheeks. "Is there nothing we can do to help him?" Annabella asked, looking up from the parchment to her husband. "Nothing at all? There has to be something."

"Nothing," Angus Ferguson said. "James Hepburn was always a gambler, and he gambled he could help the queen control her lords if he were her husband. This is one of the few times he has cast the die and lost."

"Ye hae gold," Annabella said.

"And I will use it to help make him comfortable in his prison, but if I used it to attempt to engineer his escape, to finance another rebellion, I could cost Duin dearly. Moray is in power now. He hae crowned the queen's bairn, and there, sweetheart, is an end to it. Bothwell knows that. He is nae a fool except in love."

"I understand," Annabella replied, "but it still breaks my heart to know that Bothwell will die in a foreign place, and be buried in a lonely, unmarked grave. And the queen? What will happen to the queen?"

"I think after he feels he has the reins of power firmly in his grasp, Moray will put his half sister in a more hospitable place than Lochleven Castle. He is a wily devil, but he was always treated like the prince he might have been but for the accident of his birth by Marie de Guise, who raised him with the rest of her husband, James the Fifth's bastards. He grew up at Stirling with Mary before she went to France, and he has always had a fondness for her, even if her behavior has confounded him," the earl said.

But Mary Stuart had had a year to ponder her situation. Her half brother, James Stewart, should have known better than to think he might force her to his will. Had he treated her with firm kindness, housed her as befitted her position, and allowed her small access to her little son, he might have avoided what happened next.

Mary had appealed to Parliament several times in the early days of her imprisonment. She wanted an opportunity to explain her actions. Parliament instead, under instruction from Moray and his cohorts, declared James Hepburn, Earl of Bothwell, guilty of the murder of Henry, Lord Darnley. That there was no real proof of this mattered not at all. They also declared their lawful queen his accomplice in the murder, using forged documents that they brought forth from a silver box that belonged to the queen as proof of her guilt. Even then, having gained their objective, they did not refrain from mistreating their prisoner. It was a serious miscalculation.

Mary was treated very badly. She was confined to two rooms on the third floor of Lochleven Castle. It was cold and dank. She had no privacy. Her movements were severely limited, and she was constantly watched. She had no spiritual comfort to sustain her. Angry and desperate, she reacted rashly.

Without James Hepburn by her side to temper her recklessness, Mary executed an audacious escape from her island prison. No sooner had she gained the shore of the mainland with her cohorts than her followers began flocking to her banner. She repudiated her abdication, which she said had been forced upon her. She was Scotland's queen, and she would retake her throne from those who had stolen it from her while hiding behind her infant son to justify their actions.

Moray was furious, but he knew his sister was no tactician. Without Bothwell to plan her battles, she was certain to make an error. It was that error that would cost her not just her freedom, but Scotland for good. He watched and decided what to do as Mary Stuart crossed the Firth of Forth. She had, Moray knew, two choices open to her if she were to regain her throne. She could march to Edinburgh with her ever-increasing army, forcing Parliament into session, and plead her cause in order to regain her position by legal means. Or she could make a run for the impregnable Dunbarton Castle in the west, and wait while her armies were increased before taking Scotland back by force.

Moray knew his sister was no fool, but he also knew she was ruled by her emotions. Parliament's obdurate refusal to allow her to come before them a year ago would still rankle her. She would have no faith in a Parliament that had scorned her. Mary Stuart would head for Dunbarton, and the Earl of Moray knew it, and planned for it.

He would meet her forces before she could even reach the security of that castle.

Moray had a smaller force than his half sister, but his soldiers were better trained.

Along the road to the village of Langside he positioned his men behind the tall, thick hedges lining the road. As Mary's forces marched down the road, the musketeers hidden behind the greenery fired volley after volley. Within a short time Mary's superior forces, bereft of any real commander, broke up in disarray and fled the battlefield. From her vantage point on a nearby hill, the queen could see everything. She was finally convinced to flee the scene, and did so.

Late on a mid-May afternoon, the watch atop Duin Castle saw a small party of riders coming their way. As they came closer it was noted that, while armed, they were few, and apparently not hostile. They galloped across the oaken drawbridge into the courtyard. The first man off his horse called to the servant who stood in an open door at the top of a flight of steps, "Tell yer master the queen begs shelter!"

The shocked servant turned and dashed back into the castle, running for the hall, where he delivered his message. They had been at the high board eating the main meal of the day. The Earl of Duin jumped to his feet, coming down from his place to hurry and greet the queen. She was still seated upon her horse when he reached his courtyard. He noted she looked worn and tired. He bowed.

"Madam, welcome to Duin Castle," he said.

"Moray's forces are certain to be behind me, my lord," the queen said. "Are ye sure ye would welcome me?"

"Ye are my queen," Angus Ferguson heard himself say. *Jesu!* Was he mad?

But then Annabella was there by his side. "Come into the hall, madam," she said. "I suspect ye cannot remain long wi' us, but 'tis an honor to hae ye here. There is hot food, and wine for ye in the hall." She curtsied to the queen, then looked to one of the openmouthed stablemen. "See to the horses."

"Come into the hall," the earl echoed his wife's invitation.

Once inside, the queen sank into a high-backed upholstered chair by one of the hearths. Wine was immediately brought to her. "It was a disaster," Mary Stuart said without waiting for anyone to ask her what had happened. "Argyll was a poor leader. His troops fled the field in the face of a much smaller force. We needed my husband's leadership, but Bothwell is gone. Gone." Her voice faded away.

Annabella noticed that the queen's beautiful fingers tightened about the stem of the wine goblet as she spoke. "We received a message from James late this winter. He is imprisoned in Denmark. Had he not been, madam, he would have been by yer side."

"He tried to rally the isles for me, but Moray and his ilk hounded him. He barely escaped them last summer," the queen said. "I have been told the tale by several, and each time something new is added to it. In Norway he was arrested by kinsmen of his former mistress, and jailed without charges."

"The messenger who came to Duin was from a Danish ship," the earl said.

The queen nodded. "He was taken from Norway to Dragsholm Castle in the north of Zealand. They say the conditions in which he is being kept are deplorable." She began to weep softly.

"We sent a purse to ease his days," Annabella said in an effort to comfort her guest, who was now struggling to regain mastery over herself.

"They will take yer gold and line their own pockets," Lord Claud Hamilton, who stood by the queen's side, said. "Our information is very accurate."

"What does it serve Denmark to mistreat the husband of Scotland's queen?" Angus Ferguson asked quietly.

"Perhaps ye dinna hear it, for ye are quite isolated at Duin," Lord Claud noted, dropping his voice so his words did not distress the queen further, "but James Hepburn was outlawed last summer. He is considered nothing more than a common felon. His jailers might use yer gold to better his conditions, but the Danish king has forbidden it. Denmark has already given Scotland one queen. I suspect they look to give it another. They would keep the favor of wee James's guardians for that day, for they are Protestants too. Dinna throw good coin after bad, my lord."

"We canna remain long," Geordie Douglas, another of the queen's companions, said. "We would not bring Moray to yer door. He will be a bad enemy to have."

"Ye must eat before ye go," Annabella insisted, helping the queen up and to the high board, where the servants were quickly placing bowls and platters of food.

There was sliced salmon on a plate with cress, a large roasted turkey, venison, a hot rabbit stew, a bowl of new peas, bread, butter, and cheese. Their guests ate heartily and quickly. They drank down the rich red wine. The queen smiled at the small dish of tiny wild strawberries in a thick cream set before her as the pewter plates were removed.

It was a charming and delicate touch. She smiled gratefully at Annabella, who nodded in silent understanding.

They still had several hours of daylight ahead of them. As the Earl and Countess of Duin escorted their guests back into the courtyard to their horses, Angus asked the queen, "Where will ye go, madam?"

"Why, to England to beg sanctuary of my good cousin Elizabeth," Mary replied.

Angus frowned. "I dinna think that wise, madam," he told her candidly. "Would ye nae be wiser to go to France? Ye hae family there to help ye. Ye hae lands of yer own. Ye should be far safer in France than ye will be in England."

"Nay, my good lord," Mary Stuart said. "I must not put the open sea between myself and Scotland. My sister queen is a fair woman, and wise. She will shelter me and come to my aid. I will return to Scotland. Heads must cool. Only then can we negotiate this difficulty between myself and my lords."

"I must trust in yer queenly wisdom, madam," Angus Ferguson said, bowing. Then he helped the queen to mount her horse.

"*Adieu, mon ami,*" Mary Stuart said, giving him her hand to kiss. Then, with her small party of retainers, she departed Duin.

Angus and Annabella watched her go out from the courtyard, over the drawbridge, and onto the road. Free of the castle, the riders picked up speed and headed south. Soon they were nothing more than a cloud of dust, and even the dust faded quickly away. The Earl and Countess of Duin returned to their hall.

"I hope ye haven't put us all in danger, sheltering her like that," Matthew said to his brother as Angus came into the hall. He had been absent during the queen's brief visit, but as steward he would have known she was there.

"I could hardly deny her entry to the castle," Angus said dryly. "I will plead ignorance to any who would accuse me otherwise, little brother. We know little of what goes on past the borders of our lands, Matthew. Do ye know what happened?"

"I know what I heard, and I hae surmised the rest," Matthew replied.

"Aye, 'tis obvious she escaped Lochleven," the earl said.

"Escaped, and fought a battle she lost wi' Moray," his sibling responded. "There will be hell to pay now. If anyone learns she came here, Angus . . ."

"She's fleeing into England, Matthew. 'Tis the end of it now. Bothwell is gone, and the queen is gone. She thinks the English queen will help her, but Elizabeth Tudor is too canny to involve herself in Mary Stuart's debacle. When that finally becomes clear to Scotland's queen, she will take the advice of those few around her and go back to France. 'Tis her only alternative."

"Catherine de' Medicis will hardly be glad to see her," Matthew said. "They enjoy causing difficulty in Scotland. The borders will nae forget our queen's uncle Henry soon."

"Elizabeth will nae help the woman who calls herself queen of Scotland, England, and France," Angus responded. "Remember there are still those who consider the English queen bastard-born, and if that were proven so, Mary Stuart is the true heir to England's throne through her grandmother, Margaret Tudor. As long as Mary stays in Scotland, Elizabeth remains her most beloved cousin. She will not readily welcome the fugitive queen to her shores."

"And none of it has anything to do wi' us," Annabella said. "Duin is safe, and nothing else matters."

Both men chuckled. Annabella had become Duin's greatest defender.

Several weeks later, in early June, a ship anchored in Duin's cove. A messenger brought Angus Ferguson a letter. He read it and then announced, "I must go to France. The last of my mother's family has died, and their lands are left to me. I dinna want lands in France, but it is required I appear in person to first claim them, in order to sell them to the neighbor who wishes to have them."

"Could ye nae hae Jamie do it for ye?" Matthew asked. "Scotland is in such disorder right now, I fear should ye leave us."

"James is in Rome. It is quicker for me to go to France and return than to send to Rome so Jamie might go to France for me. It will nae take me long to complete this business. Besides, Matthew, ye are completely capable of managing in my absence," the earl said. "The ship in the cove will take me, and when I have finished I will find the first vessel available to return me home via Leith."

Matthew Ferguson did not look happy, but when he spoke with his own mother, she said, "The earl knows what must be done, and he will do it. His mother's family had but one son. I do not believe he ever wed. The earl must claim those lands, even if he does not choose to retain them. I suspect it is the du Bottilier family who would have those lands. They are good folk."

Annabella was not pleased that Angus would leave them. He came to her bed that night, climbing in and pulling her into his arms. "Why can ye nae send Matthew to act in yer stead?" she asked him as his lips brushed first her shoulder and then her neck.

"It would be considered boorish and an insult if I did nae go myself. This is a matter of respect and manners, as well as commerce," he explained to her.

"Matthew is too hard a master," Annabella said. "He dinna understand that ye rule here wi' a firm hand but a kind heart. He believes he must be harsh in order to live up to yer expectations." She snuggled closer to him.

"Woman, I dinna choose to speak on ordinary household matters now. I want to make love to ye," he growled into her ear, then nipped at the lobe.

She felt a delicious shiver race down her backbone. Still, she protested softly, "But, Angus . . ."

He stopped her mouth with a long, hot kiss. "I will nae be gone long," he said, and began to kiss her again.

She didn't want to argue. His kisses were intoxicating. She kissed him back with equal passion. All would be well, Annabella decided. Matthew wouldn't have enough time to irritate too many people. Annabella gave herself over to her husband's hands and mouth with a gusty sigh.

Her perfect breasts had become even more perfect since the birth of the twins. They were rounder and firmer, especially since she had turned the bairns over to two wet nurses. He nuzzled at their nipples, and she murmured with pleasure. He licked at one, encircling the pert point with the tip of his tongue. Finally, unable to resist, his mouth closed over the nipple and he sucked hard.

"Ahhh," Annabella sighed. "And ye would leave me bereft of such pleasures while ye cavort in France."

He grinned. "Ye'll appreciate me all the more then when I return home, lass." He chuckled, lifting his head from her breast.

Wrapping her arms about him, she drew him down. "I'm filled wi' fever for ye, my lord husband," she told him provocatively, shifting so that he now lay between her thighs.

"Ye're a bad wench," he told her, sliding his big body so that he might bury his face in her and lick at her hidden treasures. He peeled her already moist nether lips open, his tongue homing in on that tempting little bit of flesh that seemed to beckon to him. He began licking at it, and when it had swollen itself, his lips closed around it so he might suck it hard. She cried out and her body shuddered. He sucked it again, twice, hard, in succession, and her body bucked beneath his mouth. He moved his head so that he might thrust his tongue into her pearl-dewed sheath, pushing it back and forth teasingly.

"Ohhh, God!" Annabella half sobbed. "Dinna taunt me so, Angus!"

"Ye taste delicious," he told her. "I want to recall the taste and scent of ye on my tongue and in my nostrils each time I think of ye while I am in France. It will but encourage me to hurry back home to ye, sweetheart." Then he ceased his torture and, mounting her, thrust deep into her eager body.

She wrapped herself about him, clinging to him, her

nails raking down his long back as he pleasured them both to extreme ecstasy. They slept briefly, and then made love again, Annabella riding her husband until he shouted with his delight, finally rolling her onto her back and fucking her until she too was screaming with pleasure. They fell asleep once again, his hand filled with one of her breasts as her delicious little bottom pressed into him.

When Annabella awoke he was gone. Instinct bade her rise and run to her windows. The vessel that had been anchored in Duin's cove had hoisted its sails, and was even now sailing past the point into the open waters of the sea. She leaned upon the stone sill, watching it go, and wept, but there was no help for it. Her husband was on his way to France. He had to go, but Annabella could not evade a tiny curl of worry that settled in her heart and mind.

Angus had been gone a week when a troop of horsemen came down the road. Matthew had ordered the drawbridge kept up ever since his brother's departure. The visitors were forced to stop at the edge of the cliff while the watch demanded their credentials and the man leading the troop demanded entry. Matthew was called for, and hurried to the parapet of the entrance.

"I am Matthew Ferguson, steward of Duin Castle, and half brother to the earl," he called down. "Please identify yerself, and state yer business at Duin."

"Why is yer drawbridge up?" demanded the unknown gentleman.

"We have been informed that there is civil war in the land," Matthew said. "It is prudent to be cautious in such times."

"I am Donal Stewart, sent by the Earl of Moray to Duin to speak wi' the earl," came the reply.

"My brother is away from Duin at this time," Matthew responded.

"I will nae discuss my business wi' Duin while standing outside of its gates, sir. We are but six men. I bid ye lay down the drawbridge and gie us entry."

"Let him in, Matthew," Annabella said, for she had followed him to the parapet to learn who their visitors were.

"We hae only his word for who he is, and from where he comes," Matthew replied stubbornly. "I am responsible for the castle."

"Lower the drawbridge," Annabella repeated. "Do ye think six men can take the castle? Do ye wish to hac Duin incur the wrath of the Earl of Moray? If ye will nae admit Donal Stewart, I will gie the order to do so. Remember I am the lady here."

"Lower the drawbridge," Matthew said. He glared at her. "Remember yer place, Annabella," he told her. "I am responsible for Duin in Angus's absence."

"Nay, Matthew, remember yers," she snapped back. "I am the Countess of Duin." Then, turning, she descended from the parapet and hurried down into the hall to grect her guest, arriving just a moment before he strode into the chamber, his men at his back. "Welcome to Duin, sir," Annabella said. "I am the Countess of Duin. I regret that my husband is nae here at this time." She signaled a servant to bring Donal Stewart wine.

He came forward, kissing the hand she offered him. Then he took the goblet the servant offered, swallowing half of it down, for his throat was parched. "Thank ye, madam," he said. "I bring Duin greetings from the Earl of Moray." She was a plain woman, but her manner was gracious, he thought. His master, who had sired him with a mistress, had sent him here after hearing several troubling reports. But this woman hardly looked like a rebel or a conspirator.

"Please seat yerself, sir, and if ye can, disclose the nature of yer visit to Duin," Annabella invited him, noting that Matthew had now come into the hall. She waved him over. "This is Duin's steward, Matthew Ferguson, who will sit wi' us, sir, while ye tell me why ye are here."

"There hae been reports that Duin hosted the escaped prisoner Mary Stuart, madam. My master, the Earl of Moray, is troubled by these reports, especially given that yer husband is known to have been a compatriot of the outlaw James Hepburn." Donal Stewart sipped from his goblet, attempting to analyze her reaction.

"Why, sir, 'tis well-known here in the western borders that Angus Ferguson and James Hepburn were old friends from their boyhood. But the last time my husband saw Bothwell was before he wed the queen. He disapproved of such a union, and returned home before it was even celebrated. I am certain my lord of Moray knows that."

"Did the queen come to Duin after her escape from Lochleven?" Donal Stewart asked her again.

"She did, but we were nae aware that she was an escaped prisoner," Annabella said. "Ye see, here at Duin we are apt to learn news of import, if indeed we learn it at all, long after the fact. The queen stopped here briefly, nae more than three or four hours, before riding on. It was she who told us all that had happened in that past year, sir. We knew it not before her arrival. And then she was gone. Some in her small party wanted her to go to France, but she seemed determined to go over the border into England. How can she be our queen if she is in England, sir?" Annabella asked him ingenuously.

Matthew Ferguson held his breath, waiting to see if Donal Stewart believed her. It had never occurred to him that Annabella could be so clever. Did his brother know?

Donal Stewart listened. The plain-faced Countess of Duin spoke candidly and without hesitation. She was obviously hiding nothing. The dour steward by her side was silent, but his face showed no emotions, which it would have if the lady were lying. "Bothwell is outlawed, and imprisoned in Denmark," Donal Stewart said. "Mary Stuart is gone into England, and it is her son, James the Sixth, who now sits on Scotland's throne."

"May the Lord have mercy on the wee laddie," Annabella replied.

"The regent is James Stewart, Earl of Moray," Donal Stewart informed her. "'Tis he who will act in his nephew's best interests."

"Of course he will," Annabella responded. "How fortunate the little king is to hae him. The wee lad is wi'out mam or da, sister or brother. I hae a son and a daughter, sir."

Then she gave him a smile. "If my simple explanations have relieved any concerns the regent might hae about Duin, I am glad. Ye will, of course, remain the night wi' us, sir?"

"Gladly!" Donal Stewart told her. "We sleep rough when we travel in the service of the Earl of Moray. A hot meal and a good bed will be a welcome luxury, my lady."

Annabella arose from her chair. "I will go and tell the cook," she said with a curtsy to him.

"The Earl of Duin has obviously been blessed in his

mate," Donal Stewart noted. "She would appear to be a wise and prudent woman."

"Aye," Matthew Ferguson said, keeping his voice impartial. He was astounded by Annabella's behavior. She had lied, to some extent, but Moray's messenger had never suspected her at all, for her manner appeared to be open and frank. Annabella appeared to be a woman with absolutely nothing to hide. Nothing at all. He would have believed her himself had he not known better. At the high board later, he watched as Annabella drew from Donal Stewart the latest news.

The lords were taking sides, for while shocked by Mary Stuart's behavior, many had disagreed with the harsh treatment that had been meted out to the queen. They saw her half brother's actions for exactly what they were: a grab for power. The earls and the lairds were choosing sides. Those who supported Mary were called the Queen's Men, and those who supported the regent Moray, who now spoke for his infant nephew, James, were known as the King's Men.

"I can certainly understand how difficult it has been for your master," Annabella sympathized. "Born a king's first bairn, yet nae a king himself. And so loyal to his sister, the queen." She shook her head. "More wine, Donal Stewart? I would nae hae ye say that the hospitality at Duin was lacking."

"Certainly nae lacking, my lady," Donal Stewart said. His belly was full with well-cooked meat, fresh bread, and good cheese. "The English queen is a clever woman," he told them. "She is calling together a conference to arbitrate between the warring parties. 'Tis to begin in October in York."

"Can she do that?" Annabella wondered aloud.

"My master says that in times past, the first English

Edward arbitrated a disputed succession when the little queen known as the Maid of Norway died," Donal Stewart answered. "My master says 'tis bold of the English queen, but a fair solution."

"I think that the English queen is very clever," Annabella remarked, "for she can surely nae find for either side wi'out incurring the wrath of the other. An infant king of Scotland will keep Scotland minding its own affairs, and nae plaguing England."

"How wise ye are, my lady," Donal Stewart said admiringly.

Annabella smiled. "Ye flatter me, sir," she told him. Then she rose from the high board. "If ye will excuse me," she said, "I must attend to my bairns now. The steward will show ye yer place for the night. Yer men are welcome to sleep in one of the barns." She curtsied, and was quickly gone.

He watched her go. "A fine woman, for all her lack of beauty. Yer earl is a fortunate man."

"Aye, my brother treasures her greatly," Matthew said.

"Yer brother?"

"Like ye, I was born on the other side of the blanket," Matthew told him. "But our da valued all his bairns."

"My father is the same way," Donal Stewart responded, nodding. "Blood is the strongest tie. He never denied me, gave me the right to his name, and I am proud to serve him in whatever capacity I can."

"They say ye Stewarts are warmhearted and hot-blooded," Matthew said.

Donal Stewart chuckled. "'Tis true," he admitted with a grin.

"Would ye like a bedmate tonight?" Matthew asked. "The bed space is more than big enough for two."

"Aye, 'tis most hospitable of ye," Donal Stewart said, well pleased. The little maidservant they sent was round, with sweet breath, and was very willing to accommodate his needs. He slept soundly after their romp. And he had learned where the earl was, which his master would find interesting.

In the morning the Countess of Duin was in the hall early to see that her guest and his men were well fed before sending them back to the Earl of Moray. Donal Stewart noted the two healthy bairns with their nursemaids crawling on clothes spread near one of the hearths. To his surprise he saw they were twins, a lad and a little lass. A trencher of bread was placed in front of him, and quickly filled with hot oat stirabout. A bowl of hard-cooked eggs and a platter with several rashers of bacon along with cheese and a fresh cottage loaf appeared.

"Ale, wine, or cider?" his hostess asked him.

"Ale," he said, spooning the hot cereal into his mouth. It had bits of dried apple in it, and the heavy cream she poured onto it made it taste wonderful. "Where is yer husband, madam?" he asked her as he ate.

"In France," she answered him without hesitation.

"Ye dinna tell me that last night," he said.

"But, sir, ye never asked me," Annabella replied.

"Why is he in France?" Donal Stewart persisted.

"His mam was French," Annabella explained. "The last of her family hae died, and he hae inherited their lands. He must appear before a French magistrate in order to claim them and then sell them to a neighbor, for Angus hae no wish to hold lands in France. He says Duin is all he can manage."

It was a reasonable explanation, and offered without any hesitancy. Still, he would add it to the report he was planning to give the Earl of Moray. One could never be certain where traitors lurked. Donal Stewart knew his father was not the most beloved of men.

Annabella walked with her guest to the courtyard, and ordered the drawbridge lowered so Donal Stewart and his party might depart. "Please tell the regent that Duin is and always hae been loyal to their king. May God go wi' ye, Donal Stewart."

"I shall give my master yer message, my lady, and tell him of yer kind hospitality, for which I thank ye," he said. Then, turning his horse, he signaled his men and they rode forth from Duin. He wondered who had brought this isolated castle and its unimportant lord to Moray's attention. But there were surely no traitors at Duin. Although the steward had been loath to allow them entry, the countess had not hesitated. He and his men had been well treated, and his questions had been answered to his satisfaction.

When they had cleared it the drawbridge was raised once again. Annabella turned to reenter her home. Angus would not be pleased when he learned of Donal Stewart's visit. Who else had known that Mary Stuart had briefly stopped at Duin?

And why would they attempt to implicate the Fergusons in some unspoken plot? She wondered if they would ever know.

Chapter 11

"*Y*e were clever wi' Moray's man," Matthew Stewart told Annabella afterward. "I wonder if my brother knows how clever ye are."

"I suspect Angus knows far more about me than ye do, Matthew," she told him. "After initial caution there was nae reason nae to admit Donal Stewart and his party into the castle. If I hae allowed ye to continue, ye would hae aroused his suspicions."

"Suspicions? Why would anyone be suspicious of Duin? We hae always lived in peace, disturbing none," Matthew replied.

"Did ye nae realize that someone learned that the queen sheltered here briefly? They reported this fact to Moray in an effort to curry favor wi' him. It is obvious that the land is nae secure. Moray must hold his position by might as well as right. Any threat must be investigated."

"Ye lied to him," Matthew said.

Annabella laughed. "Only a little bit, and nae so much as to be caught by a stranger. Would ye hae had me tell him the full truth? 'Tis true that I prevaricated a wee bit, but Donal Stewart did nae know it. I answered his questions wi'out demurring, and in such a manner as to prove our innocence in any crime that might be charged against Duin. His report to my lord Moray will calm any fears the regent might hae toward us."

"Perhaps such pure innocence will but arouse Moray's suspicions further," Matthew said. "Duin canna be put in danger. Ye hae bairns to consider, and my Aggie is full wi' our bairn."

"Duin is nae in danger," Annabella reassured him. "Angus will be back soon."

The Earl of Moray had more important matters to concern him than Duin. He listened to his bastard son's report of his visit and asked, "Did ye believe them?"

"Aye," Donal Stewart said. "Duin is a very isolated holding. I am nae surprised they did nae know what was happening. And too their earl is of nae importance. Had ye ever heard of him before this rumor was brought to ye, my lord?"

"Aye, actually I did. He was one of Bothwell's groomsmen when he wed Jean Gordon, but I had nae heard of him until then. His wife, however, is another matter. It was she who defended my sister's body from harm when that wretch Riccio was disposed of, by flinging herself in front of the queen. That is the kind of loyalty a ruler hopes for but seldom receives," the Earl of Moray said.

"Only one small matter caused me pause," Donal Stewart said. "The Earl of Duin was not in his castle, but according to his wife in France settling a family matter. His mam was a Frenchwoman, it seems. The young countess did not demur when I asked her about it, my lord. Even though the history of the Fergusons of Duin is that of a clan avoiding controversy at almost all costs, Scotland is at war wi' itself now. Was the settling of an estate so important that a man would leave his holding, his wife and bairns, to travel to France in such a time? Not being a man wi' lands, I cannot say, but I think I might have erred on the side of caution and not traveled right now."

"So the question becomes, why did the Earl of Duin travel to France?" Moray said.

"It could be for just the purpose told me," Donal Stewart replied.

"Or it could be something else entirely," the Earl of Moray said thoughtfully. "It could be for the purpose of treason, of bringing aid of one kind or another to my sister. I must learn the truth of this matter, Donal. Ye hae done well wi' this matter so far. I will leave it in yer capable hands to discover exactly what is going on. Ye hae my permission to do whatever ye must."

"And if the earl is caught in treason, my lord?" Donal Stewart asked.

"See that he does not return to Duin. I hae no time for trials and public executions wi' the Queen's Men besieging me at every turn," the Earl of Moray said.

Donal Stewart bowed to his father and departed his presence. He knew the network of spies available to him in France. He would contact them and begin his investigation as quickly as possible. It was likely to come to nothing, but one never knew what one would find.

The Earl of Duin had reached Brittany after a rough voyage that had taken him into the Irish Sea, past the Isle of Man, into St. George's Channel down the west coast of England, around Land's End, and across the English Channel to France. He landed at Saint-Pol and, hiring a horse, rode to the estate where his mother had grown up. It was near Saint-Brieuc.

The small château in which she had spent her early years was in a state of sad repair, but he was able to live in it during his stay, cared for by two ancient servants with nowhere else to go. He would remember before he left to pension them off so they would not end their days in abject poverty. He presented his credentials to the village magistrate the day after his arrival. They were accepted, and he was free then to sell the property. To his surprise he found there were two bidders for the Mont de Devereaux lands.

The village magistrate offered to advise him, and Angus accepted.

"The lands are fair enough, and arable," he noted, "and as they match Monsieur Claude's lands, I understand his wanting to purchase them. But who is this second bidder? Is he also a local man?"

"*Non*," the magistrate said. "I do not know who he is, monsieur, but his offer is twice Monsieur Claude's offer. I should take it, for it is likely you will not receive another offer so fine. What does it matter who he is? I have seen the color of his gold."

But the laird of Duin was suspicious, and asked to meet with both of his prospective purchasers.

Monsieur Claude was a wealthy merchant. He wanted the Mont de Devereaux lands for his second son and his family. Monsieur Reynaud, however, admitted to seeking to purchase the land for his master.

"What is your master's name?" the earl asked.

"Why should his name matter to you, my lord? Is the offer not enough? If it is not I am certain I can arrange for my master to increase it to your satisfaction," Monsieur Reynaud replied sharply.

"I will not sell the lands belonging to my mother's family to a stranger, no matter the amount," Angus Ferguson said in a hard voice. "That you are not willing to divulge his name leads me to consider that he seeks the land for a dishonest purpose."

"Very well, my lord, if you insist upon knowing, the name of the family seeking these lands is de Guise."

Hearing it, Angus Ferguson grew angry. "*Non!*" he said in a hard voice.

"My lord!" Monsieur Reynaud cried. "You have but to name your price."

"Do you take me for a greedy fool?" the earl said. "Or perhaps just a fool, that I would sell these lands to the maternal family of Mary Stuart? You do not wish to buy the land. You wish to buy me. *Non!* Never!"

"Monsieur, you have but to carry a single message to your queen." The agent of the de Guises looked extremely distressed.

"Mary Stuart is in England," Angus responded. "I am in Scotland. While I am not pleased by the manner in which it was done, Queen Mary has been removed from her position, and her son crowned in her stead. The Fergusons are loyal to the head that wears the crown, monsieur, and the bairn James now wears it. Should the queen be returned one day to her rightful place, then I will be unquestioningly loyal to her. Until then I choose to stay free of the entanglements of politics. *Non!* I most certainly will not carry any messages for the de Guises."

"She is not so far away that you could not cross the border to deliver my master's message," Monsieur Reynaud said. "Or if that were not possible, we could arrange to send a messenger for our correspondence. It is difficult to reach her now, and her family is concerned by this lack of communication. We suspect the English of blocking it."

Angus Ferguson snorted. "She should not have gone

into England. She should have come to France, monsieur, but she did not. Now she is caught in a trap of her own making. A disturbed Scotland fighting a civil war is more to England's liking than Mary Stuart firmly upon her throne." He turned to the astounded merchant, who had been listening to every word uttered between the earl and the de Guise family agent. "You may have the Mont de Devereaux lands, Monsieur Claude. Your offer is accepted. When the village magistrate is notified by my bankers in Paris that your monies have been deposited, then he will turn over the deed of ownership to you."

"Monsieur, I protest!" Monsieur Reynaud said.

"The lands are mine, monsieur, and I have the right to sell to whomever I chose," the earl said. "Now get you gone back to your masters. Tell them that the Fergusons of Duin are honorable men and cannot be bought. The matter is closed."

"Thank you, monsieur, thank you!" Monsieur Claude said, shaking the earl's hand and bowing profusely over and over again.

"Your offer was fair," the earl replied. "I wish your son and his family many years of happiness as the owners of Mont de Devereaux. I intend pensioning off the two elderly servants still residing in the house, but they seem capable of serving if they choose. You might value their knowledge of the château."

"Of course! Of course!" Monsieur Claude responded, his plump face wreathed in smiles. Then he hurried off with a final flurry of *merci*s.

The earl noted that Monsieur Reynaud had vanished after being rebuffed that final time. He was relieved to have the man gone, and furious to think that the family of Mary Stuart believed he could be bribed in such an outrageous manner. Speaking with the magistrate that same day, he arranged for the two old servants to receive a pension, and as an afterthought purchased two tiny cottages for them, as the estate cottages would not be available to them now. He signed the papers that, upon deposit of the purchase price, would turn over Mont de Devereaux to Monsieur Claude. Then he paid the magistrate double his fee to make certain all went as he ordered it.

The magistrate smiled toothily at him. "Monsieur is most generous," he said. "Everything shall be exactly as you have requested."

"I had not a doubt," the earl answered, shaking the man's hand. "You have been most helpful, and I am grateful."

Early the next morning Angus Ferguson rode back to Saint-Pol, where he purchased the animal he had been riding. He was not of a mind for another long voyage and had decided to follow the French coast north, checking in each port for a vessel bound for Berwick-upon-Tweed. From Berwick he could ride cross-country to Duin. It would be far quicker than retracing his steps by sea or even just sailing from Saint-Pol to Leith, and then riding southwest to his home.

Finally at Calais he found a small merchant vessel that carried raw wool and coal from the north of England. It had just unloaded its cargo a few days earlier and was ready to return home, its belly now filled with wine casks. It would be making stops at several small ports before finally reaching Berwick. Still, it was quicker than he had hoped. At each port the cargo was quickly unloaded, and they were off again on the next tide. It was the end of August when the Earl of Duin finally disembarked in Berwick. Having sold his horse in Calais, he now sought another, and with the purchase made, he set off for Duin, riding over the hills dividing England and Scotland.

After several days the landscape became more and more familiar, until he knew he was riding his own lands. Soon he was smelling the faint sweet scent of the Irish Sea, and then there was Duin below him. He stopped to enjoy the view of it. Matthew wisely had the drawbridge up. Angus Ferguson had carefully avoided several large armed parties of riders in his travels from Berwick. Scotland had obviously not settled itself yet.

He rode down the hillside at a leisurely pace, giving the men-at-arms on the walls time to recognize their master. He knew they had when the drawbridge was lowered.

Pushing his mount into a canter, he crossed the courtyard, brought his animal to a halt, and dismounted.

"Welcome home, my lord!" the stable lad greeted him as he took hold of the horse so he might lead him to the stables.

"Thank ye, lad," the earl said. Where was Annabella? Certainly someone had gone to fetch her when they recognized him. He strode into the house to the hall, where he found his family gathered, and with them a tall stranger.

"Angus!" Annabella ran to him. "Agree to whatever is asked of ye," she whispered into his ear, and then kissed him heartily.

"My lord." The stranger stepped forward as the earl released his wife. "My name is Donal Stewart. I am in the service of the Earl of Moray, who has sent me to Duin. Ye are suspected of treason against His Most High Majesty, James the Sixth."

Angus Ferguson's jaw dropped in surprise. "I hae

committed nae treason," he said. "The Fergusons of Duin are peaceable folk, and loyal to their ruler."

"Ah, and therein lies the problem. Which ruler do ye acknowledge? The royal whore, Mary Stuart, or King James?"

"He who holds Scotland is my king," the earl said quietly.

"Ye hae been in France," Donal Stewart said.

"Aye. I went to sell a bit of property I had inherited from my mother's family," Angus answered.

"Where in France exactly were ye?" Donal Stewart asked him.

"In Brittany, near Saint-Brieuc, a village called Mont de Devereaux."

"To whom did ye sell yer property, my lord?" Moray's man inquired.

"To a well-to-do local merchant, one Monsieur Claude. He wanted it for his second son and his son's family," the earl answered. "Why do ye ask?"

"Ye did not sell yer property to an agent of the de Guise family, my lord?"

How the hell had Moray learned of the de Guises' attempt to subvert his loyalty? Angus wondered. "When I went to France I was told there was but one buyer for my land, Monsieur Claude. But when I met with him and the village magistrate, there was another man, Monsieur Reynaud, in the employ of the de Guise family. He offered me double what the property was worth. In exchange I would carry a message from them to Mary Stuart. I refused. I am nae a traitor, sir."

"Yet ye came home through England," Donal Stewart noted.

"Aye, I rode the French coast north to Calais, seeking a vessel to either Berwick or Leith. It was quicker than retracing my steps from the cove beneath this castle to France," the earl explained. "I dinna wish to be away from my family any longer than necessary, but I carried nae message for Mary Stuart. How would I have gotten it to her if I did?"

"Where are the monies ye obtained in exchange for yer lands, my lord?" Donal Stewart asked him.

"They were to be placed with my bankers in Paris for the use of my brother James, who is a priest in Rome, and my sister Mary, who is in a convent in Spain."

Another man entered the hall and whispered something to Donal Stewart. The Earl of Moray's messenger seemed disturbed by what he heard, but then he looked up. "A packet sealed with the de Guise crest has been found in yer saddlebags, my lord, along with a small bag of gold coins. What say ye to that?"

"I have absolutely nae idea how they got there," Angus Ferguson said. "The château's servants packed my saddlebags. I used only one of them in my travels. I never looked in the other, but as God is my witness I did not take the de Guise commission."

Annabella was pale with shock. She believed her husband, but someone had incriminated him. Why?

"Who would seek to make ye look guilty?" Donal Stewart asked him.

"I dinna know," Angus Ferguson said. "The Fergusons hae no enemies, for we hae carefully avoided entanglements wi' our neighbors for centuries."

"If ye canna prove yer innocence, my lord, I hae no choice but to arrest ye for treason against His Majesty, King James," Donal Stewart said. His tone, however, was very reluctant. There was something about this man that made him believe that he was no traitor, but his instincts weren't enough. He needed hard evidence. "Ye rode from Brittany along the French coast," he said. "Where did ye shelter at night, my lord?"

"Sometimes I slept rough," the earl replied. "At other times I came upon public inns, or a farmer would allow me to shelter in a barn."

"I suspect someone means ye harm, my lord," Donal Stewart told him. "Did ye quarrel wi' anyone on yer journey? Did anything unusual happen that ye recall?"

Angus's brow furrowed. Then he said, "I do recall a fellow who rode too close to me upon the open road. He bumped my animal more than once, but apologized, claiming that he was having difficulty getting his own horse under control. Eventually he rode on and I thought nothing further of it."

"I must send to my master for his instructions as to what should be done in this matter, my lord. In the meantime, rather than take ye off I will house ye in yer own dungeon. Nothing will be denied ye there. Neither food, warmth, nor company." He turned to where his own men were standing. "Escort the earl to his cell," Donal Stewart said.

"Oh, please, Master Stewart, let my husband remain in his own apartment," Annabella pleaded. "The cellars are so dank. Angus will get an ague."

But Donal Stewart shook his head in the negative. "Nay, madam, I can monitor his whereabouts far easier in his dungeon."

"It's all right, sweetheart," the earl assured her. *Damn!* He wanted a bath. He hadn't properly washed since he had departed Duin some weeks ago. He wanted his own bed, for he was tired of the hard earth, hay piles, and flea-infested inns. But most of all he wanted to hold his wife in his arms after several hours of very satisfying lovemaking. But he wasn't going to have what he wanted. Grimly he followed Donal Stewart's men.

"Braziers! At least two, and the fuel to keep them going." Annabella was already giving orders. "And a feather bed and a comforter. He must have candles." She turned on Donal Stewart. "I shall hold ye responsible if he gets sick!" she said angrily. "Whatever my lord Moray thinks he knows, my husband is nae a traitor!"

"They say men are easily bewitched by Mary Stuart," he replied.

Annabella snorted impatiently. "Did ye ever meet her?" she asked.

"Nay," he said.

"Then do not repeat the drivel spouted by Master Knox and his ilk," Annabella told him. "Mary Stuart is beautiful, 'tis true. She hae great charm, and is educated, but she is nae a fair devil leading men astray. Men are fools, Master Stewart, to repeat such rumors and innuendo."

"But she murdered her husband," he protested.

"Nay, she did not. If any be implicated, it is those who plotted in the murder of Riccio, the queen's secretary. Those same men now grappling for power. Lord Darnley was not a careful man. He was debauched, and when in his cups spoke too freely. He would hae died a natural death sooner than later. Did ye know he murdered my first child?" Then she turned away, saying to Matthew, "See that someone brings Angus a hot meal as soon as possible. He was barely through the door when this nonsense began."

When the day had ended and the hall was quiet, a maidservant came to Annabella. "My lady, I would speak wi' ye privily," the girl said.

"Bring a bowl of apples to my apartments," Annabella said softly. Then she arose and left the hall to go to her own rooms.

It was there that the servant girl came, holding a brass bowl of apples as her excuse to enter the lady's apartments. Setting the apples upon a sideboard, she curtsied to her mistress. Jean Ferguson stood by Annabella's side and encouraged the lass to speak.

"I overheard the Stewart men talking as I served them this evening," the girl began. "Donal Stewart hae orders to kill the earl should treason be found. That is why he was put in the cellars, my lady. They will slay our lord, and then be on their way, and to whom can ye raise a complaint? They laughed, saying all yer preparations to keep yer husband warm and comfortable were for naught, for he will shortly be dead."

Annabella sat frozen with shock for several long moments. Then, regaining her voice, she said, "Ye are certain that is what ye heard? That they mean to do murder?"

The servant nodded. "Aye, my lady. I dinna mistake their wicked intent."

The Countess of Duin didn't hesitate. Turning to Jean, she said, "Find yer husband, and tell him to take Donal Stewart and his men into custody. House them in the dungeons. Then he is to release the earl. Angus will know what is to be done."

Without a word Jean ran from the room.

"Stay wi' me," Annabella said to the servant girl.

After an hour had passed they heard footsteps in the hallway outside. The servant grew pale, but Annabella jumped to her feet, running to the door to open it. The Earl of Duin strode into her chambers.

"Jeannie hae told me," he said. He kissed her a hard

kiss. "Ye're a clever lass, wife. We've put Stewart and his men in the dungeons until I can decide what to do wi' them. He doesn't seem the type of fellow who would kill a man in his own house."

"He's one of Moray's bastards," Annabella said. "He'll do whatever his da bids him do to keep his favor. Where did they obtain the information that makes ye seem guilty? Moray doesna need to slay an unimportant border lord to maintain his power."

"Moray will slay anyone he believes is working toward bringing Mary Stuart back to power. If she had been a less intelligent woman, if she had been a woman easily directed, if she had nae wed first Darnley and then Bothwell, perhaps things might have been different. But the plain truth is that while James Stewart, because of his birth, cannot be king, he would be king. If Mary Stuart had let him rule through her, Scotland might be a more peaceable place today. Like most of the Stewarts he is an ambitious man."

"But there is nae proof of ycr disloyalty!" Annabella said.

"Dinna forget that a packet sealed with a ring bearing the de Guise seal, and a bag of gold coins were found in my saddlebags. But why they were put there to implicate me in some plot, I dinna know," Angus responded slowly. "I'll hae to go back to France to unravel this puzzle so I may clear my name."

"I'm coming wi' ye," Annabella said.

"Sweetheart," he replied, "this is nae a trip for a woman to make."

"I can travel as a young man," she told him.

"Nay," he said in a determined voice.

Annabella looked at her husband. "I will nae allow ye to go wi'out me, Angus."

"Nay, 'twill be dangerous, for the moment Moray learns I've gone they will be after me, Annabella. I want ye here, safe wi' our bairns."

"Moray doesna have to know until we are safe in France. Matthew can keep Donal Stewart and his men confined for a few weeks. Ye know the castle is in good hands wi' him. And the bairns have their nurses and Aggie."

"Aggie is about to deliver her own bairn. She will need ye wi' her," he said.

"If we are quick we may be back before she has it," Annabella replied, knowing very well, even as he did, that such a swift trip would be difficult at best.

"Ye're remaining at Duin," he said firmly. He looked to the servant girl, who had been listening wide-eyed to her master and mistress. "Tell Mistress Jean and Master Matthew to meet me in the hall." The girl ran off. "I must have a bath before I go. And a meal, and a night's sleep."

"I'll see to it," Annabella said. "Ah, Angus, I had so looked forward to having ye home wi' us again."

He put his arms about her, drawing her into his embrace. She felt warm and inviting, her sable head against his shoulder. He considered for a brief moment eliminating Donal Stewart and his few men. Then he might settle back into anonymity and live his quiet life. Would Moray really miss one of his bastards? He sighed. He was not a man to commit cold-blooded murder. He needed to clear his name. Angus Ferguson was not one of the Queen's Men; nor would he ever be. Releasing Annabella, he took her hand, and together they descended into the hall.

Matthew Ferguson was deeply concerned that Donal

Stewart and his men were imprisoned in the old dungeons of Duin Castle. "Will ye nae bring the wrath of the regent upon us?" he asked his elder brother.

"This is nae an enormous matter. Donal Stewart was dispatched to learn whether I was a traitor, and to slay me if the facts proved it so. Whoever brought this rumor to Moray did so to deliberately add to his difficulties," Angus responded. "The regent hae many matters concerning him right now. The possible traitorous conduct of an unimportant border lord is of little import to him. He sent his son to handle the matter, and will assume it hae been done. Wi' luck it will be some weeks before Moray considers the whereabouts and well-being of Donal Stewart. Then he must make inquiries. Only after that will he send someone to Duin. If I am nae back by that time, ye will pretend confusion, and say that Donal Stewart never arrived a second time at Duin. Who is to gainsay ye?"

"This is a dangerous game ye play, brother," Matthew replied.

"What would ye hae me do?" the earl asked him. "I canna prove my innocence in this matter if I dinna return to France to learn the truth of it. Remember the packet wi' the de Guise seal, and the coins found amid my possessions. While I am gone ye will see that Donal Stewart and his men are well treated and fed. They are nae my enemies."

"And dinna let anyone into the dungeons but one or two older male servants who will serve and look after them," Annabella added. "Make certain they canna be bribed."

"I know my duty," Matthew said stiffly.

After the meal, when Angus had gone to enjoy his

bath, Jean came to sit by her mistress. "Ye spoke to Matthew as if ye would nae be here yerself to devil him. What mischief are ye planning, my lady?"

"I'm going wi' Angus," Annabella said low.

"He will nae hae it," Jean responded.

Annabella smiled mischievously. "So he hae said. But this time he will need someone watching his back. I canna allow him to go alone. He will nae know until it is nae possible to send me back," she said. "I shall dress like a young man, and ye must find the garments for me, Jeannie. Angus means to leave in the morning."

"Ye're mad!" Jean Ferguson said, but she grinned back. "I'll help ye."

"I must slip from the castle early, before Angus does, and then wait upon the road for him to pass me by before I follow him."

"Annabella, ye hae never traveled but from Rath to Duin and from there to court. It can be dangerous. Ye'll need a purse until ye can reveal yerself to Angus. And ye canna do that until ye're upon the high seas," Jean said.

"I know," Annabella admitted. She was afraid of what she was going to do, but she had to do it. If Moray learned Angus had fled to France he would take it as an indication of his guilt. And what of whoever had slipped the packet and purse into Angus's saddlebag? Certainly he was in the employ of the de Guises. If they learned Angus had returned to learn the truth, would they not seek to silence him?

"I wonder if whoever slipped the incriminating evidence into Angus's saddlebag meant to harm him," Jean said thoughtfully. "What if they were put there only to get them across the water? What if someone else was supposed to take them to Mary Stuart?"

"That would mean that someone had to be here at Duin, for whoever plotted and planned this could not be certain what vessel Angus would take, or the road he would travel home," Annabella responded. "The only thing they could be certain of is that he would return to Duin. If Donal Stewart had not been here waiting for him, I suspect the purse and the packet would hae been quietly retrieved. We would have known nothing about it. Has anyone opened the packet to see what message is written inside?"

"Nay," Jean replied. "I canna believe one of our folk would do such a thing."

"Mary Stuart has charm. Despite her short stay, there was time for someone in her party to convince an impressionable stable lad to such mischief. We must learn who this person is, Jeannie, but first the packet. Where is it?"

"I dinna know," Jean Ferguson responded. "The last person to have it was Donal Stewart. We will hae to ask him, I fear." She looked nervously at Annabella. This was a different woman from the one she was used to serving. That Annabella was calm and careful in both her thoughts and her words. This Annabella seemed bolder, even reckless, and yet whatever her mood, Annabella, Countess of Duin, would do whatever she had to do to protect her family, to protect Duin.

"Angus is bathing, and will eat in his apartments before sleeping," Annabella said. "Matthew spends this time of day with Aggie. We have time before the hall fills for the evening meal. Let us go quickly!" She hurried from the hall, and Jean ran to catch up with her as Annabella made for the door at the end of the corridor that led down into the dungeons. "There will be nae guard on duty," Annabella said, "for Stewart and his men are securely locked in their cells. Only the menservants who bring them food will come here." Opening the door, she stepped through onto the landing, and then began to descend.

Jean followed. She found herself surprised by this new and capable Annabella.

At the bottom of the staircase they found themselves in a corridor lit by a flickering torch that sat in a wall holder. There were several doors with grates in them.

Donal Stewart and his half dozen men were housed in four cells at the end of the corridor, which they discovered by looking through each grate into the cells. Finding the Earl of Moray's man, Annabella called to him to come to the door so they might speak.

Donal Stewart smiled ruefully at her. "Hae ye come to release me, madam?"

Annabella chuckled. "Nay, sir, I hae not. But I do need yer help, if ye will gie it to me, please. My husband is nae a traitor, but here ye must remain until we can prove it. I know that ye were given orders by yer sire that should Duin's earl prove traitorous ye were to dispatch him wi'out delay," she said quietly.

Donal Stewart had the good grace to flush guiltily, but he said nothing.

"Such a cut-and-dried order doesna leave room for my husband to prove his innocence," Annabella said wryly. Then she went on to explain to Donal Stewart that she thought the packet and purse had been slipped into Angus's saddlebag without his knowledge. That whoever was to take it to Mary Stuart could be certain of only one thing: The Earl of Duin would go home. "It was here wi' the aid of one of our stable lads that he meant to gain possession of the message and the purse. We will learn which of our lads it was, sir. And we must read the message in the packet. It will surely prove my husband is nae traitor, sir. Where is the packet?"

"It was on the high board in the hall, my lady," he answered her. He was very impressed by her reasoning, and her effort to save her husband. Reaching into his doublet, he drew out the bag of coins, pushing it through the grate for her. "Ye're playing a dangerous game," he warned her gently.

"Neither ye nor yer men will be harmed, Donal Stewart," she told him. "But here ye will remain for the interim. I doubt yer sire will gie ye much thought for a while."

Donal Stewart laughed. "Nay, he will not. He is far too busy consolidating his position and chasing shadows."

"Jeannie will keep ye informed as to what is happening when she is able to do so," Annabella said to him. "Dinna attempt to bribe a servant. They are loyal."

"Apparently one was nae," he reminded her.

"A stable lad offered a few coins to take two items from his master's saddlebags canna be held accountable or considered a spy. Buying men is what the powerful do best, is it nae?" Annabella said cynically. "And the poor are always willing to cooperate wi' them, especially if they think they do their own loyalty nae harm."

"Dinna ever allow yer husband or my sire to learn how clever ye are, madam," Donal Stewart said with a small smile. "I hae nae doubt that ye will see yer husband's heretofore good name cleared."

"Oh, I will," Annabella said. "I will." Then, without another word, she and Jean returned upstairs from the dungeons, careful not to be seen by any. They hurried into the hall, and there was the packet still lying on the high board. "Thank God!" the Countess of Duin said, picking it up. She broke the seal and unfolded the parchment to read what it contained. Her eyes quickly scanned the writing. It was in French, but she knew enough to be able to translate the words.

Chère cousine, *your family is most distressed by your decision to flee into England. Believe us when we tell you that the bastard Elizabeth Tudor means you no good. She is popular among her own people and careful of her position. It is very unlikely that she will help to restore you to your rightful place as Scotland's queen. What she plans, however, we do not yet know, but rest assured that you have an enemy in her secretary of state, William Cecil. We beg that you take the first opportunity to return to Scotland. Accept for the interim your place as the mother of the little king. Make peace with your lords, your brother James Stewart in particular. We will work to assuage his anger toward you so that you will be treated in a more equitable fashion. Too long have you been ruled by your heart, and you were not raised to be so foolish. Take this opportunity to renounce Lord Bothwell. Remember, a weak Scotland is much to England's advantage. As long as they hold Scotland's queen they hold the upper hand. We will continue to communicate with you, and we will pray for you.*

Annabella folded the letter back up. The signature on the letter had not been important, other than that it had been signed by a de Guise. She suspected it was one of Mary Stuart's cousins with whom she had grown up. "There is nothing here that cries treason, nor implicates

Angus in any plot against Scotland or my lord of Moray," she said. "But that is not the point. As long as Moray and his ilk believe that Angus carried the letter from France, meant to have it delivered somehow to Mary Stuart, and accepted coins for his service, it will appear that he did something guilty." She handed the letter to Jean. "Secrete it until we may add it to the rest of our evidence."

"What evidence?" Jean inquired.

"The evidence we shall obtain in France," Annabella said with a small smile.

"Ye really mean to go wi' him?" Jean said.

"I do. I must," Annabella said.

"Ye love him," Jean replied quietly.

"Aye, I love him," Annabella said, "and I'll nae be left a widow wi' bairns, like so many other border wives! I will go wi' him, and I will help him to prove his innocence, to prove that the Fergusons of Duin are an honorable and loyal clan."

Chapter 12

The servants had begun to bring in the evening meal. Angus had already eaten, Tormod told his lady, and was already sleeping. Aggie was filled with complaints this evening as they sat at the high board. She was close to delivering her first child, and her feet were swollen badly. Annabella attempted to soothe her, to no avail.

"One bairn will be more than enough for me," she whined. "There is scarce enough to leave one if it's a lad, but more than enough of a dower for a daughter. I dinna believe ye suffered as much as I do."

Annabella wanted to laugh. Agnes had never been happy when constrained from physical activity. She had not been able to ride in several months. It was late summer, and the weather had been warm and muggy. "I carried twins," she reminded her younger sister. "Ye will survive, Aggie. Ye should spend more time out of doors, rather than lying down in yer apartments. How is yer house coming along?"

"I canna walk that far," Agnes complained.

"Then ye must have the dog cart, and go tomorrow,"

Annabella said cheerfully. She turned to Jean. "Ye'll see to it?"

"Aye," Jean replied. She wondered whether Agnes would continue to complain after her bairn was born. Well, at least she would be in her own house then, for Matthew, true to his promise to his bride, was having a fine stone house constructed on his nearby property.

The meal over the hall grew empty on this summer's night. Annabella went upstairs to see that Angus was still comfortable. He was sleeping very soundly, and from the looks of it would sleep until Tormod woke him to dress before the dawn. Poor man, she thought, touching his dark head lightly. To come home to such a welcome and to have to turn about immediately wasn't fair. Angus Ferguson was not a man who enjoyed adventure, unlike Bothwell, who seemed to live for it. Well, look where it had gotten James Hepburn. A prison cell in Denmark. All Angus wanted was to stay home, shepherd his lands, and watch his family grow.

Annabella sighed. She was mad, she knew, to be following after her husband, but something deep within her told her that Angus was in more difficulty than he realized, and through no fault of his own. Although he could not realize it, or even admit to it, he would need her by his side, seeing what he did not see, hearing what he would not hear.

Jean was waiting in her apartments when Annabella entered them. "I went into the attics," she said, "and found some of the clothing Matthew wore as a lad. Try them on to see if they fit or if I must seek elsewhere." She handed Annabella a pair of breeks and a shirt, relieved to see they fit her mistress perfectly. "I'll pack two more shirts in yer saddlebag, a brush for yer hair, and a few other sundries that ye'll need. Go to bed now. I'll wake ye when it is time."

"How will I get out of the castle wi'out being seen?" Annabella asked.

Jean grinned. "There's a small back portal that's rarely used. I used to meet my Douglas outside of it when we were courting." She chuckled. "I took a horse through that gate earlier and left it at my mam's cottage. I'll go wi' ye to get it, and so ye'll hae a way around the Duin village so no one sees ye. And I hae the perfect spot for ye to wait for Angus so ye may follow him wi'out his realizing it. Ye'll hae to be very clever, Annabella, if ye dinna want to reveal yerself to him till ye're a-sea. If he catches ye he'll bring ye back."

"I've no experience in such stealthy activities," Annabella said, "but I cannot fail. He'll go to Leith, won't he?"

"Aye, he will," Jean said. "He'll take no chances going to Berwick, lest it compound his alleged guilt."

"Make certain that Donal Stewart and his men are well looked after," Annabella told Jean, "and tell Matthew I'm keeping to my quarters because I am so upset by my husband's return to France. See if ye can keep him at bay for three or four days. I can't have Matthew coming after me."

She had been removing her garments as she spoke, and now she climbed into her bed. A bed that would have contained her husband had it not been for Donal Stewart and the Earl of Moray. It had been weeks since they had made love, touched, or even kissed those long, sweet kisses she had come to love. And it would be weeks more before they did again, Annabella realized, a trifle irritated. But proving Angus innocent of treason was far more important than the incredible passion between them. "Good night," she said to Jean. "Dinna let me oversleep."

But it was not her tiring woman who woke Annabella. It was her husband climbing into bed with her, growling into her ear. "I canna leave ye wi'out tasting yer passion, sweetheart." Undoing the ribbons holding her night garment closed, his hand slipped beneath the two halves of the gown, and he sighed as he caressed the silken skin of her perfect body. "God's blood, Annabella, ye are so sweet."

She turned in his arms to face him, forgetting briefly that in a few hours she would have to arise earlier than she had ever risen in her life in order to follow after him without his knowledge. But for now all she could think of was his hard body, and his mouth now seeking to kiss her. Her lips parted eagerly for him. *Holy Mother!* It seemed as if it had been forever since their bodies had entwined in delicious conjunction, and they kissed and kissed without end.

"Angus, dinna leave me," she pleaded softly. "There must be another way we can solve this problem. Send Matthew to France to seek the answers ye need. Stay wi' me."

His hand stroked her lovely body, fondling her breasts, smoothing down the length of her spine. "Matthew wouldna know the questions to ask. He would nae hae the familiarity wi' the magistrate in Mont de Devereaux that I hae. Besides, yer sister is too close to whelping her bairn."

"She doesn't need him to hae a bairn," Annabella said. She was being selfish for the first time in her life, but she didn't care. "He did his part months ago."

The earl laughed softly, and then kissed her once

again before saying, "I am the lord of Duin, and 'tis my honor that has been challenged. I must return to France to clear my name, sweetheart. Ye know it to be so."

"Aye, I do," Annabella admitted, "but I had hoped ye might . . . Oh! I dinna know what I was thinking."

He laughed again. "I dinna want ye to think of anything but me when I enjoy yer fair body," he told her. His head dipped to her breasts and, taking a nipple between his lips, he suckled upon it. "*Only me*," he murmured against her soft flesh. "*Only me!*"

Her hand stroked his dark hair, which had become a bit unruly where it met the nape of his neck. Her fingers played amid it, stroking the sensitive flesh as he tugged upon her, his teeth gently grazing the nipple, sending shivers of delight throughout her eager body. If he could arise in the next few hours and ride off, then so could she. Her arms wrapped about him, her body encouraging him with the unspoken signals lovers learn from each other over a period of time.

He couldn't seem to get enough of her sweetness. Perhaps, he thought through the haze of passion she aroused in him, it was because they had been separated and would again be separated. His hands could not seem to cease in their caressing. His lips and his tongue followed his hands in a frantic rush of pure, hot desire. He buried his face in her mons, inhaling the elusive and seductive fragrance of her. He kissed the plump flesh beneath his hungry lips, then peeled apart her nether lips to find that tiny jewel of pure lust that he knew would explode with a mere lick of his tongue.

He licked, and she cried out. But he needed more. His lips closed over the delicate bud and he sucked harder and harder.

Beneath that wicked mouth and tongue Annabella's

need mushroomed. She gasped as the pleasure erupted, and then she begged. "Ohh, Angus, 'tis good! So good! But I need ye inside of me. Fill me full! Oh, please! *Please!*"

He was hard as rock, and the need in her voice was enough to drive a sane man wild with his own desire. He waited no more, covering her body with his own, pushing his cock slowly, teasingly into her fevered body. Then he lay still atop her.

She felt as if she were sucking him inside her. He was deep, and then he stopped. She felt the length of hard and lustful flesh throbbing as the walls of her sheath closed around him. She squeezed him, and he groaned with delight. "Fuck me!" she whispered hotly in his ear. She pushed her tongue inside the channel and wiggled it before nipping the lobe. "Fuck me hard, my dearest lord! I can never have enough of ye, Angus! Never!"

He remembered the first time she had been so bold as to instruct him. It still gave him a thrill every time she whispered the demand in his ear. "Nor can I have enough of ye, Annabella, my love, my sweet wife." And then he obliged her, thrusting himself hard and deep over and over and over until she was keening with her pleasure and his head was spinning with his. Their juices burst forth simultaneously. They cried aloud! And then all was silent in the bedchamber.

Finally he arose, bending down to kiss her a quick kiss. "I must get some rest," he said. "Dinna arise to see me off on the morrow. I dinna think I would be able to leave ye if ye did. And I must. I will nae tarry in France, Annabella." Then he was gone from her.

"Godspeed, my sweet lord," she said to him as the door between their bedchambers closed with a tiny click. Then she closed her eyes. *Merciful Mother!* Were

all women this happy, this content, with their husbands?
She was still tingling with his touch, and then she giggled to herself. How surprised everyone would be to
know they were so divinely happy with each other.

It seemed she had gotten no sleep at all when Jean
came to awaken her. Yet she knew she had slept at least
several hours. Annabella arose, grumbling, bathed herself in her basin, and pulled on her clothing. When she
had finished dressing she looked at herself in the long
looking glass that had belonged to Angus's mother. She
was wearing dark woolen breeks, a linen shirt, and a
sleeveless leather jerkin with horn buttons. Her own
leather boots were suitably worn so as to not arouse
suspicion, and beneath them she wore woolen socks.

Jean braided Annabella's long dark hair tightly, and
then pinned it up before tucking it beneath a cap with a
narrow brim. "Remember, dinna take yer headpiece off,
lest ye be discovered," she warned. "Come along now.
We must hurry. Tormod hae just come up the stairs and
gone into the earl's apartments. Ye need to be gone
before Angus."

Annabella took another quick look at herself in the
looking glass. For the first time in her life she had an
advantage in her face. As a girl, others had looked at her
and felt sorry for her plainness. But as a lad, no one
would pay her the least attention. Pleased, she followed
her tiring woman quickly from her chambers. Was she
really doing this daring thing? Leaving her bairns and
following after her husband? And if he caught her before he reached France? Would he kill her? Or have to
turn about and bring her home? It was incentive enough
to make certain she didn't get caught.

Jean led her through the silent castle. They saw no
one. In the yard she kept to the shadows, as her guide

did. Reaching a small gate Annabella had never noticed before, she waited for Jean to open it, and then passed through. Together the two women slipped down the hill and walked to the cottage belonging to Jean's mam. There in the little open stable that was really no more than a shed, they found the horse Jean had picked, waiting.

"Angus will leave his horse at the Mermaid in Leith. Stable yer animal there too. It's reasonably respectable, and the beast will be awaiting yer return. Dinna gie the stable lad any more than three coppers. Tell him that if more is needed, he'll get it on yer return."

"What will my passage cost?" Annabella asked her.

"It depends upon how far the ship is taking ye," Jean said. "It should be nae more than an unclipped silver piece. There is one in yer purse. Dinna display it, but keep it hidden in yer shirt, and dinna let anyone see where ye've put the purse lest they rob ye."

Annabella was suddenly realizing how serious her determination to follow Angus was. She was now afraid, and questioned her intent.

"Ye dinna hae to do this," Jean said.

"Aye, I do. My instinct tells me 'twill nae be as simple or easy as Angus thinks," Annabella responded. "As he would protect me, I must protect him."

"Trust nae one, and be wary at all times of yer surroundings," Jean advised.

Annabella nodded. It was good advice, and she knew it.

"There is a path around the village proper. Take the fork to the left when ye reach the crossroads," Jean said. "On the other side of Duin ye'll see a stand of trees. Hide yerself there until Angus passes by. Then wait at least a quarter of an hour before ye follow him. There is nae other road he can take until he reaches the Edinburgh Leith road. After that ye should follow more closely, for there will be more traffic and he will nae notice ye amid it. If ye lose him, dinna be fearful. He always goes to the Mermaid in Leith. He'll seek a vessel there to take him to France."

Annabella nodded. "I'll remember," she said as she mounted her horse. "Thank ye, Jeannie. Watch over my sister and my bairns."

"I will," Jean promised.

Following the careful directions Jean had given her, Annabella reached the far side of Duin village and secreted herself in the stand of trees. After a surprisingly short while Angus cantered by. Annabella began counting off the minutes in her head, and when they totaled fifteen she exited the trees and followed the road as instructed. It took several long days to reach Leith, which was the port for Edinburgh.

During much of that time she had to rely on her faith that Angus was ahead of her. She rode until it was dark each night, sheltering where she could, eating her scant rations from the packet she found in her saddlebag. She became more comfortable when they reached the main road to the port and she could keep her husband in her sight amid all the traffic coming and going. But when Angus stopped at an inn, Annabella rode by, afraid to test her disguise amid a taproom of rough males. Instead she asked permission from a farm wife to shelter in the farmer's barn.

"Why, what pretty manners ye hae, laddie," the woman said. "Aye. Hae ye anything to eat?"

"Aye, mistress, thank ye," Annabella said, lowering her voice just slightly.

The farm wife nodded, but later came to the barn

with a large slab of fresh bread with cheese. "A lad always needs food, especially one as slender as ye are."

Annabella thanked the woman for her kindness, eating her offering, saving her own oatcakes for the morning. She did not sleep heavily, afraid of missing Angus when he came riding by. She was up before the dawn, and saddled her mount, watching through the open barn door, feeling relieved to see him go by. Pulling an oatcake from her saddlebag, she mounted up and joined the early morning traffic upon the road. She ate the oatcake as she rode. At a fork in the road she saw a sign pointing in one direction to Edinburgh and in the other toward Leith. She reached the port that afternoon, going directly to the Mermaid to stable her horse. It was by good fortune she overheard her husband speaking with the innkeeper.

"What ships sail for France on the evening tide?" Angus asked.

"Two," the innkeeper said. "One for Calais and the other for Brest in Brittany. Merchant vessels both, wi' room for passengers. Which do ye prefer?"

"The ship bound for Brest," Angus said.

"Captain is in my taproom right now," the innkeeper said. "Come along, my lord, and I'll point him out to ye."

Annabella followed at a discreet distance, watching as her husband booked his passage and paid the captain. When he had completed his business the earl sat down at a table and ordered a good hot dinner. Annabella went to the ship's captain.

"I should like to book passage on yer vessel bound for Brest," she said.

"Would ye now, lad?" The captain grinned. "Ye're a wee bit young to be making such a long voyage. 'Twill be at least ten days."

"And I'll probably be sick most of the way," Annabella said, chortling. "Nonetheless I must get to Brest, sir, though I not be fond of the sea."

The captain laughed in return. "'Twill cost ye a silver piece. Unless ye would prefer to work for yer passage."

"My mistress would nae like that," Annabella said, handing him the fare he required of her. "She's a jealous woman."

The captain laughed heartily this time. "Ye're yer lady's pet, are ye? Yet she sends ye off on some secret errand." He fingered the silver piece, noting it was unclipped.

"Her husband dallies in France, and she is suspicious that he has taken a mistress for himself there. I am to go and learn the truth of the matter," Annabella said.

"The lady trusts ye, which is to the good, but yer master will nae thank ye if his wife's suspicions prove truth," the captain said.

"He'll nae ever see me," Annabella confided, suddenly enjoying her ruse.

"We sail wi' the tide just after six this evening," the captain said. "My ship is called the *Gazelle*. That gentleman over there will be sailing wi' us too." He pointed to the earl. "Be on time, lad. We'll nae wait for ye!"

"I'll be there," Annabella said. Then, taking the earl's lead, she found a quiet corner where she could watch Angus. When he got up to leave, she would too.

A serving wench came over to her table. "What will ye be drinking?" she asked.

"Cider, if ye hae it," Annabella answered, "and some bread and cheese."

"Cider, is it," the girl teased. "A fine laddie like yerself?" She leaned down, revealing a pair of very plump breasts.

Annabella swallowed hard, then said, "I've nae a head for spirits, and as I am on an important mission for my mistress, I dare not miss sailing on the *Gazelle* this evening." She chucked the servant beneath the chin with what appeared regretful interest.

The girl giggled. "And I'll wager the lady gave ye scant coin for yer travels. I'll see what I can find in the kitchens besides the bread and cheese." Then she turned about, swinging her hips as she hurried off.

Mother of all mercies, Annabella thought. *What that poor lass must do to earn her keep. I ne'er really thought about such lasses before.* She turned so that she could not be seen, and reached into her shirt to pull two coppers from her purse, one for the meal and one for the serving wench. Across the room her husband ate a small meal as she surreptitiously watched him. Her own plate came with the bread, the cheese, and a slice of goose. She thanked the barmaid, and then daringly dropped the large copper down between the girl's breasts.

The wench giggled. "Are ye sure I can't do anything else for ye, sir?" she tittered, bouncing up and down on her toes so that her big breasts jiggled.

"Nay, nay!" Annabella assured her, feeling her own cheeks grow warm. "Thank ye." If the lass only knew the truth.

The girl turned away.

Annabella ate the food on her plate quickly. Angus was still seated at his place, sipping from a pewter tankard. When he finally arose she was too fearful of losing sight of him, for she was certain he would go directly to the ship. She didn't want him catching her, especially before they sailed. He would be furious. He would feel he had to take her back to Duin, and that would delay his quest close to a month. Annabella walked slowly, keeping to the shadows. The street was still busy enough that she would not raise suspicion. Finally she saw a vessel ahead, and across its bow was written in gold letters, THE GAZELLE. The earl strode up the gangway.

Annabella waited a few long moments. She could hear her own heart pounding in her ears. Could she do this? Did she dare? But she had to, for every instinct told her that Angus would need her whether he realized it or not. She took a long, deep breath, exhaled, and walked up the gangway of the ship.

A boy of perhaps eleven years of age awaited her as she stepped onto the vessel. "Ye'll be the lad spying in France for his mistress," he said. "I'm the ship's cabin boy. Me da is the captain. Do ye hae a name? Me da dinna say."

"He never asked me, but 'tis Robert Hamilton," Annabella replied quickly, combining her father's name and her mother's maiden name. "Where am I to shelter?"

"Ye'll hae to share a space, as we only hae two cabins for passengers," the cabin boy said. "The captain said ye hae good manners, so he ordered me to put ye in the large cabin. Ye're fortunate. In the smaller cabin is a French wine merchant and his son. They've traveled wi' us before. I call the older man Master Heave and Blow, for he'll vomit and fart all the way to Brest. His son will simply vomit and moan until we sight land again. Do ye get seasick?"

"I've never been to sea," Annabella said.

"Dinna drink too much until ye get yer sea legs," the cabin boy advised. "Yer cabinmate is already on board. He's a nobleman, he is."

Mother of all mercies! Annabella swallowed back a gasp. It had to be Angus, and they were still tied to the pier. "I think I'll stay on deck until we're under way," she said. "The day has been warm. I'll welcome the sea breeze."

"Suit yerself," the lad said. "When ye're ready, just call me. Ye hae better find yerself a spot out of the way, for we are about to cast off."

"Thank ye," Annabella said to him, and he hurried off. She found a small sheltered spot, and sat down upon a barrel top to watch as the ship was made ready to sail. The gangway was drawn up. The ropes holding her to her dockage space were released. The sails were slowly raised by sailors both upon the deck and scrambling above the deck untying the rolled-up sheets, fastening them down where they should be.

They were suddenly moving away from the great stone quay. She could feel the gentle motion of the waves beneath the vessel. They were away! She remained upon the deck as they finally cleared the harbor, moving out into the Firth of Forth. The ship continued its passage, but Annabella could feel a change in the sea as the vessel moved along. It seemed deeper suddenly. Eventually a small island came into view. She knew from her own lessons as a girl that it was known as the Isle of May. Once there had been a monastery located upon it, but no one lived there now but creatures.

The sun set and the twilight filled the sky. Annabella remained on the deck watching as they left the Firth of Forth, moving out into the open sea. A light wind filled the ship's sails. It was surprisingly cool, but then, autumn was almost upon them. Annabella pulled her cloak about her. The sky above her was now dark, and bright stars began to twinkle. She shivered. She was going to have to go in sooner rather than later. Maybe Angus would be asleep.

As if anticipating her need, the cabin boy appeared. "I hae time to take ye to yer cabin, Master Hamilton. Will ye be coming along then?"

"Aye," Annabella said, standing up. "Lead on, lad." Then she followed him.

He led her below the main deck. At the bottom of the stairs he opened a door, saying, "The nobleman is wi' my da right now, but he'll return soon enough."

"I've ridden a long way the past few days, and slept along the road. Yon bunk seems fine to me," Annabella said. "I'll be going to sleep now."

"Aye," the lad said. "'Tis as good a pastime as any. Good night then." And he was gone, scrambling up the narrow ladder that served as a staircase.

The cabin had three bunks built into the wall. One stood alone, and the earl's cape lay upon it. The other two bunks were set one above the other. Annabella considered sleeping on the top, but decided against it. Instead, setting her saddlebag beneath it, she sat down upon the bottom bunk, wondering how fresh the straw in the mattress might be.

She pulled off her boots, setting them with the saddlebag. Then, hearing footsteps outside, she lay down, pulled up her cloak, faced the wall, and feigned sleep as the door to the cabin opened.

His footsteps crossed the floor to his bunk. She heard him grunt softly as he pulled his boots off and stored them beneath his bed. She heard the straw in his mattress crunch as he settled himself. She was scarcely breathing, but then Angus began to make the gentle little snuffling noise that indicated he was sliding into a deep sleep. Annabella relaxed. While she would attempt to conceal her identity from him as long as possible, the worst was now over. By morning they would be far at sea and on their way to Brittany. There was no way he could send her back to Duin now. She slid into her own deep slumber, feeling vastly relieved.

The next few days passed quickly. Annabella formed a simple routine. She would appear in the galley in mid-morning, where the cook would give her a bowl of hot porridge and a slice of bread and cheese. The food, she learned from the talkative cook, was better on voyages of shorter duration, as theirs would be. The fresh bread they took on in Leith as well as meat could be stored without going bad and becoming maggoty. She was always alone in the galley at this time of day. The earl and the captain seemed to have common interests. The seamen went about their duties. The other two passengers, the father and son, remained in their cabin, as the cabin boy had said they would.

As the earl ate in the captain's cabin each evening, Annabella was free to collect her meal when she chose. She would take it to her cabin, eat, and return the bowl to the cook. She spent her days either seated upon the barrel watching the sea, or in the cabin sleeping. She managed her personal needs quickly, and as soon as the earl left the cabin in the morning. She ate and drank sparingly, thus saving herself from seasickness.

The night before they were to land at Brest, the ship was overtaken by a storm that tossed the vessel hither and yon. Thunder roared, and lightning cracked ferociously all around them. The sails were brought down to keep them from being blown too far off course. But the storm did not last more than a few hours, and by early dawn they were sailing between Île d'Ouessant and the coast of Brittany. Annabella was amazed that her first fears when the ship began to rock had quickly subsided, and she was brought to ill-concealed hilarity at the sounds coming from the smaller cabin next door.

Her fellow passengers were really not good travelers. Their howls of anguish followed by their equally loud prayers to Saint Christopher and the blessed Mother did not allow for sleep, even if the fierce storm had. The earl had not returned to the cabin at all, and Annabella imagined he kept company with the captain. Now, as the noon hour approached, the ship entered the landlocked harbor of Brest on the Penfield River. The town was set on the two hillsides, divided by the river and dominated by its dark stone castle. The town had been part of the dower portion of Claude, the daughter of Anne, the Duchess of Brittany, when she had married François I.

Annabella made certain that her plait was securely pinned beneath her cap. She couldn't believe that she had had the good fortune to elude her husband's eye in such close quarters during their voyage. But, of course, Angus was concerned with clearing his good name. He would hardly consider that his wife had disobeyed him and followed after him. Now, however, she had to find a place to rent a horse so she might follow Angus to his late mother's home to learn the truth of what had happened. She gathered up her saddlebag and went out on the deck.

The other passengers were already assembled. The father and son looked to be a shade of pale gray-green. They were obviously not over their travel sickness. Annabella caught the sleeve of the cabin boy, asking him where she might hire a horse.

"Just follow the nobleman, sir. He is going to the stables, and the captain has already given him the directions."

Annabella thanked the lad.

The gangway was lowered. The earl strode down it, followed by the father and son. Annabella came last, her saddlebag over her shoulder as she hurried behind the earl, following but attempting not to attract his attention at the same time. He reached his destination, bargained for his mount, and waited for it to be saddled. Annabella did the same. Fortunately the animals were led out together. She paid the stable owner and mounted up first, pretending to fuss with her saddlebag while she waited for the earl to complete his transaction and be on his way.

Finally he was ready. Mounting up, he rode off. Annabella followed, keeping her husband in sight, but leaving a careful distance between them. Just as they left the town behind, she noticed a horseman enter the road from a side lane. She heard another rider behind her. She didn't know why, but all her instincts were suddenly aroused. In his travels from Duin to Leith nothing had caught her interest as did the man before her and the man behind her. Was it her imagination, or were they following after Angus?

As the late summer sun set and twilight spilled over the land, Annabella began to worry. If they had to sleep rough this night, would the other riders use the cover of darkness to attack the earl? The man ahead of her turned off the road. She rode on by him, but her ears strained for sounds of the man behind her. He turned off the road too.

Was it a coincidence? Then she saw a lighted structure ahead of her. It was an inn, and the earl was turning his mount into the innyard. She turned her horse too, instructing the stableman in precise French to check its feet for stones, then feed, water, and stable it until she was ready to leave.

He entered the inn just ahead of her. The taproom was not crowded, and the inn upon close inspection was just barely respectable. She watched as the earl sought a table in a corner that allowed him to keep his back to the wall while observing the whole room. The landlord, recognizing nobility when he saw it, hurried over to personally serve the earl. Annabella chose a small table placed in such a way that she could see both the door to the inn and her husband's table. A serving wench came to inquire what she would eat, recommending the pot-au-feu. Annabella ordered it, along with a small goblet of wine.

An elderly serving woman struggled over to the earl's table beneath a large tray of food. The landlord had obviously given the earl everything in the kitchen. Annabella hid her grin. Angus had a good appetite, but she knew he also preferred his food plain and well cooked. She watched him as she slowly ate her own pot-au-feu, which was surprisingly good. It was full of vegetables and bits of clearly identifiable poultry. If she wasn't mistaken it was flavored with both ground pepper and wine. There was a thick slice of warm fresh bread spread with butter that she dipped into the soup.

Angus, on the other hand, took a large piece of beef, bread, butter, cheese, and what appeared to be a salad of new greens. The rest he told the old woman with a warm smile to return to the kitchen. "Tell your master that I am a man of simple tastes, old mother," Annabella heard her husband say. The old woman chuckled and tottered off. Annabella watched as her husband devoured his meal. Would he remain here, or would he attempt to travel on in the dark? she wondered.

The innkeeper came and announced to the few guests eating, "Alas, monsieurs, I am a small establishment. I have no rooms to let, but you are all most welcome to remain the night where you are now seated. Or you may share the barn with your horses. Either way it will cost you a copper more in addition to your meal." He then walked from table to table to collect his coins.

The four other men in the room elected to retire to the barn. The earl, however, remained, and so did Annabella. The candles were snuffed, and only the fire remained to take the night chill from the room as well as light it. Annabella found a comfortable position, pulled her cloak about her, and nodded off after taking a quick look at her husband, who appeared to have done the same.

Annabella didn't know for how long she slept, but suddenly she was wide-awake. She focused her eyes and saw the inn door had opened. Two men quickly and quietly stepped into the inn. Even in the dim light of the single candle that had been left burning, Annabella knew they were the same men who had followed the earl from Brest. What on earth was this all about? The two hesitated briefly, looking about. Then one pointed to the Earl of Duin, who was apparently sleeping deeply as he sat hunched over behind his table.

What was she going to do? Annabella knew immediately that the intent of these two was wicked. The men stepped into the small dining room. Her eyes wide-open in the darkness, she saw one draw something from his waist. A weapon? *A knife!* They crept forward, moving stealthily, heading directly for the Earl of Duin. Closer and closer they came, and just as she shouted out a warning, Angus Ferguson stood up.

"Are you looking for me, monsieurs?" he said in a pleasant voice. His French was perfect, and even tinged with a bit of Breton.

The assassins stopped, confused, gazing up at the shadow of the very tall man. But then the one with the knife leaped forward. The earl caught him quickly, and twisted the weapon from his hand. There was the distinct sound of a breaking bone. The knife dropped to the inn floor with a clatter. The cutthroat howled in pain as his companion dashed for the inn's front door. The wounded man turned and stumbled after him.

"Are you one of them too?" the earl asked in the darkness.

"*Non*, monsieur," Annabella managed to say, but her voice cracked as she spoke. She had been absolutely terrified by what had just transpired, knowing she would have been helpless to aid her husband had he actually needed assistance. It was then that Annabella truly realized for the first time the madness of this venture she had undertaken. She should have insisted that Matthew go with him. She would have been of more use to her husband keeping the castle than trailing after him disguised as a young man. A sob escaped her with the knowledge that she had possibly put him in even greater danger.

Angus Ferguson heard the sound. It was clearly female. But the only other person in the room was a young man. Or was it? He stood up again, walking out into the entry and picking up the lit candlestick. Coming over to where Annabella sat hunched up, he reached out with one hand. Annabella drew back, trying desperately to keep her head down, but his fingers grasped her chin, and he held the candle high. Their eyes met, hers terrified, his filled with astonishment.

"*Annabella!*" he said. And then, "Jesu and Mary, woman! Did I nae tell ye *no*?" He set the candle down upon the table, and then sat next to her.

"I had to come, Angus!" she burst out. "Something deep inside me warned that ye would be in danger if ye came alone. I realize now I should hae insisted Matthew come wi' ye. When I saw those awful men just now attempting to kill ye, and I didn't know what to do, or how I might help ye other than shouting out, I realized my own foolishness, but I love ye so, my lord. I love ye so verra much. I should rather die wi' ye than be wi'out ye, Angus. Do ye understand? Can ye forgie me?"

He put his arms about her. "I love ye too, ye stubborn, wonderful woman," he told her. "I probably wouldn't hae let Matthew come wi' me, and he would hae obeyed my directives and been loyal." Aye, he loved her. And the thought of her facing any danger because of him was terrifying.

"I know," she said in a small voice, "but I couldn't let ye walk into danger alone."

"How did ye manage to get so far wi'out me discovering ye?" he asked her.

"I had to be very careful," she admitted. "If ye had caught me before ye set sail, ye would hae found some way to send me home."

"Aye, I would hae," he agreed.

"I sailed on the *Gazelle* wi' ye," she told him.

"God's blood! The young man who shared the cabin. How did I nae know ye then?" he wondered aloud.

"Ye spent all or most of yer time wi' the captain, and I was very careful not to let ye see much of me," she said with just a hint of pride in her voice. "And I followed ye to the livery in Brest, and the rest was easy. I noted those two villains following ye along the road yesterday. One was behind ye, the other behind me."

"I expected something like this," the earl told his wife, "but until we reach Mont de Devereaux and I speak to the magistrate, I cannot know for certain what is going on."

"Ye canna send me back," Annabella said.

"Nay, ye're safer wi' me, sweetheart, although ye will continue on wi' yer disguise. However, tomorrow after we hae left here, ye will ride wi' me," Angus Ferguson told his wife. "And when we return to Duin, I will beat ye for yer disobedience."

"Ye'll hae to catch me first," Annabella responded teasingly.

"I've caught ye now," he said, pulling her into his lap.

Their lips met in a passionate kiss, her mouth opening to take in his tongue, which quickly found hers, stroking it, stoking their passions to a fiery crest. His fingers loosened the ties of her shirt, his hands slipping beneath the fabric to caress her perfect breasts. He shifted her body about so that he might lower his head to suckle on one of her tempting nipples already thrusting demandingly toward him. His lips closed over it.

Annabella moaned low as his mouth tugged on her sensitive flesh. *Mother of mercy!* They were in a public place. What if someone came and saw them? Then she realized she didn't care. "I want more," she husked in his ear.

He raised his head. "So do I," he said. He tipped her out of his lap. "Undo yer breeks, lass, and bend over the table."

She quickly complied, baring her bottom to him.

"Use yer hands to balance yerself," he told her, and when she did he reached beneath her to find her little love button, which he teased and worried until she was wiggling her buttocks enthusiastically. She was already drenching his fingers with her juices. He carefully nosed his cock beneath her, finding her love passage to thrust deep.

"Ahhhhh!" Annabella sighed, feeling him fill her with his thickness.

Holding her steady with his big hands, he began to piston her, moving slowly at first, then more quickly, increasing the tempo and the friction. "Ye're a shameless piece o' goods, wife," he growled in her ear. "I love fucking ye. I love the sounds ye make that tell me I'm pleasing ye."

Her head was spinning with excitement and delight. Annabella pushed her bottom back into his groin, teasing him with the motion, tightening her sheath about him, making him groan with his own pleasure. "I love ye fucking me," she admitted. "While I hae never known another man, I cannot believe any other could or would love me as well, Angus Ferguson." She felt her crisis approaching, and knew he felt it too. When it burst over them they both sighed with equal amounts of pleasure and regret.

Withdrawing from her, he drew her breeks up and then, sitting down, pulled her back into his lap, his arms about her. They slept briefly, awakening just before the skies began to lighten. Annabella climbed from his lap and adjusted her garments. She picked up her cap from the floor where it had fallen, and, ascertaining that her plait was still tightly fastened to her head, put the cap on her head. And while she had made order from disorder, he did the same.

A servant stumbled into the room carrying an armload of wood, with which he made a new fire, the old one having burned into coals during the night. Another servant came in bringing a plate of eggs, bacon, bread, and butter. She plunked their plates before them, along with mugs of cider. Angus and Annabella ate at their separate tables, not speaking.

He finished his meal first, arose, paid the landlord, and went into the inn yard, where his horse was waiting. He then rode off. Annabella followed his lead, and found her husband awaiting her upon the road, out of sight of the inn.

It was sunny and hot as they rode along the road to Mont de Devereaux. They spoke little until he said, "We should reach the village by noon."

"What will ye do then?" Annabella queried him.

"Find Monsieur Claude, if I can. We'll go straight to my mother's old château," he said. "I sold my property to him, and not to the de Guise family. Why they would want a property in Brittany is beyond me. They are not Breton; nor should they have any use for such a property."

"Hopefully we shall soon learn the reason," Annabella said.

They arrived just after the noon hour at the village where Angus's mother had been born and spent her childhood, even as he had predicted. The dusty streets were almost deserted in the late-summer heat but for a dog here and there. They stopped to water their horses at the village fountain, then rode on to the château, which lay on the far side of the village of Mont de Devereaux. The gates to the house were closed, but a gatekeeper came forth immediately.

"Is this the home of the son of Monsieur Claude?" the earl asked.

"Aye, my lord!" The gatekeeper pulled at his forelock, and then opened the gates to allow them entry. Two unarmed gentlemen did not present a threat.

They rode through, and up the wide tree-lined road leading to the château. When they reached the circular drive they stopped before the beautiful house. A liveried servant hurried out as two stablemen took their horses. He ushered them into the building.

"I am the Earl of Duin," Angus said, "former owner of this property. I should like to see the son of Monsieur Claude."

"Please to await Monsieur Raoul in the salon," the servant replied, pointing to a double door. "I shall fetch my master at once."

"Remain standing, and do not speak unless requested," the earl said. "You are my servant. What did you call yourself when you paid your passage on the *Gazelle*?"

"Robert Hamilton," Annabella said. Then they waited in silence.

Chapter 13

Monsieur Raoul entered, and Angus knew at once he was Monsieur Claude's son, for he resembled his father most strongly.

"I am Angus Ferguson, the Earl of Duin," Angus said before the young man might speak. "This château was my mother's home, and I sold it several weeks ago to your father," he began. "When I returned home I found myself accused of treason against my king, because it was said I had sold this house to the de Guise family, the kinsmen of our former queen. I am now believed to be in league with them to restore Mary Stuart to her throne. Do you have an explanation you can give me for this misunderstanding?"

"I do not, monsieur," Monsieur Raoul replied, "but I am certain that my father will be able to enlighten you. I shall send for him at once!" Walking across the salon, he yanked impatiently upon the bell cord. "Send someone for my father," he told the servant who came at his call. "Tell him it is urgent that he come immediately." Then, turning back to his guests, he said, "We may as well sit, for my father will be napping at this time of day, and slow to rise. Will you have some wine?"

"Robert! Serve the wine," the earl instructed Annabella.

"Aye, my lord," she replied, striding over to the sideboard, whereupon a decanter and some small silver cups were set. She poured two cups, and then brought them to the waiting men.

"You may pour yourself some," the earl said.

"You speak our language well and have a tone of Breton in your voice," Monsieur Raoul noted.

"I learned the language at my mother's knee," the earl answered.

"Would it be so terrible if your rightful queen were restored?" Monsieur Raoul asked his guest, curious.

"It is the habit of the Fergusons of Duin not to involve themselves in politics. As you may know, the earls in my country are for the most part a contentious lot. We have not had a king reach old age in many years. The first James Stewart was assassinated, as was the third of that name. The second, the fourth, and the fifth James died fighting our mutual enemy, England. Only the first James was a man grown when he took his throne, but that was because on his way to safety in France as a child he was captured by English pirates, who sold him to their king. He did not return home until his late twenties. The power belonging to these child rulers is always usurped by the earls, most of whom are blood kin to the House of Stewart.

"Mary Stuart's heart is good, but I tell you truly that the woman has absolutely no common sense," Angus Ferguson said irritably. "Her choice of husbands, your own late king excepted, was abysmal. She is a woman ruled by her heart, which is not a wise trait in a queen. I am shocked and distressed by how she has been treated. But fleeing Scotland was her own choice. Her child is now crowned king, and while my sympathies may lie with Mary Stuart, my loyalty is to King James, child though he may be."

"There is much sympathy for Mary Stuart here in France," Monsieur Raoul said.

"She was well loved in her brief time as our queen."

"She has great charm," the earl agreed. He sipped slowly at the wine in his cup, thinking that it was a particularly good vintage.

Monsieur Raoul attempted to make more polite conversation. "Before you came to sell the château, had you come before, perhaps as a child?" he asked.

"*Non*," the earl answered. "After she wed my father *Maman* never returned." He concentrated on his wine once more. Where the hell was Monsieur Claude? he wondered.

He hadn't made this desperate and swift journey from Scotland to pay a social call.

Silence fell upon the salon. Finally the door opened and Monsieur Pierre Claude hurried in. His son's sigh of relief was hardly a quiet one. "Monsieur," he greeted the earl. "I had scarce expected to see you again. What is this most urgent matter that I must be roused from my afternoon nap?"

"Did you or did you not purchase this château and its lands from me some weeks ago?" the Earl of Duin asked as he stood up.

"Of course I did," Monsieur Claude responded.

"Then please tell me why the Earl of Moray, regent and guardian of King James, believes that I sold this property to the de Guise family. I have been accused of treason, of attempting to return Mary Stuart to the throne. How can this be if I sold you the property? Is it that you have some familial connection with the de

Guises of which I was not aware? I have had to flee my country in an attempt to clear my name."

Monsieur Claude looked so shocked by the earl's words that Angus knew at once that whatever had happened, the Frenchman was totally innocent of any chicanery. "Monsieur, I have absolutely no idea of what has happened. Who would do such a thing? And why would they do it?"

"I have no idea as to the who or the why," the earl answered.

"You find yourself in a very dangerous situation, monsieur," Monsieur Claude agreed. "And you have a hidden enemy."

"There were only three people involved with the sale of my mother's lands. The magistrate, you, and me," the earl noted.

"Do not forget the agent of the de Guise family," Monsieur Claude reminded the earl. "I know for a fact that he did not leave the village for several days after our transaction was completed."

"If you will give me your word that you had nothing to do with this deceit," Angus Ferguson said, "then I will accept it. The magistrate must have the answer to this mystery. I shall go to him."

"My lord!" Annabella spoke in their own tongue. "Our young host is nae comfortable wi' this topic. I believe he knows something, and is afraid to speak. Ye must question him. Look! See how he turns his face away from his father and from ye."

The earl nodded to her, and turned sharply to face Monsieur Raoul. "What do you really know of this situation?" he demanded. "You told me earlier that you had nothing to do with this matter. I believe now that you have lied to me."

"*Raoul!*" His father spoke sharply. "What do you know of this?"

"I did nothing wrong," the younger man said nervously. "A stranger, a man I did not know, came to me with a proposal. For my aid he would pay me in gold. But when I heard what he wanted, I refused. I did nothing wrong!"

"What did this man want?" the earl asked.

"He asked that I go with him to the magistrate and temporarily sign over these lands to the de Guise family. As soon as a bill of sale was drawn up, the lands would be returned to us, and I would get my gold," Monsieur Raoul said. "But I didn't do it."

"Why not?" the earl inquired.

"The gold was tempting, but there was too much of it for this to be an honest venture. My father had told me how you had a greater offer for this property, yet you still sold it to him. I realized that whatever the de Guises wanted that bill of sale for, it was a dishonest purpose," Monsieur Raoul finished.

"And yet there was a bill of sale," the earl said. "And in my saddlebags was found a bag of gold coins, and a letter for Mary Stuart."

"It is the magistrate," Monsieur Claude said with certainty. "He has always been a greedy man. He forged a bill of sale for this property, and was well paid for it by the de Guise family, I have not a doubt."

"Then I shall visit the magistrate," the earl said ominously.

"I will go with you," Monsieur Claude replied.

"*Non*, I will not involve you and your family in this, *mon ami*. The de Guises still maintain a certain amount of power, despite France's queen mother, Catherine de' Medicis. You do not want to find yourselves involved with them if you can avoid it. You have acted honorably, as has your son," Angus Ferguson said, "and I am grateful to you both."

"I will go with you," Monsieur Claude repeated. "The magistrate acted dishonestly, and must know that I know. I have more power than he has in this village."

Annabella spoke low to her husband. "The magistrate hae insulted the honor of this family. Let him come wi' ye, my lord. It will gie him an advantage that he dinna hae before over this dishonest man. That will certainly be a punishment."

"Ye're a devious soul." Angus chuckled. He turned to Monsieur Claude. "You do me honor. I will be glad for your aid." He held out his hand in friendship, and the Frenchman took it and shook it.

"Let us go immediately, monsieur. The magistrate will just now be sitting down to his meal. We can catch him unawares. He is a man who can concentrate upon only one thing at a time, and his food will be his first priority. He will be frightened and confused by your questions, and easily caught in the lies he will spew to cover his dishonesty in this matter."

"My papa does love a good intrigue," Monsieur Raoul murmured.

The earl chuckled, nodding. Turning to Annabella, he said, "Bring the horses, Robert, and follow us."

"Aye, my lord," she replied, trailing after the two men as they left the salon.

Behind them a relieved Monsieur Raoul heaved a sigh.

They walked the short distance from the château into the village. Above them the sky was a clear blue, the sun warm upon their shoulders. Annabella in her guise as the earl's servant led their two horses along the dusty path. The village was quiet in the heat of the afternoon. A large fountain in the square offered cool water to passing travelers. They stopped before a substantial stone house. Annabella tethered the animals as the earl knocked loudly upon the door of the house.

"What is it you want?" the servant answering the door said.

"We've come to see your master," Monsieur Claude said in a loud voice.

"My master has just sat down to table," the servant said. "You can wait."

"I have no intention of waiting, you insolent varlet!" the earl snarled, pushing his way into the hallway of the house. "You will take us to your master immediately or your next position will be in the eunuch's choir in Rome."

The unfortunate servant blanched. "Yes, monsieur! Come this way!" He ran down the hallway ahead of the trio. Reaching the dining salon of the house, he flung open the doors, ushering in the visitors.

"What is this?" demanded the magistrate, looking up from a fat capon that he had been slicing.

"Villain!" Monsieur Claude said angrily, shaking his fist at the seated man. "You would attempt to involve my family in your dishonest practices. You have brought dishonor and danger to the monsieur in his own land so that he must hurry back to Mont de Devereaux to clear his good name. How much were you paid by that sly agent of the de Guise family to put your signature to that false bill of sale?"

The magistrate's mouth fell open with his surprise. "How . . ." he began.

Angus Ferguson quickly stepped forward. The dirk in his hand casually speared a small piece of the carved bird. He brought it to his mouth and chewed, swallowed. "You have endangered my wife, my children, my most honorable name," he said quietly.

The magistrate, his eyes on the dagger, shrank back just slightly. "Monsieur . . ." he began again.

"I am not interested in your lies," the earl told him. "Your actions have caused me to be accused of treason against my own king. You have taken coin for this deceit."

"Judas!" hissed Monsieur Claude.

"Now you will correct your error," the earl said, "that I may prove my innocence."

"Monsieur, you do not understand," the magistrate quavered. "It was not just for the gold. My youngest son is promised a place in the de Guise household."

"That fat slug?" Monsieur Claude snapped. "How unfortunate that he will be unable to take this *promised* place."

"Why was it so important that I be implicated in this plot?" the earl asked, not really expecting he would gain an answer, but to his surprise he did.

"It was not," the magistrate said. "You simply had the misfortune to come to France at the wrong time, monsieur," the local official explained. "Ever since Mary Stuart returned to Scotland, she has been spied upon by both her former mother-in-law, Catherine de' Medicis, and her own relations, the de Guises. Both of these families are aware of everyone who comes to France from Scotland."

"And you are privy to information how?" the earl asked.

"The de Guise agent, fed enough of my good wine, had a very loose tongue. Knowledge, as you know, my lord, can be power," the magistrate said. Then he continued on with his story. "Now that this tragic queen has been driven from her throne, her family is anxious to see her returned to it. They are in the process of setting up a network of spies that will go from Scotland to England to France. But the English queen's spymaster is working to prevent them from putting Mary Stuart back on her throne, for reasons I do not have to explain to you."

"But how was it that I became involved?" the earl inquired.

"You were the decoy they chose that they might set the final piece of their plan into place. When it was learned that you were coming to Brittany to settle your *maman*'s estates, the de Guise faction decided the purchase of those lands could be used as a vehicle to convince the regent Moray that you were actually taking traitor's gold and carrying correspondence for them to Mary Stuart. They slyly planted this rumor with Catherine de' Medicis, and she informed the English ambassador, who informed his queen, who of course saw that the regent, James Stewart, was notified," the magistrate explained. "Then, while the regent's people were concentrating upon you, the de Guises were able to set up the last link in their network connecting Mary Stuart with them in France."

"God's blood!" Angus Ferguson swore.

"The fact that you were a close friend of James Hepburn, the Earl of Bothwell, did but help in this fiction," the magistrate told Angus.

"They knew about that?" Angus was surprised. He was not a man for plots, but the complexity of this plan was quite masterful, and had he not been involved, he would've admired it.

"You must undo this," Monsieur Claude said. "You cannot allow an innocent man, his family, his good name to be tarnished by these lies. He could be executed for this supposed treason! Did you think of that, you greedy dog? And you have involved me as well. The family Claude has never been known to act dishonorably. Our name must be cleared in this as well."

"If the de Guises learn I have betrayed them, my family becomes endangered," the magistrate protested.

"Sir," the earl said in a reasonable tone, "the de Guises have achieved their goal. While the finger of guilt was pointed at me, they completed their plan, and none are the wiser. It is unlikely that you will be sought out by them for correcting this lapse in your judgment, for it is unlikely they will ever learn of it; *but* should this be brought to the attention of the de' Medicis . . ." His dagger speared another bit of the sliced capon. "You have, after all, forged my signature, and the signature of young Monsieur Claude as well. The de' Medicis would be delighted to have an opportunity to strike out at the de Guise family. When they learn how this was possible, they will then take their revenge upon you." He looked about the small dining salon. "This is a fine house you have," he murmured. "How will your wife and children enjoy living in the streets when your head ends up on a pike in this village square? They will be shunned, driven away for the shame you brought on Mont de Devereaux."

The magistrate whimpered as he pictured it all.

"You can take what you know to be the honorable course to correct this error," the earl concluded. "Or you can refuse me and I will kill you."

"If you kill me my wife and children will be safe," the magistrate said smugly.

"*Non*," Monsieur Claude told him. "For I shall expose your treachery to both the de Guise family and the de' Medicis. If you cannot be punished, then your family will be in your stead. Remember it is my merchant house that supplies the royal family with salt. I have the ability to ruin you and yours, and I will do it. Cooperate and you will be safe. As for the gold you took from the de Guises, if they do not know you betrayed them, it remains in your keeping. Is that not a better fate?"

The magistrate's face crumbled. He was an older man with a younger second wife who had given him children. It was not easy to keep Celestine content these days, to keep her from making him a laughingstock in the village. "What do you want me to do?" he asked despondently.

"You will write the letter that is dictated to you to the regent of Scotland, James Stewart, exonerating the Earl of Duin of any treason. You will say the de Guises threatened the life of your family if you did not give them a bill of sale claiming that Angus Ferguson had sold his property to them for an exorbitant price in exchange for his aid in restoring Mary Stuart to Scotland's throne. You will say that you complied out of fear, but once the deed was done your conscience niggled at you. You realized that an innocent man could be condemned to death for a treason he did not commit. You will tell the regent that the Earl of Duin had refused to sell his late *maman*'s estate to the agent of the de Guise family and instead sold it to a local merchant, one Monsieur Claude, who sought it for his newlywed son."

"Does the village have a priest? Preferably one who can read?" the earl asked.

"*Oui*, we do, but we also have a Huguenot pastor in residence. I suspect your king's regent would believe the word of a French Protestant clergyman more than that of a French Catholic priest," Monsieur Claude said.

"He's correct," Annabella murmured low to Angus.

"Instruct your servant to fetch parchment, ink, sealing wax, and the pastor," the Earl of Duin said. "When this is done my servant and I must return to Brest if we are to get to Leith upon the vessel that brought us here. The captain will wait only until Thursday for us. It's a safe and sound vessel."

They followed his instructions, and within the next hour, while the magistrate's dinner grew cold, the communiqué to James Stewart, regent to King James VI of Scotland, was written, signed, witnessed, and finally sealed with both the magistrate's seal and that of the pastor.

The Protestant clergyman shook his head when he heard the tale of deceit and duplicity. He was an educated man, and understood precisely what was involved in erasing any suspicion against the innocent earl. "I shall speak to *Père* Michel about your bad behavior," he told the magistrate sternly. "I am greatly concerned that your lack of judgment may extend to the cases you oversee."

The magistrate groaned, but then said, "I make my judgments based only upon the law, Pastor. I swear it."

"Your word can no longer be trusted," the pastor said. "I shall be watching."

He then turned back to the earl and shook his hand. "May God go with you, monsieur, and save you from evil men."

Two copies of the parchment had been given to the earl. He gave one to Annabella, and tucked the other in his shirt. Outside of the magistrate's house he bade Monsieur Claude adieu. Then he and Annabella mounted their horses and rode from the village of Mont de Devereaux. Once clear of the village Angus spoke.

"We may have to shelter in a field tonight. Actually I should prefer it."

"Aye, I would too," she agreed. "We can purchase food at the inn we stayed at last night, but let us ride on beyond it. We should be able to make Brest by nightfall tomorrow. Perhaps even in time for the evening tide. The sooner we reach Scotland, the better I will feel. I heard the sailors aboard the *Gazelle* speaking of how, now that the summer is just about gone, the weather at sea can be difficult. That one storm we suffered the night before we landed was enough for me. Where were you?"

"Playing chess with the captain," he said. "The game kept getting interrupted because now and again he was needed on deck," Angus explained.

"Master Hamilton sat up most of the night listening to the retching and howling of prayers from the father and son next door," she told him.

"Ye've been so brave," he told her admiringly. "Following after me not just across Scotland, but sailing on the *Gazelle* disguised as a lad."

"As a lass my face is so plain as to cause sympathy, but as a lad no one gave me a second glance," Annabella said, chuckling. "Dinna be angry at me, Angus, for I fear once we reach the safety of Duin yer relief will turn to anger. Never before did I sense danger for another, but when ye said ye were returning to France, I felt it then. I just couldna let ye go alone. Men do not, I know, like to believe they are vulnerable, but I should not have remained behind had yer brother tied me to a stake, Angus. I would hae chewed the ropes until I was free, and gone after ye," she declared vehemently.

"I believe ye," he said quietly. "I hae come to love ye as I never loved another, Annabella. We hae forged a strong bond of passion between us."

She felt the tears filling her soft gray eyes. "Aye,

Angus, we have indeed," she agreed with him. "Will ye forgie me for disobeying ye?"

"Ye saved my life," he said. "How can I fault that? And yer judgment today was invaluable to me. Thank ye."

"I must return to the ship as Master Hamilton," she told him.

He laughed. "I heard the tale ye wove for the captain. What will ye tell him now?" He moved his mount closer to her.

"I shall say I found my master carousing in a tavern wi' the innkeeper's buxom daughter, who hae become his mistress *and* is wi' bairn. That he hae promised her marriage, according to the gossips in the marketplace near the inn. Of course I dinna allow him to see me, and having learned what I needed to know for my mistress, I am returning as quickly as I can to her."

The earl chuckled. "Ye hae a talent, madam, for telling tall tales. Should I hae cause for concern?" he teased her.

"*Angus!*" Her tone was aggrieved, but she was smiling.

They rode on the rest of the afternoon, stopping at twilight at the inn where they had stayed the night before. They ate a hot meal rather than take the food with them. Then, as there was still some light left, they rode out once again. A full moon rose, and so they rode on until finally the earl called a stop to their travels. The horses were turned out into the field bordering the road to rest and graze. Annabella and her husband curled up together near a cairn of stones.

When the skies began to lighten they awoke to find themselves surrounded by a silvery gray mist that hung in and over the fields and the trees. They could see the outline of their horses. Angus went to fetch them. Annabella noticed that even the birds were silent in this magical environment that had sprung up around them. Saddling their beasts, they rode on toward Brest, stopping at a small roadside hostelry at noonday to fill their empty bellies with hot food and good wine.

By late afternoon they had reached Brest and rode first to the livery stables to return their mounts. Then they walked through the foggy streets to the stone quay where the *Gazelle* bobbed in the water at anchor. They were greeted by the captain.

"Excellent!" he said. "We'll make the tide in another hour. 'Tis early today. If ye had not come until later, we could not hae left until tomorrow. Master Hamilton, is that ye? Hae ye accomplished yer mission for yer mistress then, lad?"

"I hae," Annabella replied. "'Twas nae difficult." And then she recited to the captain just what she had told Angus earlier that she would say.

The captain laughed heartily, for there was nothing a sailor loved better than his beer and good gossip. "Ye'll nae mind sharing yer cabin again wi' His Lordship, will ye?" he asked. "The smaller cabin is occupied by a Scots merchant and his wife going home."

"I found the earl a most considerate traveler," Annabella said. "I hope he found me the same. I am happy to share wi' him."

"Good! Good! Then ye both know the way," the captain said.

Annabella drew the fare she had paid last time from a small purse beneath her shirt and offered it to the captain. He pocketed it with a nod. "Thank ye, Master Hamilton," he said to her. She moved quickly away, now seeking the security of the cabin. The fog was growing thicker, and she honestly didn't see how they could get under way at the turning of the tide without a wind to encourage the sails. Oddly, however, there was enough of a breeze despite the gauzelike mist. They managed to get down the river and into the open sea, where the wind began to blow a bit stronger.

By the time Angus reached the cabin Annabella was fast asleep. He let her rest, for the past few days had to have been difficult for her, even if she did not complain. In the morning they found the fog gone, but the skies overhead were a washed-out blue, almost white. The pale sun was a smudge above the vessel. The wind began to freshen, and two days later was blowing strongly.

"We're racing ahead of a fine storm," the cabin boy told Annabella. "We'll be to Leith several days ahead of schedule if these breezes keep up. Ye're lucky, for ye'll be home before ye know it. Unless, of course, the wind drops."

"And if it does?" Annabella asked him.

"We'll find ourselves in the midst of that fine storm for several days," he said sanguinely. "But I think luck is wi' us, Master Hamilton."

The *Gazelle* entered the Firth of Forth seven days later, just as night fell. Their voyage had been three days shorter than they had anticipated. The ship docked. The merchant and his wife hurried down the gangway and into the dim street. Annabella disembarked as quickly, heading for the Mermaid, where she and Angus were to meet. She had not seen Angus leave the ship, but he was already awaiting. Taking her arm, he led her to a private room in the rear of the inn, where there was a fine supper already laid out for them, and off the supper room she saw a bedchamber with a large, comfortable-looking bed.

"We're remaining the night?" she asked him.

"Aye. 'Tis too dark for us to go, but we'll leave at first light. Unpin yer braid, sweetheart," he said to her. "If anyone is looking for me they won't expect a man and a woman traveling together, but rather will be seeking just a single rider."

"Is someone looking for ye?" she asked candidly.

"They should nae be, if Matthew managed to keep Donal Stewart penned up," he answered her. "But I would nae take any chances. I'd rather send Stewart to his da wi' my parchment than hae to face Moray before I can explain the truth of the matter. The innkeeper tells me there hae been more troubles along the border the past two weeks. I dinna know if they are involved wi' *her* or nae. Damn the woman! Could she nae just keep Bothwell as a lover, the way her mam did wi' Patrick Hepburn?"

"How could she hide her belly?" Annabella said as she pulled off her cap and unpinned her braid. "She was a widow, and Knox would hae pilloried her publicly again. 'Tis nae like the old days, when a queen might be indiscreet privily." Annabella went to a small table where a basin of water and a towel were waiting. She washed her face and her hands.

"What madness that both of these Marys should fall in love with Hepburn men. What is it women see in them that I canna see?" He sat down across from her.

"That's because ye're a man," Annabella said with a giggle. "I watched as he spread charm to every pretty female wi'in his ken, and his charm is genuine. Women wanted to please him just because of his charm. They couldna help themselves, and he couldna help himself." She laughed. "But I truly believe that he loved the queen, a fact that surely confused him, for I doubt he had ever really loved any woman wi' all his heart and soul. How tragic that it should be the downfall of them both."

The earl was astounded by his wife's acuity. His respect for her grew. "Aye," he said. "I believe ye're correct, but it was up to the queen to consider Scotland first, and her own heart second. Her poor wee bairn, being raised by Erskine and his cold wife. A good man and a good woman, yet they lack the kindness needed for a bairn."

Annabella sighed. "I know," she said. "But after her great disappointment in Darnley I suspect it was very difficult for her to resist James Hepburn. I dinna know what it is about the Hepburn men, but they hae always been as fascinating to women as are the Stewarts. Can ye imagine what a child of Mary Stuart and James Hepburn would have been like, Angus? I wonder if God has not spared Scotland."

He smiled at her, thinking as he did that his wife was indeed very wise. "Aye," he agreed. "God may have indeed spared Scotland."

While she spoke she had carved him a goodly piece of beef, and piled his plate with some mussels in a mustard sauce, fresh peas, a bit of breast from a fat goose, bread, and cheese. She filled his goblet with rich red wine, then placed it before him. "Eat, my lord," she said. "It looks and smells delicious. 'Tis the first good meal we have shared in several weeks." She then attended to her own plate, which contained a similar array of food. They both ate with a good appetite.

A small tartlet of apple had been left on the sideboard. When Annabella had cleared their plates away, she divided the little sweet, covering it with clotted cream. She gave him the larger portion, for she knew how much her husband enjoyed this particular treat. He devoured it quickly, and she gave him what remained upon her plate. With a guilty smile he accepted it, and ate it quickly.

"Did ye think I would take it back?" Annabella teased him as he wolfed down what remained of the sweet.

He laughed. "Matthew, James, and I always squabbled over the last bit of a treat, and usually while we did Jean snatched it for herself," the earl told his wife.

"Roosters do a lot of crowing," Annabella teased him.

He chuckled, then, reaching across the small table, took her hand in his. He kissed each finger in its turn. "I hae come to love ye so greatly that were I ever to lose ye, madam, I think my life would be bleak forevermore."

Annabella felt herself near tears with his passionate declaration, but then he continued.

"*But*, if I should ever hae to leave Duin again, and ye follow after me when I hae told ye nay, I swear I shall lock ye in the castle's highest tower, and never let ye roam free again! Do ye understand me, madam? When I tell ye nay, I mean nay."

"Ye would hae never known I followed ye had those villains nae attempted murder," Annabella said. "I could nae let them kill ye."

"I was awake, madam, for I was expecting such an attempt. Do ye think me such a fool that I was nae aware I was being followed? Actually I thought there were three of them, particularly when ye decided to remain after the meal," he told her.

Annabella giggled.

"Ye find this amusing?" he said to her, standing up.

"Aye, I do. Ye thought I was an assassin when I was

really there to protect ye." And Annabella began to laugh. "Did I really look like an assassin?"

"Assassins dinna hae a *look*," he said, coming around the table and pulling her into his arms. The feel of her sweetly rounded body against him, her plain little face looking up at him with those trusting gray eyes of hers, the subtle fragrance of her, set his senses reeling. This was *his* woman, and she had put herself in danger for him. *God's blood!* Was there a more fortunate man alive in Scotland today than he was? All he wanted to do was get them safely home to Duin to live their lives in peace, and never have to leave it again.

Annabella had grown silent, watching the play of strong emotions crossing his outrageously handsome face. What good luck had brought her this wonderful man who loved her? "I think, Angus," she said softly, "that it is past time ye kissed me and took me to bed, my dearest lord." Her fingers caressed his cheek.

He smiled suddenly, and nodded. Then his mouth took hers in a slow, deep kiss even while he picked her up and took her into their bedchamber. Together they undressed each other by the light of the fire in the hearth before crawling between the lavender-scented sheets. Annabella sighed with happiness as he stroked the length of her body.

His touch sent little shivers of delight through her. She lay on her belly while his lips pressed little kisses down the length of her spine. She lay on her back as his hands caressed her breasts and belly. His mouth suckled slowly at her nipples until they were sore, but she was so filled with pleasure that it didn't matter.

Finally he whispered in her ear as his big body began to cover hers, "I need to be inside of you, sweetheart."

She felt his length and thickness against her thigh.

Her legs opened for him, wrapped themselves about his torso as he pushed himself slowly, slowly into her wet and waiting sheath, and she groaned as he filled her entirely. "Oh, Angus!" She sighed, clinging to him, her nails digging lightly into his broad shoulders.

Jesu, he thought. She felt so damned good. His cock was throbbing with his need for her. The wall of her sheath tightened about him, clenching and unclenching, until he cried out low. He began to move upon her, slowly at first, but as his lust increased, faster and faster, deeper, deeper, deeper. He could feel the crisis approaching for them both, and struggled not to race ahead of her.

Then Annabella said hotly in his ear, "Now! Now! *Now!*"

His creamy tribute burst forth and their love juices combined, leaving them both satisfied and breathless. "God's blood, how I love ye!" he whispered hoarsely.

"Nae as much as I love ye!" she whispered back.

They slept, exhausted, for the next several hours, but, aware of their need for haste, he awoke just before first light to arise, wash, and dress. Only when he was fully clothed did he awaken his naked wife, who lay sprawled upon her belly amid the tangled sheets, her limbs askew, her sable plait undone and spread across her upper torso. Even clothed he found he was tempted to climb back into the bed and take her again. Instead he shook her gently. "Wake up, sweetheart. We've got miles to go before we reach Duin."

Annabella protested sleepily. Then with a little groan she opened her eyes and rolled over onto her back. "Come back to bed, my lord," she entreated him. "The light is nae even tinting the skies yet."

"We're leaving at first light," he told her. "Get up

now, Annabella. Are ye nae anxious to get home? We have several days' riding ahead of us before we do."

With another small groan she pulled herself up, swung her legs over the bed, and stood. Her eyes were closed again, but she smiled when he said he would leave her to her toilette.

Annabella heard him close the bedchamber door. She quickly washed herself and pulled on her garments. Then, sitting back upon the bed, she brushed her hair out with the brush she pulled from her saddlebag. Her hair felt sticky with salt from her two sea voyages, and she could feel the dust of the summer roads in her scalp. She brushed and brushed until her head and long tresses felt a little better. Then she quickly braided the long, dark hair into a thick plait, securing it with a small scrap of red ribbon. She left it hanging. Riding with her husband, she no longer had a need to conceal her identity.

He was waiting for her in the dayroom. To her surprise the supper dishes were gone from the sideboard, and in their stead upon the little table was a hot meal of oat stirabout in a bread trencher, a bowl of hard-boiled eggs, some cheese, and bread. She sat down and began to quickly eat as she saw Angus was already half-finished.

"We can take what we don't eat of the bread, cheese, and eggs wi' us for our ride," Annabella told her husband. "That way we won't hae to stop but briefly at midday, and can ride until sunset."

He grunted his approval of her plan.

When they had finished they went into the taproom and paid the landlord, who looked slightly confused as he attempted to identify Annabella's gender, for he had been certain it had been a young man traveling with the earl. But suddenly the young man had breasts that swelled generously beneath his or her shirt, and a long braid that hung down her—for he suddenly realized it was a female—back. He didn't approve of bold women, but, taking the earl's coin, he wished them a pleasant journey.

The two horses they had stabled several weeks ago were fresh and waiting for them. They mounted and turned onto the streets of Leith, making for the road that would take them southwest into the borders, and eventually to Duin. The first day was gray. The next two it rained, and they were forced to shelter in the open at night. Finally, on the fourth morning, the weather recalled it was September. The sun shone down on them as they rode onward.

The main road remained relatively safe, with its busy daytime traffic, but once they turned off of it they became warier. Now and again they saw parties of horsemen in the distance, galloping over the moors. There were several times they heard the thunder of horses' hooves before they even saw anyone. If there was a place of shelter they wisely sought it until the riders had gone by. But one afternoon a large party of men showing the red plaid of the Hamiltons caught them unawares, surrounding them upon the road.

"Do ye stand for the Queen's Men or the King's Men?" the leader asked bluntly.

"I stand for Scotland," Angus Ferguson answered them quietly.

"The queen's Scotland or the king's Scotland?" the leader persisted.

"I stand for Scotland," the earl repeated. "There is but one."

The leader of the Hamilton faction looked puzzled,

but then the man next to him laughed. "Ye hae to be the Ferguson of Duin," he said, "for only he would dare to keep himself from this fray."

"I am Angus Ferguson," the earl admitted.

"Why will ye nae declare for queen or king?" the Hamilton leader asked him now that he realized the man before him was no enemy.

"The Fergusons of Duin hae always kept themselves from siding wi' any faction," the man who had recognized Angus said. "They truly do stand for Scotland."

"The queen must be restored," the Hamilton leader said.

"Scotland must hae peace," Angus told him. "If ye want to fight, then fight wi' the English, not yer own fellow Scots. It does our country nae good when we quarrel wi' one another, but it makes England and the rest of Europe very happy."

"Ye must choose!" the Hamilton leader insisted.

"I will take sides with nae one. I stand for Scotland," the earl repeated once again.

"Leave him be," the other man said. "His wife's mother is a Hamilton." He turned to Angus. "Did ye nae wed Anne Hamilton's daughter?"

"I did," the earl replied. Then, reaching out, he drew Annabella's mount forward. "Here is my countess, who rides wi' me on family business. I have learned she is the bonniest woman alive, and I'll fight any man who says otherwise."

"Annabella Baird, I am yer cousin Jock Hamilton," the man who had defended Angus said. "Yer mother's family will be pleased to know how highly yer husband values ye. How do ye stand? For queen or for king?"

"I stand for Scotland," Annabella told him with a small smile.

The Hamiltons within her hearing chuckled at her reply, and even their leader grinned. "Travel on in safety," he told the earl and his wife as he moved his horse aside.

"We thank ye," Angus Ferguson said as he and Annabella rode by. They were just two days from Duin.

Chapter 14

They could smell the sea on the afternoon wind. The horses too sensed the nearness of home, which seemed to give more energy to their steps. And then they crested the final hill, and Duin lay below them on its cliff above the sea. Angus dismounted and, walking over to a little pile of stones, bent down, appearing to fumble with his hands. Then he stood tall once more. As he mounted his stallion a small rocket streaked from the rocks into the sky to explode over the castle.

Annabella watched in amazement as the drawbridge began to lower over the chasm separating the castle from the cliffs. "I dinna know ye had a signal fixed," she said. "How clever."

"Matthew was instructed nae to lower the drawbridge to any but me," Angus told her. "Duin is impossible to take otherwise wi'out cannon."

"Mother of mercy, may there never be cannon pointed at our walls," Annabella said. "Why would anyone want to take Duin?"

"Times change, and we are nae longer as isolated as we once were," he said.

They cantered down the hill, crossing the now lowered bridge into the courtyard, where Matthew was waiting to greet them. When he saw Annabella his face grew dark with anger. "I dinna know yer vixen would follow after ye!" were the first words from his mouth. "She tricked me, wi' Jeannie's help, Angus."

The Earl of Duin laughed. "She saved my life," he told his younger brother. "I'll hear nae more of yer complaints, Matthew. Are our prisoners still being kept comfortable? I was successful in obtaining proof of my innocence." He took Annabella's hand as together they walked into the castle.

"Aye, they're well, though testy about being penned up so long," Matthew said.

"We'll release them on the morrow," the earl replied. "Ye can bring Donal Stewart to me in the hall now. He'll eat wi' us this evening. How is Aggie?"

"Delivered me a fine son two days ago," Matthew responded proudly. "With nae help but from my mother and Jeannie." He shot Annabella a fierce look.

"We'll come see the lad tomorrow," the earl said as they entered the hall.

"I'll fetch Donal Stewart," Matthew responded, and hurried off.

"He hae never really liked me," Annabella said quietly. "Yet I know he loves my sister." She sighed.

"He's old-fashioned, like our father was. Don't pay him any mind," Angus said candidly. Then he kissed her a lovely slow, sweet kiss that came to an end only when they heard Matthew harrumph. Angus released Annabella, and they smiled at each other as he eased his hold on her.

God's bones, Donal Stewart thought, seeing them together. *How much they love each other.*

"I hope ye hae been comfortable in my care," the Earl of Duin said.

Donal Stewart nodded. "We hae been well treated and well fed, my lord. Other than the loss of my freedom I canna complain. Yer brother tells me ye returned to France." He looked curiously at Angus Ferguson. "To what purpose, if I may ask?"

"Ye may," the earl replied. "But come; the meal is ready. Let us adjourn to the high board, and I will tell ye everything."

The three men and Annabella seated themselves at the table. The servants brought in the food, and they ate as the earl spoke.

"I am nae a traitor. Today on the road we met wi' a band of horsemen who demanded to know whether I was for king or queen. I told them I stood for Scotland, and I do. The history of the Fergusons of Duin is a well-known one. We dinna involve ourselves in politics. Families who do generally meet with misfortune somewhere along the way." He ceased his speech briefly to eat. Then he told them the story of his dealings with Monsieur Claude, the de Guise agent, and the magistrate.

"Ye refused a larger offer for Monsieur Claude's offer?" Donal Stewart was slightly disbelieving. He liked the Earl of Duin. His instincts told him this man was no traitor, yet he had refused a lucrative offer to accept a reasonable one. "Why?" He needed to know that.

The Earl of Duin smiled at the frank request. "I am a rich man, Donal Stewart," he said. "Everyone knows that. What they dinna know is the extent of my wealth. A wise man keeps such things to himself lest he be envied by his neighbors. My wealth stems from the generosity of my mother's sister and her husband. They were childless, and left me all they possessed. Their lands, however, remained in his family, but the bulk of his wealth was passed on to me. I want for nothing, for I husband this wealth carefully, and hae increased it over the years. I would be a fool to lose all that I have by committing treason against the crown, to lose my home, my family, my bairns. James the sixth of his name is crowned king. He is Scotland, and I stand for Scotland."

"Mary Stuart was once crowned queen of Scotland, and she yet lives," Donal Stewart said quietly.

"Aye, she was, and she does. But she hae foolishly left her realm to flee into England," Angus Ferguson replied.

"Ye're Bothwell's friend," Donal Stewart said.

"I am, and I will nae deny it," Angus responded. "It does nae mean that I approved his rash actions, however."

"What proof hae ye brought back for my sire to judge ye?" Donal Stewart said.

The earl told Donal Stewart of his most recent travels to France, and how he and Monsieur Claude had forced a confession of fraud from the magistrate.

"But the gold, the letter to Mary Stuart?" Donal Stewart asked.

"Slipped into my saddlebag as I traveled," the earl said. "No one was more surprised to see them than I was when yer man brought them into the hall. Ye must admit that the letter itself was a bland bit of writing, making no offer to Mary Stuart of help."

"Aye," Donal Stewart agreed. "And it was probably written by the agent. The parchment showed no seal in the wax. I was suspicious, but the rest seemed to involve ye, my lord. I will need proof of some sort if ye are to convince my sire of yer innocence."

"I have documented all, and have two copies of everything. One will go wi' ye when ye and yer men leave Duin tomorrow to seek out the regent."

"Ye will nae go?" Donal Stewart was surprised.

"Yer sire's first instinct would be to throw me in prison while he considered the matter at his leisure," the Earl of Duin said. "His time is better spent governing Scotland right now. But he will sit long enough to listen to yer report and yer advice in this matter. Perhaps he will be able to come to a quick decision. He is welcome to come to Duin and speak wi' me himself. 'Tis bold of me to suggest it, but I hae been away from home long enough these last months. I wish to pick up the threads of my life and live in peace again," Angus Ferguson declared.

"My opinion counts for little among my sire and his friends," Donal Stewart said, "but I think it will be several years before Scotland is at peace again. For now my sire fears the return of his half sister, for many wish it. And the care of a child king, as ye know from our history, is a perilous one, my lord."

His companions all nodded.

"Poor wee bairn," Annabella said. "I'm sure he hae everything he needs, and is warm and dry, but where is the love in his life? A bairn needs a parent or a keeper who will hug him, rock him to sleep in her arms, cuddle him when he is frightened. The unfortunate mite is surrounded by greedy men, all eager to rule in his name."

Donal Stewart nodded. "I mean nae disrespect to my own sire, madam, but ye're correct. They all see the laddie as a pawn for their own use and the enrichment of their families."

"Yet she left him," Annabella said. "If I were asked I should nae be able to support a woman who abandoned her own bairn."

"I think yer plan a sound one, my lord," Donal Stewart said to the earl. "Ye're right when ye say my sire would toss ye in the nearest prison in fear of ye. Aye, I'll take yer proofs to him, and explain myself how ye went off to France to clear yer name. Ye hae witnesses other than the French involved."

"I was wi' my husband," Annabella said. "I know the courts will nae take a woman's sworn word, but surely the regent would if I spoke wi' him."

"Ye were wi' yer lord?" Donal Stewart didn't know whether to believe her or not.

Angus laughed. "Aye, the vixen disguised herself as a lad, binding her breasts flat and hiding her hair beneath her cap. Then she followed after me, and saved my life when a pair of villains attempted to murder me." He went on to explain in detail how Annabella had gone after him and hidden her identity. How he had learned of her deception only when she had to reveal herself to save him.

Donal Stewart was amazed. His sire would be intrigued. The young Countess of Duin was the kind of woman whom every man should be so fortunate as to possess: loyal to a fault, and loving. "Madam," he said, "I dinna think I approve of yer actions, but I must say that I admire what ye did for yer man."

It was agreed that Donal Stewart and his men would depart in the morning, and they did. The Earl of Moray's bastard son promised to send word once he had spoken with his sire on the matter. Then he rode off, and the drawbridge was drawn up once again to keep Duin Castle safe from unwanted guests. The earl was therefore surprised several days later to see a large party of men gathered on the hill above the castle. The men-at-arms stood at the alert. And then one man detached himself from the party and rode down the road to Duin. Watching from the heights, Angus Ferguson recognized Donal Stewart. "Lower the drawbridge," he said.

The visitor galloped into the courtyard of the castle, where the earl was waiting to greet him. He immediately jumped from his horse, bowed, and then said, "The Earl of Moray sends his compliments. He would like yer permission to enter Duin Castle, my lord."

"He is welcome wi' ten men, no more, Donal Stewart," Angus said. "Ye will understand I canna sanction more." Then he said, "I dinna expect to see ye for several more weeks."

"I met my sire on the road, my lord. He is due in York shortly, but diverted his travels to come to Duin, as he will tell ye."

"Fetch him, then," the earl said.

Annabella was astounded that the powerful Earl of Moray would pause in his travels. "He hae hardly *diverted* his travels to see ye," she said to her husband. "York is on the other side of England. He hae some other business in the west that he would bother to come here. Now I must know whether he is remaining the night, and surely he will. And how are we to feed that great troop he has wi' him?" She began marshaling her servants and ordering them to prepare the largest guest chamber for Moray. She hurried down to the kitchens to advise the cook of their unexpected guests. Then she dashed back upstairs to her own apartments to put on a gown more suitable to welcoming Scotland's regent than the old gown she was wearing.

Jean was waiting for her. She helped her mistress into a burgundy velvet gown trimmed in dark marten fur. The gown was one Annabella had worn at court two years ago. It was probably out of fashion by now, but would the regent Moray notice? Probably not. Jean quickly undid Annabella's plait and styled it into a chignon.

"Do ye think he'll arrest Angus?" she finally asked.

"I dinna think so," Annabella said. "He is said to be a practical man. Duin poses no threat to him or the wee king. He's simply curious, for while Donal Stewart says he met his sire on the road, he has obviously told him everything. Moray would confirm his son's judgment in the matter." She stood up and shook out her skirts. "Come into the hall and listen," she said as she hurried out.

Angus Ferguson had been there to greet his guest as he dismounted his horse in the courtyard. "My lord of Moray," he said, bowing. "Welcome to Duin Castle."

Moray's dark eyes flicked swiftly about, taking in everything. "I had not expected to find a structure of such size in this part of the land," he said.

"The late queen mother, Marie de Guise, was kind enough to grant us permission for Duin," Angus replied.

"Was that yer first connection wi' the house of de Guise, my lord?" Moray asked.

"It is my only connection wi' them, my lord," Angus replied. "Please, will ye come into the hall? My wife will be waiting to greet ye." He led the Earl of Moray and his small party inside the castle.

As they entered the hall Annabella came forward. She curtsied low to the Earl of Moray. "I bid ye welcome to Duin, my lord." She stood.

"I thank ye, madam." Again his curious eyes quickly scanned his surroundings.

"Please," Annabella invited him, "come and sit by the fire." She signaled a servant to bring the Earl of Moray a goblet of wine. "I hope ye will honor us by staying the night. I hae had our best guest chamber prepared for ye."

"Aye," Moray said. "I should like that, madam. I thank ye for yer hospitality."

"Shall I send word to yer men outside my walls to raise an encampment for the night?" Angus Ferguson asked his guest. "I will send them a sheep to roast."

"Most generous," Moray said. "Aye, have them make camp." He turned his attention to his goblet, sniffing it first, then tasting it. A small smile touched his lips. "Ye keep an excellent wine cellar, my lord," he complimented Angus.

Annabella quietly reviewed all she had known about this particular James Stewart. He was the illegitimate son of James V and Margaret Erskine, who had been married to a Douglas. Margaret Erskine had been the favorite of James V's several mistresses. He had been given the priory of St. Andrew's as a lad, which accounted for his personal income. When his father had been killed it had been the king's widow who had gathered all of her husband's bastards to be raised in the royal nurseries with her own little Mary. He had been half-grown when Mary had been born.

He was a tall man, like many of the Stewarts, with a prominent nose and chin. He had the reddish hair that distinguished them, and their amber eyes. Marie de Guise had been as proud of him as if he were her own son. The rumor was that she had planned to make him her daughter's regent if she found herself at death's door before Mary came of age in France. And James Stewart had liked Marie de Guise. He found her, unlike her daughter, a practical woman. It was a trait he much admired in women.

Like many Scots of his time, he had become a member of the Reformed Church. He had attempted to guide his half sister, but her determination to marry

Henry, Lord Darnley, set them at odds. After that he spent his time in rebellion and exile. Mary had forgiven him and pardoned him officially, but their relationship was never the same again, especially after the murders of Riccio and Lord Darnley, and Mary's hasty marriage to Bothwell. But that was all in the past now. Mary was fled, and he was regent of Scotland for his infant nephew.

After a few moments of silence he invited Angus and his lady to sit with him.

Then he said, "My son, Donal, has told me everything. Now I would hear it from ye, my lord of Duin. Evidence hae been presented that would appear to show ye in a traitorous light. Now ye bring evidence that says ye are an honest man. Which of these stories am I to believe? Both are credible."

"My lord, if I might ask a question," Angus said.

Moray nodded. "Aye."

"Who was it who brought this information to yer attention?"

"I dinna know," Moray replied. "One of my men overheard talk in a tavern."

"So ye hae no basis in fact for the accusation but a rumor on the wind," Angus said. "I deny being a traitor to Scotland, my lord. The Fergusons of Duin hae a reputation for avoiding politics and the entanglements caused by politics. Look around ye. I hae a good home and wife. Two wee bairns. I want for nothing. Why in the name of God would I endanger all I have to pursue a lost cause?"

"So ye believe the queen's cause a lost one," Moray said.

"I do. Like many of yer acquaintance I dinna like the way the queen was handled after her defeat at Carberry.

She was God's own anointed. But when she was again defeated at Langside several months ago and fled into England, I could no longer defend her actions, nor could many of her adherents. Her son was declared king in her stead. It is the natural order for a queen's heir to follow her. I stand neither for the Queen's Men nor the King's Men. I stand for Scotland, and wee James the Sixth is Scotland."

The Earl of Moray was impressed by Angus's arguments, but he said, "What of the papers and the gold that implicate ye?"

"The paper was a forgery. Both it and the gold were put deep into my saddlebag, where I was unlikely to find them, but someone searching would. As Donal Stewart will hae told ye, I traveled back to France to resolve the matter. The local magistrate had been paid to draw up the forgery. The new owner of the property had been importuned to sign it, but would not, realizing something was wrong. His signature and mine were both forged. When pressed, the magistrate admitted to it. Among the papers Donal Stewart will hae brought ye is a paper where he confesses his misdeeds.

"As for the bag of gold coins found, I do not need gold. I hae more than enough gold, a fact I will be more than willing to prove to ye, and ye alone. The Fergusons of Duin are nae traitors. I am nae a traitor. I can only rely upon yer common sense, my lord Moray, to understand that so we may both put this matter aside," Angus concluded.

"I understand yer wife went wi' ye to France disguised as a lad," Moray said. He turned to Annabella. "Is this so, madam?"

"Aye, it is," she answered him. "My instinct sensed that Angus would be in danger. I asked to accompany him, but he said nay. So I disguised myself and followed him. Only when the danger presented itself was I forced to reveal my identity to him."

A small smile touched Moray's thin lips briefly. "Ye would, it seems, be a determined woman, madam."

"Aye, my lord, I am," Annabella replied in meek tones.

He looked at her sharply, but Annabella's eyes were modestly lowered.

"My countess saved my life, my lord," Angus told Moray, and then he went on to explain exactly how it had come about.

"Your wife's lack of a pretty face was fortunate, and surely aided her in passing as a lad," Moray noted. "Your bosom, however, madam, appears quite round. How did ye disguise it?" he inquired candidly.

"I bound them flat wi' a cloth," Annabella answered shortly.

"I am curious to see ye garbed as a lad, madam," the Earl of Moray said.

"My lord!" Angus Ferguson was outraged by the request, but Annabella would not allow the regent to intimidate her, putting a restraining hand on her husband's arm.

"Of course, my lord. Wi' yer permission I shall withdraw from yer company now, and put on my male garb." She curtsied to him, and walked slowly from the hall.

Jean was beside her as they entered the corridor. "Ohh, the boldness of that man," she said, outraged. "He appears pious and sedate to all, but when was a royal Stewart ever either? Remarking on yer lack, and then asking about yer breasts!"

"Moray is testing us," Annabella said. "He would see just how obedient the Fergusons of Duin are. Angus offered the proper amount of outrage to his request, but he did not gainsay me when I offered to show the regent my disguise," she explained.

The two women hurried upstairs to Annabella's apartments, where Jean sought out the clothing her mistress had worn during her adventure in France. Soon Annabella had been divested of her burgundy velvet gown and its petticoats. She pulled on her woolen breeks and her boots. Then Jean bound her mistress's breasts flat with a piece of cloth. Annabella donned her shirt and the sleeveless doeskin jerkin. Jean plaited the dark sable hair, tightly pinning it up. Annabella then put on her cap. The lad she had been was now visible in the mirror, while the Countess of Duin had disappeared entirely.

Standing, she left her apartments, walking downstairs and back into the hall again. No one noticed her at all. She moved stealthily until she was standing near enough to both earls to be seen. But no one said anything.

Finally, after some minutes had passed, Moray said to Angus Ferguson, "How long does it take yer wife to make this transformation, my lord? We hae been waiting close to an hour now."

"And I hae been standing near ye for many minutes, my lord," Annabella said.

The Earl of Moray gasped with surprise as he turned to look at the young man now standing by his side. He stared hard. The plain but elegant Countess of Duin was not evident at all in the young man standing before him. But then she looked directly at him, and he recognized her calm gray eyes. "Madam, I am astounded by this transformation," he told her. "It is quite amazing. I dinna know whether to commend ye on yer disguise or condemn ye for yer boldness."

"I dinna mean to be bold, my lord. I only wanted to make certain my dear lord and husband was safe from harm. Anyone going to the trouble of making Angus appear a traitor would nae hesitate to kill him should their plan be thwarted," Annabella said.

Moray nodded. "Obviously someone wished to detract us from some mischief enacted on my sister's behalf. The letter in yer husband's saddlebag was quite innocuous, and might hae been sent to Mary directly. That ye and yer husband went to the difficulty of learning what small truths could be learned tells me he is innocent of all charges, as my son, Donal, believes." Then he turned to Angus. "But, my lord, before we dine I would see proof that ye have no need for gold."

"Of course," the Earl of Duin said. "If ye will be pleased to follow me. No one else may come," he told Moray and his companions. "Only ye, James Stewart." Moray nodded in agreement, for his curiosity was great. He followed Angus Ferguson from the hall, through a small door hidden behind a large tapestry in the wide hallway outside of the hall, and down several narrow, twisting flights of stairs. Angus carried no torch, for the stairwell was well lighted, and the corridor below as well.

They stopped before a door at the end of the short corridor. The earl took a small ring of keys from his doublet, searched among them, and, selecting one key, fitted it into the lock in the door. The key turned easily without the slightest sound. Angus Ferguson took a torch from the holder nearest the door and flung the door wide. He stepped in, Moray behind him. The torch lit the small stone chamber, whose walls were lined with chests.

The Earl of Duin moved from chest to chest, lifting

the lid of each. When the fifteen containers had been opened he waved his torch over them.

James Stewart, the Earl of Moray, gasped in amazement. The small trunks were filled with gold and silver coins. "How . . . how is this possible? Are the stories that are told of yer family's sorcery true, my lord?"

Angus Ferguson laughed. "Nay, my lord, those tales are false. This wealth comes from mines that I inherited in the New World. They originally belonged to my mother's sister and her husband, a Spanish lord. They were childless, and I was their heir. This is the secret I harbor, and now you are aware of it, my lord. You see how I live. Simply but comfortably. I could not spend all the coins contained in these chests if I live to be a century old. Why would I risk all that I have and be branded a traitor as well for a wee bag of coins that might to some represent a fortune, but to me is but little?"

He had to be dreaming, James Stewart, Earl of Moray, thought. He had never seen so much gold and silver in his entire life. It was surely enough to support Scotland's government for years to come. He was tempted to confiscate the chests in this chamber, but he would not. He was a canny man. He had always made certain to keep free of any plots, although he had certainly known about enough of them, and even sanctioned them. But he could not be accused of partaking in them. He had been in England when both Riccio and Darnley were murdered. James Stewart, Earl of Moray, was a careful man.

He was also a leading member of the Lords of the Congregation, a respected member of the Reformed Church of Scotland. *Thou shalt not covet* was a commandment he could not break. He took his faith seriously, for the most part. Even his bastard son was the result of a youthful dalliance long before his marriage to his wife. Once wed he had never committed adultery. But God had certainly punished him for that peccadillo. His wife had produced only three daughters. If he had a weakness at all, it was his lasses, Elizabeth, Annabel, and Margaret. But he had always been good to his lad too.

"I will donate two chests of coins to the royal treasury," the Earl of Duin said.

"Yer secret is safe wi' me, Angus Ferguson, even wi'out yer generosity," Moray said. "Perhaps ye will now and again gift the royal bairn wi' something. A pony. A sword made just for him. A velvet doublet," he suggested slyly. "As ye did wi' his curst mam."

"I will do so gladly," Angus replied. "And I will gift yer brother John's laddie, Francis, as well, for Bothwell's sake. He is his uncle's heir, and his uncle was my friend."

Moray nodded. "I understand," he said, "but dinna ever say his name in my presence again. I canna forgie him for marrying Mary. He brought about her downfall."

Angus Ferguson said nothing, just nodded. In a sense, he held himself partly responsible for the queen's behavior. It had been his wealth that had made it possible for the queen of the Scots to have any- and everything she wanted as she grew up in France as the adored and pampered bride-to-be of the young dauphin. She was beautiful, and she was charming. The French court had adored her. She could not be faulted for believing all men would be dazzled by her youth, beauty, and manner. But Scotsmen were different from other men.

To give her credit, she had tried to get on with those hard, cold lords who surrounded her. In becoming members of the Reformed kirk, Scotland's nobles had lost their joie de vivre. John Knox's thunderous sermons preached on sin and punishment, hellfire and damnation. And the bishops of Holy Mother Church, with their mistresses, their many bastards, and their lavish living, had not helped their own cause at all.

Knox had grown used to his power, but he could not keep Mary Stuart from returning from France to rule Scotland. Mary, unfortunately, was ruled by her heart and not her head. It was, Angus considered, a great tragedy all around.

"Come," he said, leading his guest back upstairs to the hall.

Once there Moray gratefully accepted a large goblet of the earl's good wine, and sat down by the fire to drink it.

Donal Stewart came to stand by his sire's chair. "Ye're satisfied that the earl is innocent of any attempts at treason?"

"Aye," Moray said.

"He showed ye his gold?" Donal pressed.

Moray nodded, but then he said, "Ask me no more, for I am sworn to keep the confidence, and I will." He drank deeply from the cup in his hand.

Across the hall Annabella stood by the other hearth. "Is he satisfied?" she asked her husband. "How much did ye reveal to him?"

"Just the one small chamber at the foot of the tapestry stairs," Angus said. "To hae shown him all would have probably killed him wi' too much knowledge. He dinna need to see the other chests with their gold and jewels. 'Twas more coin in one spot than he had ever seen, or is apt to see. It convinced him I am an honest man. He is free of suspicion. He will depart tomorrow, and we will go back to living a normal life."

In the morning the Earl of Moray left Duin Castle

for York, where the English queen, Elizabeth Tudor, had set up a conference chaired by the Duke of Norfolk to settle the dispute between Mary Stuart, queen of the Scots, and her half brother, James Stewart, Earl of Moray. This event was of such interest and importance to the people of Scotland that news of what was happening even reached Duin on a regular basis. Mary was not allowed to attend, although she was represented. Moray was there to speak for himself, which infuriated her, and many thought it unfair. The conference began in early October, reconvening in late November at Westminster, and holding its final session at Hampton Court in the middle of December.

Moray's rebellious behavior was suddenly less and less important, while the matter of Lord Darnley's murder became paramount, even though it had been settled in Scotland.

James Stewart suddenly formally accused his half sister of partaking in the murder. He brought forth her treasured silver casket that King Francis I of France had given her as a child. Inside was a small stack of rather salacious letters said to have been written by Mary that clearly indicated her involvement in the murder, which was now said to have been committed by James Hepburn, Earl of Bothwell, who for lack of evidence earlier had been cleared of this deed by the Scottish courts.

All of this information was brought to Elizabeth Tudor. She personally examined it, and then said, "They might have done a better job of the forgery, Cecil. 'Tis rubbish! I don't believe a word of it! The verdict has certainly not been proven to anyone with intelligence. Give Moray five thousand pounds, and tell him he is to return to Scotland in his position of regent. It is my wish that he keep his nephew, our most royal cousin King

James, safe until he is grown and able to govern for himself."

"And Mary Stuart?" Sir William Cecil asked his mistress.

Elizabeth Tudor considered in silence for several moments, her long, elegant fingers drumming on the arm of her chair. Finally she said, "Another matter altogether, Cecil. Mary cannot be allowed to return to Scotland. That northern land is better ruled by an infant king and his quarrelsome lords. The Scots will not declare any wars on England until they have a king who can lead their armies. That will not be for many years, Cecil. And my cousin, his mother, must not be allowed to flee to France, where Catherine de' Medicis and her son will use the queen of the Scots as a pawn in whatever game they would play with England.

"I think that Mary Stuart must be moved to Tutbury Castle. It has not the graciousness of her former abode, but it is better defended. It will be difficult for anyone to help her escape from Tutbury. Let the Earl of Shrewsbury and his wife, Bess, oversee the care for the queen of the Scots. They own that old heap of stones."

"Will you see the Earl of Moray before he returns to Scotland?" Cecil inquired.

"Aye, I shall greet him warmly, and he will go on his way, content that England will leave him to his own devices," Elizabeth Tudor said with a chuckle.

In late February the word reached Duin of the no-fault decision in the matter between Mary and her half brother, James Stewart, Earl of Moray.

"How clever this English queen is," Annabella said admiringly. "She hae found her cousin guilty of nothing, and Moray free of sin as well. She hae sent him back to resume his place as regent, and found a more secure place to keep Mary Stuart, taking her deeper into England. She will nae escape to France now."

"And perhaps we will finally have peace," the Earl of Duin said. "Moray is sly, but he is honorable. He will keep the little king safe, and rule in a reasonable fashion."

"There are those who dinna like him," Annabella replied. "And are envious of him. The Queen's Men are nae yet ready to concede defeat. The Hamiltons in particular."

"Moray is firmly in control," Angus replied.

"None of our kings who came to the throne as bairns lived till their majority wi' just one regent," Annabella reminded him. "Only Marie de Guise was able to hold the reins of power firmly in her hands long enough to get Mary Stuart to safety. Too many men, most of them involved in Riccio's murder, hold positions of power. They are ruthless and would think little of slaying a bairn."

"The king is Moray's own blood."

"As if kinship ever stopped a usurper," Annabella replied dryly.

"He'll keep the laddie safe," Angus insisted.

But the borders remained restless, with the Hamiltons stirring up discontent in their unceasing efforts to restore Mary Stuart to power. Immediately after her flight into England, Mary had been housed in Carlisle Castle, then moved to Bolton Castle. Both were located in the north of Yorkshire. After the verdict rendered at Hampton Court, the Scots queen was moved to Tutbury, an inhospitable stone keep located farther south in Staffordshire. Surrounded by marshes, it was a less than gracious abode. But it did not keep Mary's partisans from planning her escape. First, however, several routes for messengers had to be established.

A young man, one William Hamilton by name, came to Duin. They knew him as nothing more than a traveler seeking border hospitality, but that night in the hall he took Angus aside and asked for his help. "We hae several routes for our messengers to take between Scotland and England, but this western route is one that would nae be seriously considered by those seeking to thwart us," he explained.

A chill ran down Annabella's back as she listened to William Hamilton.

"And what purposes do yer messengers serve, Master Hamilton?" the earl asked.

"Why, they serve to keep us in communication wi' our brethren who are even now down in England working for the queen's escape," the young man replied. "We hae come to Duin for two reasons: yer isolation and the fact that yer own wife hae Hamilton blood in her veins. Surely ye canna refuse yer aid to her kinsmen."

"Aye, I can, and I do," Angus Ferguson said to William Hamilton. "Yer cause is lost, yet ye continue to foment trouble in Scotland. We hae a king on the throne. The queen's own bairn. This constant warring between the Queen's Men and the King's Men plays havoc here in the borders. It has to cease, yet it won't as long as men like ye continue to pursue this foolishness."

William Hamilton looked at the earl. "I was told ye were nae a man to take sides. That ye stood for Scotland."

"I do," Angus responded. "And there is a king on Scotland's throne now."

"And the Earl of Moray behind the king's throne," William Hamilton answered.

"If it were a Hamilton behind that throne, would this be less of a problem?" Angus Ferguson asked him candidly. "The Fergusons of Duin follow the laws of Scotland. Ye're welcome to shelter wi' us and eat at our board, but I will nae put my family in jeopardy for what I truly believe is a lost cause."

"Then ye hae chosen sides, my lord," William Hamilton said stiffly, and he moved away from the earl and his wife.

"What if by some miracle Mary were restored to her throne?" Annabella asked her husband in low tones. "Would Duin be at risk?"

"Nay, sweetheart, we would not," he replied. "We are neither a great nor a powerful clan. Mary Stuart, when not ruled by her heart, is an intelligent woman, which unfortunately few men realize. She would understand my position, and then too, the kindness I did her and her mother is nae something she will ever forget."

"That kindness was rendered long ago, Angus," Annabella reminded him.

"Aye, it was," he agreed, "but while I will nae allow Duin to become a post stop for treason against Scotland's king, neither will I act aggressively toward Mary Stuart. I hold to my position, as the Fergusons of Duin always have."

"Ye're a wily fellow, Angus Ferguson," Annabella told him with a smile.

He took her hand up and kissed it. Then he said as he looked across the hall, "Do ye think that Matthew seems in deep conversation wi' young Hamilton?"

"They are of an age," Annabella replied. But she had noticed it too.

In the morning after William Hamilton had gone on his way, disappointed, Angus took Matthew aside, but before he might speak his younger brother did.

"Are ye mad?" Matthew demanded. "Ye hae refused

the queen's request to allow Duin to be a resting place for her messengers?"

"It was nae the queen's request, but the Hamiltons'," Angus said. "I would remind ye that Duin is nae above the law. Mary Stuart, for good or for ill, hae been deposed. 'Tis her son who is crowned king of Scotland. To aid Mary Stuart would be seen as treason. Would ye hae me put us all in danger?"

"She is Scotland's anointed queen," Matthew responded. "Where is the treason in helping her, Angus?"

"Her son is now anointed king," Angus said quietly.

"In a Protestant ceremony," Matthew answered scornfully. "Is that even legal?"

"In Scotland it is," the earl replied, amused by Matthew's suddenly deep faith.

"Yer Protestant wife influences ye, I fear, brother," the younger man said.

"Does nae yer Protestant wife influence ye?" Angus replied mockingly.

"Agnes hae repented of her lapsed faith. Would that that plain-faced wife of yers would do so," Matthew snapped. "How long hae ye been wed, and but twin bairns to show for it, one a lass. I know the woman is nae fair, but ye need to apply yerself to her more often, that ye may get another son or two on her. Or will she nae do her duty?"

Angus Ferguson felt his anger rising. Matthew had always had difficulty in accepting Annabella, but his words were intolerable. Still, he held himself in check. "Why is it that ye canna get along with my wife?" he asked his brother.

"She is too bold, nae at all womanly, like my Aggie. She speaks her mind even when she knows a woman should keep silent unless required to speak. She is nae a good wife to ye, Angus," Matthew said. "Why, I believe she considers herself yer equal, if such a thing can be tolerated."

"She is my equal," the earl told his younger brother. "It is nae yer place to judge me, or Annabella, by yer own narrow standards, Matthew. I love my wife, and I do for Duin what I believe is the right thing to do. Ye will nae criticize either of us again. Ye forget yer place, brother."

"They call the Fergusons of Duin sorcerers, *my lord*," Matthew said scathingly, "but 'tis yer wife who is the witch, for she hae besorceled ye."

They both heard the gasp of shock, and turned to see Annabella standing there. She was paler than usual.

"Leave the hall," the Earl of Duin said in icy tones. "For now ye will keep yer place, but dinna show yer face to me until ye are prepared to apologize to my countess, Matthew. I would remind ye that ye hae nae the right to speak for Duin."

"Angus, nay! Ye must nae quarrel wi' yer brother," Annabella cried.

"Ye see!" Matthew's tone was accusatory. "She canna keep her place!" He stormed from the hall.

"Oh, my lord, I am so sorry to be the cause of dissension between ye and Matthew," Annabella said.

"He is jealous," Angus told her. "Until we wed it was always his counsel that I listened to, sweetheart. Now I listen to yers, for ye are thoughtful and wise. He is a good steward, and he is loyal to Duin. But he hae his own wife, and must learn to accept mine."

"He loves ye dearly," she said. "He feels ye could hae made a better match than me, I fear. And especially as he now is wed to my beautiful sister, I seem even plainer by comparison." She laughed ruefully. "But ye must reconcile yerself with him, Angus."

"Nay! He must reconcile himself wi' me, sweetheart," the earl said. "I wed wi' the best woman in this world. The virtues ye possess, Annabella, dinna—" He took her in his arms, looking down into her plain face with a warm smile. His eyes met hers as he told her once again, "I love ye." It was said simply. Then their lips met in a tender kiss.

He was the best of men, Annabella thought, but she was concerned about Matthew. She knew he would not be deliberately disloyal, but she had noticed how earnestly he had engaged William Hamilton in conversation the previous evening. Angus was doing what was right for Duin. He understood the politics of the situation far better than did his younger half brother. If Mary ever by some stroke of good fortune came to power once again, she would indeed forgive the Earl of Duin.

Moray, however, would not. If he believed that the Fergusons were colluding with the Hamiltons, and knew the secret of their wealth, Moray would fall on Duin with a vengeance. She could imagine how difficult it was for him to keep the secret that had been revealed to him. His religion kept him from plundering Duin, but given an excuse to do so, Moray would not hesitate. Annabella could but pray Matthew's anger would ease, and that he would accept the judgment of his elder half brother, his laird, the Earl of Duin.

Chapter 15

$\mathcal{H}$e wanted to believe himself neutral in this war that swept the borders. But the truth was, he could no longer remain neutral. He soothed himself by saying that as the king represented Scotland, and he stood with Scotland, he must therefore stand by little James VI, a lad but slightly older than his own wee son. In his heart Angus Ferguson knew it to be the right thing to do. Mary Stuart had left them.

Of course, she had had no real choice in the matter. Beaten in her last battle at Langside, Mary did not wait this time to be incarcerated in some moldering heap of stones once again watched over by pious folk hostile to her and everything for which she had stood. She had trusted to the nobility of her lords once before. A miscarriage and her imprisonment for a year at Inchmahome had been the reward for her faith in them.

After Langside she had fled south into England. Angus often thought that if she had just holed up in Dumbarton and negotiated with Moray and his ilk, she would still be queen. But her half brother, anticipating that she would make a run for Dumbarton, had blocked her way. She hadn't so much fled, Angus thought in retrospect, as she had been driven from Scotland, and by the very men who were her own kin and had colluded in the murders of both David Riccio and Henry Stewart, Lord Darnley.

And these men had gained exactly what they wanted: An infant king who would need their protection. A lad who could be educated and molded to suit them. A king who would not rebel against them but would be like them, think like them, act like them, and defend the new Reformed kirk of Scotland. And his mother would not be there to interfere with them as they produced this creation of theirs. Nay. They would not want Mary Stuart back in Scotland to thwart all their plans.

Matthew Ferguson didn't understand this, however. All he could see was a beautiful and tragic woman forced from her throne. He did not approve of her marriage to his brother's friend James Hepburn, but that was an error that could have been remedied. Mary Stuart was a devoted and devout daughter of Holy Mother Church.

She had allowed these men who called themselves the Reformed Church to practice their faith. But Knox and his ilk were yet suspicious of her, and could not refrain from taking the slightest thing they did not understand about the queen and declaring it ungodly or unchaste. They had stolen her bairn from her—driven her from Scotland. It was unjust!

How could his elder brother not understand the truth of all that had happened? William Hamilton had explained it quite clearly to Matthew Ferguson. The queen, their good Catholic queen, had had her throne usurped by her Protestant bastard half brother. They had imprisoned her. Caused her to miscarry. Fought against her and then driven her from their land. It was certainly God's will that she be restored to her throne.

Her misalliance with Lord Bothwell would be annulled by the pope in Rome. England's Duke of Norfolk, a good Catholic, would wed the queen. The queen would give to him what she had not given to either Lord Darnley or Lord Bothwell: the crown matrimonial. Scotland would have a good king and queen. Norfolk would be a good father to little James, and with luck there would be more children. The queen was still young enough. But first Mary Stuart must be restored to her rightful place.

"Duin is isolated," William Hamilton said. "All we ask is a safe resting place for our messengers. Moray's people will look to the east for our messengers. Perhaps they will even look to the center region of the border, but the west is the least likely place they will look. They will be no danger to the Fergusons, and the queen is certain to show her gratitude, Matthew, my friend. Would ye nae like a title of yer own to pass down to that fine laddie yer fair lady bore ye? Why should an accident of yer birth prevent ye from such a prize?"

And Matthew Ferguson listened, and was tempted. He had seen the queen when she had stopped briefly at Duin in her flight south. She was beautiful and royal, but she had looked so frail and tired. She was Scotland's rightful queen. If his brother could take sides, then so could he. He would shelter the messengers needing rest and nourishment at his own new stone house. There was no need for Angus to know anything.

"I'll help the queen," he said.

Afterward he told his wife, Agnes, expecting to be praised for his chivalry. To his great surprise Agnes was horrified, and chastised him sharply.

"Are ye mad, Matthew Ferguson? What hae ye done? Ye've put me and our bairn in danger, not to mention yer brother!"

"Angus would nae help the poor queen," he answered her.

"Of course he wouldn't, ye dolt! The queen is finished. Do ye truly believe those cold, hard men clutching the royal bairn in their paws will gie way and allow her back?"

Matthew Ferguson was astounded. She had berated him, called him a *dolt*. His beautiful and sweet wife had suddenly become a harsh scold. "Madam," he said, "am I nae the master in my own home? Dinna remonstrate wi' me, for I hae made my decision. Offering shelter and food to a passing messenger, if indeed one should pass through Duin, can hardly be countenanced as a crime. I am involved in nae plots. I simply offer border hospitality, as any man would to a stranger."

"Matthew, do ye nae realize that messengers coming over the border will always stop here, knowing that ye hae offered to shelter them? They will all be headed for Dumbarton Castle, for the Queen's Men still cling to that pile of rocks. The plot comes from there, nae from England, ye great fool!"

"Madam," he shouted at her, "I will nae be spoken to as ye hae been speaking to me. Hush yer mouth, and say nae another word."

Agnes looked at her husband, outraged. "I'm taking our wee Robbie and going to the castle," she told him. "I'll nae abide another night beneath the roof of this dwelling that is to be used to house traitors to the little king. I'll nae hae my bairn put in danger of ending up on the end of a soldier's pike because his pudding-headed da canna see the truth. I'm nae coming back until ye repair this disaster."

"Jesu! Mary!" Matthew swore. "Ye're just like yer plain-faced sister!"

"Dinna criticize my sister," Agnes snapped back. "Annabella is wonderful, and yer own brother hae seen it. The bond between them is so strong nothing could break it. Would that our marriage could be as strong."

"Yer damned sister hae turned my brother away from his duty to our queen," Matthew said. "She hae bewitched him, for no man could love such a simple face."

"Is that why ye wed wi' me, Matthew? Because I am beautiful? Did ye see nothing else in me but my face?" Agnes was near crying. "If I were as my sister, would ye hae loved me? It seems ye would nae." Then she ran from the little hall of their stone house.

He watched her go, puzzled. What was the matter wi' his beautiful Aggie? And then a thought struck him. She was breeding again. Certainly that was it! Breeding women were always given to odd fancies. But then the next day Agnes and his son were gone missing from their house. He found her servant woman packing Agnes's possessions. "Where hae she gone?" he demanded.

"To the castle," the woman replied.

Matthew Ferguson mounted his horse and rode the distance between Duin and his stone house. He found his wife in the castle hall with her sister. "Where's my son?" he demanded to know. "Ye may remain here if ye choose, but Robbie is coming home wi' me," he told her in a hard voice.

"Robbie will remain wi' me," Agnes said obdurately.

"Matthew," Annabella said, "I dinna know what hae precipitated this rift between ye and Aggie, but perhaps ye both need a few days to cool yer fiery heads."

"Dinna tell me how to manage my wife, madam," Matthew snarled.

"Manage?" Agnes's voice had become a screech. "Am I a horse or a dog to be managed? How dare ye, Matthew Ferguson!"

"I want ye and my son home," he replied.

"Then ye know what ye must do, sir, for I'll nae be home until ye do it," Agnes said in firm tones.

He realized then that she had not revealed his secret, and for that he was grateful.

"I'll nae besmirch my honor, Agnes," he informed her.

"I hope yer honor will keep ye warm this winter," she snapped.

With a snarl of impatience Matthew left the castle hall.

"What hae happened to put ye and Matthew at odds?" Annabella asked. "I realize that he can be a difficult man, but he loves ye."

"He is nae difficult!" Agnes defended her husband. "But sometimes he is foolish."

"How hae he been foolish?" Annabella probed gently. It had to be something very foolish to have sent her sister racing with her bairn from the fine stone house Matthew had built for her to the security of Duin Castle. But Annabella knew her sister would say nothing—indeed, if she said anything at all—until she had resolved the conflict, at least in her own mind.

Angus took his wife aside when he saw his sister-in-law and her bairn had moved into his home. "What hae happened between them? They're mad in love."

"I dinna know," Annabella admitted. "She is nae ready to tell me, but she will. We hae but to be patient. She is verra angry and hurt by something he hae done or said."

Several weeks passed. The days were growing notice-ably shorter as the autumn arrived and began to deepen. Then one day Jean's husband, who was captain of the castle men-at-arms, came to the earl.

"The men on the heights hae noticed something, my lord, that I believe should be brought to yer attention. There is traffic coming across the border, single riders, but more in the last two weeks than we usually see in a twelvemonth's time."

"Do they seem headed in a singular direction?" Angus asked his captain.

"Aye, toward yer steward's house. They make an ef-fort to bypass the castle, my lord, but those headed both north and south seem intent on that direction and pos-sible destination. I knew ye would want to know."

"Thank ye. I should like to be notified the next time one of these riders is spotted so I may see for myself," Angus told his captain.

"Aye, my lord, I'll see to it at once," the captain re-sponded.

Several hours later a man-at-arms came to report that a rider had been spotted on the horizon coming north. The Earl of Duin followed the man up the stairs and finally up a ladder to the roof of his castle. There on the heights, in a driving wind coming off the sea, he stood for the next hour watching the horseman come, and he did indeed make an obvious effort to avoid the castle, instead turning toward Matthew Ferguson's house.

Angus finally came down from the heights and called for his horse. With two men-at-arms accompanying him, he rode to Matthew's house. "Check his stables for a weary and lathered mount," he instructed the men-at-arms. Then, without another word, he went into his brother's home. He stood silently in the entrance to the little hall for several long moments. At a trestle a stranger was seated in earnest conversation with Matthew as he ate.

The Earl of Duin stepped into the hall, making his presence known as he greeted his younger sibling. "Good afternoon, Matthew," he said.

Matthew Ferguson jumped up from the bench where he had been seated. There was guilt written all over his face. "Angus!" he exclaimed. "What brings ye here?"

"The stream of riders heading to yer house these last few weeks," the earl replied dryly. "What mischief hae ye gotten yerself into, brother? Is it the mischief that I expressly forbade ye to involve yerself in? Is that why yer wife left ye, taking yer bairn wi' her? Who is this man who eats at yer board, Matthew? Do ye even know his name?"

"I had to help!" Matthew exclaimed.

The Earl of Duin's face grew dark with his anger. "Nay!" he thundered. "Ye dinna hae to help. Yer disobedience hae endangered us all. Dinna ye understand, Matthew? Ye are consorting wi' rebels. Engaging in treasonous conduct."

"How can helping Scotland's rightful queen be treasonous?" Matthew demanded.

"Scotland hae no queen, ye thick dolt! Scotland hae a king. His Majesty James, the sixth of that name," the earl said angrily. Then he turned to the man still eating at the trestle. "Finish yer meal and then be gone back from whence ye came. I'll take the packet ye carry first, however."

The messenger stood up. He was almost as tall as

Angus Ferguson, and looked him directly in the eye. "'Tis nae for ye, my lord, but bound for Dumbarton Castle."

"I know where it goes, but 'twill nae get there through my lands. I'm nae above throwing ye in my dungeons, man. Now hand me yer packet so I may destroy it and rid my foolish brother's house of treason. Tell yer masters in England that neither Duin Castle nor the house of its steward will be open to them, ever. My brother hae defied my direct orders to nae consort wi' the Queen's Men. I told William Hamilton nay, and I meant it. Whether the Hamiltons and my brother wish to accept it, these actions are treasonous. The Fergusons of Duin will nae involve themselves in this treason."

The messenger looked the Earl of Duin over. He noted the dirk in his belt, and he could see the earl was a man used to handling a weapon. Though he considered himself one of the Queen's Men, his first loyalty was to himself. It wasn't worth getting killed or maimed over a single message. He had no idea what was in it, but the Hamiltons would have to get it to its destination another way. Reaching into his shirt, he pulled the packet containing the message out, handing it to Angus Ferguson.

The earl took it, then, turning to his brother, said, "I'll deal wi' ye later. Ye're forbidden the castle until I call for ye to come, Matthew."

"Angus . . ."

The earl gave his younger brother a hard look, and left the little hall.

Angus and the two men-at-arms rode back to the castle. He ordered the drawbridge up as soon as they crossed it. His anger with his younger sibling was burning white-hot. Never had Matthew questioned his judgment before, or disobeyed him. His brother had grown restless and reckless of late, and he didn't understand why that was. Even Annabella's little sister had disapproved of his actions, and wisely removed herself and her bairn from the stone house Matthew had built for her. And that was another thing: Why had Agnes not told them what was going on instead of simply coming to Duin for safety's sake?

Annabella greeted him as he came into his own hall. "What has happened?"

He told her, asking when he finished, "Where is yer sister? This is why she left him, and she was wise to do so, but she might hae told us the mischief he was up to, yet she did not." He called to a servant, "Fetch the lady Agnes to me."

"I believe she was torn between her loyalties," Annabella said, seeing his anger was high, and attempting to spare her sister the scolding she was about to get.

"She is the wife of a Ferguson of Duin," the earl replied in a hard voice. "Her first loyalty must be to Duin itself, and then to Matthew, nae to my brother alone. She came to us for protection while allowing the danger to continue."

Agnes came into the hall. She was pale and looked frightened. "My lord?" she said in a soft voice. "Ye wished to see me?"

"Why hae ye left my brother?" Angus demanded of her. "The truth now, madam! I'll hae no shilly-shallying about it."

"He's allowed our house to become a stopping point for the Queen's Men," Agnes answered. Then she burst into tears. "I told him it was wrong. I told him he endangered us all wi' his actions, but he would nae listen to me."

"Aye," the earl roared, causing the poor lass to tremble where she stood. "Ye told him, but *ye dinna tell me*! Damn it, Agnes, I am Duin! Everyone on these lands defers to me first. Nae to Matthew. *To me!*"

"Angus." Annabella spoke, putting a restraining hand on her husband's arm.

He looked into her soft gray eyes. For all her plainness she did bewitch him.

She smiled softly at him. "Angus," she repeated.

"Oh, verra well," he said low. Then, turning to his weeping sister-in-law, he told her, "Ye will remain in the castle until I can make certain yer disobedient husband hae nae brought the wrath of the King's Men upon us. Wi' luck no one hae noticed yet."

"Th-thank ye," Agnes quavered, and without permission or another word she picked up her skirts and fled the hall, sobbing.

The earl took his wife's hand and led her to the chairs they favored by the blazing hearth. They had eaten earlier, and the hall was quiet now. The twins had been put to bed before their father's encounter with their pretty aunt. The dogs were sprawled near the two fireplaces. The cat who had occupied Annabella's chair now jumped into her lap and settled itself comfortably amid her dark green velvet skirts. She stroked it absently.

"I brought back the packet the messenger carried. Let us see what treason it contains before I burn it," Angus said as he opened the square leather container and drew out a folded and sealed parchment. Undoing the letter, he spread it out on his knees to smooth any creases; then, picking it up, he silently read the contents.

"What does it say?" Annabella asked him.

He looked up at her, his face deadly serious. "They

are planning several assassinations," he told her. "Those who hold or are likely to hold the reins of power for the wee king: Lennox, his grandfather; Moray; the king's guardians, Erskine and his wife. They believe if they can rid themselves of these few they can bring the queen back into power once again."

"Erskine and his wife are good folk," Annabella said. "Perhaps they dinna gie the little king the warmth and love a parent might gie him, but they do their duty by him admirably. Moray is ruthless, but all he hae done to date hae been in the king's best interest. They hae taken to calling him the good regent. As for Lennox, I hae never liked Darnley's father. He betrayed Marie de Guise, and took the English queen's gold, remaining in England for many years. His own wife, though Scots born, was the daughter of the English princess Margaret Tudor and her second husband. His interests are not, I believe, Scotland's interests. He simply wants the power that would come with being a royal regent. Still, I dinna think they should be murdered. If they are, who knows who will grab the power?" Annabella said. "Who do they say is to be killed first? And when? Ye canna destroy this evidence, but must warn Moray and his counsel."

"They dinna say," Angus replied, looking carefully through the message again.

"Would the messenger know?" Annabella wondered aloud.

"Nay, 'tis unlikely he even knows what he carries. He is just a courier for the Hamiltons," Angus said.

"We must learn the truth," Annabella replied.

"*We?*" He looked directly at her.

She gave him a saucy grin. "Remember that I make a good lad," she said.

"I will nae hae ye in danger," he responded.

"I hae a plan," she countered calmly.

"Annabella!"

"Angus!"

He laughed. Matthew was right: She was bold, but he couldn't resist asking her, "What plan, madam? And if I refuse ye, will ye run off as ye did when I went to France?"

"Probably," she admitted, "but hear my plan first, husband. We must incarcerate the Hamiltons' messenger for our safety's sake, after learning from where he came. Then we will ride togcther to the Hamilton lair, but while ye remain hidden outside of their walls, I will ride in to tell them that their messenger was injured by the time he reached Matthew's house. I will say he was set upon by bandits, and destroyed the contents of the packet rather than allow it to fall into the wrong hands. I will bring the empty packet wi' me to prove my veracity. I will say that if they want me to, I will take another message to Dumbarton. That Matthew sent me to them. Riding boldly into their stronghold and having the leather case wi' me will prove the truth of my tale."

"If they send the same message we will still nae learn the time and place or the first of their victims," Angus said. "That is what we must discover."

"I dinna believe they would be informing Dumbarton unless the time was near to begin implementing their wicked scheme," Annabella noted. "Take the courier now, and then let us wait a few days before questioning him. *Or* better, I could simply bring the message that ye hold to Dumbarton myself. Perhaps I could learn something there."

"It's too dangerous," Angus Ferguson told his wife. "What if ye were caught?"

"Someone is going to die, my lord. And Scotland is

going to be thrown into chaos again. We hae the ability to prevent that, and we must."

"We could send Matthew to Dumbarton," the earl suggested. "He needs to repent of his disobedience."

"Forgie me, my dear lord, but yer brother can no longer be trusted," Annabella said bluntly. "His heart is good, I am sure, and he would go wi' the best of intentions, but then he would be swept up in the patriotic fever of those who wish to restore the queen. He would betray ye, betray us, and then he would repent, but it would be too late."

"I could go," the earl said.

"Nay," Annabella replied, shaking her head. "The Hamiltons may have informed those at Dumbarton of yer refusal to help. They would nae believe yer change of heart. There is nothing for it but that the lad I can be must go."

"Nay! I canna allow it, sweetheart," he told her.

"Dumbarton is easier than having to find the Hamiltons' hidey-hole," Annabella said, as if he had not spoken at all. "Come, my lord; the hour grows late. It is past time we were abed, Angus." She stood up, and the cat on her lap hissed at being displaced once more. It stalked off, its ears turned back.

"Jesu, woman, are ye attempting to seduce me?" he demanded of her.

"Oh, may I?" she teased him, and, laughing, took his hand to lead him upstairs.

"I will not be ensorcelled by yer charms, Annabella, many as they may be," he said sternly, but he did not pull away. Indeed, he was smiling. How he loved his lass!

"Nay, nay, my lord, of course not." She whirled about, standing upon her tiptoes, and kissed his mouth a quick kiss.

"I will take a hazel switch and beat ye," he threatened.

"And if I am deserving, ye should, my lord, ye should," Annabella agreed.

They were on the stairs now. He stopped and pushed her against the wall, his hand sliding beneath her velvet skirts along her silken thigh. He pressed his big body against hers as his fingers tangled in the dark curls covering her mons. "Oh, ye are deserving, my love, of a great deal," he told her. "And I intend on seeing ye get all ye deserve." A finger slipped through her nether lips to touch her love button, to rub it teasingly.

Annabella drew a sharp breath. She loved it when he touched her there. She wiggled against the ball of his finger. She was already moist, and growing wetter with the teasing pressure and friction of that finger. "Angus," she moaned against his lips.

The finger was withdrawn from the sensitive nub, leaving it tingling but not at all satisfied.

"Oh, nay, madam," he said softly into her ear. "Ye will nae hae yer way wi' me so easily before I hae had a full measure of my own back." He took his hand from beneath her skirts and continued up the stairs, this time leading her through her apartments and into her bedchamber. Turning her back to him, he unlaced her gown, pushing it down to her waist. His hands reached around to undo the ribbons of her chemise, which he peeled away over her shoulders and down to meet the fabric of the gown. Then, holding her by her shoulders, he bent to slowly trace a line of kisses down her backbone.

Annabella sighed, feeling his warm lips moving across her flesh.

His hands dropped from her shoulders to cup her breasts, which he fondled at his leisure. Now his hands were moving to clasp her waist so he might lift her from her slippers and the pile of fabric that had covered her glorious body. She was naked but for her stockings with their silk ribbon garters.

Free of entanglement, Annabella turned about and began to undo the sleeveless leather jerkin that he wore. She unlaced his shirt, pulling it from him, and then, bending to press kisses all over his chest and torso, she slipped to her knees before him. She could feel his various pulse points jumping beneath her lips as she moved lower and lower. Her hands worked to undo his breeks, beneath which he wore naught. Her breath caught briefly in her throat at the sight of his wonderful manhood. She gave his taut buttocks a quick fondle as, now fully kneeling, she reached for him.

His cock was yet a wonder to her. Annabella could not know for certain, but she assumed its size was of a larger variety. Whether it was or not made little difference to her, as it gave the greatest of pleasures, for he wielded it skillfully. Taking a gentle hold on it, she licked its length several times while her other hand played with his sac. Angus made a small murmur as the message of her tongue was conveyed to him. Annabella next licked the tip of his cock with several seductive sweeps of her tongue before taking that tip between her lips, pressing down on it, rolling it between those lips.

His hand slipped to her dark head. He had taught her months before how to suck his cock, but something instinctual had taken over and she had refined the task into the sweetest of tortures. He felt her mouth opening now to absorb as much of him as she could. She began to tug upon the peg of flesh within her mouth with delicate pulls that grew stronger and stronger. Then, sensing his excitement, she would pull back, her tongue caressing his length and his thickness as it lay imprisoned between her lips. The wicked bit of flesh stroked him, encircled him, but never allowed him release. Finally he could bear no more of this deliciousness. "*Enough!*" he growled in a hoarse voice, and as she released him he pulled her up to kiss her hungrily.

She loved teasing him. She had discovered almost immediately that she had an instinct for pleasuring him without bringing him to completion. Now it was her turn, and Angus Ferguson did not fail his wife. He kissed her until her lips were bruised. His tongue ravaged hers until she was weak. Then he stopped and, seating her upon the edge of the big bed, he pushed her gently back, pulled her shapely legs up over his shoulders, and buried his dark head between her thighs. The tip of his tongue found her love button, touching it lightly at first, then with delicate, quick touches, until Annabella could not refrain from making small noises as his tongue began to stroke her strongly. Then his lips closed over that sensitive little nub of flesh and sucked hard, releasing the first flow of her juices. Annabella shuddered with the tiny burst of pleasure.

Now he raised himself up. Holding his swollen cock in his hand, he guided it into her welcoming sheath with a single hard and deep thrust. "God, ye feel good!" he groaned as he filled her full. Then he began to piston her.

Annabella couldn't speak at first. His cock moved slowly but steadily, its speed increasing slightly with each strong stroke until it flashed in and out of her with incredible rapidity. Then he would slow his pace again, and when he did Annabella squeezed him, the walls of her sheath closing about him so tightly that he cried out at one point. Then the movement began once again.

Back and forth. Back and forth. Back and forth until they were both drenched in utter pleasure.

"Dinna wait," she whispered hotly in his ear.

"I canna," he admitted, increasing the tempo that shortly sent them both over the edge and into paradise as his juices flooded her secret garden and she cried out with her need fulfilled. He fell on the bed next to her then.

For some minutes they lay motionless: Annabella with her legs now fallen over the edge of the bed, Angus on his belly near her. Finally she managed to crawl up and beneath the coverlet, tugging at him to do the same, for the night air was becoming chill.

He pulled her into his arms with a groan into her long loose hair, and whispered that he adored her.

"I love ye too, Angus," she responded. "But send someone to catch the Hamiltons' messenger before he escapes us."

He laughed softly. "I hae just loved ye verra well, wife, and ye canna enjoy the afterglow?" he teased her. He released his hold on her, climbing from their bed to yank upon the bellpull. To his relief his serving man, Tormod, appeared immediately, entering through the small door that connected the earl's bedchamber to his wife's. "Send several men-at-arms to catch the Hamilton messenger who came to my brother's house. Treat him well, but put him in the castle dungeon. He may still be at Matthew's or he may have departed either back south or toward Dumbarton."

"At once, my lord," Tormod replied with a quick bow, and was gone again. He was not in the least disconcerted by his master's naked state.

Angus Ferguson climbed back into bed to pull his

wife close. She murmured sleepily, for she was already slipping into rest. In a few hours she would want to play again, he knew. Annabella had gained a healthy appetite for bed sport, he considered with a grin. He chuckled, and concentrated on sleep. The demanding wench would be awake soon enough.

But to his surprise they both slept until Jean awakened them just as dawn was breaking. "They caught the messenger," she said by way of greeting. "Get up now, for the day is beginning, and yer breakfast will soon be in the hall."

The earl got up and, walking to the little door separating the bedchambers, passed through it so that he might have the services of his serving man.

"He still has a fine ass," Jean remarked pithily. "I remember when we swam together as children. What will ye wear today?"

"Something that doesna make me look all female and fragile," Annabella said.

"Ahh, ye're planning some naughtiness," Jean remarked, "aren't ye?"

"The lad I once was must be resurrected," Annabella said. Then she explained everything that had happened yesterday.

"Aye, Ned told me of Matthew's lapse in judgment," Jean said. "Did Angus really forbid him the castle?"

"Aye, until his anger cools. I think that once we can correct this situation, Jean, Angus will nae be quite so angry, but questioning the earl's judgment was not a wise thing for Matthew to do. It is his antipathy toward me that seems to direct this. Why does he persist in disliking me so, Jeannie?"

"Because he's a fool," her tiring woman said. "Matthew has always almost worshiped Angus. He felt Angus should hae a woman as beautiful as Angus was handsome, and wi' a large dower to match his brother's wealth. Instead Angus took ye, a plain-faced lass, to wife for a piece of land he coveted. I think my brother thinks ye are nae worthy of his idol."

"He told Angus I was too bold," Annabella said as Jean laced up her gown.

Jean laughed. "Matthew is an old-fashioned man. He thinks women should be silent, yet neither our mother nor Angus's mother was meek and mild. Is Aggie?"

"Aggie is like our mother: quiet to a point, but she will speak up when she hae had enough, and believes a situation needs correcting," Annabella explained. "I think she may hae given poor Matthew quite a piece of her mind when she learned what he had done. Angus scolded her severely for nae telling him what she knew until it was almost too late. She is nae used to a woman's first loyalty being to her overlord, nae her husband. I think Angus hae made that quite clear to her now, however."

"Aye, I expect that he did," Jean agreed. "He hae had the responsibility of Duin ever since he was a young lad. He is a good lord."

"Aye, he is," Annabella said.

Jean dressed her mistress's hair. "Ye're ready," she said.

"Thank ye." Annabella got up and hurried from her apartments down into the hall. Angus was not yet there, but Agnes was already seated at the high board. Annabella joined her younger sister. "Feel better this morning?" she asked Agnes.

Agnes nodded, but then she said, "I think I should

take Robbie and go home today, Annabella. Angus is certain to be angry until he can straighten out Matthew's foolishness, I fear."

"Angus hae told ye ye're to remain in the castle until he gives ye permission to leave," Annabella reminded her sibling. "He is the earl, the laird here, sister. It is his word that prevails, nae mine nor yers nor Matthew's. Ye are nae stupid, Aggie, and this is nae Rath, where our da is laird, husband, and father. This is Duin. We owe our very existence to its earl. Why can ye nae understand this?"

"I do, and yet Matthew is my husband. It seems odd that yer husband must approve his every move." She sighed. "I know 'tis nae different than the household of any other lord, and yet I chafe, as I know does Matthew," Agnes replied.

"When this crisis is over," Annabella said, "I will ask Angus if we may do something that could change all that, but for now ye must obey him."

"I will," Agnes promised.

The earl came into the hall. He did not look pleased as he joined them. He gave Agnes a quelling look as she concentrated upon her oat stirabout.

"Eat before ye interrogate the messenger," Annabella said to her husband.

"I hae already spoken wi' him," Angus said. "Now that he believes he faces nae real danger from us, he will nae cooperate and tell me from whence he came. When I hae eaten I will see he is disabused of the notion that we are weak."

"Angus, ye canna torture the man," she said.

"Of course I can, and I intend to," he told her. "Going to Dumbarton is a better idea than going into the Hamiltons' lair, wherever it may be, but I need to know if this man came from Dumbarton originally. We dinna need any surprises."

"What will ye do to him?" she asked, fascinated in spite of herself.

"A wee beating will loosen his tongue," the earl said, helping himself to a large portion of eggs and several rashers of bacon. He pulled a piece off of the cottage loaf, buttering it generously with his thumb.

"Nae too hard," Annabella pleaded for the man.

The Earl of Duin laughed. "Ye're too softhearted, sweetheart. We need to know what he knows, and we need to know it in relatively short order." He began eating with a good appetite, his good nature restored by just being with Annabella.

"Gie the man a day or two to consider his position," Annabella suggested. "Surely we hae a little time, particularly if this messenger does not arrive as promptly as those waiting at Dumbarton expect. And unless he originally came from there, went to the Hamiltons, and is returning to Dumbarton, it's likely he isn't on a fixed schedule. A messenger comes when a messenger comes, Angus."

"I'll gie him a day to reconsider his fate," the earl said.

But by the next day the courier still remained obdurate. Annabella, however, could not bear to know the man would be beaten. She insisted upon going down into the dungeons to speak with the fellow herself. He was surprised to see this plain-faced woman standing looking through the cell door grate.

"I am the Countess of Duin," she introduced herself.

Her husband's prisoner jumped up and bowed politely.

"I dinna want to see ye beaten, sir," she began.

"I can take a beating," he answered her.

"I'm certain ye can, for ye appear to me to be a strong man," Annabella agreed. "But what we seek to learn is hardly vital."

"It seems to be for ye," he said with a cheeky grin.

Annabella laughed. "If you answer a question for me," she said, "I'll answer one for ye, sir. And ye may go first."

He was surprised, and curious to see whether she would actually keep her word. Offering to allow him to query her first was certainly reassuring. "Verra well," he said. "Tell me how such an attractive man like yer husband came to wed such a plain lass? Ye must be verra rich to hae gained the wedding band on yer finger." It was a bold question, and even a bit insulting. Of course she wouldn't answer it, and then he did not have to answer any query she put forth.

Annabella was startled by the inquiry, but she knew if she did not answer their prisoner she had no chance at all of learning what she needed to know. Looking the man directly in the eye, she said mischievously, "I'm nae rich, sir, but my da had a wee bit o' land Angus wanted for his cows. The cows gained the pasturage; and I got a husband."

The prisoner chuckled at her explanation. She had, to his great surprise, answered him honestly, he knew. And the truth was, the questions they wanted him to answer were really of no importance to him. "The Hamiltons hae an encampment in the hills along the border. They move it every few days in order to avoid being discovered by the King's Men. I am a paid courier and was nae expected to return there, but to make myself of use to Lord Fleming at Dumbarton. I hae never been there before. I dinna care which side in this war prevails, as long as I earn my coin. The Hamiltons dinna pay me. Lord Fleming was to do that." His tone was slightly aggrieved when he said it.

"The earl will see ye are paid when we release ye," Annabella told the prisoner.

"And when is that to be?" he asked her.

"When we hae completed yer commission, sir," she said with a twinkle. "Ye'll be comfortable until that day. Hopefully 'twill nae be long."

He nodded understanding, and smiled a small smile. "I thank ye for visiting wi' me, madam. To hae the lady of the castle concerned wi' my welfare is comforting."

"I hae always attempted to be a good chatelaine, although my purview hae nae before extended so deep into my husband's castle," Annabella said, smiling back.

"He knows ye're here?" the prisoner inquired.

"Aye, he does," she replied.

"He must trust ye a great deal, madam."

"I hope he does," Annabella answered him. Then she turned and hurried away.

The courier felt a sudden loss at her departure. She was nae a pretty woman, but by God she had such great charm a man could forget that her face was plain. He wondered just what the Earl of Duin would do with that small scrap of information he had given the countess. And what had been in the message that the earl needed to know from where he had ridden, and whether he had ever been to Dumbarton before. Turning from the cell door, he lay down on his cot. It wasn't likely he would ever get the answers to his questions, but he had enjoyed his brief conversation with the Countess of Duin.

Annabella had returned to the hall to find Angus

waiting. "The Hamiltons move their encampment every few days," she told him. "And our courier is for hire. He had never been to Dumbarton before. It's perfect, my lord! I can dress as the young man I was in France and carry this message to Lord Fleming. The castle will afford me its hospitality until they need me to carry a message for them. I will be able to overhear all sorts of gossip, for no one pays particular attention to servants or men who carry messages. And then I will return to ye wi' the answers we seek!" Her voice was excited, and her eyes alight with her enthusiasm.

"Nay," he said. "'Tis too dangerous for ye. Listen to me, Annabella. When ye followed me to France ye had little contact wi' others. Aboard ship ye were careful to avoid the company of the other passengers or the crew. Ye kept well to yerself. It was easy for ye to pass yerself off as a young serving man under those circumstances. But Dumbarton is a large fortress, and 'tis filled wi' many soldiers. Fleming's family will be there, but they are few. Mostly 'tis a male population. It will be difficult to keep yer identity hidden, and if ye are found out, God help ye. If ye can even reach Lord Fleming to beg his mercy, he is nae apt to give it. Instead he'll gie ye to his soldiers. Ye'll nae survive in their tender care."

Annabella gasped as the implication of her husband's words struck her. Then she said, "But we need to know when these assassinations are to take place so we may gie Moray warning. We canna just let them happen, Angus."

"We may hae no choice in the matter, sweetheart," he told her.

"I'll go," a young voice piped up.

They turned to see Annabella's protégé, Callum Ferguson, who was now fifteen, standing there. "I overheard," he said apologetically, blushing slightly. In the years since Callum had come to live in the castle, he had grown tall, and become very clever with his mathematical skills, helping out in the household steward's office now.

Chapter 16

N ay, 'tis too dangerous for ye!" Annabella cried. "Ye're still a lad!"

"I can do it," Callum insisted. "Ye need a pair of sharp ears inside of Lord Fleming's fortress. There are couriers as young as I am, my lady. I can do it!"

"He could," the earl said; then he looked at the boy, who was now almost six feet in height. "But it is indeed dangerous, lad. Ye dinna hae to do it."

"Lady Annabella hae educated me. I can beg a place of the castle steward, and when he learns I can read and write and do numbers, he'll consider himself lucky. He'll gie me a place in the household, and I'll learn much."

"Aye!" Angus said enthusiastically. "He could do it, sweetheart!"

"But what if they discover he is a spy?" Annabella fretted.

"I think if Callum is careful, and takes nae chances, there will be nae reason to suspect him of anything," the earl said.

"But should he overhear something that will be of value to us, how will he be able to leave Dumbarton wi'out causing suspicion so he may tell us?" Annabella wanted to know. She was not about to send this intelligent young lad into needless danger. She had not educated him to face death, but rather life.

"I will place someone in the town below the castle," the earl said. "Callum will determine an excuse to go into the town, meet up with our agent, and pass the information on to him. Then he will return to the castle to tell the steward that while he was in the town he met up with someone sent from his village, come to tell him his mother was dying. He will ask permission to return home. They will gie it to him and he will be back at Duin before we know it, safe and sound."

"Ye make it sound simpler than I suspect it really is," Annabella said.

"I can do this, my lady," Callum repeated. "I can!"

The Countess of Duin looked to her husband. "Angus?"

"He's a braw lad wi' a good head on his shoulders, sweetheart. All he needs do is listen, remember anything of import should he hear it, and return home to Duin wi' whatever small knowledge he hae gained," the earl said.

"How long must he remain at Dumbarton?" Annabella wanted to know.

"No more than two months, laddie," Angus Ferguson said, "and ye're to come home earlier if ye learn what we need to know sooner. The Queen's Men plan to assassinate several important lords. I need to know when this wickedness begins. The three men who are likely to be targeted are James Stewart, the Earl of Moray, the regent; Matthew Stewart, the Earl of Lennox, the wee king's grandsire; and John Erskine, His Majesty's royal governor. The targets I am certain of, but I know not when these murders are planned. If I am to warn Moray, I must learn that if I can.

"Do ye understand, Callum? Ye are nae to put yerself in any danger. Ye'll tell them at Dumbarton the messenger took ill upon arrival at Matthew Ferguson's house. That because he believed the message to be urgent he asked Matthew to send one of his serving people to Dumbarton with the packet he carried. When ye hae delivered the message, linger about for a day or two before ye ask the household steward for a place. Remember to tell the steward ye read, write, and can do numbers."

"Aye, my lord!" Callum Ferguson was very enthusiastic and excited to be entrusted with this mission.

"And when ye return," Angus Ferguson told him, "I'll want ye to help me wi' my correspondence, if it would please ye to remain at Duin. I find I am in need of a secretary, Callum Ferguson. If ye're old enough now to take on such a mission as ye're about to take on, then ye're old enough to serve me."

"Thank ye, my lord!" The young man's eyes were shining.

"Ye'll leave Duin early on the morrow," the earl said. "Tell the stable master I said ye are to hae a swift and sturdy horse."

"Aye, my lord!" Callum hurried off.

"Are ye certain he will be safe?" Annabella asked her husband.

"If he follows my directions, he will be," her husband answered her. But later in the evening, when Annabella was seated with her sister and their children, he sought out the lad, reminding him once again not to take any chances.

The following morning Callum Ferguson rode forth from Duin and took the road to Dumbarton. The horse he rode was young and quick. Callum carried no coin, only the packet for Lord Fleming. There was a dirk in his belt but nothing more. He reached Dumbarton after almost two days of riding. He could see it long before he reached it. The great fortress of a castle had been there in one form or another for so long that no one could quite remember when it had first come into existence. Massive and built of dark rock, it sat high on a great black cliff above the River Clyde, a town at its feet.

Callum urged his horse up the narrow path leading to the castle's entry. "Urgent message for Lord Fleming from the Hamiltons," he called out, and he was admitted through the portcullis gate. He dismounted in the courtyard. His animal was taken from him and led away. A man-at-arms came up to him.

"I'll take yer packet," he said.

"Nay," Callum replied. "I have been told to put it into Lord Fleming's hand, and nae one else's."

The soldier shrugged. "This way," he said, leading the boy into the castle.

Callum carefully memorized the way so that, should he need to retreat in a hurry, he would know it. They went upstairs and through ill-lit corridors, finally stopping before a door. The soldier knocked, waited, and the door was finally opened by a small man who looked rather harassed.

"Messenger for His Lordship," he said. Then he went off.

"Well, give me the message, lad," the rumpled man said.

"Are ye Lord Fleming?" Callum asked, suspecting he wasn't.

"I am my lord's secretary," the man said, peering closely at the boy.

"I was told to only place this message in His Lordship's hands," Callum replied.

"His Lordship is a busy man," the secretary said.

"I've ridden two days wi' little rest for me or my horse," Callum said politely. "My master told me to place this packet in His Lordship's hands, and His Lordship's hands only. I would be a poor servant if I disobeyed him because I am hungry and tired."

"Let the lad in, Allan," an amused voice called from the depths of the chamber.

"Very well, come in then," the secretary said irritably. "There is His Lordship." He pointed across the chamber, where a man sat in a high-backed chair before a rectangular table spread with parchments.

Lord Fleming beckoned Callum. "What is it ye hae for me, lad?" he asked.

"I carry a message from the Hamiltons, my lord," Callum answered politely, holding out the leather packet.

"Ye look young to be a messenger," Lord Fleming said as he took it from the boy. "From where do ye come?"

"I am nae the Hamiltons' original courier," Callum said. "Their messenger was verra ill when he reached my master's house. 'Twas my master who sent me to ye, my lord. The Hamiltons' man seemed to think the message was of some importance."

Lord Fleming had opened the packet and taken out the parchment within, which he spread open before him. He scanned it quickly, then refolded it. "'Twas nae really that urgent," he said to Callum with a smile, "but I thank yer master for his diligence in seeing it was brought to me. Who is yer master?"

"The steward of Duin, my lord," Callum answered

him. "His dwelling is a way station for the Queen's Men coming from the borders."

"Ahh," Lord Fleming said with a nod. "I hae heard that, though I am told yer earl does nae support the queen."

Callum said nothing.

"Well, then, lad, go to the hall. Tell my steward I said ye were to be fed and sheltered for yer service," Lord Fleming told the young man. He turned to his secretary. "Allan, direct our young messenger to the great hall. Then come back. We have much work to do, and the day is almost gone."

"Thank ye, my lord," Callum said with a small bow.

Grumbling beneath his breath, the old secretary led the boy to the wide corridor leading to the great hall. "It's at the end of this hallway," he said. Then he turned about and hurried off.

Callum found the great hall easily. He inquired of a servant for the castle's steward, who granted him a place at one of the lower trestles and said he might sleep in the hall itself. The boy lingered for the next few days, speaking little but listening a great deal as he moved discreetly about the hall itself. He learned that while, discouraged, she had fled into England, where she was now more prisoner than honored guest, Mary Stuart was still beloved by those within the castle. He heard whispers of a plot to restore the queen to her throne, but he learned nothing that was not really common gossip in all of Scotland. Finally, after two days, he sought out the castle steward once again.

"Would ye consider gieing me a place here?" he asked the man.

"Who are ye?" the steward said.

"I'm the courier who brought a message to Lord

Fleming several days ago," Callum reminded him. "I can read. I can write. And I can do numbers. There is opportunity here for me. If I return home I must toil in my father's smithy."

"I dinna know," the steward said slowly. He looked the boy before him over. His hair was a bit shaggy, and his clothing was hardly elegant, but if he told the truth about reading and writing, he might very well be of use. Allan, His Lordship's secretary, had been complaining about having to write letters for Lady Fleming when he was so busy with more important things to do for His Lordship. His hair trimmed, the rough clothing replaced, the boy might serve as Lady Fleming's scribe. "Perhaps I have a place for ye," the steward said. "But first I must hae yer hair trimmed, and find more respectable garments for ye." He then went on to explain to Callum that Her Ladyship could use him to write her letters. She was a great letter writer.

"Thank ye, sir!" Callum bowed to the steward, who was further pleased by this show of manners.

The boy was sent to the kitchens, where his hair was trimmed and he was bathed so that the stink of horse would not offend Lady Fleming and her woman, and then he was given fresh garments of a more suitable sort for a lady's scribe. Callum made certain, however, to retain the breeks and shirt he had formerly worn. The old laundress told him she would wash his garments and return them to him. He had to admit he was surprised by all this fuss just so he could serve Lady Fleming.

He returned to the hall, presenting himself to the steward once more.

The steward nodded, pleased. The lad had cleaned up nicely. "Follow me," he said, and led Callum to Her Ladyship's apartments, where Lady Fleming and her women were now gathered. He bowed, and Callum followed his lead. "Here is the lad I've found to be yer scribe, my lady," he told her. "His name is Callum and he will serve ye well."

"I must see an example of the boy's writing," Lady Fleming said. "Ye say he can write, but how he writes is more important than the fact that he can." She spoke directly to Callum. "Go to the table there. There is parchment and ink. I would see an example of yer skills, Callum."

"Aye, my lady," the boy said, going immediately to the desk, seating himself, and taking up the quill. He spread a piece of parchment out carefully, thought a moment, and then wrote quickly. They could see the words forming upon the vellum. When he had finished he silently handed it to Lady Fleming. She read it and laughed.

"What did he write? What did he write?" demanded her women.

Their mistress read from the parchment: "'Madam, I will consider it an honor to be in yer service. Yer most humble servant, Callum Ferguson.'"

"Ye write very well," Lady Fleming said. "Who taught ye?"

"The Countess of Duin," Callum answered truthfully.

Lady Fleming nodded. The name was vaguely familiar but of no importance to her. "He will do very nicely," she told the steward.

Callum was pleased that so far the plan formed by the earl and his wife was working so smoothly. Now a part of the family's household, he was apt to hear things he might not otherwise hear. He made certain not to be absent from Lady Fleming's presence. He was always available when she needed someone to fetch something for her. He was young enough that she felt no shyness in speaking before him. Soon Lady Fleming found Callum, her scribe, indispensable. He was allowed a place at the far end of her table, even as Lord Fleming's secretary was given a place at the opposite end. He ate quietly, and he listened.

And then one day his listening was rewarded. When Lord Fleming spoke at his high board, those seated with him did not speak over or around him, so Callum heard him quite clearly as he spoke with his wife.

"It hae been decided," he said.

"Must more blood be shed?" Lady Fleming said.

"Do ye truly believe that Moray will ask his sister back to take up her throne again now that he hae all the power in his own hands?" Lord Fleming said. "It will nae happen, madam. They want a Protestant king, and the only way to gain one is to raise one."

Lady Fleming sighed. "How soon will it be?" she inquired. "And how soon before we may welcome our dear queen home?"

"Moray will be the first," Lord Fleming said. "As soon after Twelfth Night as we can. Then the others as quickly as we can run them to ground. Once Moray is dead the others will know the hunt is on and make provision to defend themselves. And remember too that they hold the wee king. The queen cannot return until we have destroyed her enemies. And after that we will have to go down into England to rescue her. It will be several months, but hopefully by summer Scotland's queen will be restored."

"She is fond of James Stewart, despite everything that has happened between them," Lady Fleming noted. "She is sentimental when she recalls her childhood before France at Stirling. He was the oldest of the bairns. She looked up to him."

"Which is why it is better to dispose of him quickly, and first," Lord Fleming said. "She detests Lennox and will weep no tears over him. As for Erskine, it is a necessary evil we face, for he also is kin, but it must be done."

Lady Fleming nodded. Then she crossed herself and continued eating.

At the far end of the table Callum listened while he ate, and stored away the small nugget of information. In the days that followed he heard nothing more. When Lady Fleming asked him to go into the town to fetch her a supply of a particular sweet she loved, he knew he must use this opportunity to execute his escape. He visited the sweetshop and was pleased to learn he would not have to come back.

"She always orders these sweets near the holiday," the sweetshop owner told Callum. "We have them in readiness for her," he said, handing the lad a large square box. He thanked the man and then continued on his way, walking through the town until he heard a familiar voice at his elbow. Turning, he saw one of his kinsmen and stopped. "Rafe, 'tis time for me to return to Duin, isn't it?"

"Aye, lad, it is," Rafe said.

"I'll tell them, and meet ye on the morrow just after dawn on the road to the borders," Callum said.

Rafe nodded, and then disappeared into the crowded marketplace near where they had met. Callum rode back up to the castle. He brought his mistress her sweets, saying, "May I speak wi' ye, my lady?"

Lady Fleming popped a sweet into her mouth, and a look of delight passed over her features. She waved a hand at him. "Aye, Callum."

"I must beg yer permission to leave ye. When I was in the town I was approached by a kinsman who had come to find me. My mam is very ill, Rafe said. They think my mam may be dying. He was sent by our priest to fetch me home to Duin," Callum said.

A look of distress passed over the good woman's face. "Then ye must go if the priest calls ye," she said. "Will ye return?" She took another sweet from the box.

"If I can, my lady, for it has been a pleasure to serve ye," Callum said with a bow.

"Inform the steward of yer departure," Lady Fleming told him. "Tell him I have said he is to hold yer position for ye until Twelfth Night."

"Thank ye, my lady." Callum hurried off.

The castle steward was not happy to see him go. "She likes ye, and ye've served her well, but still, we only hae one mam, and if the priest sent for ye, then it is serious."

Callum ate a larger than usual supper. In the very early morning he arose from the pallet that had been his in a corner of Lady Fleming's apartments. He had dressed the night before in his own clothing, carefully folding the garb he had been given and laying it on the pallet. The false dawn was lighting the skies as he came out into the courtyard and made his way across it to the stables. There he sought out his horse, saddled and bridled the beast, and led it outside.

To his surprise Lord Fleming's secretary, Allan, approached him in the half-light. He thrust a small packet at Callum. "His Lordship wants this delivered to the Hamiltons. If their messenger hasn't died and is still at yer master's house, have him take it. Otherwise tell the steward of Duin he is to arrange for its delivery himself."

"Aye, sir, gladly," Callum replied, taking the leather packet and tucking it in his shirt. The Earl of Duin was going to be very interested to see what this message contained.

He mounted his horse, Allan walking him to the barred gate.

"Let the lad through," Lord Fleming's secretary said.

The portcullis was raised, and Callum Ferguson departed Dumbarton. He met his kinsman eventually on the road to the borders. Together they rode home to Duin, riding in as the late-November sun was setting over the sea. Callum went immediately to find the earl and tell him what small information he had discovered, and to deliver the packet meant for the Hamiltons. He found both his master and his mistress in the hall.

Annabella jumped up from the high board when she saw him. "Oh, lad, thank God ye're back safely!" she said. "I hae been so worried." She collapsed back into her seat.

Callum bowed to the earl. "I bring some small news, but more important, I bring a message meant for the Hamiltons," he said, laying the leather packet on the table before Angus Ferguson. "They plan to assassinate Moray as soon after Twelfth Night as they can, Lennox next, and then Erskine. They dinna believe they can bring the queen back until this is done. And they said they will hae to rescue the queen from the English."

"Did ye learn where they will accost Moray?" Angus asked the boy.

Callum shook his head. "I heard Lord Fleming complain to his wife that Moray never remains in one place long enough to catch."

"Moray knows the dangers he faces," the earl said grimly. "Ye've done well, lad, and I thank ye. Go and get something to eat. After the old year turns ye'll come into my personal service."

"What did ye do at Dumbarton?" Annabella asked him, curious.

"I was assigned the task of scribe to Lady Fleming," Callum said. "She writes letters each day to her family and her friends. I learned nothing, however, from her dictation. Mostly gossip and her thoughts on being cooped up in Dumbarton. She dinna like it, and fears the castle will eventually be taken."

"Dumbarton's impregnable," the earl said.

"Everything hae its weak spot," Annabella said.

Callum went off, and Angus Ferguson reached to open the packet. Taking his knife, he carefully slipped it beneath the seal, easing it from the parchment enough to open. If he decided to send the message on, he could reseal it in such a manner that no one would realize that the letter had been opened.

The inside revealed little new but for one important thing: Lord Fleming had learned that Moray would be spending the twelve days of Christmas at Stirling, where the little king was now housed, as his mother before him had been. Sometime in mid- to late January he would go to Edinburgh. An assassination at Stirling with the king in residence was unthinkable. But a watch would be kept to learn of the departure of Moray for the capital. And when that date was learned, a messenger would be dispatched to the Hamiltons. It was up to them when and how the deed was to be done.

Angus read the message aloud to his wife. "They are being cautious," he noted.

"Will ye send the message on?" Annabella wanted to know. "And where will ye send it, as we never asked our guest from where he came?"

"Remember he said the Hamiltons move around quite a bit to avoid the King's Men. But he must know some way of getting in touch with them," Angus answered her.

"Shall I ask him?" Annabella teased. "He seems to be willing to speak wi' me."

The earl laughed. "Let me try first."

The dungeons were colder now with the onset of cooler weather. Angus Ferguson was not a cruel man, however. His prisoner had both a brazier heating his small cell, and blankets. He was seated on his bed, finishing a bowl of what appeared to be lamb stew.

"Good evening," the earl said.

The courier jumped to his feet as his spoon clattered to the floor. "My lord!"

"Sit down," the earl said. "Finish yer food. Lamb stew is nae good cold. I hae a few questions for ye."

The prisoner picked up his spoon and sat back down. "I will answer whatever I can, my lord," he said.

"Are ye a kinsman in any degree to the Hamiltons?" Angus asked him.

"Nay, I am just a messenger," came the answer.

"Hae ye any loyalty to the Hamiltons?"

"My loyalty, my lord, is to he who pays my fee," came the candid reply.

"Yer message was delivered safely to Dumbarton," the earl told the man. "It was said you fell ill and could nae continue on, so my brother sent one of his own people in yer place. He hae now returned wi' a message for the Hamiltons, but we dinna know how to reach those who dispatched ye." Angus Ferguson paused to see how this news was affecting the face of his prisoner. He saw curiosity, nothing more.

"I was told that if I received a return message for them that yer brother would know how to direct me," the courier replied.

The earl was both astounded and furious. Matthew had shown a proclivity for taking Mary Stuart's side in this, but Angus had assumed from his brother that he had only offered Duin as a way stop. Now it would appear his brother was involved more deeply than he had admitted, and by being so Matthew had endangered them all. He focused his gaze upon his prisoner. "I may require yer services. I will pay ye far more than the Hamiltons will, for I need your complete loyalty. I think ye have learned in these last few months that I am a man of my word."

"Aye, my lord, I have," the messenger said quietly.

"I will pay ye in gold for yer services, and should ye choose ye may make yer home here at Duin. A man should hae a safe place, and yer accent tells me ye're an Edinburgh man," the earl said with a small smile.

"I am," the courier replied, "and yer offer is generous. I will serve ye loyally, my lord, but Edinburgh is a better place for a man of my profession. However, I will gladly accept ycr gold in payment for my services," he finished with a grin.

"'Tis fair," the earl agreed, smiling. He instinctively knew he might trust this man he had held prisoner for these last months. "I will bid ye good night then," he said. Then he stopped. "Ye hae never told me yer name."

"My name is Ian Elliot," came the answer.

"Good night, Ian Elliot," Angus Ferguson said a second time. Then he returned to the hall from the dungeon. Arriving there, he called to Jean's husband. "Fetch Matthew to me immediately," he said.

"What is it?" Annabella asked anxiously, for she had heard the severe tone in her husband's deep voice.

"Matthew is deeper into this treason than he has admitted," Angus said.

"Oh, sweet Lord!" Agnes half whispered. "What hae he done, my lord?"

"He is in contact wi' the Hamiltons. He can get in touch wi' them. This goes deeper than just assassinations, and I mean to learn everything he knows. I think it best that ye take the children and leave the hall, Agnes," the earl told her.

"I hae a right to know!" Agnes cried out.

"Aye, ye do. And ye will, but not until after I hae spoken wi' my brother. Please obey me. Take the bairns and leave the hall."

"I'll go wi' her," Annabella said quietly. She could see the panic and fear in Aggie's beautiful blue eyes.

"Nay," Angus told her. "I want ye and Jeannie here. Agnes! Go now!"

Very frightened now, Agnes gathered the twins and her own infant, and hurried them all from the hall.

"What do ye mean to do?" Jean asked her brother. "Remember our mam, my lord. Remember Matthew's devotion to ye, to Duin all these years," she pleaded for her brother. "He would nae be disloyal to ye, to us, to Duin."

"He hae been disloyal, Jeannie," the earl responded. "I dinna know why, but he hae betrayed us. I must know why if I am to even consider forgieing him."

Jean's lips pressed together as she fought to control her emotions. She said nothing more as they waited for Matthew to make an appearance in the hall.

He came, and his stance was one full of defiance. "Am I to finally be recalled to my position as Duin's steward?" he asked bluntly.

"Nay, ye will nae serve me ever again," the earl told his young brother, and derived satisfaction from the look of complete surprise upon Matthew's handsome face. "Ye've committed treason, and put Duin and all of its inhabitants at risk, including my wife, my bairns, and yer own wife and bairn. Why, Matthew? Why hae ye involved yerself wi' the Queen's Men? They fight a losing battle. Can ye nae see it? The King's Men hold the wee king. They hold Stirling. The power is wi' them. I care nae a whit for who rules Scotland as long as Duin and its folk are safe. Yer actions hae put us all in danger."

"She's the queen!" Matthew burst out.

"Mary Stuart is dethroned. Finished! It is my opinion that she will never again sit on Scotland's throne. The people loved her for her beauty, her kindness, her daring, her love for Scotland. But it was nae enough when she disappointed them wi' one bad marriage after another. I believe her innocent of Darnley's murder, but her association wi' James Hepburn tainted her purity, for Bothwell hae many detractors only too glad to defame them both. I believe that even if she hae converted from the old Church to this new Protestant faith, Knox and his ilk would hae hated her. Mary Stuart is an intelligent and educated woman. Those who advised her had a difficult time wi' that."

"England's queen rules supreme," Matthew said. "Why is Mary Stuart so different?"

"England's queen hae nae husband," the earl said.

"There is the Dudley scandal," Matthew countered.

"Suspected, but nae proven," Angus retorted. "Mary Stuart, on the other hand, hae publicly paraded her marriages and love affair. They will nae take her back. And for this ye hae endangered us all. Worse, however, ye lied to me, Matthew."

"I dinna!" he exclaimed.

"Ye dinna tell me the entire truth of yer involvement

wi' these misguided men," Angus said. "My whole life I hae loved ye. I hae done my best by ye because of that love, and because of the love our father held for ye, but ye hae betrayed Duin. Ye show nae remorse for this. I dinna know what hae happened to ye, Matthew, but ye are nae the brother that I knew."

"How stiff-necked ye've become," Matthew said bitterly. "All ye can see is Duin, nothing more. They hae driven our queen away. Our beautiful queen wi' her good heart, who generously gave freedom of faith to us all, old kirk or new kirk. They imprisoned her and stole her bairn. Why can ye nae see the wrong in it, Angus? Why?"

"I see the wrong. But 'tis a wrong that canna be righted. Much of Mary Stuart's fate was of her own making. She was advised strongly not to wed Darnley, but she did. She was advised even more strongly nae to wed Bothwell. She did. Now she must live wi' her decisions as ye must live wi' yers. Ye will leave Duin on the morrow. I am banishing ye from my lands. Where ye go or what ye do is yer own choice. But ye will nae longer make decisions for Duin that ye hae nae right to make and put at risk all here."

"No!" Agnes cried out, and then she flung herself at Angus's feet. "Please, my lord, I beg ye. Dinna send Matthew away! Hae mercy!"

"Get up, Aggie!" Matthew Ferguson took his wife by the arm and yanked her roughly to her feet. "I need nae mercy of him. We'll go to the Hamiltons. They are yer mam's kin, and will surely take us in for our faithful service to the queen."

Annabella had listened to it all, never speaking once. This was a tragedy. Now she spoke. "Angus, my lord and my love," she began, putting a restraining hand on his arm, "surely if Matthew will repent of his errors in judgment, ye can forgie him."

"I dinna need yer intercession, madam," Matthew said angrily.

"Aye, ye do," Annabella replied sharply.

"I dinna want it, then! Ever since ye came to Duin my brother hae changed. That is yer doing. He might hae wed a woman whose beauty matched his own. A fair lass wi' a large dower. Instead he wed ye for a bit of land he could hae eventually bought. Ye hae turned him from Ferguson ways and now he takes sides wi' murderers and usurpers instead of our true anointed queen. I hae committed nae sins from which I must repent, madam, but yer husband hae. When the queen is restored I will be given a title that I may pass on to my son, and he to his son one day."

"Oh, Matthew, I dinna know what I hae done to gain yer enmity, but however I hae offended ye, I beg yer pardon for it. I want things to be as they were when I first came to Duin. I want ye and Angus once again to be loving brothers. I hae nae changed Angus. He hae done what he had to in order that we all might survive these changing times."

"My God!" Angus Ferguson exclaimed, shocked by his younger brother's words. "Is that how they turned ye? Is that the bauble they dangled before ye? A title? Jesu, Matthew! Mary Stuart will ne'er again sit on Scotland's throne, and ye're more likely to end up at the end of rope than gain a title. But I will nae allow ye to bring the rest of us down wi' ye! Nor will ye blame my sweet good wife for imagined faults. I love this woman, Matthew. She hae no beauty that is visible. Her beauty is a different kind. It is one of the heart and of the soul. She is the best, the most perfect wife any man could hae, and she is mine. I am sorry ye canna understand that, brother." He turned his gaze on Agnes, whose shocked face told him she had known nothing of the depth of her husband's betrayals. "Aggie, ye may remain at Duin wi' yer bairn. I'll nae send ye into danger with this fool to whom ye're wed."

"I thank ye, my lord," Agnes said with as much dignity as she could muster, "but I must go wi' my husband. I will, however, ask sanctuary for our bairn until it is possible for us to establish another home." When Matthew made to protest, Agnes said in soft but firm tones, "Nay, Matthew. I will follow ye into danger and the unknown, but I will nae expose our son to yer folly; nor should ye. Come now. We must pack if we are to leave on the morrow."

"Wait!" the earl said. "I want to know how to get in touch wi' the Hamiltons."

"Why would I tell ye that? So ye can tell the King's Men?"

"So I can release to them the messenger I have held imprisoned these past months. Lord Fleming sent a message that needs to go on. Since I hae already read it and found it harmless, I would let it pass on, for this is the last time Duin shall be used as a way stop."

"Do whatever ye choose wi' the courier," Matthew said coldly. "I will carry the message myself to John Hamilton. It will help to ingratiate me wi' him."

"If the Queen's Men should catch ye, brother, there will be nae doubt of yer treason. They will hang ye at the side of the road, and heaven help yer wife then," the earl said quietly. "The messenger is paid to take the risk."

"I'll tell ye nothing," Matthew said stubbornly. "Either ye gie me the message from Dumbarton, or it will nae be delivered, for ye'll nae find the Hamiltons."

"Angus, nay," Annabella murmured low. "For my sister's sake I beg ye to find another way. The countryside is so dangerous right now. Ye hae said it yerself."

The Earl of Duin thought for a long moment. He was not of a mind to argue, and he wanted Matthew Ferguson gone. Though it broke his heart, he could no longer bear the sight of his younger brother. "Go to Brittany," he said. "Yer mam still hae kinsmen in Mont de Devereaux. I will write a letter to Monsieur Claude. He could use a man of yer many skills. Go to Brittany, and avoid the Hamiltons for yer own sake, and that of yer family," the earl advised.

"Go to hell!" Matthew said. "I will help to restore Scotland to the glory it lost when our beautiful queen was driven from this land." Then he turned on his heel and left the hall, Agnes hurrying after him.

"Aggie!" Annabella cried.

Agnes turned to see her eldest sister with her arms outstretched. Unable to resist, she flew into Annabella's embrace. "There is time for farewells, sister," she said, and she kissed her sibling several times upon the cheeks. "Take good care of my wee Robbie." Then she pressed her lips together to attempt to stave off the tears she felt near.

"Dinna go!" Annabella said. "It is too dangerous." Her eyes were welling up.

"I am his wife," Agnes said simply. "I go where he goes, no matter the danger."

"Dinna stay wi' the Hamiltons. They are at war, and their living will be rough. Their own women will be housed in hidden places to keep them and the bairns safe. The women in the encampment are whores and camp followers. They are nae fit company for ye. Go to our parents at Rath for shelter. Ye will be safe from the

King's Men there, Aggie." She hugged her sister a final time, then released her.

"I'll remember yer advice," Agnes said, and then she was gone from the hall.

Annabella burst into tears when she had gone. The earl took his wife into his arms. He said nothing, allowing her to weep against his shirt. His eyes met those of his sister Jean, whose own eyes were filled with tears that now silently slipped down her pretty face.

"How hae this happened?" he asked her.

"His jealousy got the better of him, I fear," Jean said, wiping her face with her apron. "It started when ye wed."

Annabella, hearing this, stopped crying and said, "But I did nothing to make him dislike me so verra much."

"Ye didn't hae to do anything," Jean explained. "When Angus took a wife everything began to change, and it would hae changed even if ye were the most beautiful woman on earth. That is what Matthew never realized. But he expected that since ye were plain of face there would be nothing between yer husband and ye but enough coupling to produce bairns for Duin. Instead ye and Angus fell in love. Ye forged a strong bond. Matthew felt cut out. The incident of his birth, being bastard-born, suddenly began to affect him. And then he wed Agnes.

"His position rankled him even more, especially after she bore him a son. Matthew wanted more for his son than just the stone house he built on the bit of land our father deeded to him. The Hamiltons were clever. They knew just how to turn him, and especially after he hae seen Mary Stuart as she fled Moray. I doubt the woman said more than a word or two to Matthew, and yet he was enchanted wi' her, as so many men before him have been. None of us hae done anything to Matthew. He hae done it himself."

"Ye must tell yer mam," the earl said.

"In the morning," Jean told him. "'Tis night, and I'll nae bring her bad news now that will keep her awake till dawn."

"Go to yer man, then," Annabella said. "I can undress myself."

"Thank ye," Jean replied, and, turning, departed the hall.

Annabella sighed, putting her head against her husband's shoulder. "How will ye get the message from Dumbarton to the Hamiltons?" she asked him.

"The courier will find a way. I suspect he knows more than he is willing to admit. We'll send him on his way on the morrow. Actually, he can follow along after Matthew. I'll warn him to be careful of being caught by my brother."

"Angus, I am so sorry," Annabella said.

"As am I, my love," he responded. "But Duin will be safe, and I must find a way to warn Moray that he is being stalked and marked for murder. I may go to Stirling myself before the weather gets too wintry."

"I'll ride wi' ye!" she answered enthusiastically.

"Nay," he said. "I need ye to remain at Duin. Wi' no steward now, ye must manage it all for me while I am gone. The beasties need to come from one pasturage to another nearer the castle before being brought into the shelter of the courtyard should a storm come. There should be one more boat from the New World due before winter sets in, my love. I need ye here. Promise ye will not attempt to follow after me this time. I should nae be gone long."

Annabella sighed again, but this time from the knowledge that he was right. With no Matthew to shepherd everything, she must become the shepherd. Callum wasn't old enough yet, although he would come into his new position sooner than he ever anticipated. "Verra well," she said. "I promise I will remain at Duin, my lord."

Chapter 17

$\mathcal{A}$ngus went off to speak again with the messenger. He would, she knew, bribe the man heavily so he would be true. Annabella went to find her younger sister, who she knew would now be packing her possessions, having made her peace with Matthew and her plans to go with him. She found Agnes, as she expected, in her own apartment.

Agnes looked up as she entered. Her eyes were red rimmed from crying. "He agrees that the Hamiltons' lair is nae the place for me. He will take me to Rath."

"Stay here!" Annabella said. "Ye are more comfortable here, and yer son is here."

Agnes shook her head in the negative. "Nay, Annabella, I would be as close to him as I can. I will never forgie myself for quarreling wi' him, leaving him. I should hae understood him better, but I behaved like a spoiled bairn."

"Ye behaved like a sensible woman," Annabella said sharply. "Matthew is wrong, Aggie. He endangered everyone here wi' his foolish actions. Ye need hae no regrets."

"What if he is killed?" Agnes asked her sister.

"He is apt to be if he persists in choosing sides," Annabella said.

"Angus chose sides," was the reply she received.

"Nay, not really. What Angus has done is accept the facts in this matter. Mary Stuart is gone from Scotland, and unlikely to ever return. James the Sixth, for all he is a wee lad, now sits upon the throne, while Moray stands behind it. Those are the facts. Angus neither lobbies for the king nor seeks to bring the queen back. He simply accepts what is."

"Matthew hae explained it all to me now. Our poor queen was driven from her throne by wicked and ambitious men," Agnes said.

Annabella found herself exasperated by her younger sister's sudden conversion. "That is nae the complete truth, Aggie. Ye hae lived wi' us, and ye know the full truth. I shall nae go into it wi' ye. I would like ye to stay, but go if ye will wi' yer husband. At least yer son will be safe here at Duin."

"I will send for him when I am resettled wi' Da and Mam at Rath," Agnes said.

"Of course," Annabella said. She seriously doubted that Agnes would send for her son, and if she did it was unlikely the Fergusons would turn the boy over to her. They would not allow one of their own to be placed in needless danger. As it was, her parents were not going to be happy to have Agnes bringing treason into their house. "I'll ask ye to carry a letter to our parents, if ye will," she said.

"I will be happy to do so," Agnes answered her. "It is little enough, considering all yer kindness to me."

Later that evening, as she and Angus lay abed after a delicious bout of lovemaking, she told her husband of her sister's change of heart regarding Matthew. She was sitting between his long legs, her back against his chest while he played with her full breasts.

"She loves him," Angus said dryly. "Women do odd things for love."

"I never did!" Annabella protested, then purred as he dropped a kiss on her rounded shoulder. "Umm, that's nice."

"Ye dressed as a lad and followed me to Brittany," he said with a chuckle. "Since ye hae nae business in Brittany, I must assume that ye love me, madam." He gave the two round breasts a gentle squeeze, tweaking the nipples as well.

"Ohhh!" The tweak sent a flash of sensation to her nether parts. She could feel his cock growing harder against her lower back. Removing his hands from her breasts, Annabella rolled over, kneeling first in order to push him fully onto his back. Then she grasped the towering flesh, swung over him, and guided it into her wet sheath. Sinking down upon him, she sighed with satisfaction as she began to ride him.

At first he held her hips to steady her, but eventually she found her perfect balance, and his hands reached up to grasp her breasts again. His eyes closed slowly, and he groaned with the outrageous pleasure she was giving him, not just with her luscious, perfect body, but with her long sable hair that swung back and forth, brushing his sensitive flesh until he was almost ready to scream with delight. He groaned again.

Annabella loved feeling as if she were in total control of their passion. Her knees and thighs squeezed his torso. Her hot sheath squeezed his thick length. She watched the lust build and spread over his gorgeous, handsome face. His dark, thick eyelashes quivered against his wind-tanned cheekbones. He groaned once, and she knew she had him. When some minutes later he groaned again, she could feel his cock trembling within her, and then as her sheath tightened about it one final time, his juices burst forth. Unable to help herself, Annabella threw back her head and screamed. Then she collapsed atop him.

After a few moments he rolled her over onto her back. "And now, madam, you will pay the piper for your wickedly skillful torture of your master."

"Ye're still hard." She gasped and shuddered in a final burst of pleasure.

"Aye," he whispered hotly in her ear, the tip of his tongue teasing at the whorl of her ear. His teeth nibbled delicately on her lobe. "Hard and hot and hungry still, madam."

He began to move on her once more. The rhythm was very, very slow at first, a teasing hard thrust followed by a leisurely withdrawal that after a few moments had her gasping with a burgeoning need she couldn't quite believe. Then his movement increased in its tempo, becoming faster and faster and faster. Her legs wrapped about him. Her fingers dug into his muscled shoulders. She moaned with a need that kept growing greater and greater and greater. "Dinna stop!" she cried softly.

"I dinna intend to," he growled back.

The world was suddenly changing around her. The air was sweet and hot by turns. A myriad of colors flashed behind her closed eyelids. She was flying. Aye! Flying and flying straight up into the bright golden sun. Stars burst all around her, showering their glittering bits over her head. Annabella cried out as she shuddered again not once, not twice, but three long shudders of utter perfect pleasure. It was too much. Too, too wonderful! And then everything went black.

With the last bit of his strength Angus rolled off of her and lay gasping on his back like a large salmon pulled from the water and tossed upon the grassy bank. Reaching for her small hand, he squeezed it tenderly; then, bringing it to his mouth, he kissed it several small kisses. The most passionate woman in the borders hid her gorgeous, shapely body behind a plain face that most men wouldn't give a second look. And she was his till death parted them. He meant that to be a very long time.

This time they both slept soundly until the morning. But as much as they wanted to remain abed, they knew they must arise. Annabella hurried to dress so she might see Agnes off personally. Angus, she knew, would not come to the courtyard. He would stand on the battlements of the castle and watch his brother and Agnes depart. He had said all he had to say to Matthew. If his damned fool of a younger brother could not see the error of his ways, then he must go forth from Duin before he brought trouble down on all of them. If Angus Ferguson felt any regret in his actions, it was for the sorrow this would bring old Jeanne, Matthew and Jean's mother. But Jeanne would understand.

She was loyal to Duin and always had been.

Annabella hurried into the castle courtyard, where Agnes was embracing her small son and promising to send for him one day. Robbie Ferguson didn't really understand, for he was still too young. He squirmed away from her and ran off to find his twin cousins. Annabella hugged her youngest sister. Then she handed her the sealed parchment she had written to their parents.

"Write to me, and tell me whether Rob has found a wife yet. And if he has, tell me if you like her," Annabella said. Then she hugged Agnes. "I'll miss ye, Aggie."

"My place is with Matthew," Agnes said primly. "He awaits me on the other side of the drawbridge. Ten young Duin men are going wi' us. They are loyal to the queen."

"I am glad ye will hae protection. 'Tis a long ride to Rath," Annabella said.

Ten men! She must remember to tell Angus. He would want to know.

"Farewell, sister," Agnes said in a calm voice. She clambered up onto her mare.

"Farewell, Aggie," the Countess of Duin said quietly. Then she watched with sadness as her sibling, back straight and stiff, rode from the courtyard and out across the castle drawbridge, where Matthew and his men waited for her. She never looked back.

Annabella began to cry softly.

Jean came to her side and quietly slipped her hand into that of her mistress. "This is Mary Stuart's doing. Her charm hae torn another man from his family."

"Better than allowing her to destroy the Fergusons of Duin," Annabella said in a suddenly hard voice. She was angry at what had happened. Angry at Matthew first and foremost. Then she remembered. "How is old Jeanne taking all of this?" she asked.

"She is furious, thank God! But better than sorrowful. She swore in her Breton tongue," Jean said with a chuckle. "I haven't heard her swear like that since our father died. Some of her words I didn't even understand." She gave Annabella's hand a squeeze. "We will survive this. The Fergusons always survive."

While the two women had seen Agnes off, the earl had dispatched the now freed courier with a promise and a warning. "Come back to Duin," he told the man, "and these five gold pieces, full weight, are yers. Betray me, and I *will* find ye."

The messenger had been returned all his possessions, including a small purse with a silver piece and some coppers. His formerly scrawny horse was now fat and ready to travel. The messenger had been given a warm cloak, for when he had arrived at Duin he had not needed one, and didn't own one anyway. Both he and the earl knew that there would be no five gold pieces from the Hamiltons. His mission was to reach the Hamiltons before the earl's brother, and be gone as quickly. "I'll be back," he said, and he would. The promised gold pieces would buy him a small cottage on the outskirts of Edinburgh, where he might bring a wife and have a peaceful old age. The Earl of Duin had proved himself a trustworthy man. The courier rode off.

It was December now, and although it was not the custom of the new Reformed kirk to celebrate all the feasts and fasts of the old kirk, the country folk were apt to do it, although to a lesser extent. Inside the castle the hall was decorated with boughs of pine and holly. Two enormous logs that would burn at least until the new year were dragged into the hall and lit with much ceremony. There was a modest amount of feasting and much music and some dancing, although the new kirk disapproved but had not yet forbidden it entirely.

Little Jamie and his twin sister, Annie, were now past three, and their cousin, Robbie, almost two. The children toddled about the hall accompanied by a large watchful deerhound who had appointed himself their guardian. The patient beast had been seen pulling the little ones away when they got too close to the hearth. This Christmastide old Jeanne came to reside in the castle for what promised to be a difficult winter. With her came Jean's two bairns. Looking about his hall, Angus Ferguson was content. His family was as paramount as was Duin's safety.

It was in the interest of his family that he decided to go to Stirling to warn the Earl of Moray of the plotted assassination. It was cold, and there was snow on the ground, but the weather was dry and would remain so for the interim, according to the old man in the village who predicted these things. Annabella was not happy about his going, although she knew he would not send anyone else.

"It is my way of proving to Moray our loyalty," Angus told Annabella. He rode out even before the sun was rising on the fifteenth day of January. But while the weather remained dry at Duin, its earl found himself having to shelter from a snowstorm several days later. He managed through sheer effort of will to reach Stirling at last, only to learn that the Earl of Moray had decamped for Edinburgh. Angus Ferguson turned his horse again, but when he reached Linlithgow he found the town in a terrible uproar. There were men-at-arms rushing about everywhere. The taverns were overflowing. He stopped a soldier wearing the Earl of Moray's badge.

"I'm the Earl of Duin," he identified himself. "I'm seeking yer master, as I have news of great import for him."

"The Earl of Moray is dead, my lord," the soldier answered him. "Killed by James Hamilton as he rode through the town."

Angus Ferguson felt his heart sink. It had all been for naught. He had thought he had plenty of time, and he would have, had the sudden snowstorm not delayed him. "When?" he asked the soldier.

"Not more than an hour ago, my lord. My master was passing a house owned by the archbishop of St. Andrews when he was shot from an upper-floor window. The coward hid behind a line of laundry."

"God hae mercy on his good soul," the earl said, and caught himself before he crossed himself, lest his Catholicism make him guilty by association with the Catholic cleric. "Are ye certain he is dead?"

"They carried him to a nearby house, my lord, but there was no hope. He died shortly thereafter. The wicked archbishop hae already fled, probably to Dumbarton."

"What of the assassin?" Angus asked.

"Fled too, but we'll catch him and hang him, ye can be certain."

"Who is in charge now?" Angus inquired.

The soldier looked befuddled; then he said, "I dinna know, my lord."

The earl thanked the man and moved on. He was tired. His horse was tired. He would need to find a place to rest where he might hear all the gossip. Then in the morning he would turn his horse's steps toward Duin. The Fergusons were not involved in all of this. If he told anyone now that Moray had been assassinated that he had known of the plot to kill him, to kill Lennox, to kill Erskine and others, it would be assumed that he was somehow involved, but had had a change of heart. Nay! He was not going to say a word now to anyone. He would return to his anonymity.

He found a large and prosperous inn, where he might have a bed for the night and several hot meals. His horse was well stabled. Angus sat in the taproom, eating a good supper, drinking his wine, and listening to all the gossip that was being reported. He quickly learned there was nothing more to know than the soldier in the street had reported to him. Moray was dead, but the little king was safe at Stirling. Moray's funeral would be a state one. Angus Ferguson had no doubt that a battle had already begun to fill the boots of the good regent.

He arrived home at Duin, a great snowstorm on his heels. He called all of his clansmen and -women into his hall after the snow ended several days later to tell them what had transpired. They were shocked and concerned. They wanted to know whether Moray's death meant that the queen would return to Scotland, be restored to her throne.

"It would take a miracle, for although Mary Stuart believes herself a guest of her cousin Elizabeth Tudor, she is more a prisoner. Since she left us they have drawn her deeper and deeper into England," the earl explained. "It is unlikely they will be able to extract her from the castle in Staffordshire where she now resides."

Duin settled down into a quiet winter. There was no news, for the weather made it impossible. The courier sent to the Hamiltons in November returned in March as soon as the melt began. The road was muddy, but patches of green were beginning to take hold on the hillsides, and the days were longer, brighter now as the messenger rode into the courtyard. He carried several messages with him. One was for Annabella from her mother, and she opened it eagerly.

Dearest daughter, her mother began.

While happy to see Agnes, we are distressed by her reasons for coming to Rath. We have told Matthew Ferguson of our disapproval of his behavior in endangering Agnes. Sadly, he seems to think of nothing but restoring Mary Stuart to her throne.

Thank God wee Robbie is with ye. I am shamed by the disloyalty my kinfolk are showing. My own brother is involved, to my great sorrow. Thank ye for advising us of the situation surrounding Matthew Ferguson. No matter how much Agnes begs it of ye, do not send our grandson to Rath. The countryside is not safe. I am happy to tell ye that your brother, Robert, will wed Alys Bruce in the coming summer here at Rath. She is a pretty lass, amiable and most sensible, which suits your brother well. It is my hope that James, Anne, and Robert thrive, and that you and Angus are in good health. Your father and I send our love to ye all,

Your mother, Anne

"She says not to send Robbie even if Agnes begs," Annabella told her husband.

"I don't intend to. My nephew is a Ferguson, and he will learn to behave like one," the earl said. "We dinna involve ourselves, but neither do we commit treason." He was holding a second open parchment in his hand, and looking extremely irritated.

"What is the matter?" Annabella asked him.

The earl held out the letter and shook it as a dog might shake a piece of prey. "*This* is the matter," he said. "It is from Matthew. He informs me that a vessel will shortly be anchoring in the harbor beneath the castle. We are to grant its captain and crew our good border hospitality." He flung the parchment from him. "Who the hell does my brother think he is? This ship bodes no good, and once again Matthew endangers Duin wi' his arrogance. I hae no intention of granting it permission to anchor in my harbor." He called the courier to him. "Ian Elliot, tell me what ye heard in the Hamiltons' hall. What do ye know of this ship?"

"I heard them speaking about a plan to rescue the old queen from England. They mean to bring her to Duin, where she will board the waiting vessel and be taken to France," the messenger said. "From there the Hamiltons will restore her to Scotland."

"Jesu!" the earl swore. "What wily fools these petty conspirators are. If they mean to restore her, why send her to France? Nay, they mean to take control in her name while keeping her in France waiting for the proper time to return. It will nae come, of course."

"And Duin will be implicated in this new treason, because the ship will anchor in our harbor," Annabella said, as angry as her husband. "We canna allow this to happen, Angus! But how can we stop them?"

The earl smiled a wolfish smile. "I possess two cannons that sit on the battlements," he said. "That is why the Irish stopped raiding here. We shall make certain the cannons are primed and ready for our guests."

"Your boat from the New World never came," Annabella said.

"It hae been delayed, then," the earl said. "It will come."

And it did, sailing into the harbor several days later, looking rather battered and damaged. When the tide was out enough to allow for a landing, a small boat was lowered into the waves and rowed to the narrow strip of beach. A man got out and climbed the interior steep cliff staircase up to the castle. When he arrived in the hall he went directly to Angus Ferguson and bowed.

"My lord," he said. His accent was light but there.

"Captain Diego, 'tis good to see ye once again, but

the ship is obviously the worse for wear. Ye encountered difficulties."

"Aye, my lord, we did. We are fortunate to be here at all, but thanks be to God, the lord Jesu, and his blessed *Madre* Maria, we have survived. I bring bad news, however." The captain took a silver goblet of wine from the servant with the tray and drank deeply before continuing.

The earl waited politely for Captain Diego to continue. He saw his wife signal for food to be brought. Good lass, he thought. Hot food and wine were exactly what the seaman needed to become more comfortable, to loosen his tongue.

Finally, his thirst assuaged, the captain spoke. "My lord, yer mines are finished. The gold and the silver I bring is the last of it. I was fortunate to get it out, for all properties owned by foreigners are now being confiscated by His Most Royal Majesty King Philip. I had to run a gauntlet of Spanish warships several times before I was finally able to escape, and then it was as if the devil himself had put every storm upon the face of this earth in my path. Then we were accosted by pirates off the west coast of Ireland, and escaped only when a thick fog blew in, allowing me to navigate around Mizzen Head and Cape Clear before they might find us again. There were English ships in St. George's Channel to avoid as well. I've never been so glad to see Duin in all my life."

"Come to the high board," Annabella invited him, and then saw him made comfortable with a round bread trencher filled with lamb stew.

Captain Diego ate the food eagerly. His cup was refilled once.

"Ye went to the mines yerself?" the earl asked.

"Aye, my lord, I did. There were more Indians in their village center than inside the mines. I have noticed over the last three years the workers being fewer and fewer. I had spoken to yer steward about it the last time I was at Duin. Did he not tell ye?"

"Nay, he did not," the earl said grimly. "My half brother has unfortunately chosen to disagree wi' me at every turn in recent months. He hae now departed Duin."

The seaman nodded as he scraped the last of the stew and bread from his trencher. "It is sometimes difficult for the younger ones to obey the elder," he said.

Then he became all business once again. "We will off-load your cargo in the morning, my lord, if that will suit ye."

Angus Ferguson nodded. "And ye will remain in the safety of my harbor until yer vessel can be restored and is seaworthy once again," he said. "I'll send a servant to tell yer man ye stay the night here in the castle. Tomorrow we'll ride into my village for workers and materials for the repairs."

"I'm grateful, my lord," Captain Diego said.

"I'll want ye to hae the ship," the earl said. "'Tis nae use to me any longer."

"My lord!"

"Ye've served me well these past years, Captain Diego. I'm a reclusive Scotsman. What use would I hae for a sailing ship?"

"'Tis too generous, too generous," the seaman said. There was just the hint of tears in his eyes, and his voice almost shook.

"Nay, ye've risked yer life many times to bring yer ship to safety in my harbor," Angus Ferguson said. "Now, I'll hear nae more about it. Ye'll hae the vessel's papers transferred into yer name when ye're ready to depart. And my wee harbor is always open to ye, sir. Come! We'll drink on it!" And he raised his own goblet.

No wonder men loved her husband, Annabella thought. His sense of fair play, his generosity, was that of a great ancient lord. Few men if any behaved like that now. She asked for the courier, who was now planning to depart Duin to carry a message to Rath, and then she wrote to her mother, saying that if it were possible she would come to her brother's wedding in the summer. She begged her mother to plead with Agnes to return to Duin, where she would be safe, and not endanger her family at Rath. The Countess of Duin was very surprised to receive a letter back from her mother that was carried by one of Rath's servants.

Dearest daughter, the lady Anne wrote,

> *Ye need have no further concern about your sister Agnes. She has departed for France with her husband. The Hamiltons have been hounded vigorously since Moray's murder. They could not successfully hide this time while waiting to strike again. Their forces have been scattered, at least temporarily, for now. I am certain Agnes will write to you when she has been safely settled. We have heard that a rescue attempt was made to free Mary Stuart from her imprisonment early this spring. It failed, and the young men involved were all killed. Your brother and his bride have chosen the week after Lammastide in which to wed. It is dearly hoped that ye and Angus will be able to come. I remain as always your loving mother, Anne.*

Annabella placed the parchment in her lap and looked to her husband, to whom she had just read the letter aloud. "If," she said, "Mary Stuart is nae free, then I suspect we may nae have to contend wi' any other vessel anchoring in our harbor."

"They may come yet," he said, "for it is possible they hae nae heard that the escape attempt failed."

With the opening of the roads again now that winter was over, news began to trickle into Duin. There was no regent agreed upon yet for the king. His paternal grandfather, the Earl of Lennox; Lord Erskine; and the Earl of Morton were all locked in a fight to gain control of the little lad's power.

"What a trio," the earl said, shaking his head. "Mary Stuart hated Darnley's father, and Morton is said to have been involved in the murders of both Darnley and Riccio. Erskine's a good man, but surely not powerful or strong enough to handle the regency."

"He holds the king at Stirling," Annabella said quietly.

"Aye, ye're right, sweetheart," Angus answered her. Her astuteness continued to surprise him even after several years of marriage.

"Let us concern ourselves wi' matters closer to home," Annabella said. "What will ye do if Agnes and Matthew want the return of their child? We must consider this."

"Robbie remains at Duin," Angus told her firmly. "He is a Ferguson. If my brother chooses to continue in his foolish ways, I'll nae hae this bairn dragged into a nomadic life. Robbie belongs here wi' us, his family. But the household is yers, madam, so the final say will be yers as well."

"I agree wi' ye, my lord," Annabella said.

At that moment a man-at-arms hurried up to the earl. "My lord," he said, "a ship hae just entered yer harbor, and 'tis nae Captain Diego returned."

"I'll come," Angus Ferguson said. He turned back to Annabella. "May this be the last battle for Duin, sweetheart."

"I'm coming wi' ye," she told him.

The Earl of Duin did not argue with his countess. He knew better than that now.

They climbed the stairs to the top of the castle, and then scrambled up the ladder through a trapdoor to the heights. Angus immediately began the business of seeing that the two small cannons were loaded properly in preparation for firing. It had been some time since these guns had been fired, and even though they were well maintained, there was always the danger of one or both of them exploding.

Annabella, however, was once again astounded by the beauty surrounding them as she gazed from the battlements of the castle. The low green hills, the winding streams crisscrossing the landscape, the vast blue sea beyond. She could see both the village and Matthew Ferguson's house in the distance. Tears touched her thick, dark lashes. Agnes should be here in her own home, not wandering a foreign countryside, friendless and separated from her family. Silently Annabella cursed the enchantment that surrounded Mary Stuart, causing men to follow her blindly.

When the guns were loaded and prepared, Angus ordered that both of them be fired at once: one cannon shot to fall just beyond the ship's bow, the other its stern. That would be the vessel's only warning. The cannons were to be reloaded immediately, for if they were forced to fire a second time, their aim would be deadlier.

The earl gave the order, and both of the small guns fired simultaneously. They heard the booms echo across the water, watching as the shots dropped exactly as they should. Now they waited to see what this ship flying Mary Stuart's flag would do. Suddenly a small white flag was raised, and at the same time a small boat was lowered into the waves and rowed toward the narrow strip of beach at the foot of Duin's dark cliffs. The Earl of Duin and his wife hurried from the battlements back down into the castle. In the hall the earl ordered his wife to remain while he traversed the steep, narrow interior passage leading to the beach.

He stepped from the hidden door in the cliffs as the small boat reached the shore.

A gentleman stepped out of the craft and came forward. "Monsieur, I was told we would be welcomed at Duin," the man said. "Is this your vaunted border hospitality?" The man spoke French.

"You are not welcome here, sir. We are loyal Scots at Duin," the earl replied in that same language. "I am sorry to tell you that you are mistaken. I am informed that Mary Stuart's escape has failed. I advise you to return from wherever you have come, for the English will surely be even more vigilant than ever now."

"I thank you for not damaging my ship," the man replied.

"I wished only to warn you," the earl responded with a small smile. "Now, pray allow me to escort you to your cockle." He walked the man to the little boat, where an oarsman waited patiently. The man stepped into his transport and sat down. "Farewell," the Earl of Duin said formally. He then stood watching as the little vessel made its way back to the larger ship. He remained watching as his visitor reached his destination and climbed up to the deck. The sea anchor was raised, along with a large sail. The ship began to turn itself about and exit the little harbor. It was only then that the

Earl of Duin reentered the passage in the cliffs that led back up to the castle.

In the weeks that followed they heard nothing of any import, and so they decided to travel to Rath to young Robert Baird's wedding. Their trip took them a little longer than if they had just gone alone, but they decided to bring the children to see their grandparents, who had not laid eyes on them since shortly after their birth.

The laird of Rath and his wife were overjoyed to see them. To Annabella's delight, both Sorcha, who lived nearby, and Myrna, who had traveled down from the Highlands, were at Rath. The tower house was overflowing with family. The sisters and their children would sleep in their old chamber high in the tower. Sorcha had two little ones, both boys; and Myrna had brought her daughter, a little freckle-faced lass with auburn curls.

"She looks like her da, worse luck," Myrna said pithily. "She's a wild Highlander."

"Are ye so unhappy then?" Annabella inquired of her sister.

"Unhappy?" Myrna sniffed. "Why would I be unhappy? I've a good man, a good home, a daughter, and the hope of another bairn in the coming year. Nay! I am not unhappy, sister."

The men slept in the hall. The bride would not arrive with her family and clan folk until the wedding day. Rob's mother and his sisters cleaned and refurbished the chamber that had been his, and that he would now share with his wife.

The wedding day dawned sunny, for it was August, and August seemed to be a bright month in the borders. The Bruces of Cleit arrived in early morning with flags flying and pipers piping. The blushing bride was on a pale dun-colored mare being led by her father. Annabella thought Alys Bruce a pretty girl, although she had not the beauty of the lady Anne or her three younger daughters. The pastor from the nearby village kirk came to unite the young couple in a plain and simple ceremony.

Then they returned to Rath Tower to celebrate this new union between the Bruces of Cleit and the Bairds of Rath. The feast was held in the hall. There were roast meats: beef, venison, lamb, and boar. There were trout and salmon from the nearby streams and rivers. There was an enormous pie filled with rabbit, carrots, and tiny onions surrounded by a rich wine gravy, and topped with a flaky crust. There were ducks roasted until their skins were crispy, and swimming in a plum sauce. There were capons stuffed with sage, bread, onions, and celery. There were two roast turkeys, and platters of quail eggs. Lettuces had been braised in white wine. There were bowls of tiny peas. The trestles had small wheels of hard yellow cheese. The high board had two cheeses: a hard yellow, and a soft white French cheese. There were ale and cider and wine to drink.

They ate, and they toasted the bridal couple. Annabella thought her brother looked genuinely happy, as did his new wife. And when the feasting had ceased they went outside into the summer sunshine, where an archery contest was in progress. In a nearby field a group of men were kicking about a ball made from a sheep's bladder. A group of musicians played, and there was dancing. Annabella and her sisters briefly joined in the round, catching hands with the villagers and cavorting in a circle, first this way and then the other.

Angus watched his wife, thinking that although her sisters had great physical beauty, Annabella was truly the most beautiful of them all, even if they didn't know it. Her goodness radiated from her plain face. Her gray eyes sparkled, and her smile was sweet. The laird of Rath came and stood next to his son-in-law. "It pleases me to see the love ye hae for her," he murmured softly.

"She's yer daughter," Angus answered quietly. "Ye know what she is like."

"Aye, I do," the laird replied, "but most men could nae get by her plain face. Ye did, and discovered the treasure that I gie ye. I am glad, for she loves ye too."

Angus Ferguson smiled. "Aye!" he agreed. "Are we nae the most fortunate couple, my lord?"

The day began to wane, and they returned to the hall to feast once again. It grew near the hour that the bride and groom would be put together. But first Rob and his three brothers-in-law danced amid the swords laid out upon the floor as both the Baird and the Bruce pipers played. As their dance was coming to an end, there was a small disturbance at the far end of the hall. The mournful sound of the pipes died away as a gaunt figure stumbled forward toward the high board, hands outstretched.

Myrna and Sorcha screamed softly. Alys clung to her bridegroom. The lady Anne looked to her husband. It was Annabella who recognized the visitor. "Agnes!" she cried. Then she rushed to catch her youngest sister, who was collapsing to the floor. She sat on the hall floor, cradling her sibling in her lap. The girl was covered in the dust of the road. Her hair was matted, her garments shabby, and she was very pale. "Agnes," Annabella said again. Her hand smoothed a strand of hair from her sister's face.

"Am . . . I . . . home?" Agnes whispered hoarsely.

"Aye, ye're home, and in time for the end of Rob's wedding day," Annabella said.

Agnes sighed deeply, and then her eyes closed as she fell into a deep sleep.

The lady Anne was now by her eldest daughter's side. "What hae happened to her, Annabella?" She gave a little shriek. "She is barefoot! Where are her shoes?"

"We need to get her upstairs and into bed," Annabella said.

It was then Myrna's big Highlander husband, Duncan MacKay, stepped in, saying as he gathered Agnes up into his brawny arms, "Where do ye want me to take her, my lady? God's blood, the lass weighs nae more than a bag of feathers," he exclaimed.

The lady Anne looked distraught. The tower was not spacious. The chamber she shared with her husband was on the floor above the hall, their son's chamber above that, and his sisters' at the top. For the first time in her life the lady of Rath didn't know what to do. She looked helplessly to Annabella.

"We must make a bed here in the hall for her," Annabella said quietly. She called a manservant to her side and gave quick instructions. In just a very few minutes a small cot had been put next to one of the hearths. It was then covered with a feather bed, pillows, and a down coverlet. Duncan MacKay gently set the sleeping girl down on the narrow bed. "Thank ye," Annabella said, smiling at him. Then she turned back to attend to her youngest sister.

"We must get her out of those filthy clothes," the lady Anne said.

Together, amid the finish of the wedding feast, the two women worked to divest poor Agnes of her clothing, bathe her as best they could, and dress her in a clean night garment. The women servants had thoughtfully brought a screen to give them a modicum of privacy.

When Agnes was settled, her old nurse patiently comb-
ing the tangles from her hair, the lady of Rath and her
daughter, the Countess of Duin, came back to the high
board, where the rest of the family was awaiting them.

The lady Anne collapsed into her high-backed chair.

Annabella sat down, quietly saying, "As soon as Agnes knew she was safely home, she fell into a deep sleep.
She hae said nothing, and so we must possess our souls
of patience now until she awakens and can tell us what
happened."

"I think, with both families' permission, we may dispense wi' the putting-to-bed ceremony. Alys and I will
just go to our chamber now," young Rob Baird said.

The Bruces agreed with the Bairds. Everyone at the
high board wished the bridal couple a pleasant night,
and then they were gone from the hall.

Myrna stood up. "I will sit by Agnes's side for the
next three hours," she said without even being asked.

"I will sit by her for the next three after that," Sorcha
said.

"And I will do the hours before and into the dawn,"
Annabella told them. "Ye must rest, Mam, for yer nurs-
ing skills will be needed on the morrow, I am certain."

She was right. Agnes finally awoke the next day with
a low fever. Her mother cured it with a mixture of herbs.
They were all horrified by her wasted appearance, but
she was not yet ready to explain it, or how she had gotten to Rath. Several days passed before, finally convinced that their youngest sibling would survive, Sorcha
and her family departed for their nearby home. Myrna
and Duncan MacKay, along with their curly-haired
daughter, Meggie, left the day after. They had not yet
allowed little Robbie Ferguson to see his mother, for
fear her meager appearance would frighten him. The

Bruces had also departed two days after the wedding was celebrated.

"When she is strong enough to travel," the earl told the laird, "she will come home to Duin wi' us. She is my brother's wife. She hae her own house there, and her bairn. Taking care of Robbie again will help her to recover."

At first the laird protested. "She is my daughter, Angus. She is Rath born."

"Aye," he agreed, "but she is a Ferguson's wife, and she does love Duin. What is there for her here now, wi' yer heir married? 'Tis nae a grand house, Robert. 'Tis just large enough for a small family. At Duin she can live either in the castle or the fine stone house that my brother built for her. She is her own woman, beholden to neither her da nor her brother. Alys seems a sweet lass, but how long will she tolerate her husband's sister in the same house? Nay, Agnes will come wi' us."

"Leave the choice to her," the laird said.

Angus Ferguson laughed. "Nay, Robert. Agnes is a stubborn young woman. She left Duin to follow after my brother, despite our best advice, despite our pleading that she remain. She is too proud to beg to come home wi' us. She must be told she is coming and has nae choice in the matter at all. 'Tis better that way for all of us."

The laird thought a long moment, and then he agreed that perhaps the earl was right. That evening Agnes sat among her kinfolk and finally told them her tale. The color had begun to come back into her cheeks. Her feet, which had been cracked, roughened, and covered with blisters, were now healing. Her little son nestled in his mother's arms as, sitting up against a pile of pillows at her back, she told them what had happened.

"When James Hamilton murdered the Earl of Moray," she began, "the Hamiltons were almost immediately besieged by the King's Men. There was nae place they could hide. Matthew managed to escape and come for me here at Rath. Then we went on again to France, to the village from where old Jeanne had come."

"Why did ye nae return to Duin?" the earl asked quietly.

"Matthew no longer felt welcome at Duin," Agnes said, lowering her eyes. "I begged him to go back, but he would nae. He said that in France he would make a new life for us. He had been a steward in a great castle, and he could hire his sword. But we never reached Jeanne's village. We never got past the port where we landed, Harfleur. Though we had little coin, we managed to gain shelter in a waterfront tavern. But then Matthew heard some sailors disparaging his queen. They called her a whore. Matthew got into a quarrel wi' them over it." Here Agnes stopped briefly, her beautiful blue eyes filling with tears. "He . . . he was killed before my eyes. They slit his throat and left him to die in my arms." She began to sob softly. Then she continued.

"When they tried to rob him as well, I began to shriek to the high heavens. The innkeeper and his lads came to my defense, and what coin we had was saved. I used most of it to hae him buried in the churchyard, and for the priest to say prayers for him. Then I sought a vessel to bring me back across the water."

"Ye had enough coin for it?" Annabella said.

Agnes flushed and said nothing for a few moments as they all waited to learn what else she would say.

"Thank ye for seeing that Matthew was properly buried," the earl said to her. "I regret the pain my brother hae cost ye."

Agnes looked up, and he could see both sorrow and

anger in her lovely blue eyes. "By some miracle I found a vessel going to Leith. I told the captain my husband had just died, and showed him my few coins. 'Twas all I had for my passage, and I told him I would travel on the deck, and eat only the scraps from the table." She paused, then went on. "He suggested another arrangement, which I at first refused, but after two nights of rain and wind I weakened, for I knew I would get sick and die if I had to endure another night on the open deck. He was a kind man, and I no virgin."

The laird's wife grew pale at her daughter's words. Annabella reached out and took Agnes's hand in hers. Agnes threw her sister a grateful look and continued onward.

"When we reached Leith I sold my boots for enough coin to purchase bread. I had been able to eat little aboard the vessel, for my belly is nae a good sailor, I fear. I began walking, and I walked and walked and walked until the countryside began to look familiar again. I passed many villages and homes burned out, for they were obviously supporters of the Hamiltons. Three days ago I ran out of both bread and coin. I made certain to shelter secretly in barns, where I was able to steal eggs to eat raw. And then I reached Rath, praise God! There were times," Agnes said as tears began to roll down her cheeks, "that I thought I should never see home or family again."

There was a long silence as her words concluded, and then the laird of Rath told his daughter, told them all, "Ye're a brave lass, Aggie. I'm proud of ye."

"We'll gie ye another week to gain yer strength back," the Earl of Duin told his sister-in-law, "and then ye're coming home wi' us, Agnes."

"Nay!" Agnes quickly cried.

"Aye, ye are, lass," Angus Ferguson said. "Ye should

hae never left us, and yer son needs his mam, but he's a Ferguson, Aggie, and he remains at Duin, where he hae his family, his grandmam, his cousins, his aunt and uncle."

"But how can I live?" Agnes said. "I hae no monies."

"But ye do," the earl surprised her by saying. "Matthew would hae accessed his gold when ye got to France and were settled. Now it is yers. Ye hae a stone house on lands belonging to him. Ye can live in the castle if ye prefer. However, there is nae question of ye living anywhere else but Duin. We want ye home again, Agnes. Yer son wants his mam."

Agnes began to weep again, but this time the sound she made was one of relief. She looked up at Angus Ferguson. "I am grateful to ye, my lord. I will gladly come back to Duin, for I love it. It almost broke my heart to hae to leave it."

"Then it is settled," the earl told her.

Afterward, as Agnes lay sleeping again, the lady Anne came to where her eldest daughter and Angus Ferguson were seated together by the other fireplace. The flames were blazing brightly, the warmth of the fire taking the chill from the summer's evening.

"How can I thank ye," she said to the earl. "When I think how concerned I was when it was decided ye were to marry Annabella . . . Yer family's reputation for sorcery frightened me. Yet my husband assured me ye were naught but a man who sought his privacy. I was but partly reassured. And then I met ye, and I could see yer deep and abiding affection for my child. Everything I had heard of ye was put to flight, for ye are a man of honor, of principle. Now, seeing yer kindness and forgiveness for Agnes, I think ye are nae a sorcerer but an angel come to earth, my lord. Thank ye."

The Earl of Duin stood and took the lady Anne's two

hands in his. His handsome face turned to look into her blue eyes. "Let me assure ye, madam, that while I am nae a sorcerer, neither am I an angel." He flashed her a warm smile. "I have done little, but even fearful ye gave me Annabella, who is the best of all women. I will do whatever ye need for that reason and that reason alone," he assured her. Then he kissed her two hands before releasing them.

Afterward, when she had gone, Annabella told him, "Ye hae made her so happy, my darling. Thank ye for reassuring her."

A week later, Agnes settled in a comfortable cart, the Fergusons of Duin began their journey to the southwest. With the good late-summer weather they reached Duin in good time, considering the baggage that followed them along with Agnes's cart. Agnes had decided to live in her own home. She and her son would live in the castle until the house had been opened up again and the servants returned to serve her.

That first night back, after she had made her rounds through the hall seeing that doors were barred, candles and oil lamps snuffed out, the fires in the fireplaces banked, Annabella went to her apartment. She had dismissed Jean, and now stood gazing out upon the sea, which was silvered by a glowing full moon. Angus came up and began to unlace her yellow gown. He kissed her shoulder and the nape of her neck with slow, heated kisses. Annabella sighed.

"Ye're happy to be home," he said.

"Aye, and I never want to go anywhere again, my lord. Duin suits me well. The autumn is coming, the winter will follow, and by midsummer we shall hae another bairn, for I am certain now that I am breeding. If it is a lad, we shall call him Patrick or Ian or Charles or David," she said.

"But what if it is a lass," he teased her, pushing her gown and chemise down, cupping her wonderful firm, round breasts in his two hands.

"I dinna know what I will call a lass," she replied, "but I know what I will nae call a wee girlie," she told him.

He chuckled. "What will ye nae call her?" he asked.

"Mary," Annabella said firmly. "I shall nae call a daughter Mary."

The Earl of Duin turned his wife about to face him, laughing as he did so. "Madam," he said, "I am in full agreement wi' ye. We will never call a daughter Mary." And then he kissed her hard. Nay, there would be no more Marys causing difficulty in his family. If the bairn were a lass, they would name her anything but Mary.

But on midsummer's eve next, the Countess of Duin was delivered of a strapping son who was called Patrick. And the question of the name Mary never came up again among the Fergusons of Duin.

Epilogue

The question of the boy King James VI's regent raged on for six months. Finally, in the summer of 1570, the Earl of Lennox, the king's paternal grandfather, was chosen on the strong recommendation of England's Queen Elizabeth. Mary Stuart, imprisoned in Tutbury Castle, was furious, but there was nothing at all she could do. She held the earl responsible for his son's character and behavior. She did not want her own son falling victim to the same man, but the choice was no longer hers to make.

The gentlemen of the Queen's Men would not accept Lennox, for as much as Mary Stuart hated him, he hated her as well. In her youth he had been suggested as a possible husband for the child queen, though he was twenty-six years her senior. When he had been refused he had gone into England, where he had lived for many years. His son's marriage to Mary Stuart had returned him to the limelight. Lennox held her responsible for his son's death. With the power of the regency in his greedy hands, it was a matter of concern to many how he would treat the little king.

The Queen's Men formed a rival parliament at Linlithgow. The Gordons came forth under the command of their earl and met the forces of the Duke of Lennox at Brechin, where they were defeated. Several months later, in February of 1571, another Hamilton rebellion was put down at Paisley. In April of that same year a group of daring commandos scaled the heights of Dumbarton in the dark of the night, capturing the formerly impregnable castle. All that was left for Lennox was Edinburgh, which was held by Kirkcaldy of Grange, now Mary Stuart's most devoted adherent.

When the duke attempted to hold his parliament in the Canongate beneath the castle, Kirkcaldy's guns quickly chased the parliament away. Edinburgh found itself a divided city, with two town councils and two kirk sessions. John Knox wisely withdrew from the city entirely, and the King's Men set up in Leith, where they were besieged for the next fifteen months.

In August of that year a parliament was held at Stirling, the little king's home.

In early September a raiding party of over four hundred men from the Queen's Men got into Stirling in the middle of the night. They rounded up all the lords who had come for the parliament, and then remained. The king's guardian, John Erskine, the Earl of Mar, managed to regain control of Stirling and keep the little king safe. The Earl of Lennox, however, was shot in the back and died several hours later.

The Earl of Mar quickly became the king's new regent. It was unfortunate that a little over a year later John Erskine died of natural causes. He had been the most moderate member of the King's Men, and until Darnley's murder a devoted supporter of Mary Stuart. Now the regency fell to the Earl of Morton, a proper villain who had been implicated in the murders of both

Riccio and Lord Darnley. Morton hung onto his power until 1580, during which time Elizabeth Tudor sent a large force of men who helped him to regain control of Edinburgh Castle once again. Kirkcaldy of Grange and his kinsmen were hanged. The King's Men had triumphed. There was no absolutely no hope that Mary Stuart would ever regain her throne.

In the years that followed her son grew up under the influence of a group of hard men. He was well educated, but timid, having spent his early years surrounded by war. It was a hard and loveless childhood, but the boy survived and even learned to think for himself. Finally, after several more years of peril during which he was influenced by his French cousin Esme Stuart, the new Earl of Lennox; and a brief captivity at Ruthven, from which James escaped; the young king declared himself emancipated and took up his throne to rule Scotland by himself. He married Princess Anne of Denmark shortly thereafter, and several years later, at the age of thirty-six, found himself not only king of Scotland, but king of England and Ireland too. His reign is well documented.

As for the Fergusons of Duin, they quietly faded once more into the anonymity that was their custom, and which they preferred above all else. But if you seek Duin Castle today, you will not find it. The legend says that that both castle and village disappeared one day into the mists that came off the Irish Sea. Neither was ever seen again. Some, however, claim to have heard ghostly pipes gaily playing in the vicinity of Duin on clear winter nights. So perhaps the Fergusons of Duin were sorcerers after all.

About the Author

Bertrice Small is the *New York Times* bestselling author of fifty-four novels and four novellas, as well as the recipient of numerous awards, including a Lifetime Achievement Award from *Romantic Times*. She lives on the North Fork of eastern Long Island in Southold, which was founded in 1640 and is the oldest English-speaking town in the state of New York. Now widowed, she is the mother of a son, Thomas, and grandmother to a tribe of wonderful grandchildren. Longtime readers will be happy to learn that her beloved felines, twelve-year-old Finnegan, the long-haired black kitty, and eight-year-old Sylvester, the black-and-white bed cat, are still her dearest companions. Readers can contact the author by going to her message board on her Web site, www.bertricesmall.com, or writing to her at P.O. Box 764, Southold, NY, or bertricesmall@hotmail.com.

Read on for a look at the first in a brand-new
historical romance series set in
Renaissance Italy by Bertrice Small.

Bianca
The Silk Merchant's Daughters

Available from New American Library
in print and as an e-book.

$\mathcal{S}$he was the fairest virgin in Florence. Or so it was said of Bianca Maria Rosa Pietro d'Angelo. High praise considering that red-gold or blond hair was considered the height of beauty, and Bianca had ebony tresses. She also had flawless features, an ivory complexion, a heart-shaped face, and eyes that were a startling shade of aquamarine blue. As she crossed the Piazza Santa Anna from her home with her mother more and more, gentlemen came to catch a glimpse of what they could of her features, which were carefully and modestly concealed by a bowed head and a light veiling. An audible sigh of regret arose as mother and daughter entered the church for morning Mass.

"They will be waiting when we come out," Bianca said to her mother.

"*Sempliciottos!* They are wasting their time," her parent replied. "I do not mean to waste my daughters on Florentine marriages. I was sacrificed by Venice to this dark city. I will not allow my girls to be. Only my love for your father has kept me here."

They found their way to the chairs set aside for their family and knelt in prayer on the embroidered red and gold kneelers. Mass began. They had music, which many smaller churches in the city did not—but Santa Anna Dolce was the family church of the Pietro d'Angelo family. It had been built by them a hundred years ago across from their large palazzo, which stood on the opposite side of the piazza. Upon its walls it had murals that depicted the life of Santa Anna, mother of the blessed Virgin. Besides the main altar, there were two other small altars. One to Santa Anna herself and the other to Santa Maria. The windows were stained glass. The floor, squares of black and white marble.

The Pietro d'Angelo wealth generously paid the livings of the three priests and the small choir that served it. The choir was a mixture of eunuchs and ungelded men with rich, deep voices. As long as they sang, they received a small stipend and were allowed to live in a dormitory attached to the church. The choir was a particularly excellent one, and much envied by its neighbors.

As their voices died, Orianna Pietro d'Angelo sighed softly with relief, Mass concluded. She had a busy day ahead of her and little patience for piety except where it benefited her. Father Bonamico was waiting for them at the door to the church. He was a chatty old man, and fond of the Pietro d'Angelo children. "Bianca's prospective suitors grow more each day," he noted, nodding approvingly. "Word of her beauty spreads."

"It is ridiculous," Orianna said irritably. "Have they nothing better to do than hang about like dogs after a young bitch? I must speak to Gio about seeing that the piazza is cleared when we cross to the church and back. Next they will be stomping and hooting at her. Her reputation will suffer then, though she be as innocent as a lamb."

"They have too much respect for your husband to do that," the priest responded.

"They are afraid of him, you mean," Orianna answered drily.

Father Bonamico chuckled. "Perhaps that too, gracious lady. Young men will be young men. The lady Bianca is quite lovely. You cannot blame them for looking."

A small smile touched the mother's lips. "Well," she allowed, "perhaps not." Then she gracefully descended the church steps, her daughter behind her. "Walk next to me, Bianca," Orianna instructed the girl as they reached the bottom of the stairs. She linked her arm with her daughter's, and the two moved back across the square together towards the palazzo. They had almost gained their destination when a young man sprang in front of them holding out a small beribboned nosegay to Bianca.

"For you, *madonna*!" he said eagerly, smiling, his brown eyes shining.

Bianca looked up, startled, but her mother slapped the flowers away.

"Impudente! Buffone!" she said, scolding him sternly. "Where are your manners? We have not been introduced, *but I know your mama*. She shall hear of this breach of etiquette on your part. She did not raise you to accost respectable maidens in the public square, or to offend their parents, as you have now done."

"Your pardon, *signora*, *madonna*," the young man said, bowing shamefacedly.

The two men who guarded the palazzo's main doors, finally remembering their duties, rushed forward and beat the young man away. He fled howling across the piazza while the others gathered and laughed at his retreat. Then they too began to disperse, hurrying after

the daring one to learn what he had seen when Bianca
briefly lifted her eyes to him.

"You should have come and escorted us from the
church," Orianna told the two servingmen furiously.
"You saw that crowd of ruffians leering at the lady Bianca. If you do not do better in the future, I shall tell
your master that you are dilatory in your duties and
have you both dismissed." She swept past, stopped, and
then glared at them, waiting for the palazzo's main portal to be opened so she might enter her home.

Bianca gave the two men a sympathetic look and
hurried after her mother.

"A sweet maid," one of the men said as he pulled the
door closed behind his mistress and her daughter. "It
will be a fortunate man who gains her to wife."

"And a rich one," the other man replied.

His companion shrugged, the motion conveying his
thoughts as clearly as if he had spoken them. Of course
the girl's bridegroom would be a wealthy man. Her father was a wealthy and important man. Master Pietro
d'Angelo was not likely to give any of his four daughters
in marriage to a man lacking in distinction. The one who
had just passed by would surely be matched soon. She
was just fourteen, the second eldest of her parents'
seven children. Her brother Marco had been born nine
months to the day after their parents married. The lady
Bianca had come thirteen months later, to be followed
by Georgio, Francesca, the twins, Luca and Luciana, and
finally the little *bambina* Giulia, who would be four
soon. The *signora* had produced no more children after
that.

Like a good wife, the lady Orianna had given her
husband seven healthy children. She was content with
her privileged status as the wife of the man who ruled

the Arte di Por Santa Maria, the city's silk merchants. Their guild was named for the street on which the city's many silk warehouses were located. The lady was aware, as all rich wives were, that her husband had a mistress he visited discreetly at a house he owned in a section near the river. It was the custom of important men to keep a mistress. One who did not was considered either parsimonious or less than a man. The master respected his wife publicly and, it was said, privately. He never flaunted his mistress, though her identity was known. He set an excellent example for his sons. Giovanni Pietro d'Angelo was a good master.

The servingman drew the great door closed once the women had hurried through. The city was becoming alive around them, although Piazza San Anna was a quiet enclave. The church and its musicians' dormitory took up a side and a half of the square. The family's palazzo took up another two sides. There was only one way both in and out of the piazza, which took up the remaining angle of the square. There was also a small park that was open to any whose behavior was respectable. The greensward had a beautiful white marble fountain with a naked marble naiad seated at its center. She was brushing her long hair. The water nymph was surrounded by fat, winged cupids, several of whom held porphyry vases from which water poured into the fountain. There were lime trees and terra-cotta pots of peach-colored roses that the family gardeners kept in bloom most of the year but for the winter months. There were three white marble benches for visitors to rest upon, and white crushed-marble paths for strolling.

From inside the palazzo, you could see the park only from the windows at the very top of the building, for the marble edifice had no windows on its lower floors. It was a Florentine belief that only a foolish man encouraged robbers by putting windows where someone could peer in from the outside and view your possessions, thus tempting theft. The Pietro d'Angelo palazzo was built around a large garden.

As in all families of wealth and importance, respectable adult women did not leave their homes except on rare occasions, such as attending Mass or going to their villas in the countryside outside of Florence. Privileged daughters might accompany their mothers to church, as Bianca did, but their only other foray outside of their father's homes would be when they were married or entered a convent. The garden served as a place for recreation and fresh air. It was there that Bianca now found her sister Francesca.

"Were there men again today waiting for you?" she eagerly asked. She was seated with her nursemaid, who was brushing her blond hair. Francesca's golden tresses were a source of great pride to her. They were washed weekly and rinsed with fresh-squeezed lemon juice and warm water. And she always dried her hair in the bright sunlight while her nursemaid slowly brushed the long locks so they might gain the full advantage of the sun.

"Yes," Bianca answered. "A larger crowd than before."

"I heard that one accosted you," Francesca said, her face turned to her sister's. "I don't know why our mother does not let me come to Mass with you."

"How do you learn such things and I am barely back in the house?" Bianca asked.

Francesca giggled. "Whenever they know you are returning from church, a bunch of the housemaids run to the top of the house and the windows overlooking the square to watch your passage back across the piazza.

Ohh, I wish I could be with you. Did you keep your swain's bouquet? Let me see it!"

"I would not take any kind of gift from a stranger, or any man for that matter, but our father and brothers," Bianca replied primly. "Such a query tells me that you are far too young to be allowed out, Francesca. You have only just turned ten. I was not permitted to accompany our mother until I had celebrated my thirteenth birthday last year. Remember, you are the daughter of an important man of business from Florence and of a Venetian *principessa*, Francesca."

"Oh pooh," came the airy reply. "You have become so stuck-up of late. Well, you'll be gone soon enough, for our father is even now arranging a marriage for you. By summer you will be wed, and mistress of your own house. Then our mother will take me across the piazza to Mass with her."

"What do you mean our father negotiates a marriage for me? What have you heard, little *ficcanaso*?" She grasped a lock of her sister's hair and yanked it hard. "Tell me at once! Who is it? Do you know? Is he handsome? Has he come with his father to negotiate with our father? Speak, or I will snatch you bald!"

"Ouch!" Francesca protested, retrieving her hair from Bianca's grip. "I only overheard a little by chance. I was passing by our father's library yesterday when I heard voices coming from the chamber, and the doors were closed."

"You eavesdropped!"

"Of course I did," Francesca said. "How else would I learn anything that goes on in this house? I put my ear to the door and heard our papa say that our mama did not wish their daughters to marry within the Florentine community. That he agreed, and planned for our marriages to benefit the Pietro d'Angelo family to the maximum. Papa said he had all the influence he sought or needed in Florence.

"The man, his voice was hard, and he told Papa that a marriage to *him* would ensure the security of the Pietro d'Angelo family. He reminded our father that a debt was owed to him. It would be paid in full when his marriage to you was celebrated. Father asked that he request anything else of him but such a union. The man laughed. Oh, Bianca, I did not like his laugh. It was cruel." Francesca shivered with the memory.

"Madre di Dios," the older girl whispered almost to herself. Then she said, "What else, Francesca? What else did you hear?"

"Nothing. I heard someone coming. I didn't want anyone catching me. You know Papa would have whipped me for it. I didn't dare stay," was the regretful reply.

Bianca nodded. "I will speak with our mother," she told her sister.

"Ohh, please don't tell that I eavesdropped!" Francesca begged.

"I won't," Bianca promised. "I'll say I heard the servants gossiping. Mama will tell me if any such arrangements for my future have been made. She will know."

"I don't want you to marry and leave us," the younger girl admitted. "I didn't mean it when I said I'd be glad to have you gone."

"I know that, little *ficcanaso*," Bianca assured her sibling with a small smile. Then she went off to find their mother and learn the truth of what her sister had heard.

"Your mother is closeted with the master," Fabia, her mother's servingwoman, told Bianca. Then she lowered her voice to speak in a more confidential tone. "It is something serious, for I heard your mother raising her voice, which is most unlike her."

"I have heard rumors regarding a marriage for me," Bianca said softly.

Suddenly the door to her mother's privy chamber was flung open, and her father, his face dark with anger, strode out and past them, exiting Lady Orianna's apartments.

"I will never forgive you for this, Gio!" her mother shouted after him. *"Never!"* Then, seeing Bianca, she burst into tears, turned, and slammed the door shut behind her.

"I must go to her," Fabia said.

Bianca nodded, and left her mother's rooms. Her mother had shouted. Orianna never shouted. And she had looked positively distraught. Orianna Rafaela Maria Theresa Venier, a *principessa* of the great Venetian Republic, never raised her voice, never allowed her emotions to show, and yet she had done both within hearing of not only her eldest daughter but a servant as well. Whatever was happening was not a good thing.

Also available from

New York Times bestselling author

BERTRICE SMALL

The Silk Merchant's Daughter Novels

BIANCA

After being used as the pawn in a blackmail scheme and traded as a bride to a debauched brute, the beautiful Bianca flees the cruel union and seeks shelter in a seaside villa. The shocking murder of her husband proves even more liberating. Unfortunately, Florentine society will never approve of the new man she's chosen: Prince Amir, grandson of Mehmet the Conqueror. How can two lovers from two cultures find happiness in a world determined to tear them apart?

FRANCESCA

Bertrice Small continues her historical romance series of close-knit, marriageable sisters in Renaissance Italy. For Francesca, her intended is a duke's heir—but she has no plans to marry him. Only when she flees the family does she find an unlikely lover. But the future holds many surprises for this runaway bride who is promised to another...

Available wherever books are sold or at
penguin.com

facebook.com/LoveAlwaysBooks

S0437

Also available from

New York Times bestselling author

BERTRICE SMALL

THE BORDER VIXEN

This novel in the Border Chronicles
series "reaffirms her standing as a
historical romance stalwart."*

Aware of the covetous interest in his land, the laird of
Brae Aisir announces that any man who can outrun,
outride, and outfight his headstrong granddaughter
"Mad Maggie" will have her as a wife—along with her
inheritance. His proposition causes more chaos than
resolution, especially when King James II sends his
cousin, Fingal Stewart, to compete for Maggie's hand.
The competition brings out the fire in both of them, and
it doesn't take long for the rivals to become lovers. But
there are those who will do anything to gain control of
Maggie's inheritance—even if it means getting rid of
Fingal Stewart and his border vixen.

*Publishers Weekly

Available wherever books are sold or at
penguin.com

Also available from

BERTRICE SMALL

Contemporary erotic romance from the
New York Times bestselling author

PRIVATE PLEASURES

FORBIDDEN PLEASURES

SUDDEN PLEASURES

DANGEROUS PLEASURES

PASSIONATE PLEASURES

GUILTY PLEASURES